LADY'S
RANSOM

LADY'S RANSOM

THE FIRST ARGENTINES

JEFF WHEELER

47N⬤RTH

Text copyright © 2021 by Jeff Wheeler
All rights reserved.

No part of this book may be reproduced, or stored in a retrieval system, or transmitted in any form or by any means, electronic, mechanical, photocopying, recording, or otherwise, without express written permission of the publisher.

Published by 47North, Seattle

www.apub.com

Amazon, the Amazon logo, and 47North are trademarks of Amazon.com, Inc., or its affiliates.

ISBN-13: 9781542027403
ISBN-10: 1542027403

Cover design by Shasti O'Leary Soudant

Printed in the United States of America

To Angela

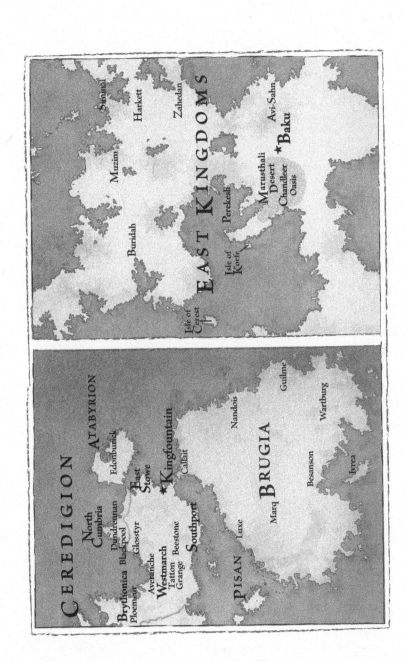

There is a storm at sea, which has prevented us from leaving Glosstyr. Every time I see clouds in the morning, I long to curse the Aos Sí for whatever conflict beneath the waves has caused such a commotion in the water. Ransom is more patient than I. He rises with the sun every morning to practice in the training yard. He works so hard all the day long as he seeks to learn how to be a duke of the realm. His fear of failure drives him to spend hours poring over records, reading missives—even the ones I've already gone through and answered. He wants to know the why of things. I've enjoyed teaching him.

Emi has stayed with us here in Glosstyr. She didn't return to Kingfountain with King Benedict or his council, and that is because he has given her his most important charge: to find him a wife to be his queen and rule Ceredigion with him. He told her that he trusts her judgment, her wisdom, and her canny sense of politics to find someone suitable. She has chosen to seek an alliance with Genevar, and thus she waits for the seas to calm before she voyages west. She will stop in the Vexin on the way now that she is its duchess once more. In all honesty, I'm grateful she has been delayed. She's been my closest friend and confidante for years, and the separation from her will be painful. Thankfully, I have Ransom to fill that void.

I'm grateful to him. For him. I had lost hope that we would be together, but he has always brought hope back to *me. And yet, he is so quiet. So reserved. He's still hurting from the death of the Elder King. Whatever happened, at the end, he's kept to himself. He carries a wounded heart. I hope I shall be able to heal it.*

—*Claire de Murrow, Duchess of Glosstyr*
(watching the ships from the window)

PROLOGUE

Master of the Wood, Keeper of the Gradalis

The call of a seabird came in through the open window, rousing Ransom from a fitful sleep. He opened his eyes, confused by the smell of the salty sea air. In his dream, he'd been back at Tatton Grange, enduring the scent of sick and sweat in a stuffy bedchamber, curtains shut, as King Devon lay dying from poison. The horror of that scene had chained him to the nightmare, and once again he was a knight about to lose his master, worried about a possible future in exile, listening to the morbid groans of a dying man.

Ransom sat up in bed, breathing hard, trying to shake off the lingering feelings the dream had evoked. The sun was rising in the east, early still, for it was late spring, and light glowed through the silk curtains hanging on the windows on that side of the room. On the other side of the chamber, the window was open, and he could hear the surf crashing against the shore. He loved falling asleep to that sound each night.

Looking next to him, he saw Claire fast asleep still, and his heart ached with a feeling of joy as well as the fear that this might be the dream and not the other scene. Her beautiful hair was nested against the pillow. Bending down, he gently kissed her shoulder, not wanting to awaken her. She murmured in her sleep, shifting slightly, and then the faint whistle of her breath resumed. His heart nearly burst with feelings of tenderness and gratitude. She was his wife, his duchess, and soon—so very soon—his new queen.

Ransom eased himself off the bed, moving carefully and quietly. He dressed in his breeches and a tunic, then tugged on boots and belted the Raven scabbard holding his bastard sword around his waist.

As he dressed, a feeling of danger, of warning, began to bubble inside his chest. He walked to the window, staring out at the seabound horizon. Not a cloud in the sky anymore. The storm had finally moved on. He glanced at the ships docked in the harbor, ships from the Vexin, a few from Brythonica, and the vessel waiting to bear him and Claire to Legault, where they would reclaim the title that was Claire's birthright.

All looked well, but something *felt* wrong. It twisted inside his stomach, making the peace he'd felt upon seeing Claire sleeping beside him vanish. He did not sense the presence of Lady Alix, the poisoner who served King Estian of Occitania. This was something else, a preternatural warning unanchored to any specific object or person. Was it from the Fountain?

Ransom left the room and walked down the hall. The servants were already hurrying about, preparing for the day. Although nothing seemed unusual or out of order, the strange feeling did not lift.

When he reached the training yard at the castle, he noticed Guivret sparring against one of the other knights. Each wore a hauberk, bracers, and a helmet. Others were practicing beyond them, some doing drills, some dueling with each other. A few were even preparing their horses to practice lance work, something they accomplished by hitting a wooden target fixed with a counterweight.

Ransom's mesnie had grown considerably since King Benedict had made him Duke of Glosstyr. Almost all the Elder King's household knights had asked to join his mesnie—men like Sir Harrold, Sir Axien, and Sir Thatcher. But others had come too, seeking the favor of the man who had overnight become the most powerful lord of Ceredigion. He had more than enough income to pay for their service, but he did not allow the knights of his mesnie to lay abed and dream. Discipline was his expectation, for them and for him.

When Guivret saw him arrive, he stopped his duel with the other knight and joined Ransom as he approached a table to the side of the yard that held pieces of armor and weapons. Ransom put on a hauberk, and Guivret helped him buckle on a pair of bracers.

"May we fight, Lord Ransom?" the young knight asked. He had become Ransom's squire after the death of his former master, Sir Terencourt of Brythonica.

"Just the two of us?" Ransom queried.

"Yes, my lord. I think I'm going to win today."

"You expect so? A knight should be more humble."

"If you say so, my lord."

Ransom could hear the smile, although he couldn't see it through Guivret's helmet visor. He picked up his own helmet and put it on; then he and Guivret made their way to an open corner of the training yard. They drew their bastard swords and faced each other.

Ransom admired the lad's pluck, but the nagging feeling in his chest had doubled. What was causing his unease? He glanced around the training yard, but all appeared as it should. With his Fountain magic, he sensed Guivret was about to attack him and raised his blade as the younger man lunged.

As their weapons clashed, a peal of thunder boomed over the cloudless blue sky. It was so loud, Ransom backstepped, swinging up his visor, his sword arm going down. Had lightning struck the castle? He looked up at the sky but found nothing to warrant such a sound. Not a single wisp of white lay above. A quick glance revealed the other knights were still going about their business, practicing alone or fighting. As if nothing had happened.

"Is something wrong, my lord?" Guivret asked, lowering his weapon.

"Did you hear that?" Ransom asked him.

"Hear what?" Guivret also raised his visor, a look of confusion now evident on his face.

"Thunder," Ransom said, turning around in a circle.

Recognition dawned in Guivret's eyes. "Get ready, my lord," he said. "Prepare yourself."

"What is happening?" Ransom whispered, feeling a strange nausea in his stomach. Wind began to kick through the courtyard, swirling fallen leaves and debris. It whistled past the stones.

"I should have warned you about the summons," Guivret replied sheepishly. "Here, let's go over there, where we're less likely to be seen."

Ransom didn't understand what was happening, but he followed Guivret to the corner of the yard that was partially concealed by the weapons table.

And then he was gripped by the sensation of falling—as if he'd tumbled off a cliff—and a shock wave of pain roiled through him as though a shard of lightning struck him partway down. The episode ended as swiftly as it had begun, and he found himself standing in another place, one sheltered by thick woods. The dawn was just beginning to stab its light through the branches. The pleasant smell of trees surrounded him. Had time gone backward?

For a moment, he was struck by the oddity of the scene before him. A thick grove of trees. A small trickling stream. Some massive boulders, flecked with moss and lichen, were huddled together in a heap that was higher than him. There were hailstones everywhere, and a massive oak tree stood sentinel by the boulders. Several men lay in a heap, groaning and writhing. Through his Fountain magic, he sensed their weaknesses, their injuries.

In a rush, he remembered that the Duchess of Brythonica had told him that when he became the master of the wood, a position Sir Terencourt had passed on to him, he might someday be summoned to defend the Gradalis, an ancient relic of Wizr magic.

"Who is that?" someone asked in Occitanian from behind him.

Ransom turned and saw three knights in hauberks and dusty gray tunics. If they had any affiliation, they didn't care to show it.

"Kill him," one of the others said, also in Occitanian.

Ransom lowered the visor of his helmet and felt the churn of the Fountain rush within him. He caught a whiff of sweat as the first man charged at him, swinging his sword around to cut off Ransom's head. In reaction, Ransom ducked and then smashed the pommel of his sword into the fellow's skull. A skull that was not wearing a helmet. The man dropped instantly, and the other two swarmed at Ransom, coming at him from either side.

Jumping backward, Ransom swung his sword and blocked a blow from the man on his left, then kicked the one to his right in the chest, knocking him down.

The knight who was still standing grabbed a fistful of turf and tossed it against Ransom's visor. He managed to turn his head to avoid being blinded, but the sharp edge of the man's blade bit through his armor and sliced his arm. The man who'd been kicked had already found his feet again and was rushing forward. Ransom caught his downstroke with the bastard sword and then blocked another attack with his arm bracer from the other man.

Driven by a surge of anger, he blocked their next attacks and then skewered one of them with his sword. The survivor started to run toward the boulders. Ransom saw, in the shadows nearby, the dull metal of a large serving bowl etched with designs around the rim. The man raced toward it, and Ransom felt a compulsion to go after him, even though his arm was throbbing in pain.

The fleeing man reached the metal bowl and lifted it. It was attached to a long chain, the other end driven into a stone plinth on the ground, something Ransom hadn't noticed at first due to the woodland detritus in the grove.

The Gradalis.

With a look of fear and determination on his face, the man tried to wrench the bowl from the chain. Ransom ran up and struck him down with a single blow. The man crumpled and fell, and when the bowl struck the plinth, it made a harsh metallic noise that grated down Ransom's spine.

He stood near the plinth, breathing quickly, looking around at the bodies strewn about the grove. There were eight in all, some still writhing and moaning. He hadn't fought that many. The other five had been dead or injured before he'd arrived. Ransom stepped onto the plinth and dropped to a knee by the man he'd just killed, whose eyes were fixed and gazing blankly. He hoped to find a clue, some evidence of who had sent them.

A little flash of metal around the man's neck hinted at a bit of jewelry. Ransom lifted the knight's visor and prodded through his clothes until he found it. A necklace, with a charm shaped like a fish.

He was pulling against the chain to get a better look when he felt a swelling of Fountain magic around him. Suddenly, the ground seemed to churn, as if invisible plows were at work in a farmer's field. Although he felt no sucking sensation against his own boots, the bodies and hailstones began to sink into the ground. One man, still partially conscious, began to wail with terror as he sank beneath the surface, his gloved hands reaching for something to hold on to. Then the earth smothered his screams.

The man whom Ransom had just killed was also sucked into the earth. He felt the tug of the necklace, but he gripped it more tightly. The chain snapped, leaving the necklace in his hand as the body was subsumed by the forest. In a few moments, no evidence of the battle or its victims remained. Ransom knew he had done the right thing in protecting this place. As he knelt there, gazing at the silver charm in his hand, he felt a lifting sensation. No more could he feel the premonition of danger that had weighed on him all morning. Those men had violated a sanctuary of sorts, and they'd paid the price. Now that they were gone, he could hear the birds again and the wind as it rustled the leaves.

He rose and stuffed the necklace into his pocket and sheathed his sword in the Raven scabbard. The sigil on the scabbard was glowing. When he looked at his arm, he saw the deep cut that had penetrated his hauberk. No blood came from the wound. The scabbard, which he had been rewarded with at the Chandleer Oasis, had remarkable healing powers. The wound would mend on its own.

Standing on the plinth, he stepped around in a circle. He sensed he was inside the borders of Brythonica, but he knew not where. Why had these men come? And why did one of them have a necklace with the sign of the fish? He thought of Alix and her castle at Kerjean. The castle of the ancient Fisher Kings. Had she sent these men to steal the Gradalis?

He turned and stared down at the silver bowl. After it had fallen, it had righted itself. In appearance, it was a simple thing, but he sensed the immense power coming from it. There were droplets of water inside. Was it from the morning dew?

Ransom felt compelled to set the heavy bowl back on the center of the plinth, so he did, handling it reverently. Upon closer inspection, he realized the markings on it were decorations. A few of them were animals—he recognized one as a sheep, another as a lion. After setting it down, he turned and glanced around the clearing again.

He had no horse, only his two legs. Did he have to walk back to Glosstyr? Or should he walk to Ploemeur and seek out the duchess? Something told him she was the only one who'd be able to explain what had just happened to him.

Turning around, he gazed at the huge boulders. The plinth looked man-made, but not the boulders. How long had they been there, and where had they come from? He gazed at them and stepped forward, intent on touching one.

As soon as he stepped off the plinth, the feeling of falling and lightning caught him again.

Suddenly he was back in the courtyard of Glosstyr. He stumbled and went down on his knee, finding cobblestones instead of earth. Guivret bent down and hooked his arm.

"You're wounded," he exclaimed, seeing the gash on Ransom's arm. Their eyes met, and a look of understanding passed between them.

"Sir Terencourt used to disappear at times," Guivret explained. "He never told us where he went. I think only the duchess knows."

Ransom winced and rose again, rattled by the experience. The warning feeling was gone now, but it had not put an end to his worries. What if he'd been asleep in bed when it had happened? Touching his leg, he felt the necklace in his pocket still. What had happened was real, not some vision.

Tell no one where you were. Or the Gradalis will be stolen.

I had a nightmare that I was back in the tower at Kingfountain. The feelings of despair and helplessness choked me. I tried scratching at the walls until my fingertips were bloody, then I awoke to the feeling of a kiss on my shoulder.

—Claire de Murrow, a Prisoner of Memories
(I hope we can depart today)

CHAPTER ONE

Terrible Is the Sea

When Ransom reached the top of the steps and arrived at the master bedchamber, he saw that Claire was already up and dressed and talking to one of her maids, a Gaultic lass by the name of Keeva. He loved hearing the lilt of their accent—Claire's became stronger, he found, whenever she spoke with someone else from Legault.

"And Keeva, make sure my father's bow is stowed for the voyage. I want to have it mounted when we get back to Connaught."

"Yes, mistress, is there aught else?" She smiled when she saw Ransom. "Mornin', milord."

"Good morning, Keeva," Ransom said, walking to his private closet, where he could change out of his sweaty tunic and see to the injury on his arm. Although he needn't do anything to heal it, he didn't wish to attract anyone's notice.

"Ransom, she brought some qinnamon torrere for breakfast," Claire said. "To celebrate. Captain said the weather should hold. We can leave today." The excitement in her voice would have normally made him smile, but he was still rattled from his experience in the grove.

"I'm glad to hear it," he answered, still going.

"Stay and eat," Claire pleaded.

"I smell like a boarhound. Let me change first."

She pouted and then nodded, turning back to Keeva as he shut the door. There was a marbled-glass window in the closet, providing sufficient light. He made his way to the basin on the table and splashed some water on his face. Then, wincing, he pulled off his tunic to examine his arm. The cut was long and deep, in the upper part of his arm, and the raven's-head scabbard still glowed as it worked to heal him.

Once he'd collected himself a little, he picked up a rag and dipped it into the bowl of water. Slowly cleaning his neck and his throat, he thought about the magic that had swept him away. He'd considered the possibility it might transport him while he was sleeping, which would surely set him at a disadvantage, but what if it swept him away during an important moment?

The door of the closet opened. He glanced over his shoulder and watched as Claire stepped inside.

"I don't care if you smell like a boarhound," she quipped, offering a mischievous smile. She sidled up to him and kissed his back. The feel of her lips on his skin made gooseflesh prickle down his arms. Her hands wrapped around him, and he felt the anxiety begin to melt away, replaced by much more pleasant feelings. But the familiar ache in his heart had not been dispelled—he feared losing her the way he had lost so many other people.

Her hands deftly unbuckled the scabbard belt, and before he could stop her, the sword, scabbard, and belt dropped to the floor. Pain flared in his shoulder, and he tensed before he could conceal his reaction.

"Why did you flinch? I sent Keeva away and locked the door. No one will—*mallacht*! You're bleeding!"

Blood was streaming down his arm. He grabbed the rag and pressed it against the cut.

"Brainless badger, why didn't you say you'd been hurt? Let me see it."

"It's nothing," Ransom said, turning his shoulder away from her.

"Nothing? I'll be my own judge, thank you. Remove the rag."

He did, gritting his teeth. The thrum of his heartbeat could be felt from the wound. "I've had much worse than this."

She examined it, her brow furrowing with concern, and then nodded for him to cover it again. He pressed the bloody rag against it, knowing the bleeding would stop as soon as he put the scabbard back on.

"I know you've had worse," she said, meeting his gaze. Her hand touched his chest, and she traced one of the scars near his collarbone. "I've kissed them all." Her finger pointed to the center of his chest. "But the ones on the inside worry me most. The kind that pastes and poultices cannot heal. Still, I'll take the chance to help where I can. I can work a needle and thread, Ransom. Let me stitch it closed. You don't have to do it yourself."

Her words reached through the pain and tugged deep at his heart.

"You don't have to," he said, feeling tenderness that was sweeter than the dish she'd ordered for their breakfast.

"I want to," she said, stepping closer.

He closed his eyes and smiled. "I didn't mean it like that. Could you pick up my scabbard belt?"

There was a confused look on her brow, but she bent down and retrieved it. He raised his arms so she could wrap it around his waist and buckle it. As soon as that was done, the dormant raven's head began to glow again. The pain and dizziness faded, and he dipped the bloodied rag into the dish.

"The bleeding stopped," Claire said in wonder, gazing at the line of the wound and then at him.

He squeezed the rag above the dish and began wiping the blood off his arm, but she stopped him and bathed his arm herself.

"This scabbard came from the Chandleer Oasis," he told her. "It is unlike other scabbards, Claire. It heals wounds."

"The Aos Sí must have made it," she said with interest. Her gaze took it in, and she started nodding, bright eyed. "It's one of the thirteen treasures."

"It was a gift from the Fountain," he insisted.

"Ransom," she said with a little patient condescension in her voice, "I've read about the treasures, and I'm telling you it's one of them. Look what it's done! The wound is there, but it does not bleed." She pressed against it with the rag, and he winced. "Sorry."

"You say there's thirteen of them?"

"Yes, I've read about them in the legends of my people. And you found one of them in the East Kingdoms. I'm agog." Her enthusiasm was charming. He didn't resent her the certainty she felt, yet he knew what he knew. The Fountain had spoken to him.

After she'd finished wiping his arm, she examined the wound again and then kissed the tip of her first two fingers and pressed them next to the wound. Their eyes met.

He took her hand and kissed her knuckles. "You have healed me," he told her. "More than you'll ever know."

A sudden pounding on the outer chamber door broke the intimacy of the moment. Claire huffed and stormed out, ready to scold whoever had intruded on them.

He grabbed another linen undershirt and held it in his hand while he looked at the tunics spread out before him, symbols of his wealth and royal office.

Claire poked her head around the door. "As much as I enjoy seeing you like this, Ransom," she said with hungry eyes, "you'd best hurry. Emi is leaving!"

$$\mathbb{X}$$

Claire and Ransom walked with the queen dowager down the wharf toward the ship bearing the lion sigil of the Vexin. She was taking the early tide, and Ransom and Claire intended to take the later one. A crowd had gathered to bid the renewed duchess farewell. She had been given the warmest welcome of any of the noble wedding guests, owing to her close connection to Claire.

Her knights stood at the gangway, ready to escort her up, but she stopped and turned to Claire. "We leave as equals now," she said. "Duchess to duchess. When we next meet, it is I who will be beneath you, the Queen of Legault."

"But you are forever taller than I, Emi, so that can never happen," Claire bantered cheerfully. The two embraced, their long captivity and confinement over. The shared suffering had forged an unshakable bond between the two women.

There were kisses and tears as the two held the embrace. Ransom felt a surge of admiration for the queen dowager. Had she not taken a chance on him all those years ago by paying his ransom to DeVaux, he wouldn't be here. All he had, he owed to her. The obligation he felt to her went beyond mere duty. He would do anything for her.

Emiloh broke the embrace and then turned to Ransom. "My heart is heavy leaving the two of you," she said, touching his arm. "You are both still very young, still very much in love. Be wiser than Devon and I were. Be true to each other. I want so much for both of you."

Ransom felt his throat catch at her words.

The queen's eyes peered into him, her gaze so deep he felt it in his soul. "Thank you for staying with my husband until the end, Ransom. He needed someone. I'm glad it was you."

He tried to speak, but words failed him. He swallowed and tried again. "Remember his last words to me, my lady. You were in his thoughts at the very end. He regretted that he hadn't forgiven you sooner."

The queen nodded, although she did not shed any tears. "Being imprisoned was a heavy burden. But those days are past us now. The sun has risen in the east, as it always does. I look now to fulfill the wishes of the new king. I hope you can show as much devotion to Bennett as you did to his father and brother."

"I shall, madam," Ransom said, and he meant it. He'd learned long ago that loyalty empowered him—it triggered his Fountain magic. Besides which, the new king could have punished the Elder King's favorites but had instead fulfilled his father's promises to Ransom. It was why he'd been allowed to marry Claire.

"No doubt you will," Emiloh said, then patted his cheek. "Claire will hold you to it."

Claire huffed, squeezing his arm. "He's as stubborn as a broken-legged ox, my lady; I can't sway him at all."

Emiloh gave her a fond look. "Oh, I've a feeling you can sway anyone if you have a mind. Farewell." She turned to leave and then paused, looking back at Claire. "I understand from my steward, Jex, that Lord Dougal of the Reeks has been a continual menace to the Vexin shores. If you would coax him to stay away, my dear, I should be grateful."

"Lord Purser Dougal? Has he indeed? He has been a problem for us in the past. Thank Master Jex for the kindness of this information. It will stop, I assure you."

"Of course," said Emiloh. Then, offering them another proud smile, she took the arm of one of her knights and mounted the gangway to the ship.

Ransom and Claire stayed and watched as the ropes were coiled, the staves were used to shove off, and the wind began to ripple the sails.

"You know Lord Dougal, then?" Ransom asked.

"Yes, he was a thorn in my father's side," Claire answered. "Always skulking about like a rat whenever there was trouble." She hooked her arm with his, and they started walking back toward the fortress of Glosstyr.

"How did your father handle him?"

"Increased his taxes, I believe," Claire said with a smile. "I imagine he hasn't paid them in years. He's probably built up quite a debt."

"I doubt he's the only one," Ransom said. As they neared the gates, he was surprised to see Sir Simon of Holmberg coming their way.

"Sir Simon?" Claire asked with a laugh. "What are you doing here? Did you come to see us off?"

Like Ransom, Sir Simon had served first the Younger King and then the Elder, although he had been with the Elder King for much longer. He had an affinity for managing money, for which he'd earned a position on the king's council. He was also one of Ransom's closest friends. The haste of Ransom and Claire's wedding had prevented him from coming to the ceremony.

"I hoped to catch you before you departed," he said. His hair was windblown. "I rode all night for that purpose."

"Why didn't you take a ship from Kingfountain?" Ransom asked, looking at his friend with a questioning expression.

"Ah, I would have, you see, if I were still serving the king." His shoulders slumped, and he shrugged. "I've been dismissed from the council. So has Lady Deborah. She left for Thorngate yesterday."

"Who is managing the treasury?" Ransom asked.

"King Benedict has brought in his chancellor from the Vexin, a man named Longmont. And so I find myself . . . unfortunately . . . with limited prospects."

Claire looked at Ransom and then nodded subtly.

"I would be grateful to have an old friend nearby," Ransom said, bringing a smile to the other man's face. "Would you be willing to stay in Glosstyr and look after our interests while we sort things out in Legault? You'd be welcome to bring your family, of course."

Simon rubbed his hands together. "I would be honored, my lord. Thank you. I have lands of my own, but the challenge isn't enough to fully occupy me."

"You will always call me Ransom, not 'my lord,'" Ransom said to his friend, putting a hand on his shoulder.

"What other news do you have?" Claire asked with interest. "What else has changed at Kingfountain?"

"Well, Lady Claire, Duke James, our mutual 'friend,' was finally dismissed and sent back to Dundrennan. He hoped to ingratiate himself with the king, but the king wants little to do with him. James was spending an inordinate amount of time with the king's brother, Jon-Landon."

Claire gave Ransom a waspish look. "I can't stand either of them."

"Not many can," Simon admitted. "There was a good deal of carousing going on at night. But that's stopped now that James has been removed. Jon-Landon is pushing for his own land. Wants to be part of the king's council too."

"He doesn't deserve it," Claire sniffed.

Simon chose not to comment on that. Turning to Ransom, he added, "You remember Master Hawkes, don't you?"

"I do," said Ransom. "The master of the rolls."

"I heard he's advised the king to send Jon-Landon to Atabyrion. The king has a daughter who is coming of age soon. An alliance with them would be a boon, for certain."

"It would also stop Jon-Landon from meddling," Claire said. "However, it's not wise to keep your enemies too far from sight."

"Truly said, my lady," said Simon, grinning. "Well, I'll not be a nuisance to you before you leave. If I can bother the cook for some breakfast, I'll be set up for the day."

"Indeed, and glad we are to have you," Claire said. "Did Master Hawkes say anything about Ransom's sister?" Her tone shifted to one of concern. "She's the king's ward now."

Ransom was grateful to Claire for bringing that up. Although he felt he was in no position to make demands, he hoped to talk to the king about it the next time he went to court.

"Not that I've heard," Simon answered. "I will keep alert for any information, though."

"That would be good," Ransom said. "We'll make arrangements with our steward to provide a room for you. I had anticipated needing to travel back and forth frequently to handle our duties here, so your coming is a blessing."

"I'm grateful to you both. The blessing is on both sides." He gave them a parting nod, then headed back to the castle ahead of them, intuiting they wanted some time alone.

Claire squeezed Ransom's arm, and then her eyes widened. "Does it hurt? I'd forgotten about the cut. I'm sorry."

"Don't be. Thank you for suggesting he stay. We need men we can trust."

"It was foolish of Bennett to let someone like that go. Someone who already knows the ways of court, has the history and experience."

"Kingfountain is not the Vexin," said Ransom with a smile.

"No indeed. I also find it interesting, and a little loathsome, that the king is so impartial about finding a wife. As much as I loved my father, I wasn't keen on letting him choose for me. I wanted to choose for myself." She took his hand and squeezed it.

"Thank you," he said, feeling a pulse of love for her.

With her other hand, she brushed some of her crimson-streaked hair behind her ear as the sea breeze blew it astray. Her hair looked brighter than usual in the sun. She glanced back toward the wharf.

"Are you ready for your next adventure, Sir Ransom?" she asked him with a wily grin. "Legault won't be tamed easily. We may have to crack a few skulls."

"Just tell me which ones, and it will be done," he told her.

"I can't wait to show you *everything*," she told him. "I hope you aren't afraid of the ocean. 'Terrible is the sea' is a saying of my people. Crossing the sea is always dangerous, even in the spring."

"I don't think we came this far to drown," he said. "To Connaught it is, my lady fair."

Neither of them had any idea what to expect when they got there. What they found was a castle in ruins.

X

The crossing went calmly, which brought a false sense that all was well. I stood on the deck with the sailors, too eager to wait down below. My heart brimmed as the coast of Legault came into view, the hills lush and green, full of ancient trees and their ancient memories. Connaught stands on a bluff with a dominating view. It was built by the Gaultic kings of ages past, back in the days of Wizrs and their battles with the Aos Sí.

But my childhood memories were dashed the closer we came. The building that once stood so tall and proud is falling apart. One of the towers is nothing but a heap of stone. My heart cannot bear the grief of knowing my long absence has caused this neglect. It could take years to rebuild. Years lost that cannot be reclaimed.

I didn't weep when I realized the work that lay before me. My blood is made of fire now. We will do this. Ransom tried to comfort me, but I do not want comfort. I want my castle back.

—Claire de Murrow, a Queen without a Palace
Landfall in Legault

X

CHAPTER TWO

Connaught Castle

Even damaged, the castle was a wonder to behold, perched on a rocky green bluff with a cove behind it. It made Ransom think of Claire's tales of growing up in Legault surrounded by hundreds of shades of green. The building was a contiguous structure with a few rounded towers, some of which had fallen, adjoining a larger structure with arrow slits and pyramid-shaped roofs, sloping gables, and chimneys popping up throughout. The front facade of the castle was a triple-arched structure with a circular window made of stained glass at its apex. Because of its position, Ransom imagined that when the sun rose, it shone off that circle of glass like a beacon, making the castle visible for leagues distant.

It had clearly been built for defense, with a lower outer wall circumscribing the top of the hill. That wall was damaged in several spots, which fed his suspicion that the damage had not only come from neglect. Parts of the building and its defenses had deliberately been broken down to make the keep less defensible.

After examining the ruins briefly, Ransom and Claire rode their horses down to a little meadow at the base of the hill, encircled by enormous trees that were centuries old and fared much better than the castle walls. All the knights in Ransom's mesnie had come on the journey, save Dearley, his close friend and the first member of his mesnie.

Dearley had just married Ransom's ward, Elodie, and the two would be joining them soon. The rest of the knights had been ordered to explore the grounds and set up watch to prevent any surprise intruders. Sitting on Dappled's back, Ransom looked up from the meadow at Connaught and the teeth of stone protruding from the grassy knoll leading up the rise.

Claire rode up next to him on a chestnut stallion she'd taken from the stables of Glosstyr. It had a long white stripe down its nose. Her countenance had fallen, and he felt her disappointment keenly.

"I'm so sorry, Ransom," she said, gazing up at the castle. "I don't know why I thought it would still look the way it did. That was foolish of me."

He cocked his head slightly. "It's a beautiful thing, Claire. It's on good ground, and at least part of it is still standing."

"Don't joke," she said with a mournful sigh. "It's going to cost a fortune to repair. And years. Many years."

"Whatever it takes, whatever it costs . . . we'll get it done."

"You say that now, but after a fortnight you'll be wanting to go back to Glosstyr."

"Why? Do you have plans to travel so soon?"

She shook her head, a little smile curving her lips. "You saw what it looks like in there. We don't even have a bed to sleep on, Ransom. Everything is ruined."

He shrugged. "All the barrels have been dragged away, all the chests broken open. But I think I saw a curtain rod still hanging. It's something, at least."

She grinned. "Does nothing dampen your spirits?"

"I once had only a broken suit of armor and a second-rate horse. My fortunes have improved drastically. Besides, we won't bleed Glosstyr dry to repair Connaught. Those who allowed this neglect to happen have a duty to fix it. The council of lords meets in Atha Kleah every new moon until winter. We will go there and seek recompense."

"What if they won't pay?" Claire said with a dark look. "They know our position is weak. They'll take advantage of it and say they've got naught to spare from having to fortify their own castles over the years."

Ransom stroked Dappled's mane. "Those who ally themselves with us early will receive the greater benefits. I think our first appointment should be a sheriff—one who collects the taxes. Do you have anyone in mind?"

"Someone who doesn't mind being hated?" Claire laughed. "Da always trusted Lord Toole. He's the first one who comes to mind. But it's no good having a sheriff if you cannot enforce the taxes."

"I agree. But that won't be Lord Toole's duty. It is mine." He gave her a dangerous smile. "We need to find out the biggest dog in Legault and humble him. The others will heel. Who might that be?"

Claire's brow furrowed. "It's not like the tournament circuit, Ransom. They are more devious here."

He thought of the poisoner, Lady Alix, who could influence a person's thoughts, and King Estian the Black. Although he couldn't say he'd defeated them, neither had they defeated him. "All it will take is one example, Claire," he insisted. "The rest will fall in line."

"I'll think on it. You're my husband. Not just my champion."

"While you are thinking of whom you'd like to have pay taxes first, I've another suggestion."

"What is it?"

"My brother, Marcus, has spent much of his life working on the Heath. He's learned quite a bit, and he knows all the best castle builders. I expect he can recommend people to help us restore Connaught. I could send Dawson to deliver the message." Dawson was another member of his mesnie, one of the knights who'd been with him almost since the beginning.

"Yes, indeed," Claire said, smiling brightly. "That would be lovely. It will take time, but I want to see this castle like I did as a child. I want our children to see it that way."

"We'd best get started, then," he said, smiling.

"Rebuilding?"

He felt a throb of love in his heart. It was good to see her smiling again. "No. I meant the other thing."

※

It was back-breaking work, clearing stone and hoisting timbers. Ransom worked from dawn until dusk, leading by example, and Claire toiled every bit as hard, although she and her ladies focused on fixing the interior of the castle. Stone masons from Atha Kleah arrived on the second day and quickly constructed the scaffolds needed to repair the broken walls. Although they all bedded down at night on a straw pallet like servants, Ransom found it rewarding to build rather than break, and going to bed exhausted helped chase away nightmares.

One morning after their arrival, Claire announced she was going hunting and asked Ransom to join her. Workers continued to arrive, responding to the incentive of easy and abundant coin, and there were enough of them that the knights were needed for guarding and patrolling rather than laboring.

Hunting was not a sport Ransom had done much of, but he did have good childhood memories of riding in the royal woods with his mentors, King Gervase and Sir William Chappell. She packed two bows, one for each of them, as well as bedrolls so they could camp beneath the stars. They set off midmorning, heading northeast into the wooded peninsula that was a dedicated hunting land for the rulers of Legault. Their knights had previously scouted the area to make sure no one had created any forbidden dwellings in that land.

Claire wore a blue-green hunting cloak over a pale blue chemise, and a quiver was strapped to her back, full of arrows with dark fletching. Ransom kept staring at her hair, brown or red depending on the light, distracted by it as they rode deeper into the woods. The ancient trees towered above them, large crooked branches and a canopy of leaves protecting them from the sun.

After midday, they stopped to feed their horses and eat the provisions that had been packed for them. After that, they began to hunt.

They'd tethered their horses in a glen and set off searching for beasts, Claire impressing him with her silent stalking as she ducked beneath branches and crept around rocks, an arrow fixed to the string of her bow. He followed suit, holding her father's bow in his hands. The air was pristine, smelling of the dense undergrowth and rich soil, and fat jackdaws squawked in the branches overhead while bushy-tailed squirrels clambered up the massive trunks. He reached out with his Fountain magic and felt no danger anywhere. The peacefulness of the place stirred emotions of gratitude and contentment in him.

She gestured for him to halt as she came up behind a tree. He did as she asked, listening to the trickling sound of moving water. The source, he discovered when she waved him forward, was a fresh spring in an enormous pond covered with lily pads. Wildflowers grew in patches of sunlight nearby.

"This is where the moose elk come to drink," she whispered in his ear. "We'll wait here. They get thirsty in the afternoon and come to the pool."

She nestled down in the thick meadow grass, resting her bow on her lap. He sat by her, hearing the clicks of insects and smelling the breeze.

"I used to come here with Da," she said, her voice soft. "I loved going hunting with him. It's been too long." She reached for his hand and squeezed it. They sat like that for a long time, listening to the frogs croak in the pool and the shushing water, watching as the sun began to crawl to the west.

"There's one," she whispered at long last, her eyes fixed.

Ransom had seen elk before, but none like this. Instead of elk horns, it had the wide horns of a moose, with jagged prongs that looked wickedly sharp. The bull crunched through the terrain to their left, then began to gulp from the pool. Claire grinned at him. That monster could feed an army.

She rose slowly, carefully, and lifted the bow. He did the same, coming around the other side of the tree. A branch snapped beneath him, and he looked worriedly at the moose elk. It didn't even flinch, though, unaccustomed as it was to the presence of danger.

Claire pulled the string back and let her arrow fly, hitting the moose elk in the shoulder. The animal groaned and began to charge away, the arrow jutting from it, but Ransom lifted his bow and took a shot at it. His arrow went true and hit one of the hind legs. The moose elk fell in its flight and began thrashing while he and Claire hurried toward it.

"First shot!" she cried excitedly. "I haven't lost it entirely!"

They had to stay at a distance to avoid its massive antlers as it twitched and thrashed. After hurrying around to the other side of the beast, Claire shot it again in the neck to end its misery, killing it instantly.

"How are we going to get that back to Connaught?" he asked her, shaking his head. "It's too heavy for both of our horses."

"We won't need to take it far," she said. "But let's gut it first so it doesn't spoil."

"Not far?" he asked with a chuckle. "It's half a day's ride back to Connaught."

"We're not going back to Connaught tonight," she said, giving him a sly look.

He wrinkled his brow. "Oh?"

"I failed to mention, deliberately, that there is a hunting lodge we'll be staying in. I sent Keeva and two knights ahead to make sure it was still there. It was undisturbed, unlike the castle. Keeva told me yesterday it was cleaned up and ready for us. They'll bring a wagon for the moose elk in the morning. All we need to do is have the horses drag it to the lodge." She walked up to him and cupped his cheek. "I wanted to surprise you."

He set his bow down and embraced her. "You did indeed. A hunting lodge?"

"Yes, but first I want to show you something. The barrow mounds. How I've wanted to share these memories with you! Come on! Let's clean the animal quickly."

"And we'll leave the carcass?" he said, gesturing at the dead elk.

She knelt down, withdrawing a knife from the sheath at her waist, and prepared to make the incisions. He lowered onto his haunches next to her. He'd butchered a few animals before while hunting, but never one this big.

"There are no bears or wolves in Legault, Ransom. Just badgers, stoats, and foxes. The most dangerous creatures in this land are men. And the most dangerous of them all is *you*."

After a bit of work, they removed the entrails and tossed them farther away. The smell would attract foragers. After they finished, they cleaned their hands and knives in the pool.

"Come, my love," Claire said. "Let me show you."

He did, and they left their bows and quivers near the kill and followed the edge of the pool hand in hand. She kept looking at him expectantly, smiling, and his heart ached with the wonderful pain of loving her. It felt as if they were alone in all the world.

After walking around the pool, they entered the woods on the other side. The Fountain magic started to churn within him. He could sense something ahead, not a person—a place. A prickle of warning went down his back.

"Are the barrow mounds that way?" he asked, pointing in the direction of the feeling.

"Yes," she said, smiling at him.

After passing through a screen of ancient trees, they arrived at a small man-made clearing carved into the forest. It appeared as if a patch of trees had been uprooted, their stumps removed, and a large mound of dirt stood where they once had. A few small saplings had sprung up, but they were much smaller than the remaining trees. At one end, facing them, boulders had been gathered at the base of a hill. Some had been set vertically, forming a little doorway. It was so narrow, a person would have had to walk sideways to enter it. There was a cave of sorts beyond, beneath the dome of the hill.

He swallowed, feeling the sensation of Fountain magic crawling up his arms, making his skin pucker with gooseflesh.

This had a similar feeling to another grove he'd visited, the one in Brythonica.

It felt dangerous.

The hunting lodge wasn't despoiled after all. I'd tried not to hope for a bit of good luck. Wishing for luck never helps. But two good things have come to pass—Lord Toole replied by messenger that he'd accept the role of sheriff, and Keeva told me the lodge is clean and intact. A day or two is all it will take to furnish it and make it a proper dwelling for us. The castle, of course, will take much longer.

I'm eager to surprise Ransom. He's been working so hard since we arrived. The lodge might not be much, but it will be a good start for us, for our marriage. And truthfully, I cannot wait to be surrounded by the woods instead of cold palace walls.

But before I take him to the lodge, I intend to take him to the barrow mounds. There are many in Legault, but this one is for the kings and queens of Legault. In Gaultic, it's called the Elf Barrow. It is where my mother's bones lie.

—Claire de Murrow
Connaught Ruins, the Fair Isle

CHAPTER THREE

The Elf Barrow

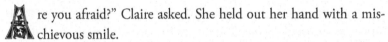 re you afraid?" Claire asked. She held out her hand with a mischievous smile.

Ransom stared at the dark gap in the stone and felt another shiver go down his back. Something in the air whispered of warning, of danger.

"What's in there?" he asked her.

"Just bones, Ransom. With my people, we don't send corpses to sea on boats. They are burned on a pyre, and the bones are brought to the barrow mounds. This is where my ancestors are buried. Where my mother rests."

"This is a wicked place," Ransom said, shaking his head.

Claire looked at him with hurt and surprise. "Hardly. It's a sacred place." She gestured again for him to take her hand. "There are magical protections that safeguard this place from trespassers, but my family belongs here. No harm will come to either of us."

His stomach clenched with dread, but he couldn't deny her, nor did she seem in the least concerned by the dangerous feelings battering him. He took her hand, and they started forward together.

She tugged him by the hand, smiling at him, although there was a look of worry in her eyes. "I've been here before, Ransom. It's not dangerous."

He did not agree. It felt like they were surrounded by invisible beings, and the closer they got, the more oppressive the feeling became. Sweat began to trickle down his cheek. The dark gap between the arch of stones seemed alive, menacing.

As they reached the first stones, he saw they had been carved with designs similar to the silver ends of the braided bracelet he wore on his left arm. The entire face of the stone was carved with a whorl-like pattern. The markings were indistinct, like ivy, but the lines wove around the rock, each one leading to the entrance. He felt he was going to be sick. Weakness overpowered his joints.

Claire touched the first stone, grazing her hand across it, and continued forward.

Ransom's mind went black with terror. The impulse to flee was immense, but he kept moving forward—one hand grasping Claire's, the other grasping the hilt of his bastard sword. The opening in the stone seemed to sigh.

Claire turned sideways so she could slip through the narrow gap. Ransom balked, his arms trembling, but she turned to face him, smiling at him as if nothing at all were wrong.

"Come on," she said.

His stomach heaved as he looked at the designs on the nearest stones. A black serpent slithered by his foot. He cried out, but it had already disappeared from view.

"What's the matter?" she asked.

"I saw a snake," he said.

"There are no serpents in Legault," she told him. "It was probably just a lizard."

He was breathing fast. Releasing the hilt of his bastard sword, he touched the stone as he, too, shifted sideways to enter. It felt as if the boulders were teeth, and he was about to be swallowed by a giant, but he made it into the barrow mound after Claire.

The darkness closed in around him, then Claire said a single word in Gaultic. *"Solas."*

Two burning coals appeared in the blackness of the tomb. Ransom watched as the fiery coals gradually brightened, revealing another boulder at the end of the barrow, about a stone's throw from where they stood. The two points were actually the eyes of a face carved into the rock. It was a menacing face, a bearded man with wild hair and an awful visage. The light from the burning eyes revealed stone shelves containing urns.

As the barrow mound brightened, the feeling of dread and gloom dissipated. Relief calmed him.

"You can let go now," Claire said to him, and he realized he'd been clenching her hand too hard. He relaxed his grip, and she massaged her palm but didn't scold him or tease him.

The walls were full of intricate carvings, some of beasts, some of moose elk, each image wrapped in lines that twisted and wove. It was amazing handiwork, and now that the strange fear had left him, he could admire it with new eyes.

Claire walked into the middle of the chamber. "This is where my ancestors sleep. Their bones are sacred to us. The name of this burial place is called the Elf Barrow—though none of us know why." She approached one of the stone benches and touched a stone jar etched with designs similar to the rest. "This jar was my mother's," she said, stroking it with fondness.

Ransom looked around, feeling more and more at ease. There were many such jars throughout the chamber, each one representing a life long gone.

"I used to come here to feel close to her," she said. "That's why I've never understood why your people cast away the bones of the dead."

"My people?" he asked, feeling a wrinkle in his heart at her choice of words.

"There is more Gaultic blood in me than any other kind," she said, looking over her shoulder at him. "I've always remembered my heritage. I need but look in a mirror to see it, after all," she said, reaching and twirling some hair around her finger. Her gaze grew serious, then intense. "*Is bred liom an iomarca duit,* Ransom."

"What does that mean?" he asked in confusion.

"It means 'I love you too much.'" She shook her head. "I want so much to show you this world, but I'm afraid you'll reject it because it's not what you were born to know. Our customs are so different from those of Ceredigion." A pause. "I could tell the safeguards bothered you earlier. I'm sorry for that. I've only been here with my father, and I don't remember whether they affected him. My bloodline protects me."

He gazed down at the ground. "I want to learn, Claire. Truly." He hesitated. "But the Fountain is real. I know it is."

She approached and then took his hands in hers. "The stories of the Fountain began when the Lady gave a sword that could spurt flame to the mortal world. They called it Firebos, did they not?"

"The sword of King Andrew," Ransom said, nodding. "I believe it's real."

"I do as well, Ransom," she said. "The Lady came from the waters of a pool. A pool not unlike the one we just came from, thick with lily pads and frogs. The sword was made by the Aos Sí, Ransom. Their stories go even further back than the legends of the Lady. They existed long before people began throwing coins into pools. If the tradition you believe in is ancient, might it not be possible there is one even more ancient?"

Her words made sense, but they also felt blasphemous. What was it she'd said? *When something is new, it can feel like a threat.* Perhaps the followers of the Aos Sí had felt the same way many, many years ago, when new traditions had sprung to life. Might there not be middle ground between them?

"Who is that bearded man in the carving? It seems very old."

She turned and beckoned him to approach it with her. He did, for it no longer felt as threatening as it had.

"He has many names. You'll find this visage carved into trees as well as stone. He's known as *an Fear Glas*—the Green Man. Others call him *an Ridire Glas*. The Green Knight. He's immortal, having learned the secrets of undying life from the Aos Sí, and cursed to roam the world for all time. The legend is that if you cut off his head, he will not die. It's a frightening story, actually."

As Ransom stared at the carving with its burning eyes, he understood that fear.

"Others call him the Green Druid," she said somberly. "The first Wizr."

Ransom gazed around at the stone jars on the shelves. So many years were represented here. So many generations. "I wonder if that's connected to the legend of King Andrew in some way?" he wondered aloud. "The Green Knight who can come back to life? The legend of King Andrew says he was mortally wounded and taken away to a distant land to heal so he could be born again and rule once more. What sort of magic could make that possible?"

She tilted her head and smiled at him. "I know the legend. People will believe anything so long as it gives them hope."

He felt a little stab of discomfort, the fear their beliefs might be incompatible.

"Let's go drag our kill to the hunting lodge," she offered. Then she turned to the stone carving of the Green Man and said, *"Dorcha."*

Everything went black again, except for the pale strip of light coming from the narrow exit. She took Ransom's hand, and they left together.

Once they were past the stones, he felt the terror rising in his chest again. He didn't understand the magic of the place. Nor did he particularly want to, other than as a way to understand Claire.

A pleasant fire crackled inside the hunting lodge. It was a single-chamber structure of stone and wood, a lacework of beams forming a tall sloping roof. It was sturdy enough to have survived many winters. There was a bed, enough ground for knights to sleep on, and a table and chairs for meals. It had been stocked with plenty of food in anticipation of their visit.

Ransom and Claire lay on a fur blanket before the fire, enjoying the solitude it afforded, away from servants, duties, and the pressures of life. She propped her head up on her arm and looked at him with affection.

"How is your wound?" she asked him. "Is it fully healed?"

"The cut on my arm? Yes. It was healed the following day."

"That scabbard is a wondrous thing," she said. "Tell me how you got it."

He was lying on his chest, propped up on his elbows. "I found it at the bottom of a well, actually."

"What were you doing climbing down a well? Were you that thirsty?"

"We'd crossed a desert," he said with a smile, "so yes, I was thirsty." He gazed at the flames. "A deconeus had told me to travel to the Chandleer Oasis if I sought a blessing from the Lady of the Fountain. I went there and felt guided to that spot. I was wearing armor, you know. Climbing into a deep well wasn't my idea."

"It doesn't sound very wise to me. And it was in there?"

"That's when I lost the bracelet," he told her, looking at her again. "And then you found it by the cistern."

"Water is important in both of our traditions," she said, glancing at him in the warm light from the hearth. "It is where the Aos Sí were banished. They have dominion over the waters."

"You mentioned the Aos Sí made thirteen treasures. There's a sword, the scabbard. Do you know about any of the others?"

She reached over and touched the edge of his collarbone. "I think this is another little scar. I haven't noticed this one before." She bent closer and kissed it. "Thirteen . . . I don't remember all of the artifacts, but they're very powerful, Ransom. There was a . . . cloak. I remember that one. A lady's cloak. Then there was the magic Wizr set. The game played itself, the pieces moving as if invisible fingers controlled them."

Ransom's eyes widened. "A Wizr set?"

"You've heard of it?"

"I have. I believe the King of Occitania has it."

She lifted her brows, her mouth pursing into a frown. "I hope not. It would give him an unfair advantage. The legend says it's not just a game. It controls the destiny of kingdoms. I only remember two others. The Fault Staff, a piece of wood that can cause earthquakes, and the most powerful artifact was the Grochan."

"It sounds like 'broken,'" Ransom said.

"Perhaps, but it's not. It's a cauldron, a silver bowl used for cooking. Its power was used to make rifts between worlds. It's how the Aos Sí were able to come here. But it was stolen by a human, something that caused a war between our kind and theirs. The war finally ended when they were banished to live below the sea. It is their goal to end their curse by flooding the earth with water and regaining dominion over the land again."

Ransom couldn't deny Claire's stories were interesting. It explained the origins of the Wizr set, which he'd never seen but had learned of from Alix. And was the Grochan the same as the Gradalis? Just a different translation of the same thing? Its power had indeed summoned him from a distant place. He wondered what artifact Alix possessed since she had gone on a pilgrimage like he had.

"So you are saying the Aos Sí flooded Leoneyis?" he asked her.

"I have no idea," Claire answered. "It could have been an earthquake. It could have been a storm. Perhaps it was the Wizr board. It happened so many years ago, we've no way of knowing. What I do know is that the myths of our people attribute the same things to different causes. And the legends of my people, here, are older than yours. There was a time when Connaught was equivalent to Kingfountain, when other kings came and paid tribute to my forefathers to keep them from invading their realms."

He rested his cheek on his forearms, looking at her. "Are you planning an invasion, Claire? Is that your aim?"

"Don't be an eejit, Ransom," she said, rolling her eyes. "It is Occitania's goal to rule the world, not mine. Connaught and Kingfountain have been allies for a long time. I'd like to keep it so. My father treated Legault like it was only another duchy. They tolerated him because he was a powerful lord, but many of them were resentful. The people here will look to me to lead them. I speak their tongue, and I know their traditions. Try not to scoff at them, Ransom. Learn what you can."

"Tell me how to say 'I love you' again, in Gaultic."

"*Is breá liom an iomarca duit.* It means 'I love you too much.'" She smiled as she said it, a smile that made his heart thump harder in his chest.

He tried to say the words, but they tumbled out of his mouth like stones, making her laugh. He attempted it again and failed the second time as well, but Claire leaned over and kissed him, a kiss that continued to grow in intensity and excitement, drowning out the sound of the horse riding up to the hunting lodge.

It wasn't until they both heard the jangle of spurs and march of steps toward them that they broke their kiss.

Claire's faced flushed with anger. "I warned Keeva—"

"Maybe there's trouble," Ransom said. He rose and walked to the chair where his belt and scabbard lay. He put them on as a fist started pounding on the door.

He approached it, Claire joining him with a scowl, and raised the crossbar. Ransom didn't feel a warning of danger, but part of him worried he'd find a towering man painted green standing there.

Instead, it was Guivret. He looked worried and anxious.

"You rode hard to reach us before nightfall," Ransom said. "It must be important."

Guivret nodded. "A boat just arrived at Connaught from Kingfountain," he said, breathing fast. "King Benedict has summoned his council. You're to go there at once."

"No!" Claire said, gripping Ransom's arm tightly, her face flushed.

"I wasn't supposed to go to the palace until autumn," Ransom said in confusion.

"The messenger is expecting an answer," Guivret said. "He needs to be able to tell the king you're on your way."

Ransom didn't know the nature of the emergency. But he knew the king wouldn't have summoned him unless there was one. Although Bennett hadn't been his king for long, the king had impressed upon him the importance of reclaiming Legault—something he'd wished for Claire and Ransom to do together.

Ransom looked at her and saw the anguish in her eyes, her silent pleading for him to refuse the summons. But he was now the Duke of Glosstyr. He *had* to go.

I had so looked forward to sharing the barrow mounds with Ransom. I have vague recollections of Father being stern when we went, but Ransom was positively spooked. Why would the barrow have more of an impact on him than they did Father? Maybe it is because Ransom is more superstitious about such things. We'll have to try it again in the future to see if those feelings persist. I want to be able to take my children there someday, Aos Si willing. To teach them the lore of our people.

These ancient woods hold so many memories. How many knights have brought their ladies beneath these boughs? How many kisses have been stolen or claimed? The woods are precious to me. I will always remember our time here together, our early days as husband and wife.

—Claire de Murrow
the Hunting Lodge, in the Woods

CHAPTER FOUR

Call of War

The look on Claire's face caused a wrenching feeling in Ransom's heart, as if his loyalties were pulling him in different directions. She wanted him to stay, but how could he disobey his king?

Guivret fell silent, seeing the tension between his master and his master's wife.

"Rest your horse, give it something to eat," Ransom said to Guivret. "We need a moment alone."

"Of course," Guivret said, bowing and quickly striding away from the conflict. Ransom pushed the door shut.

"It isn't fair to ask this of you," she said, her voice hot. "Are you a hound to be summoned with a whistle? Is he proving how promptly you'll obey him?"

"I'm not a hound," Ransom said, anger spiking in his chest. "He is a *king*, and he has the right to summon his vassal whenever he wishes to."

She frowned, her anger rising to match his. "Am I less in authority? My kingdom may be smaller, but my rank is equal to his."

This was not what he wanted. He had to leave—they both knew it—so why part with an argument?

"If not for Bennett, you would still be in the tower at Kingfountain," he reminded her. "You may not have to pay him allegiance, but you owe him some respect."

She flinched, her cheeks flushing. "What if I forbid you to go?" she asked softly, her voice suddenly calm and dangerous.

He closed his eyes. "Why would you do that?"

"What if *I* wanted to test your loyalty, Ransom? Would you come if I called?"

"You know I would," he said, staring at her pleadingly. "But why make it an ultimatum?"

She buried her face in her hands, but not to cry. He saw her fingers digging through the hair at the crown of her head. When she lowered them again, the fury was obvious in her expression. "The brainless badger! Why now? Why do this to us now!"

He wasn't entirely sure whether she referred to him or the king.

"I have to go, Claire," he said. "But not until tomorrow. Let me find out the cause of this summons. It must be serious, or he wouldn't have done it."

"Wouldn't he?" she asked doubtfully. "He's testing you, Ransom."

"Shall I not pass the test?" Anguish ripped through him—he did not like being at odds with her, not now, not ever—but he held firm.

She pursed her lips and began to pace. "I'd looked forward to staying here at the lodge with you. I thought we'd be here at least a fortnight while they repair our rooms at the castle. A fortnight of bliss, of waking by your side each morning." She sighed. "Of hearing you learn endearments in Gaultic and teaching you about the ways of my people. That vase of hopes is now dashed to the floor, broken to pieces."

"I'm sorry, Claire. Truly I am."

"But not sorry enough to stay," she said. Her brow furrowed. "It better be a war, Ransom! Anything less, and I'll feel jilted. Would Estian have broken the truce so quickly? He promised two years of peace. I thought he'd last more than a month."

"It *has* been more than a month," Ransom reminded her. The final days of King Devon's reign felt like a blur now. The once mighty king had tumbled quickly in the end. He remembered the list of names of those who'd betrayed him in the last hours of his rule, the king's youngest son's name being foremost.

"I could just spit in his soup," Claire said, stamping her foot. "Barmy . . . how I hate this!"

"Believe me, I have no desire to go back to the palace right now."

She blew out a breath and gave him an arch look. "You'd rather stay with me?"

He took a step closer. "Need you even ask that?"

Claire came to him. One moment, she was all raw fury and squeezed fists, and the next she slumped her shoulders and sagged against him, sighing dramatically.

"It isn't fair, Ransom."

"No, it isn't," he agreed, running his fingers through her delicious hair.

"I don't want you to go," she said. "I'm afraid to sleep alone. Maybe I should go with you?"

"You can," he said, feeling a spark of hope.

Then her eyes darkened again, signaling another shift in mood. "The woman wants to. But the queen can't. Don't leave until the morning. Give me one night at least in this place. One night to remember."

He stroked her cheek with the edge of his finger. "I'll tell Guivret. Tomorrow."

She still looked wounded, but she nodded, and he walked to the door and left the lodge. It was almost eventide, and the night birds were starting to make their sounds.

"I'd invite you to come in," Ransom said with a sigh and a smile, "but I—"

"I wouldn't dare intrude," Guivret said. "When are we leaving?"

"I'm leaving at dawn," he said. "And you'll accompany the queen back to Connaught once she's ready. I'm trusting you with her safety, Guivret. Guard her with your life."

Guivret swallowed, nodding in agreement. "Yes, my lord. With my life."

"I'll sail back to Kingfountain with the messenger. Then return as promptly as I can." He glanced back at the lodge, seeing the glow of the firelight through the heavy curtains.

"That big elk," Guivret said, nodding to the kill, which they'd dragged from the woods to the lodge earlier. "It's the biggest I've ever seen. Did you kill it, Lord Ransom?"

"No," he replied with pride. "*She* did."

𝄞

As the ship reached the palace docks at Kingfountain, which were situated on the other side of the waterfall and protected by lower towers armed with massive crossbows, Ransom stared up at the palace. This was the first time he'd come in at the royal docks, which would hasten his arrival at the palace. The roar of the falls welcomed them, and he felt the strong, steady thrum of power within him. He'd come as called. Duty had prevailed.

He wished that he and Claire hadn't argued. Although they'd settled things between them, he regretted bringing up her imprisonment. It was a painful subject for her, even more so because she'd known he was returning here, where her tower prison could be seen from almost every part of the castle. Storm clouds were visible coming from the north, so he hoped his return wouldn't be hampered by the weather.

The messenger, one of Bennett's household knights, had not been able to give him any further information. He had been sent to summon Ransom for reasons unbeknownst to him. That made Ransom wonder if Claire were right—the king was just testing how promptly his vassals would respond to a call.

He made his way to the palace, where he was received by servants who brought news of his arrival to the great hall. They promptly returned and informed him his presence had been requested. The king had assembled his council.

By the time Ransom arrived, the others were all present. His gaze traveled through the room, taking in the faces of those who'd gathered. His mother's cousin Lord Kinghorn was present, and so was Ransom's childhood enemy Sir James Wigant. He met Ransom's eyes for only an instant, giving him a bemused smile. In keeping with Simon's report, Lady Deborah was missing, but Jon-Landon was present, and so were Duke Ashel of East Stowe and Duke Rainor of Southport, both of whom had sat on the Elder King's council. There were two open chairs, one on each side of the king. One for Emiloh, Ransom intuited, and the other for himself.

Only one face was unfamiliar to Ransom, that of a clean-shaven man in a costly tunic. He had an arrogant look about him. Was this Lord Longmont, the king's chancellor?

But Ransom's attention shifted to the king, who had shorn his hair and trimmed his beard and looked like an altogether different man from when Ransom had last seen him. Dressed in royal robes of state and fur-lined boots, he was more merchant lord than soldier now. Benedict was undeniably handsome, but the transformation had made him more regal and self-assured. His eyes were shuttered, however, and it was impossible to tell what he was thinking or feeling.

Ransom swallowed and approached the large ornate chair, and the king gestured to the empty seat to his right.

"I thank you all for responding so promptly to this summons," said the king, leaning forward in his seat. "Whatever reason you may suppose is the cause of it, I assure you . . . you are wrong."

Ransom lowered himself into the chair, feeling the hard back against his spine. Glancing at the faces around him, he took note of the others' expressions, most of which were not as difficult to read as Benedict's. The king had kept most of his father's council, but they did not all share the same degree of loyalty to him.

"And why did you summon us, Your Majesty?" Lord Ashel asked with a baleful look.

"I did so, Duke Ashel, because of news I received from Genevar. From my mother." He paused deliberately, letting his words sink in. He looked from face to face, studying each person in turn, projecting a sense of dominance. "As you know, I sent her there to negotiate a marriage alliance. She has done so, with the doge's own eldest daughter. But I did not summon you here because of my nuptials. You would not think so little of me as to assume that."

Benedict paused again, then leaned back in his throne. "The East Kingdoms are at war, and the Chandleer Oasis was overrun by one of the factions. Every single Genevese merchant present was murdered, and all trade has come to a halt. Worse, they have declared worship of the Lady a heresy punishable by death." He strummed his fingers on the armrest.

Ransom was sickened by the news. He wondered if Kohler and the merchants he'd traveled with on his pilgrimage had been slaughtered in the attack.

The king leaned forward. "The doge fears they will bring war to our lands if we do not keep them from coming. He has proposed an alliance between Genevar, Brugia, Ceredigion, and Occitania to lead a force to reclaim the oasis. All three kings will join him in this conflict, for if even one of us were to remain behind, it would cause suspicion and animosity. We strike a common foe. That is why I've summoned you."

The king's words sent a collective gasp through the room. Ransom could hardly believe his ears. A knot of dread formed inside his stomach. He'd hoped to return to Claire soon, but he knew the oasis—it took a year to get there, a year to come back. He tried to keep his emotions from showing on his face, but he couldn't prevent a worried frown.

"War with the East Kingdoms?" blurted out Duke Rainor. "Because of trade?"

"This is a problem for the Genevese," said James with a smirk. "Not us."

"My lords, please," said the king with a tone of reproof. "My father may have suffered such outbursts of emotion, but I will not. I value calm and decisive action. Look to Lord Ransom as your guide in what will please me. Temper yourselves. Or you will lose your place on this council."

The rebuke caught everyone by surprise, Ransom especially. He shifted in his seat uneasily as the others exchanged glances.

"This is not just a matter of coin and trade," said Benedict. "Yes, it affects Genevar. But let us not forget who supplies us with grain, fruit, and spices. If their trade routes are cut off, then every kingdom will feel the bite of it. But it won't end there. After they have weakened us, the infidels of the East Kingdoms will come here next. They will violate our sanctuaries and befoul our fountains." He made a gesture with his hand, as if he were holding a sphere and examining it. "We must look ahead to these things. For many years I have wanted to go on a pilgrimage to the East. In the ancient tongue, my name means 'blessed.' I say the Fountain has called me as king for this very purpose. To defend our beliefs from our enemies."

As he spoke, Ransom felt a ripple from his magic, a sense that what was being spoken was true and necessary. The pit in his stomach deepened. He didn't want to go back to the oasis, but he could hardly refuse. He was the only one in the room who had been there before.

"What do you propose?" asked Lord Kinghorn, who had a look of zeal in his eyes. Ransom knew that he had long wanted to go on a pilgrimage himself. One of his greatest wishes was to hear the voice of the Fountain.

Sir James looked ill at ease, and he leaned back, rubbing his upper lip with his finger. Jon-Landon had a neutral expression. It was unlikely that he would be allowed to go, since there were only two heirs left in the Argentine family, Jon-Landon and Goff's son, Drew.

"My mother, the queen dowager, will be arriving in two days. She has been instrumental in negotiating this to our advantage. Brugia doesn't share our faith, but they are wholly dependent on Genevese trade. They will be the counterbalance we need with Occitania. Estian and I . . . do not see eye to eye as we once did." As he said this, he glanced at Ransom, a silent communication that he had not forgotten their conversations about the Occitanian king. "Estian knows that I would take advantage of his departure if he were to sail to the East, just as I know he would target us if the situation were reversed. We both must go, and Brugia will come with us to prevent any problems. We shall leave imminently and winter in the East. I will leave my authority vested in one man to rule in my stead. To act in my interests and command in my name."

Sir James glanced at Jon-Landon with a startled look. But Ransom saw that Jon-Landon wasn't excited. It wasn't going to be him.

"I name Lord Longmont justiciar of Ceredigion. He has been my chancellor for many years and knows my every thought. He will act as proxy for me and keep those who remain behind in obedience. But I will not trust one man, even one I trust as much as Longmont, to have sole command. I name protectors who will check his authority. My lady mother, Duchess Emiloh, and Lord Ransom, Duke of Glosstyr. The three of them will rule Ceredigion while I am away."

The king looked pleased by how his announcement had shocked everyone in the room.

All except for Jon-Landon. As Ransom looked at the younger brother, he saw a glint of mischief already forming in his eyes.

John Dearley arrived from Glosstyr today. He is not just Ransom's first knight, but also a stalwart friend to us both. He had not heard about the summons to court, so he was surprised to learn Ransom wasn't at Connaught. His wife, Lady Elodie of Namur, came with him. They were wed not long before Ransom and I. Seeing my husband's friends made me miss him all the more. No word has come, but then it hasn't been long. I keep wondering what the king wants.

Progress on Connaught is going well, I suppose. Lord Toole is due to arrive for his official commission so that he might begin collecting taxes. There are a lot of workers here, many mouths to feed. We need coin soon. I don't want to draw on the largesse of Glosstyr for too long, or it will incur the animosity of the people there.

Write to me, Ransom. I long to hear from you.

—Claire de Murrow
Connaught Castle
(anxious for news)

CHAPTER FIVE

Damian Longmont

When the business of the council was concluded, the king left the chamber with his chancellor at his side. The rest of the council broke into small groups as they all tried to process the king's decision. War against the East Kingdoms would be a monstrous undertaking. But a temporary alliance with Brugia and Occitania as well? It seemed a stone too heavy to lift, and everyone brooded over the coming task.

Ransom approached Lord Kinghorn. The big man was coughing, something he did often when exposed to smoke from torches. His steel-gray hair was swept back on his head, and his beard was streaked with gray. Fourteen years before, Ransom had come to him as a stripling, freshly dismissed from court after King Gervase's death. Now they were serving together again.

"I thought we might enjoy a season of peace, no matter how brief," Lord Kinghorn said, shaking his head. "This is unexpected."

"It is a long journey," Ransom replied. "Bringing a host of men out there will be difficult. Nigh on impossible."

"You've been to the oasis. I must admit that my imagination is fired up. For years I've longed to make a pilgrimage there. I'd about given up hope."

Ransom felt a strange brew of emotions. He didn't wish to go back—indeed, he'd dreaded it—but he still felt overlooked. No, "overlooked" was not the right word. He'd been given an important task, but he was a warrior first and foremost, and he had been taken out of this fight. "I wish you luck on your journey."

He'd tried to conceal his conflicted feelings, but Lord Kinghorn picked up on them. "You want to go back."

"Not really, to be honest," Ransom said, shaking his head. He fidgeted and then sighed. "There is so much to do here. Legault is in shambles." The other's observant eyes bored into Ransom. "There are troubles enough without adding more."

Lord Kinghorn put his hand on Ransom's shoulder, a fatherly gesture. "I think the king should have taken you," he said. "You are, after all, the strongest knight in the realm. In any realm, I should venture. I don't say this to fill you with pride. I just speak the truth. The king has been envious of your reputation. He goes to war to secure his own."

The words brought a small measure of relief to Ransom's heart. "Thank you."

Lord Kinghorn lowered his hand. "Bennett is still very young. I'm impressed, so far. Even though he serves his own ends by keeping you away from your share of the glory, he is pragmatic enough to put you to good use. Keeping you in Ceredigion . . . or at least nearby . . . will help prevent treachery. I don't trust the Brugians any more than I do the Occitanians. You remember when they invaded us all those years ago. You proved a formidable knight even then. And the Fountain knows Estian the Black fears you. Whatever mischief he might plan will be tempered by the knowledge that you stand in the way."

Ransom swallowed. "I cannot protect the king if I am not with him."

Lord Kinghorn's brow furrowed. "What do you mean?"

"I speak of Estian's poisoner, Alix of Bayree. She's killed two kings so far. She is cunning and deadly. If she travels with Estian, our king will be vulnerable." Ransom wanted to confide in him that she was also the queen dowager's illegitimate daughter, but he didn't dare share the news without the king's permission. Benedict knew the truth, of course, and understood the nature of the threat.

There were only three remaining descendants of Devon Argentine, and the Fountain had warned Ransom that he was all that stood in the way of the line failing. Perhaps the king had also chosen to leave him behind because he feared what might happen to Jon-Landon and Drew in his absence.

"You've shared your concern with the king?"

"I've told him. And he believes me. Both of us have fallen victim to her treachery before."

Lord Kinghorn nodded thoughtfully. "I will make sure no harm comes to him. I know he sent an emissary to Pisan to see if he could learn the nature of the poison used to kill his father. I suspect it was the same one used on his brother. Their response? Send someone to the school. With war happening right now, we cannot afford the cost or the time."

Alix had offered to heal the Elder King if Ransom did her bidding, which indicated there was an antidote, but it could have been another lie. The school would keep its secrets carefully guarded.

"I'm grateful you'll be with him," Ransom said. "And frustrated that we cannot gain the information we seek. But perhaps you will find something else you seek on this journey. There are many fountains at the oasis. Be sure to choose the right one." Ransom chose not to reveal the one he'd found. The Fountain had whispered its location to him. That was part of the test, he imagined. Whether someone would listen to the voice and follow it.

"We will speak again, Ransom, on this matter. I know the king said he wants to leave soon and winter with the fleet farther east, but we must take time to prepare and plan. As you said, the logistics will pose a challenge."

Someone approached them, and when Ransom turned, he saw the smooth face of the chancellor, Longmont. "I'm sorry to intrude, gentlemen," he said in a somewhat condescending tone, "but His Majesty wishes to speak with Lord Ransom."

"We've just finished," said Lord Kinghorn, inclining his head.

"I'm grateful I didn't interrupt, then," said Longmont. He was, by Ransom's estimation, about ten years older than himself, but had a youthful face that belied his age. The styles he wore were too flashy for Ransom's taste, from his gloves to the foppish velvet hat angled across his brow. The man bowed to Lord Kinghorn and then gestured for Ransom to follow him.

The two walked out of the great hall, using not the main door but the back one that led toward the king's private chambers. The chancellor walked quickly and confidently with a bit of a hurried pace.

When they were alone in the passage, the chancellor said, "If I understand the situation well, and correct me if I don't, you found Connaught castle in a bit of a mess, Lord Ransom. Is that true?"

"It is, but I'm curious how you know of it."

"One of my special talents, my lord, is to acquire knowledge and information that I feel could . . . in my best opinion . . . be of service to His Majesty. Are you in need of funds, my lord, to help refurbish the castle? I can secure you what you need for a very modest rate of interest."

Ransom felt a ripple of distrust. "Thank you for your offer, Lord Chancellor, but I must decline."

"I'm not surprised. I'm also informed about the state of your wealth. In fact, I may solicit a loan from *you* depending on how this war turns out. The king has asked me to summon fifty thousand livres to finance this expedition. That does not include the amount the Genevese are investing, which is sizable."

Why was the chancellor telling him this? "I imagined it would be costly," he said.

"There is rarely any profit to be taken in war," said Longmont. "But do let me know if I can be of any service to you, Lord Ransom. I should consider it a particular honor if you were to ask."

They reached the door at the end of the way, guarded by two of the king's knights, who nodded at them as they passed. Benedict was pacing the chamber in a way that summoned a strange ripple of memory. How many times had Ransom seen the Elder King pace in this manner? The presence of the hollow crown, resting on a cushion on a small end table, only deepened the impression.

Bennett turned when he heard the noise and offered Ransom a friendly smile.

"I have brought him as you commanded. Is there anything further you require, my lord?" said Longmont with sudden meekness and deference.

"Thank you, Damian. I would speak with Sir Bryon next. Have him meet me in the solar."

"Of course, my lord. I am your humble servant." He bowed deeply and then exited, leaving the two of them alone.

"Are you disappointed, Ransom?" the king asked him, folding his arms and tilting his head in an inquisitive way.

"My lord?"

"Are you disappointed not to be going?" clarified the king. "I had assumed, being so newly married yourself, that you would prefer to remain here."

Ransom clasped his hands behind his back. "I am yours to command as you wish, my lord."

"We're alone, Ransom. Drop the pretenses. I'll put it more bluntly. Are you disgruntled that you aren't coming to war? There can be no doubt as to your suitability or capability for it."

"I am not. Not for the reason you are implying. My concern is the danger to you."

"You speak of my half sister?"

Ransom nodded.

Benedict turned and walked to the curtained window. He looked outside, and the sunlight glinted on the streaks of gold in his hair. "I don't know if Estian will bring her. He might. Her skills may prove useful in such a conflict." He turned and looked at Ransom seriously. "I don't need you as my protector, Ransom. I would have no compunction killing her if she tried to murder me."

Ransom frowned but said nothing.

"I've increased the watch on the decorative fountains throughout the palace," the king continued. "Some of the servants confessed they have, at times, seen a noble lady wandering the halls. Based on where she was seen, I've stationed more guards at a particular fountain, which may be the source of her supernatural ability to travel here." He inclined his head. "Father always wondered if he had a spy in our midst. I suspect it was her all along."

"I'd come to that conclusion," Ransom admitted.

"I've taken action based on the information you gave me. I hope that instills you with some confidence in my judgment. And also that I've chosen you to check my chancellor's authority."

"I'm grateful for the faith you have in me," Ransom said.

"Then speak your mind. Do you feel it is wrong to go to Chandleer? I *want* to go. I've wanted it ever since I heard about your voyage. I hope my desire isn't overruling my good sense."

"I think the threat you learned of from Genevar is real. I trust your mother's wisdom."

"She learned of it shortly after arriving there. It could soon affect all of our lives, but it'll hit the poor the hardest." He paused, then added, "I agreed to marry the doge's daughter. Do you know about how their rulers are chosen?"

"They have a council of forty who chooses the ruler from among the nobles," Ransom said. He'd learned much about the Genevese from traveling with Kohler's caravan.

"Indeed. But the appointment is for life or until impairment makes it impossible to rule. The doge is Domenic Orio. His daughter is Portia." He shrugged and sighed. "At least you chose who you married, Ransom. But as I said, I trust my mother's wisdom. I need a strong alliance to strengthen our position, and Mother said Portia will be wise and a suitable partner. She is going on this war with us."

Ransom was taken aback. "Truly?"

Benedict shrugged. "Why should she not? My brother's wife joined in the war when . . ."

His words trailed off at the mention of Noemie, Devon the Younger's wife. There was still a scar of pain in Ransom's heart from those days. Benedict caught his mistake, and he had the good grace to look away.

"I know the rumors weren't true, Ransom," he said softly. "It was that other knight, not you."

But there were still people who believed Ransom had seduced his master's wife. He had left Ceredigion to go to the oasis because of it. Strange how things from the past kept coming up again, as if the tide were bringing them back.

"That was long ago," Ransom said. The man who *had* cuckolded the king, Sir Robert Tregoss, had already met his end on a bloody meadow. "I do congratulate you on your upcoming marriage. When do you expect to meet your bride?"

"Within a fortnight," said the king. "You and Claire must come to the wedding."

"I will extend your invitation to her myself," Ransom said with a hopeful look.

The king gazed at him. "Missing her already? Like every other lovestruck fool I've known. I can say that now because I've not even met Portia yet. Devon changed after he was married. Maybe it will happen to me; I can't be sure. I'd like to think that I won't become sentimental." He chuckled. "I trust you, Ransom, just as I trust Longmont and my

61

mother. I do *not* trust my brother, Jon-Landon. That's why I'm sending him to Atabyrion." His gaze became more serious. "Am I wrong to distrust him?"

Ransom shook his head. "No, Bennett. He will use this war and your absence to his advantage."

The king sniffed and nodded firmly. "Longmont has been a faithful servant to me for many years. He's clever and always thinks the worst will happen. With men like DeVaux in the Vexin, the worst often does. I trust that you and Mother will not let the troubles of your own domains prevent you from keeping an eye on things in mine?"

"I have Simon of Holmberg serving me now in Glosstyr," Ransom said. "I hope that doesn't offend you . . . I know you dismissed him from the council."

"Sir Simon is a good fellow and all," said the king, "but he's a knight who has learned politics. He's not as capable as Damian Longmont. I'm sure the two of you will get along. He knows I favor you, and so he will seek your good graces. You'll see."

Ransom already had. And he didn't like the way the chancellor had tried to insinuate himself.

"When may I return to Legault?" Ransom asked the king.

"Oh, not quite yet," said the king with a grin. "We have maps to peruse, supplies to raise, and fish to catch and cure. You'll be going home by way of Brythonica. I want you to tell my sister-in-law how much money she needs to donate to the cause. Then you may return to your wife. But you're not to tell her the news until you see her. What you learned in council today must remain a secret for now. Guard it well."

He made a dismissive nod, which was Ransom's signal to leave. The trip to Brythonica was welcome—he was eager to talk to the duchess about his experience in the grove—yet he felt wearied by the burden of another secret. Ransom felt them wriggling inside his chest, squirming to get out.

Lord Toole is a worldly man, seasoned in years and experience. He's rather gaunt, but his voice is strong, forceful, and he has an implacable sense of justice. I'm pleased with his appointment. He's to immediately ride to Lord Tenthor in western Legault and demand the boor pay his due. It's a strategic move, to be sure, for Tenthor is a disagreeable man with bad breath and a developed muscle of pride reminiscent of Devon Argentine. Ransom said we must choose the top dog, and so we did.

Lord Toole said that each lord should be responsible for bringing the tax to Atha Kleah in person. Such a strategy prevents them from hiring brigands to intercept Lord Toole's tax collectors and steal the money back. He said that he's seen such wily tricks before and may have played them himself during his younger years.

Starting with Tenthor and adjusting the method of affairs of collection will benefit us in the short term, but Toole advised me that new measures must always be employed to keep the lords of Legault guessing. "They look at tax evasion as a sort of game," he said.

He also advised that Ransom be there in Atha Kleah when Tenthor arrives, for a show of strength might be necessary. I smiled and told him that his counsel was appreciated.

But thanks to King Benedict, I may be unable to fulfill his wishes. Still no word from Kingfountain.

—Claire de Murrow
Connaught Castle
(on commissioning the high sheriff of the Fair Isle)

CHAPTER SIX

The Tides of Ploemeur

everal days after the council meeting, Ransom left for Brythonica on a merchant vessel whose huge square sail was emblazoned with the Lion of Benedict. They stopped at the fortress of the Steene in Atabyrion to inform the king of Jon-Landon's imminent arrival, but even though the hour grew late, Ransom refused the captain's suggestion that they anchor in the Steene for the night. He didn't want to further delay his return to Claire. He thought he'd never rest, but the swell and fall of the sea calmed his mind and coaxed him to sleep at last.

The next morning, he awoke to find the ship at anchor. The feeling of forward momentum was gone, and he wondered why no one had roused him. Getting to his feet, he marched out of his stateroom and up the stairs to the squawking of angry seabirds. His heart sank when he saw Ploemeur in the distance, the palace rising on a hill inside the cove.

The captain ambled up to him, looking apologetic. "I'm sorry, my lord, but we were too late." He pointed. "The tide is ebbing, and all of the ships are leaving Ploemeur. We'll have to wait until they're gone." True to the captain's word, Ransom saw dozens of ships leaving port, creating an enormous scene. He hadn't considered the possibility of such a delay, but he should have—Brythonica was a strong trading duchy.

"So we have to sit here and wait?"

"I'm afraid so, my lord. We'd risk an accident if we tried to force our way in right now. Again, I'm sorry."

They were forced to anchor off the coast near a spit of land and wait for the ships blocking the way to depart. The wait was maddening, and he paced restlessly on the deck until the captain whistled for his attention. Two smaller boats were rowing toward them. When they came alongside the cog, he saw a knight wearing the Raven badge.

"The duchess was informed about your ship," said the knight, cupping his hand around his mouth to amplify his voice. "You bear the king's emblem."

"Aye," said the captain. "We're from Kingfountain. Lord Ransom has a message for the duchess."

"She thought that might be the case," said the knight. "We were ordered to row out and bring him in. When the shipping lane clears, come into the harbor."

Grateful for the reprieve, Ransom took a rope offered by one of the sailors and used it to climb down into one of the boats below. They rowed hard, keeping a distance between their small craft and the ships exiting the cove, and made their way toward the docks.

The knight escorted Ransom to the Hall of Justice, where he found a boisterous crowd had gathered to speak to the duchess. His stomach dropped when he saw the crowd, but the knight took him to an antechamber and told him to wait there.

Another indeterminable stretch of time lay before him, and he sighed with growing unease at having to wait again. What was Claire doing? How was the work on the castle progressing? He longed to be there.

But his concern proved unwarranted when Constance opened the door moments later, entering the chamber hand in hand with her son, Drew. She still wore black, as she had at Ransom's wedding, but the dress had a stately cut, and her jewelry added a splash of color.

"Welcome back to Ploemeur, Lord Ransom." She squeezed the boy's hand. "Be courteous, Andrew."

The little boy smiled at him. "Hello. Can I hold your sword?"

"Andrew," the mother scolded.

"But I want it. Look, Maman, it has the Raven on the sheath!"

Ransom approached the two of them and bowed his head in greeting.

She beheld him with a serious expression. "You were at the grove recently. Weren't you?"

"I was, my lady. How did you know?"

"When the Gradalis is used, it sends out a tremor of sorts, like a distant peal of thunder. I felt it in my bones. It happened in the morning."

"Yes," Ransom agreed. "I was summoned to defend the grove."

"I thought so. I sent knights to investigate, but there was nothing there when they arrived. It has caused me a few sleepless nights. What happened there?"

He was grateful no one was there but the three of them. "There were men there, swordsmen trying to take the Gradalis. They attacked me as soon as I arrived. Some were already dead when I arrived. I'm not sure what caused it, but the rest . . . I killed, my lady. And then the ground swallowed the corpses."

"The grove has its own magical protections," Constance explained. "Those who try to use the Gradalis summon a hailstorm, brought on by the bowl's magic. Anyone caught unawares can be smitten severely, even killed." Her lips pressed together tightly. "Do you have any idea where they were from?"

"I did get a clue. One of them had a necklace with the emblem of a fish—"

"Kerjean!" she said suddenly, interrupting.

"I think you have it right. I've been to Kerjean, and it was the same symbol." He reached into his pocket and produced the necklace and charm. It was something he carried with him, a reminder of his obligation to protect the Gradalis from those who would steal it. It served as a reminder also of Alix's treachery and his commitment to avenging the deaths of Devon the Younger and Elder.

"The symbol of the Fisher Kings," she added when she saw it. "They were the original guardians of the Gradalis, as I told you before." Her fingers played distractedly in her son's hair. The boy looked so innocent that Ransom felt a surge of protectiveness toward him. He put the necklace back into his pocket. "They're hunting for it. They will continue to. It concerns me that they made it this far. Have you told anyone?"

"No, my lady," Ransom said, shaking his head.

"Not even Lady Claire? Not even your wife?"

"I haven't," he said. "The Fountain bid me not to."

She let out a worried sigh. "If you've come from Kingfountain, then you've already heard the news about the Chandleer Oasis. Is that correct?"

"Yes, and I come bearing orders from the king and the new justiciar."

"Longmont?" she asked, her voice betraying a feeling of loathing.

"Yes. Do you know him?"

"Oh yes, to be sure. You know that our duchies border each other. He was a frequent visitor to Ploemeur. He has expensive tastes. When he was with Duke Benedict, he was all grace and agreeability. But when he came alone, he was rather imperious. He acted as if *he* were the Duke of Vexin."

Ransom wasn't surprised, and his worries now multiplied. Although he thought Benedict had the makings of a fine king, he didn't always exercise good discernment. As when he'd trusted Estian when he shouldn't have. "I'm sorry to hear it."

"I learned about the East Kingdoms because of the trading alliances we have with Genevar. In fact, I knew of it before the queen did. As a result, we've been saving grain and preparing for famine should this affair end poorly." She gave him a worried look. "Has the king asked you to accompany him?"

"No, I'm to stay and defend the realm. Longmont was made justiciar, but the king has given his mother and me the power to check him."

Her eyes closed with relief. She knelt by her son and kissed his cheek. "Go bring some berries for Lord Ransom. Would you do that, please?"

"Yes, Maman," the boy said and quickly hurried out of the room.

"I'm relieved," she said after he was gone. "For selfish reasons, to be sure. My son means the world to me. If anything were to happen to him . . . but I also fear for the king's life. Is it true that the kings of Brugia, Occitania, and Ceredigion are going to fight together?"

"That's what the king said," replied Ransom. "None of them trust each other. But Genevar has brought everyone together to fight for a mutual cause. Benedict is to marry the doge's daughter."

"Yes, Lady Portia," said Constance. "I had news of it last night."

"The king said they're to be married in a fortnight."

"Not that soon," she replied with an enigmatic smile. "The doge is clever. The wedding will not happen at Kingfountain but at the Isle of Cerest, a Genevese stronghold east of Brugia. And the doge will not allow the marriage agreement to be consummated until all three kings have set out for the East Kingdoms. Benedict will march south with our Genevese allies. Estian will command the vanguard and march through the desert to strike from the west. And King Rotbart of Brugia will attack from the south."

Ransom glanced at her in concern. Did Benedict even know this information? It certainly hadn't been shared at court. "My lady, this information . . . how did you come by it?"

She gave him a pointed look. "From the doge's ambassador. He sought out an audience with me to ask whether Benedict is a man of his word. The threat from the East Kingdoms is real, Ransom, though none of us know what spurred it. When I learned Benedict was going to fight, I assumed that you would go with him. If he were wise, he would take you. But I must say that I'm glad he decided not to." She lowered her voice. "If he perishes in this war, then my son may someday become King of Ceredigion. I don't trust Jon-Landon. So I am grateful that you are staying."

"It will be difficult to get word back in a timely way."

"It will indeed. But as I told you, the Genevese are very liberal in their sharing of information with me. If something should happen to Benedict, I'll know before Jon-Landon does, and I will summon you to Ploemeur. I'm grateful the Gradalis called on you to defend it. Perhaps the prison will be open at last."

Ransom's brow furrowed. "Prison?"

She shook her head. "More secrets . . . for another time. What orders did you bring me from the king?"

Ransom withdrew the scroll from his pocket and handed it to her. She broke the seal and began to read it. Drew returned with a plate of berries and offered them to Ransom. He ate the delicious fruit while she read.

"I don't know how I can afford to pay this," she said, shaking her head. "But that is my problem, not yours. Two hundred knights to join the war . . . that will leave Brythonica vulnerable. But the king has commanded it, and so I will obey." She looked at him. "Will you stay the night? It's always dangerous attempting a night crossing."

"No, I must get back to Legault. Thank you for your trust."

Drew came up and stood by her again, staring up at Ransom with a look of admiration. Constance stroked his hair again, and the protective look on her face made Ransom's soul tremble.

Waves crashed against the side of the cog, rocking it violently. A storm had struck after they left Ploemeur and rounded the tip of the Brythonican peninsula. The tranquil sea was tranquil no more. The captain fought to reach Connaught, but the wind kept driving them away. Ransom's face dripped with rain, his clothes soaked from the waves pounding against them. He could see the castle in the distance, but it might as well have been on another island.

"We can't make landfall in such a storm!" the captain shouted to him, clinging to one of the ropes. "The waves will crush us into the rocks! We need another harbor!"

Frustration mounted inside him. "What other port is there?"

"Only Atha Kleah. We can be there before nightfall. The wind will push us right there. I'm sorry I can't deliver you to your lady, but it would be safer if we didn't try to fight it any longer!"

Another huge wave struck the hull of the cog, dousing both of them.

He'd wanted to see Atha Kleah with Claire. They'd planned to bring several of his knights and make a statement. But Claire wasn't here, and he had neither servants nor knights to accompany him. The four who'd traveled with him from Kingfountain had ridden home from Brythonica on borrowed steeds. Entering Atha Kleah like this might be the most foolish thing he'd ever done. But it made him queasy to watch the gray surf pounding against the cliffs. What had Claire said? *Terrible is the sea.* Besides, Lord Toole was in Atha Kleah. He could call on him.

"Let's do as you say," Ransom yelled. Then he went belowdecks before he could be swept off to sea to find out for himself whether the Lady of the Fountain was real or the Aos Sí.

They did reach Atha Kleah before nightfall. It was the largest city in Legault, a dank and miserable-looking place. Ransom's normally iron-hard stomach had been dented by the storm, and he was only too grateful to disembark.

Until he saw the crowd that had gathered on the wharf. The cog bore the royal emblem of Ceredigion, and passersby were pointing at it and standing around. Ransom walked down the dock, listening for any strains of Ceredigion or Occitanian, but they were all speaking in their ancient tongue, and he felt more and more uncertain.

"Oy, Sir Knight!" said a man missing a few teeth, accosting him in the language of Ceredigion. "You lost?"

Ransom reached for his blade, and the man quickly held up his hands. "I'm no blighter! Give a man a few livres? I'll guide you wherever you're going."

"Lord Toole," Ransom said. "Where is he?"

"Ah! Lord Toole. You know the high sheriff, eh? What's the purpose of that ship, eh? Is it going to take the taxes to Kingfountain? Is that what it's for?"

"Can you bring me to Toole or not?" Ransom said.

"I can. For a few livres. That's not too much to ask."

Ransom didn't trust him, but he felt a strange compulsion to follow him anyway. "Lead the way."

Clenching his hand around his sword hilt, he followed the oily man through the throng of people talking and laughing. Many were drinking a honeyed sort of drink that smelled sickly sweet to Ransom's nose. Ransom's neck prickled with warning as they entered the cobblestone streets of Atha Kleah. He looked to the side and saw several dark-clothed men trailing after them. His stomach was still ill from the voyage, but he prepared himself to fight.

The man brought him to a stately-looking home with a wrought-iron fence in front of it, the iron forming a woven design. The man jogged up the steps and quickly banged on a door. He looked down at Ransom, who remained at the level of the street. There were many such homes crowded close together.

The door opened, and the man spoke in Gaultic to the servant, who answered in the same manner. Some money exchanged hands surreptitiously, quickly pocketed by the guide. Ransom scowled. He felt the presence of the men in the shadows behind him, watching him closely, but they were not near enough to strike at him.

The fellow jogged down and opened his palm. "You're here. Some livres, mate?"

"Weren't you already paid?" Ransom asked him.

"Oh, that's nuthin'. I pick up coin where I can. You said you would. You're a man of honor?"

Ransom dug into his purse and dropped two livres into the man's palm. He looked disappointed by the offering.

Ransom marched up the steps, but the door opened before he could knock. The servant was dressed in a green tunic with gold thread. He had carrot-colored hair and a little beard. "Welcome, mayster, welcome," he said, speaking in Ransom's language but with a thick Gaultic accent.

Ransom was sopping wet when he entered the fine home. The noise of the street quieted. He smelled varnish and a cooking meat dish. A huge two-handed sword was mounted above the hearth, the naked blade gleaming in the candlelight.

"This way, mayster." The servant guided him to a room and opened the door.

Inside was a huge man, taller even than Ransom. The big man paced back and forth while four other knights in hauberks stood watching. They looked at Ransom with disdain. The huge man had a qinnamon-colored beard and scars across his brow. His hands were enormous.

"Lord Toole?" Ransom asked, but he already knew it wasn't him.

"No," answered the man in a deep, thrumming voice. "My name is Tenthor."

We arrived in Atha Kleah today. It's been so many years since I came here that I hardly recognized it. The amount of trade that goes through this city will soon rival that of Ploemeur. There are Genevese ships everywhere and huge imposing hulks on the lookout for brigands who prey on the waters between the Fair Isle and the continent.

The fortress of Atha Kleah still stands in the northeast corner of town. From the view of my tower window, I can see Scath Pool, which is the broad moat beyond the castle walls. I can also see the Wood Quay just to the south. That's where all the ships are moored. It's a busy town. Lord Toole, who is at the fortress with us tonight, said that the city is dark after the sun goes down. It is kept so because of the brigands. All the castle windows have thick wooden shutters.

Tomorrow we will meet with the first group of nobles who are to pay their taxes. I've been so ill in the mornings, but I mustn't let it show. I'll not breakfast in the morning. It wouldn't do well to earn their respect if they saw their queen spewing her food.

—Claire de Murrow
Royal Fortress, Atha Kleah

CHAPTER SEVEN

Shadows in the Sun

Ransom looked from man to man, realizing that he was in a dangerous situation. He felt his Fountain magic ripple in a belated warning he was surprised hadn't come sooner.

"I had a feelin' de Murrow's brat would take the treasure by ship," the lord said to Ransom. "I've had men stand watch on the quay. It's worth a thousand livres to me to gain your cooperation. That's more than you'll earn in ten years, Sir Knight. Who do you serve?"

Ransom met the steady gaze with one of his own. They still didn't know who he was. That was to his advantage. "I serve Glosstyr," he said simply and watched for their reaction.

One of the men seemed shaken by the information, but the others just sneered.

"Glosstyr, eh?" said Tenthor with a chuckle. "A thousand livres. No one will know about our arrangement. You were looking for Toole. He's at the fortress with *her*. All I want is to know the day the ship you came on will set sail. I'll pay my taxes, but I want the money back. It's worth a thousand to me, you see. Do we have an understanding, lad?"

Ransom glanced at the man to his left, then looked back at Tenthor. "You think I'd betray my lord for a thousand livres?" he said softly.

"I'm counting on it," said Tenthor. "Men disappear in Atha Kleah all the time. Especially if they sail under the wrong banner."

Now it had turned from a bribe to a threat.

"I'll not help you," Ransom said, shaking his head. The sense of danger increased, making the skin at the back of his neck prickle. "It's for the best if we end this conversation now. I'll be on my way to the fortress."

Tenthor gave him a menacing smile. "As you will, Sir Knight. Lads . . . show him the door."

Ransom felt their intent to maim and harm him. So he didn't wait for them to attack. He lunged to the left and smashed his fist into the jaw of the closest knight, snapping the man's head back. The commotion that ensued became a blur as his Fountain magic responded to the danger. He kicked another man in the abdomen before he was grabbed around the middle. Instinct overcame him, and he knocked his head back into his attacker's nose and felt the weak bone crack.

Then Tenthor was in front of him, punching Ransom in the gut in a vicious blow that took his breath away. Another fist, hard as a stone, collided with his forehead and sent a blinding flash of light before his eyes. The others crowded in, grabbing at his arms to hold him back. Ransom used their grip to his advantage and lifted himself up, kicking Tenthor in the face and knocking him backward. When his own feet were back on the floor, he levered the man holding his right arm with pure strength and hurled him down.

Another fist came at Ransom's jaw, but he ducked, and the man punched the wall instead, letting out a yelp of pain. As the knight still holding his left arm released it in shock, Ransom punched him on the cheekbone with his left fist. The invisible ring on his finger sliced the man's cheek open, and blood began to spill.

Tenthor, who'd recovered and regained his feet, roared and charged at Ransom again like a bull. The two collided, and Ransom was shoved back into the wall. The massive man grabbed Ransom's throat with one hand, his face curling with rage as he raised his fist to punch.

Ransom kneed him in the groin twice before pain finally slackened the man's grip. The moment it loosened, Ransom caught hold of the giant's collar and shoved him face-first into the wall.

He saw a flash of steel, and a dagger came at his ribs. Ransom turned, catching the man's wrist, and then brought the edge of his hand into his throat. The dagger clattered to the floor an instant before the knight did, holding his neck and struggling to breathe.

Ransom turned and saw everyone else had fallen to the floor. His breath came hard and fast. Lord Tenthor held his loins with one hand, grunting in pain, and pushed away from the wall, blood oozing from his eyebrow. The giant's shoulders quivered as he began to stand again.

Ransom sensed his host's desire to continue the fight, so he grabbed him by the shirt with both hands and shoved him into the wall again. The Gaultic lord fell to the ground, unconscious.

Ransom gazed across the room at the other men, some writhing and one cringing from him. He walked to the door and opened it, and the servant who had led him upstairs backed away in terror. Grabbing the man by the neck, Ransom hauled him to the front door.

"You're taking me to the fortress," he said. "Now."

"Yes! Of course! Can I check on my—?"

"No," Ransom barked. He kept a firm grip on the servant, and as they made their way onto the busy street, people pointedly ignored them. The men who had followed him were gone, or at least he couldn't sense them any longer.

They wove through the crowds as dusk faded into darkness and the streets began to clear. Shops closed, as did all the shutters. There were still others walking about, only now they were hurrying back to their dwellings instead of reveling in the street. Darkness brought danger, Ransom sensed.

"Where is it?" Ransom demanded.

"A little farther. You can see the towers?" He pointed to a sturdy structure, surrounded by timber-and-plaster homes. They turned another corner, and the fortress gates lay ahead. Ransom let go of the servant, who fled like a frightened animal.

As he marched up to the gate, he saw several knights standing guard. He recognized one of them as Sir Axien, one of his own mesnie. He couldn't imagine what he looked like, waterlogged and approaching them in the dark, his boots still squelching.

"You may be lost, friend," said one of the knights good-naturedly. "Go back the way you came."

"He probably only speaks Gaultic," said Sir Axien and then stopped when Ransom drew near. "By the Lady! It's Lord Ransom! Did you come on the king's ship? The one that docked at Wood Quay?"

"Aye," he answered. "I was a little lost. Is Claire here?"

"Yes," Axien said, grinning broadly. "She'll be only too grateful you came in time. We're collecting taxes on the morrow. You're soaked! Let's get you inside."

They walked through the gate, and Ransom was immediately surrounded by servants eager to attend to him. They had all heard of him, but none had met him. He heard Gaultic expressions left and right. The throng followed him inside, where he saw Dearley gaping at him in astonishment.

"What are you doing here?" Dearley asked, flummoxed.

"Is this not where I should be?" Ransom answered, arching his eyebrows.

"You know what I mean! I thought you were still in Kingfountain! Was that your ship? We heard about one of the king's ships docking at the wharf, but no messenger came. Come on, Lady Claire will be just as astonished as I am!"

He led the way up a set of stairs, past several smoking torches that would have given Lord Kinghorn a coughing attack. Once at the top, they entered a solar, and the first thing he saw was Claire holding her stomach and leaning over a bronze dish, one arm pressed against the wall. Although her back was to him, he could see a glimpse of her pale cheeks. His anticipation turned to concern—Had Alix attacked her while he was away?—but he reached out with his magic and could sense no evidence of warning or danger. She was queasy, nothing more. He watched Elodie hand her a cup of water. Claire rinsed her mouth out and spat in the dish before handing the cup back with a grateful smile.

Another man rose from a chair, a gaunt-looking fellow with a lot of silver in his hair.

"Is this the messenger?" Lord Toole asked, looking at Ransom with expectation.

"No. It's the Duke of Glosstyr," Dearley said.

Claire straightened, turned, and looked at Ransom as if she didn't recognize him. Then she blinked with surprise. "Ransom!" she gasped and hurried to him, rushing into his embrace. Although she was pale, she felt warm, and the ache caused by their separation began to fade.

When they kissed, he felt a sense of peace wash through him. He hooked his hand around her neck and then noticed the wet spots on her dress from his tunic.

"I'm soaking wet," he apologized.

She drank him up with her gaze. "Oh, you eejit. I wouldn't care if you were *sáithithe*—soaked to the skin!"

It was nearly midnight. All the windows in the fortress were shut, and the remains of a fire crackled in the hearth. Ransom had changed into dry clothes, and he sat next to Claire on a small sofa, Lord Toole and Dearley across from them on a pair of chairs. He'd told them all about his trip to Kingfountain, the king's betrothal, the upcoming war with the East Kingdoms, and the storm that had prevented him from landing at Connaught—which was, it turned out, a blessing instead of an inconvenience.

Because of Atha Kleah's status as a trading port, word had already reached them about the trouble at the Chandleer Oasis. But none of them had heard news of the war, so they'd listened eagerly to his story. Claire was grateful, relieved even, that Ransom had not been chosen to go with the king into the war.

Lord Toole had given Ransom a briefing on his new role as high sheriff of Legault. The results, of course, would be revealed on the morrow when the most powerful lord of the realm, Lord Tenthor, was due to bring his taxes to the palace. Ransom smiled and nodded and did not mention his encounter with the nobleman.

If the man didn't show up, he fully intended to bring him in. He knew where he was staying.

"It's after midnight," Lord Toole finally said. "I suppose we should let the queen and her consort have some time to themselves. Shall we depart, Sir Dearley?"

"I'd completely lost track of time," Dearley said. "Of course. No doubt Elodie is fast asleep herself. Atha Kleah is very quiet at night. I prefer it."

"The quiet is not peaceful," said Lord Toole. "We'll have to do something about the brigands soon, my lady. But let us control the roads before we try taming the seas."

He rose from his chair, and Dearley followed suit, both men taking their leave.

Ransom, still holding Claire's hand, rubbed her knuckles with his thumb.

"Is that a bruise?" she asked him, touching his cheek. "I didn't notice it under your scruff."

"Is it?" he asked, lifting her hand and kissing it. "You were unwell when I arrived."

"I've been unwell for over a week," she said with a sigh. "But now my mood has improved."

"I'm sorry we quarreled before I left."

"It was my fault," she said softly, looking down. "I'm glad you did your duty. And that fair winds blew you home in time."

"I hope Longmont isn't as dreadful as Lady Constance said he is," Ransom murmured. He'd told them about his stop at Ploemeur, although he hadn't disclosed the secret that bound him. He couldn't, however much he hated keeping it from his wife.

"He's not the one I'm worried about," Claire said, sidling closer to him. She leaned her head against his neck, her hair tickling his throat. "It's Jon-Landon. Do you think he'll stay in Atabyrion?"

"No, I don't," Ransom answered with a sigh. "But what's to be done about it?"

"I suppose it's Longmont's trouble. But the oasis is very far away. And what if the king doesn't return?"

"Hush," Ransom said, feeling suddenly ill. Constance had already mentioned that possibility, and he didn't wish to think about it. Already two kings he'd served had died. "Let's talk of more pleasant things." He took a goblet and filled it with a little wine.

"There is one bit of news that I wanted to share with you. Now that we're alone, it's probably as good a time as any."

"What?" he asked, stroking her arm, enjoying the feeling of being alone with her at last.

She turned her head and whispered something in his ear. The surprise made him drop his goblet.

Ransom held Claire's hair out of her face as she vomited noisily into the basin. He could hear the rumble of conversation in the audience hall beyond the heavy wooden door. Claire's maid, Keeva, fetched her a drink of water for when she was finished. The nobles had been assembling, and the furor was growing louder as they waited for their queen to finally arrive. Knights patrolled the gates and the grounds, on the lookout for any trouble.

"I can do this," Claire gasped, nodding her head. She took the proffered cup and swallowed some water. Then she took a deep breath and gripped Ransom's hand. He squeezed back, staring at her with love. Now he knew the reason for her sickness. A child was coming. A child that would arrive before Benedict even reached the East Kingdoms. What if it was a little girl with hair like her mother's? The thought made him grin like a fool.

The wooden door opened, and Dearley entered. "Everyone is here," he said solemnly. "They look none too happy."

Ransom pressed her hand to his lips. "You are their queen. I believe in you."

She let out a pent-up breath. "Hopefully, it won't end in a brawl."

Ransom thought about Lord Tenthor, who would surely recognize him despite his change in clothes. "I don't think it will."

They walked hand in hand toward the door.

"Good luck, my lady," Keeva said, beaming.

Even after vomiting in a bucket, Claire had a regal look about her. As Dearley opened the door for them, a hush fell over the hall. Everyone rose in unison as the couple entered the hall. There were lords and ladies standing before wooden benches, which had been arranged for the occasion. Lord Toole stood by the double throne at the head of the room, and he bowed his head to them, prompting everyone else to do the same.

Ransom and Claire walked together, side by side, climbed the dais, and seated themselves. The queen's throne was more prominent, which was as it should be—Ransom was a king's man, not a king. They sat in unison, and their audience followed suit. At the front bench was a huge man with a qinnamon-colored beard. He had dark scabs on his nose and cheek, a purpling bruise on his forehead, and a split lip.

He looked up at them and saw Ransom sitting next to the queen. A look of recognition came over his face. His lip began to tremble with dread as he realized just who had given him a beating the night before. Ransom bowed his head slightly to Lord Tenthor.

"That big man is Lord Tenthor," Claire whispered to Ransom. "He's in an awful state. I wonder what happened to him?"

Ransom squeezed her hand and said, "We met last night when I arrived."

Claire's brow shot up as she turned her head and looked at Ransom in disbelief.

The leaves on the trees have begun to change to their more brilliant hues. Ransom says this is his favorite season because the leaves remind him of my hair. So much has happened this summer, I have not had a chance to pick a quill up to write before now.

I'm pleased to say that the renovations of Connaught castle are going well. The roof and outer walls have been repaired, which means we can winter here. Lord Toole has successfully been established as high sheriff, and taxes continue to flow into our coffers. Even better, we now have an ally in Lord Tenthor, who, despite the drubbing he received—or perhaps because of it—has been a strong voice for unity in Legault. That doesn't mean other lords aren't acting like complete eejits, but each disruption has been put down, the culprit fined for breaching the peace. Each fortnight, we ride to Atha Kleah to hear complaints and dispense justice. A boat is faster, but the mere thought of sailing makes me ill. The vomiting is coming less and less now, and my belly gets firmer and firmer, like it's becoming the rind of some strange fruit.

Things are not as well back in Ceredigion. The justiciar, Lord Longmont, has managed to offend nearly everyone, including the queen dowager. They say he is relentless in collecting taxes to support the war with the East Kingdoms, but he pockets plenty of the proceeds for himself. He has a new *wardrobe made every other fortnight, rides expensive stallions, and makes people bow as if he himself were king. So far, the queen has tried to temper Longmont's impulses with warnings, but he's utterly deaf to them. She doesn't want to countermand Benedict's decision so soon after the appointment, but the lord chancellor is showing no signs of self-awareness. If he continues in this way, he will give Emiloh and Ransom no choice but to act.*

Benedict and Portia were married on the Isle of Cerest, as the doge insisted in his terms for the wedding, so none of us have even seen her. It is unclear whether they will try and cross before the winter storms begin. It seems a foolish risk to me, but I imagine Benedict's impatience will prevail.

I'm grateful we are so far away. Sir Simon sends us news from Glosstyr regularly. But Longmont hasn't provoked Ransom. In fact, he has put two new royal castles under Ransom's stewardship, providing us with additional income. My husband didn't ask for them. I think it's Longmont's way of trying to keep those happy who could do him the most harm.

—Claire de Murrow
Connaught Castle
At the turn of the season

CHAPTER EIGHT

Fell Return

The noise of birds awoke Ransom from his slumber. They'd kept the windows open again that night, and by morning, a chill had settled into the room. He opened his eyes and found Claire turned away from him, the quill scratching softly in the little book she kept. A book that she'd not let him read.

He nestled closer to her, hooking his chin on her shoulder. Turning her head, she gave him a smile and then took his hand and placed it over her womb.

"Are you very sick this morning?" he asked her. Some mornings it was the sound of her retching that awakened him, not the noise of the birds.

"Surprisingly, no." She blew on the page to dry the ink and then gently closed the book. She set both the book and quill down near the ink bottle on the table beside their bed.

"What were you writing about?" he asked her.

"I was describing how loudly you snore," she said with a teasing grin. Then she snuggled back against him. "I jest. I was writing about Longmont."

"Are you sure it wasn't a love poem?" he asked, teasing her back.

"Am I to be a minstrel for you? We can send for one if you would like to hear yourself praised all day long."

He circled his palm around her belly, still finding it strange to think a living being had quickened inside of her. There was no sure way of knowing if they would have a daughter or a son, although Keeva believed it was a girl because she'd dangled a ring on a chain over Claire's womb, and the ring had gone in a circle instead of swinging back and forth. Part of him was overjoyed, but the prospect of fatherhood terrified him. His own father had bet his life on King Gervase's compassion. And Ransom had watched as the Elder King's sons turned against him, one by one. Even months after his death, the horror of watching the man die had stamped an imprint on Ransom's soul.

He didn't want to repeat the mistakes of the past, but life had a cyclical nature he did not quite understand. Wishing to avoid something wasn't the same as doing so.

"You're quiet of a sudden," Claire said, turning. "Are you brooding?"

"I suppose I am," he confessed.

"About what, my love? Where shall we start? Lord Purser Dougal is acting like a brainless badger again. He's been stealing from his neighbor in the middle of the night and then attacking with his knights when the man attempts to reclaim what he took. Lord Crowen just fell off his horse and broke his leg, leaving him vulnerable to attack. It's costing more to fix Connaught than we were told in the beginning, which has strained our coffers here as well as in Glosstyr. There is a heap of missives to be read and answered that only grows fatter . . . as do I. Some days I wonder if we should even bother getting out of bed."

He smiled at her banter and kissed her earlobe.

"What's troubling you?" she asked, more solicitously that time.

"It's nothing," he said, shaking his head. "Why borrow trouble?"

She shifted and lay on her back, looking up at his face. To him, she was breathtakingly beautiful, even in the morning when her hair was disheveled and she wore a simple linen chemise instead of a royal gown.

Reaching out, she touched his chest with her hand. "Will you ever share your heart with me, Ransom?"

"You have my heart," he said, looking at her in confusion. "All of it."

"But you hide things from me. Like right now. You hide your feelings."

He put his hand atop hers. "What kind of father was Lord Archer?"

"That's a different question from what kind of *man* he was. He was strong in front of others, like you, but he was a caring and indulgent father. He'd listen to me prattle on about stories of the Aos Sí, even though I'd repeated them dozens of times before, and he'd smile as I assume most indulgent fathers do. He trusted me. He let me make my own decisions, even if they annoyed him." A smile of memory touched her lips. "Remember when we met in Chessy? After all those years of not seeing each other? You gave me a taste of penuche, and I gave you the bracelet."

"Of course I remember. That's the night I began serving Emi."

"And now you serve another queen," she said with a wicked smile. "My father could have forbidden me to walk with you. From his perspective, you weren't a suitable husband back then. But he didn't forbid it. He gave me his counsel and let me make my own choice. He trusted me not to be foolish. Not many fathers would have."

She painted such a lifelike picture he found himself wishing he'd known Lord Archer better.

"So are you going to tell me what you were brooding about?" she asked with entreating eyes.

"I was worried about being a good father," he said simply.

Her look softened to one of deep tenderness. "That you even have that worry is a good sign, you fool eejit. I've never had any brothers or sisters, and my mother died when I was very little. So I have the same fear. But Emiloh was a good example to me. You will be a wonderful father, Ransom Barton. Or else!"

He chuckled softly and took her hand and brought it to his lips. He felt the calluses on her first two fingers from the bowstring. He liked that she practiced so much, even though he worried that the strain of effort might not be good for the baby growing inside her. But he didn't say anything about that worry, since he knew nothing about what her body was going through. Sometimes she'd get cramps in her legs for no reason at all. It was all rather baffling.

"I should get up and go to the training yard," he told her, releasing her hand and touching the tip of her nose.

"I suppose I should let you," she sighed. "There is much to do today."

⋈

A ship from Glosstyr came with the morning tide, which wasn't unusual since Sir Simon sent updates regularly from Ceredigion. But this time he came in person, and when Dearley announced him, Claire and Ransom looked at each other in startled surprise and pushed aside the breakfast dishes.

Sir Simon strode into the room, tugging off his gloves and stuffing them into his belt as he approached their breakfast table in the great hall. He bowed quickly.

"What brings you all the way from Glosstyr, Simon?" Ransom asked, feeling a pit inside his stomach. For Simon to have arrived with the morning tide, he must have left Glosstyr the night before. Night voyages were risky, especially at the change of the seasons, so this was not idle news.

"I couldn't entrust it to a messenger," Simon answered. He looked at Dearley and then back at them. "Can we speak privately?" Claire motioned to the servants to disperse, and they did. Dearley bowed to take his leave, but Ransom asked him to stay. As the first knight of

Ransom's mesnie, he was given more liberties than some of the other knights.

After the servants had left and shut the door, Simon began to pace.

"This is ill news indeed," Claire said, "if you begin in such a manner. Out with it, Simon."

He sighed and turned to face them both. "Last night I had a message from Lady Deborah. Jon-Landon showed up at her castle."

"He left Atabyrion," Ransom said with growing dread.

"But why did he go to Lady Deborah?" Claire asked in confusion.

"You know she was part of the Elder King's council," Simon answered. "She's also in charge of Thorngate castle, which Longmont has tried to claim as a royal castle. It's hers by right, of course, and she isn't a young lady who can be taken in wardship, although that was exactly what Longmont tried to do. He wants to increase Benedict's power and weaken those who were once loyal to the Elder King. Believe me, I haven't passed on half of the complaints I've heard from Ashel and Rainor. They both feel they're being edged out of the king's council. Jon-Landon is using the unrest to insert himself. He's seeking allies. You know he and Lord James have long been friends. So he went to Dundrennan first and then to Thorngate. She sent me word right away and asked that I get a message to you."

"Does Emiloh know?" Claire asked.

Simon shook his head. "I don't think so. I thought it best to come here first. You and the queen dowager were to put a check on Longmont's power. I tell you, Ransom, he's a conniving, duplicitous powermonger. And that's being generous. He's done nothing to alienate you because he's afraid of you. But he's acting like an arrogant git and giving Jon-Landon an opening. If the prince isn't back in Atabyrion before winter, he won't go back at all. He could try to seize the throne."

Ransom closed his eyes, feeling the queasiness increase. The king had only been gone for five months, and already the situation was deteriorating.

"How long would it take to get a message to King Benedict?" Claire asked.

Simon shrugged. "Four months with a fast ship? By the time the messenger would reach him, he'd already be wintering on the Isle of Korfe."

"I can't send a message to him without talking to Emiloh first," Ransom said. "She could command her son to return to Atabyrion."

"But will he listen to her? Their relationship is strained, Ransom." Claire tossed her head. "Jon-Landon may be gambling that Benedict has committed himself too much to the cause to come back. He could be gone for years and then out of earshot if something happens."

"Ransom, you have to come," Simon said, putting his hands on the table. "This is a moment of crisis. If you return, it changes the situation."

Ransom looked at Claire's pale cheeks. Simon was right, but what if he couldn't return before the winter storms? What if they would be separated for the entire season? He wanted to clench his fist and slam the table in frustration.

"I have to concur with Simon, Ransom," she said in a resentful tone. "This is Jon-Landon's best chance at stealing power. Even a half-brained lackwit like Jon-Landon can see that." She put her hand on Ransom's clenched one. "If you go now, it may frighten him back to Atabyrion. And something has to be done about Longmont. Sadly, it is the nature and disposition of some men to let power go to their heads. Longmont drinks it like some men drink wine. He's an eejit. Knock some sense into him."

Ransom rose from the chair. "Were there any signs of storms when you left?"

"No, but there were some ugly-looking clouds behind us. We might have to follow the coast toward Ploemeur."

That made sense as well. The open sea between Connaught and Glosstyr could be perilous, although it was a shorter distance.

Claire rose from her seat. "You brought ill news, Simon of Holmberg. Next time, you owe us something better."

"I'll try my best, my lady," he said.

"Any word from Brugia or Occitania?" she asked him.

"Estian has arrived at his position for the winter. And King Rotbart has reached the coast to establish a beachhead. It's not too late for any of them to turn back. If Benedict returns, the others will as well. But I don't think he will. He married Portia, so he's committed himself to this war. He's trusting in you, Ransom, to defend Ceredigion while he's away."

"And he couldn't have chosen a better man to see it done," Claire said. "Did you rest during the voyage, Simon? Do you need some sleep?"

"I am exhausted," he confessed. "I don't sleep well on boats."

"I don't blame you. Dearley?"

"I'll see it done, my lady," Dearley said, responding quickly to the need. As the two of them left, the door shutting behind them, Ransom looked at Claire in concern.

"I will do everything in my power to be back before winter," he said.

"I know; it's not that," she said, shaking her head.

"Then what is it?"

She turned to him. "Don't go to Ploemeur."

He pushed his chair backward and looked at her in surprise. "Why not? It would be safer to follow the coast."

"I know, Ransom. You're going to think ill of me, but I must speak from the heart. I have an unfounded fear of the duchess. Her husband is dead, she has a little boy, and you're kindhearted to a fault. I can see you have some feelings of loyalty to her, and I fear . . . I don't know . . . that those feelings might cloud your . . . I'm being foolish." She closed her eyes, her face twisting with concern and worry. When she opened them again, she gave him an imploring look. "Don't break my heart,

Ransom. So many husbands stray. If I mean anything to you, don't ever be unfaithful to me." She looked down, tears thickening on her lashes.

The loyalty she sensed was real, but he couldn't explain the reason for it without sharing the secret of the Gradalis. However much he wanted to tell her about his secret duty, he knew he could not. The Fountain had warned him the Gradalis would be stolen if he spoke of it to anyone.

Reaching out, he tilted her chin so that she looked at him. "If it concerns you this much, we will not go that way."

She bit her bottom lip. "Now *I'm* the fool eejit. If there is a terrible storm raging and you need a safe harbor, by all means go to Ploemeur to avoid shipwreck. I shouldn't have let my fears leave my lips. I trust you, Ransom. Truly, I do. Maybe every woman with child has these fears. I worry I've become grotesque and you'll lose your desire for me."

He gave her a knowing smile. "Never. I will return as soon as I can."

She nodded and then thumped his chest with her fists. "You'd better not miss the birth of your child, Ransom Barton. I'm giving you fair warning."

◊

Before Ransom left with Simon of Holmberg, we rode horses into the meadows beneath Connaught castle. On the north side of the meadow a farmer had grown an enormous harvest of pumpkins. Some of them were too big for a man to lift. Many were carted up to the castle for winter storage, but there were several left. And so the young squires were brought down from the training yard with their swords, and they practiced the knightly art of decapitation on these orange husks.

We watched the lads, after placing stumps to hold up the pumpkins, swing and cleave and otherwise decimate their orange foes. Cattle would be allowed to graze in the field afterward, for the milch cows consider pumpkin a delicious feast. The boys were between the ages of ten and fifteen, many of them the sons of the noble houses of the Fair Isle. Not hostages, not like we were as children, but because their parents wish to gain favor with us by showing their trust in letting our knights train the lads.

As I watched them from horseback, I could not help but wonder if there is a son inside my own pumpkin belly. Strange feelings came over me, with Ransom seated on his ugly destrier, Dappled, next to me. Will the father train the son? Or will he be sent to serve in another household when he is barely more than a lad?

Or will this boy, if the Aos Sí grant it be so, be an archer and not a knight? I always ride with my bow and a quiver of arrows, and so I loosed a shaft across the meadow and struck one of the fattest pumpkins in the field. Many of the lads raised their swords and waved at us. At that moment, they felt like my sons, and my heart constricted as a mother's. These lads will grow up and fight to defend Connaught. And some of them will die. It's such a strange thing to think of. It made me wish Ransom weren't leaving so soon.

—Claire de Murrow
Connaught Castle
The pumpkin war

CHAPTER NINE

The Man Who Listed to Be a King

The storm smashed into their ship like so many hammer strokes in a blacksmith's forge. The turbulent sea rocked and tormented the boat and the passengers. Lightning streaked across the northern skies. A spray hit Ransom in the face as the boat tilted ominously to one side. He gripped the rope tightly, teeth clenched, the taste of salt in his mouth.

The captain barked orders, his words drowned out by the loud rustling of the square sail and creaking timbers. Simon gripped the rail and vomited over the side of the ship. Ransom felt queasy too, but his stomach had more iron in it, and he endured the buffeting wind and erratic plunges from the boat to better end.

"Get belowdecks!" Ransom called to Simon.

His friend looked at him with misery on his face. "It feels even worse down there where I can't see. Shouldn't we be there by now?"

"We might be wrestling this storm half the night," Ransom answered. Due to the change of season, it was getting dark earlier and earlier. They'd risked open sea to get to Glosstyr faster, but now they were in the teeth of the storm, and he regretted not turning south to Ploemeur. His promise to Claire had rendered that a less favorable option, but would the winds or the Fountain itself drag them there regardless?

A prickle of warning went down his back. At first he thought the Gradalis was summoning him again, but this felt more like the warnings he'd received from the Fountain in the past, the premonition of a threat he could not yet see.

Holding on to the rope, he left Simon to his misery and crossed the slick deck to where the captain managed the rudder. The crew fought against the sail to keep it steady.

The captain was leaning against the tiller with all his strength. He grinned like a maniac at Ransom as he approached. "Fine eve at sea, my lord!" he shouted, water droplets dripping from his beard.

A sudden pitch made Ransom sway, but he held on tight. "Is everything well?" he asked.

"Well? In a storm such as this? I've been in worse, my lord. The waves are rough, but we'll ride them."

Ransom looked behind the captain into the dark throes of the sea. And that's when he saw the other boat closing in on them. And the throb in his heart told him this was the source of the warning he'd felt.

"We're being followed," he said.

The captain turned his neck in confusion, and when he saw the other ship, he spluttered an oath. "Gag me, a brigand ship! They'd be daft to try and take us in the middle of this nonsense, but brigands are too greedy by half. Curse the moon, they're slicing through the waters like a knife!"

"What do we do?" Ransom demanded, wiping spume from his mouth. The salty taste of the sea sickened his stomach further.

"Hold the rudder, my lord. We need to prepare to fight them off."

Ransom took the captain's place, clenching his hands around the tiller and leaning his body weight against it. The captain scrambled ahead, calling out to the crew to prepare for action. As the brigand vessel came nearer, Ransom could see the braided hair and beards of the brigands in the fading light. There were a dozen or so, wearing leather armor, and some had the orange hair mostly found in Legault.

The captain returned to him and took his place. "My lads are fetching bows. That's the kind of warfare we'll have first, my lord. But it'll be mighty hard hitting anything with the waves rocking us to and fro! They'll jump aboard when they're close or use ropes to swing across." He looked at the scabbard strapped to Ransom's waist. "You'll be needin' that."

An arrow whistled past them, and the captain flinched.

"You're makin' a fine target, my lord! Get down!"

Ransom squatted near the captain, watching as the smaller vessel veered toward them down the side of a wave. More arrows began to pelt them, some sticking into the mast, others piercing the wooden side of the ship.

Lightning streaked across the sky overhead, illuminating the sea with a brightness that blinded.

"Oh, by the fells!" gasped the captain.

"What?" Ransom demanded.

"When the lightnin' went overhead, I was looking at the ship. That's Ryain Hood."

"A friend of yours?" Ransom asked with black humor.

"No, my lord! He's the worst of the brigands. I know him from the peasant hood he uses to disguise himself. The Genevese pay him an awful tribute so he won't attack their ships. He mostly preys on lords, though. If I had to guess, he saw us come in from Glosstyr and followed us back out. He's known for his skills with a bow."

As he said the words, an arrow struck the tiller with a jolt.

Ransom unsheathed his sword, gripping the rope again to steady himself. He squatted low and held himself sideways, giving the archers less of a target.

Another streak of lightning gave him a clear view of the brigands bearing down on them. A hooded man with a longbow stood at the prow, his face cast in darkness except for his chin and the tip of his nose. He had an arrow aimed straight at Ransom. The bow flexed, and the captain cried out in warning.

Ransom leaned on instinct, and the arrow sailed past him, missing him by a hair. The waves leveled again. A spurt of Fountain magic shot down his arms and legs, filling him with courage and preparing him to do battle. He rose, holding on to the rope with one hand and his sword with the other. The hooded archer took aim again. Another lightning flash revealed how close the other boat had come.

With his eyes fixed on the brigand's dark cowl, Ransom stared him down. An arrow would hurt, but it wouldn't kill him. As long as he wore the scabbard, he couldn't bleed.

The hooded brigand lowered his bow without loosing the arrow. The two ships went up the next wave together, one after the other. And then the archer waved his bow, and the brigands' ship turned another way.

The captain grinned like a madman. "They broke! They're not going to board us! Thank the Lady and all the Fountain's blessings!"

Had the brigand chief recognized Ransom? But if so, why had he turned away? Taking him prisoner would have won the man untold wealth. Maybe his reputation for violence had garnered him some wary respect.

"Land! Captain! Land!"

Ransom and the captain turned together and saw the watch flames burning from the fortress of Glosstyr in the distance.

Even though they'd arrived late at Glosstyr, the sound of the birds and the smell of the sea roused Ransom at dawn. He went down to the training yard and was pleased to see the castle knights drilling. He worked up a sweat himself and then went to bathe and change clothes in his room, which felt lonely without his wife.

Breakfast was brought to him, and Simon arrived soon afterward. When Ransom offered to share the food, his friend waved off the suggestion.

"I'm still queasy from last night," he said. "I'm relieved those brigands didn't try to board us. I should probably spend more time in the training yard. I haven't drawn my sword in years. I'm out of practice."

Ransom sipped from his goblet before setting it down again. "But if they'd come, you would have fought."

"True. Are you riding to Kingfountain today? The roads are pretty muddy."

"At least they don't rise and fall like the sea. The weather doesn't bother me. I'll head to the palace. Is Emiloh still there?"

"From what I've heard, yes, although she was planning to winter in Auxaunce. I hope she hasn't left yet."

"Do you think I should send a courier ahead of me?" Ransom asked, cutting a piece off a strip of pork.

"It might be better if your arrival surprised Longmont. You can see for yourself how he comports himself."

It was a good point.

"How many knights will you bring with you?" Simon asked.

"I was thinking a dozen. Can you choose the men to ride with me?"

"Gladly. When will you depart?"

"As soon as I finish eating," Ransom said with a smile and wolfed down the rest of his food.

The weather was foul all the way to Kingfountain. They stopped at Beestone to spend the night and then rode hard all the next day to try to reach the castle by dusk. With the ugly drizzle and inconsistent harder rain, they were all soaked and mud-spattered by the time they arrived. Water dripped from the wooden signs on the city streets as they passed them. Once, it had felt like home, but now the memories were bittersweet. It felt as if Devon the Younger might ride up beside him, laughing about some trifle, or his father, Devon the Elder, might be pacing restlessly in the throne room. And he couldn't help but think of Claire whenever he saw the tower where she and the queen had been imprisoned for years.

While crossing the bridge, he sank into the noise of the falls and let the sound fill him up and strengthen his determination. They rode up the hill to the castle proper, and their sudden arrival sent a shock wave through the knights guarding the gate, many of whom he knew from previous journeys.

"What are you doing here, Lord Ransom?" one of them asked with a nervous laugh.

"Is the queen dowager here?" he asked.

"Aye. Did you come for her . . . or to see Lord Long-Fur?"

Ransom furrowed his brow in annoyance.

The knight flushed with chagrin. "Sorry. He's a blasted fool. We mock him with many names. I beg your pardon, my lord."

That Longmont was being openly ridiculed by the knights didn't bode well. Ransom dismounted, travel weary but grateful he'd arrived. He marched into the castle while his knights attended to the horses. Torches burned in racks on the walls, and he observed the murals had been changed. New tapestries had been added, along with fine silk curtains hung from filigreed iron rails tacked into the stone walls. The walls had been scrubbed of soot—recently—and he noticed servants still bustled about, though it was late, scrubbing and arranging things with a look of nervous dread on their faces. They seemed too harried to even notice him as he passed.

Ransom's tunic and cloak were soaked through, so he went to change first. As he walked toward the stairwell, he heard gasps of dismay and turned around, finding servants on their knees, frantically wiping up the trail of mud he'd brought in with him. Sighing, he continued up the steps and went down the hall to his private room in the palace. Devon the Elder had allotted it to him due to his frequent stays at the palace, and Benedict had upheld the decision. It served as yet another reminder of how much gratitude he owed his king.

He grabbed the handle and pushed it open, earning a scream of dismay from a young woman inside in the midst of changing into a nightgown with the help of her maid.

"How dare you!" shrieked the lass.

Ransom, startled and mortified, froze for an instant. He didn't see any immodesty, but he quickly shut the door and backed away from it. Bewildered, he glanced up and down the hall, wondering if he'd made a mistake, but the room was in the same location it had always been.

A moment later, the door flung open, and the outraged young woman stood there with a shawl over her nightdress.

"Who are you! How dare you spy on me while I'm changing!" she said to him.

The maid looked abashed and backed away from the girl, who behaved like a lioness but was probably no more than twelve.

"I beg your pardon," Ransom said, still trying to understand. "I didn't know—"

"You could have knocked! Or were you *trying* to spy on me? Callum! Callum!" she yelled, her voice rising.

Another door opened, and a knight with a tunic and sword came charging out with a confident look. It took a moment for the name and the face to register, but Ransom *knew* this knight. Callum was one of Lord DeVaux's knights. Ransom had been DeVaux's hostage for months until Queen Emiloh herself paid his ransom.

The knight approached with a swagger. "What's this fuss about, Lady Léa?"

"This fool burst into my room while I was dressing!"

"Actually," Ransom said, trying to control his anger, "it is *my* room."

The girl gasped in outrage. "Insolence! It's my room! Lord Longmont gave it to me himself. I should have you flogged. Callum! No . . . Father!"

Ransom saw someone else coming down the hall. The sight of Lord DeVaux made his stomach clench with pent-up revenge. What was *he* doing at Kingfountain? This was his daughter?

"Whatever is the matter, child?" said Lord DeVaux as he approached. When he looked at Ransom, his eyes bulged with recognition, and his skin turned pasty with fear.

"Take this man to the yard and flog him!" the girl said, stamping her foot.

Callum grabbed Ransom by the cloak, but Ransom yanked him by the front of his tunic and shoved him into the wall.

"Unhand me, Sir Callum," Ransom said in a voice barely under control. "I'm not defenseless this time."

"Do as he says," commanded Lord DeVaux, who had finally reached them.

"But, Father!" Léa complained.

"Be silent!" he barked at her. "He is the Duke of Glosstyr! Not a man to be trifled with. He's Fountain-blessed." He sized up Ransom, his eyes shifting from fear to ambition. "Well . . . we meet again under different circumstances."

"But he said it was his room," the girl said in a sulky voice.

"It is," rebuffed the father, his eyes not leaving Ransom's fierce gaze. "Out. Now."

Callum had long since released Ransom's cloak, his face registering horrified recognition, and Ransom unclenched his hand from the man's tunic.

"Hello, Ransom," he said in a shaky voice, holding up his hands in a submissive gesture.

"What is all this commotion about?" came another voice from the stairwell. It was Longmont. He arrived on the scene next, wearing the most gaudy outfit Ransom had ever seen. A puffed tunic, lace at the throat, and a vest striped with green and purple. He looked like a courgette squash in all its color.

He went pale at the sight of Ransom.

"Lord Ransom! What are you . . . why . . . it is so good to see you! You hadn't said you were coming! What a terrible mistake. A message must have been delayed. I'm absolutely mortified. Lord DeVaux, please forgive me. I had no idea Lord Ransom was due . . . for a visit."

Longmont's smile was a pained one, his attempt at cheer as convincing as a seasick man pretending his stomach wasn't about to overturn.

✕

A storm pounded the sea after Ransom left. I hope he made it to Glosstyr safely. Alas, the storm caused us trouble as well.

We left for Atha Kleah to handle the final judgments before the winter months made travel too difficult. Going by sea wasn't an option because of the storm and my own discomfort, so we rode on horseback. I did not think a large escort necessary, but I should have been more cautious. We were ambushed on the road, and several knights were injured in the skirmish. Sir Guivret remained by my side and showed excellent courage. I used my bow to good effect as well. Our enemies were defeated.

When we questioned our prisoners, we learned they were in the service of Lord Purser Dougal. Somehow they knew Ransom was gone, and he took advantage of the opportunity to attempt to kidnap me. Or worse. That's when more riders appeared from the woods, and we had to turn and flee back to Connaught with Lord Dougal hot after us. We made it there first, if only barely, and called to arms all the knights in my service.

The castle is under siege. It's a desperate gambit on Lord Dougal's part. He rolled his dice and must bear the number of pips on the face of them. But then, he's always been the desperate sort.

—Claire de Murrow
Connaught Castle, the Fair Isle of Eejits

CHAPTER TEN

The Espion

Longmont brought Ransom to the king's own chamber as a temporary alternative lodging. Servants brought food and fresh clothing, while Longmont repeated his apologies to the point that it became annoying.

"I wish I knew you were coming, Lord Ransom. Truly, I would have had trumpeters lining the streets of Kingfountain to welcome a favored duke home. In the future, and this I plead most humbly, I would greatly appreciate if you made me aware of your intention to come for—"

"Trumpeters?" Ransom interrupted. "I would rather drown in a river than endure such a spectacle." It felt good to be in warm clothes again, and the shock of his arrival had ebbed.

"Duly noted—no trumpeters. But you are held in such high esteem. Will you tell me why you came? What prompted this surprise visit?"

"I have matters to discuss with the queen dowager. Now that I'm in a more presentable state, I should like to see her at once."

Longmont's brow furrowed. "Of course," he said after an awkward pause. "Might I inquire as to the nature of the matters you wish to discuss with her? Have I offended you in some small way, my lord?"

"Just ask her if she will see me. If not tonight, then on the morrow. I will not sleep in here. I'd be more comfortable in a stable than the king's room."

Longmont opened his mouth to speak, only to immediately shut it. He bowed once and then hurriedly left the room. Ransom took some grapes from a tray the servants had brought in and enjoyed their sweetness. He paced, looking at the decorations, especially all the lions throughout the chamber. There was even a table with two carved lions as the supports.

Before long, the high justiciar returned with Emiloh, and Ransom approached and knelt before her.

"Ransom, we are equals," she said, gesturing for him to stand. "I am a duchess, and you are a duke."

He rose, taking note of the aging around her eyes, the worries on her brow. She looked tired.

Longmont folded his arms and showed no intention of leaving. His expression was guarded but informal.

Emiloh turned to him. "Good night, Damian."

The only sign of his anger was a slight pursing of his lips. He bowed to them both and then departed the room. How it must have galled him to be so dismissed. But their rank superseded his role as justiciar.

"So it was *you* who caused such a commotion after arriving," said Emiloh with a wry smile. "It's a long way from the Fair Isle, Ransom. This must be important, or you would have sent a messenger."

"I thought it best to come in person. What I have to tell you—"

She interrupted his words with a surreptitious gesture of her hand. "It's a beautiful night, Ransom. Might we stand on the balcony?"

It seemed an odd request on the surface, especially since it had been raining all day, but he suspected she had her reasons, so he followed her out onto the balcony. The smell of wet stone greeted his nose, and his boots splashed in little puddles on the tile. The rain had stopped, but clouds still blotted out the stars.

"Longmont has a group of servants called the Espion," Emiloh said in a lowered voice. "It's an Occitanian word and a borrowed custom. Lewis had many in his service. There are passages built inside the walls of the palace intended as a way for the occupants to escape if the fortress were ever to come under siege. It's supposed to be a secret, but his Espion use them now to wander through the castle and study people unawares. He pays men well for information. I find it . . . too much like the court at Pree." Her tone revealed her disdain.

"And you were concerned that they were watching us in the king's own room?"

"I can't prove it, but yes . . . I did suspect it. He hates not knowing things. And I'm glad you didn't send a letter, Ransom, if the news is dire. I suspect his people are opening letters sent to me. There are little details that seem off, like creases in the seal. He's been quite a bother since he came to Kingfountain."

"I've heard that as well. But that's not why I came."

Emiloh ran her hands along the balcony edge, which was still wet from the storm. "Tell me."

"Jon-Landon is back in Ceredigion."

She looked at him in surprise. "That's something the Espion *should* have known. I've heard nothing of this. Where did you get your information?"

Ransom stood alongside her so that their backs were facing the chamber. They'd left the door open, but both of them were speaking in low tones.

"Simon told me. He had a message from Lady Deborah. Jon-Landon came to her."

"Then it's more than just a rumor," Emiloh said softly. "I don't think Deborah would have lied about that. I'm grateful she chose to confide in you."

From the way she said it, he suspected there was an unspoken rivalry between Emiloh and Deborah. While Emiloh had been confined in the tower prison following Devon the Younger's failed rebellion, Deborah had been given a seat on the king's council and shown favor for her valuable advice. But Bennett had dismissed her straightaway upon becoming king, replacing her with his mother.

"Why do you think Jon-Landon has returned?" he asked her.

She sighed. "No doubt to cause trouble. Longmont has been heavy-handed, especially against people like Deborah who used to support Devon. He's been trying to alienate them, perhaps to prod them into rebellion so he can prove his might." She said it with more than a touch of derision. "I'm sure my husband told you that he'd considered making Jon-Landon king instead of Benedict?"

"He did, my lady." In fact, the king's final words to Bennett had been that he hoped Jon-Landon would seize the throne from him so he might learn the sting of humiliating defeat. When Jon-Landon had changed sides at the end and betrayed his father, it had robbed the king of his will to live.

"How do you feel about Jon-Landon?" she asked him, staring at the view, her tone thoughtful and probing.

"I don't particularly care for him," Ransom said honestly. "I know he doesn't like me."

"He was too spoiled," Emiloh said. "He should have been sent to live with another lord, like you were sent to train with Lord Kinghorn. But Devon wanted to keep him near. He needed someone in his family to give him the respect he hungered for. Devon taught Jon-Landon to despise me. I've tried to rectify that, but it'll take more time." She turned her head and looked at him. "I cannot allow him to threaten Bennett's authority. He must be brought to Kingfountain."

"I agree. I doubt Lady Deborah is the first noble he visited."

"Oh no," Emiloh said with a chuckle. "He went to James Wigant first, no doubt of it. And it makes sense, being that North Cumbria is so near Atabyrion. The Atabyrions may not even realize he's missing yet."

"Would you like me to find him and bring him here?" he asked her.

She shook her head. "You're a duke now, Ransom. That is a duty for others. In fact, we should tell Longmont and have the dock warden notified as well. It shouldn't be too hard to catch him."

"He is clever," Ransom said, remembering how he'd tricked everyone into believing he was carrying on a dalliance with a woman when he was really negotiating terms with his brother.

"Clever but not wise," Emiloh said. "But before we call for Longmont, there's something you and I should discuss."

"Yes?"

She wiped the moisture from her hands and turned to face him. Then she smoothed his tunic, just as she would if he were her own son. The tender gesture softened his mood.

"The decision to make Longmont the justiciar has been disastrous. Bennett made it without consulting anyone. He wants to be seen as a strong leader, a decisive one, but he's too much like his father, although that comparison would offend him. Still, he made one wise move—he gave us the power to balance Longmont's influence. It's my verdict that power has gone to the man's head like a man giddy from too much wine. He doesn't see his excesses, nor does he recognize that he's making decisions better left to Bennett. If we don't do something now, we could have a rebellion on our hands. Deposing Longmont later would prove ever more difficult. Do you agree?"

Ransom gave a single, decisive nod. "What do you suggest we do?"

"Bennett is wintering on the Isle of Korfe. I propose sending him a message detailing Longmont's abuses and that we'll bring him to heel. Another can be called to take his place. It seems the most sensible thing to do. I've wanted to discuss the situation with someone but lacked a trusted confidant. Your surprise arrival is truly a blessing from the Fountain. If we act now, we can solve this problem while we deal with the one regarding Jon-Landon."

"It's a thorny situation. If we depose him too soon, it will open the king to ridicule. The nobles may lose faith in his judgment." He rubbed his lip. "It won't surprise you to hear Longmont hasn't done anything against me personally. In fact, he's given me additional lands and income, although some of that is on the king's orders."

"Of course. He's shrewd."

"And so are you," Ransom said with a smile.

The queen dowager dimpled with the compliment. For a moment, he flashed to another face—Alix, her daughter. King Estian's poisoner. The two looked disarmingly similar.

"Do you agree with my reasoning?"

"I do," Ransom said. "Who would you recommend to replace him?"

"I think one of the deconeuses would suffice. Someone who can balance the ambitions of Bennett and Jon-Landon. Or do *you* want the position?"

"I definitely do *not*," Ransom said in surprise.

"Which makes you all the more suitable. But you have problems enough of your own. How is Claire doing? Is she still sick all the time from her pregnancy?"

"She is. I didn't wish to leave her again so late in the year. I don't want to be trapped here when winter comes."

"That makes you a good husband," Emiloh said, pleased. "Your loyalties are divided, something I understand well. But such is life, Ransom. A person cannot be in two places at once. We must neglect some things to accomplish others."

"I was afraid you'd say something like that," Ransom said, slumping his shoulders. "The only time I have clarity of thought is in the mornings when I'm in the training yard. There's something about the art of killing that clears the mind."

She put a hand on his arm. "It is always easier to fight, Ransom. When passions get raised, it's more natural to pick up a shaft of heavy steel and swing it than a delicate quill and scratch ink stains with it. But diplomacy, while the harder solution, lasts longer. It causes less destruction. It leaves fewer grieving widows."

He heard the pain in her voice and knew she spoke from the vast well of her own experience.

"How would we get a message to the king without Longmont's Espion finding out?"

She smiled again. "After we tell Longmont about Jon-Landon's return, I'll insist on sending a message to the king to inform him. One of my trusted knights will deliver it, although it'll be Longmont's responsibility to deliver the knight to the king. The official message will be transported in a fancy scroll with gilt caps on it. But another message, sewn into his boot, will be delivered after he arrives at the Isle of Korfe."

"That should work very well," Ransom said. "Longmont is so focused on pomp and circumstance, his focus will be on the first message."

"Then we're agreed?"

"We are."

"Let's go talk to Longmont. No doubt he's chafing outside the door in the corridor, anxious to accost either or both of us."

She was about to leave, but he caught her arm.

"What is it?" she asked.

"Why is Lord DeVaux at the palace?" he said, still feeling shards of resentment from a long-ago wound.

Her brow furrowed. "Longmont says it's to keep DeVaux out of trouble in the Vexin while I'm here. But honestly, I think he plans on marrying his daughter, Léa."

Ransom recoiled. "She's very young."

Emiloh nodded. "Indeed. Very young. But she will not always be. I think Longmont has convinced himself that he will become the Duke of Vexin someday. Shall we?"

Ransom let her precede him back into the king's room, which felt comfortably warm after their time on the balcony. He went to the door and, without surprise, found Longmont pacing outside, rubbing his chin. When the door opened, he startled and gave Ransom an expectant look.

"Come in," Ransom said.

"So there is news! Yes, of course!" He promptly joined them, his eyes wide and eager.

"Have you heard any rumors recently about my son, Jon-Landon?" Emiloh asked him archly.

Longmont's brow wrinkled, and he chafed his hands together slowly as he turned in a half circle. "He's at the Steene in Atabyrion, ma'am."

"No, he isn't. He's back in Ceredigion."

His brow wrinkled further. "That's not possible. I would have—"

"No, I don't think so," she rebuffed. "He was with Lady Deborah recently. He may still be there."

"At Thorngate?" Longmont said, perplexed.

"Yes, that's the castle. The one you've tried to take from her. Thankfully, she is loyal to the crown and sent word to Lord Ransom at once." She cocked her head. "What good are all of your Espion if they think my son is still at the Steene?"

"A thousand pardons, ma'am," Longmont said, looking greensick. "I don't think it would be wise if your son were allowed to—How shall I say this?—roam freely. He may start an insurrection."

Emiloh shot Ransom an exasperated glance.

"Which is why we've told you," she answered, stepping forward. "Find out where he is, and bring him to Kingfountain at once!"

It was the second time that night that Longmont looked humiliated.

"If it pleases you, ma'am, I shall send riders immediately. He will not be harmed." He was about to turn and rush out of the room, but Emiloh's gaze restrained him.

"One more thing," she said. "I'm going to craft a letter to the king."

"I could do that, ma'am, for certain!"

"Yes, I know, but I wish to write it and send one of my knights to deliver the message. Make preparations so that he can leave with the tide for the Isle of Korfe."

"Of course," he said, bowing low. Then he scuttled from the room. As soon as the door was closed, they heard the noise of his boots running down the hall.

Lord Dougal continues his attempts to breach Connaught. There have been three raids so far, and I must admit his determination is impressive. I wish it weren't. There is a certain ferocity in this attack, a knowledge that he will seize us or die trying. My advisors have suggested I board a ship and risk the sea to get back to Glosstyr, but I cannot back down. We must prevail.

We have enough knights to defend ourselves. I wish we had enough to attack them. But Lord Dougal has at least ten times our number. He's clearing the woods at the base of the hill for firewood and siege weapons. Every tree that falls makes me want to curse him more. I've sent a ship to Kingfountain to get word to Ransom. But I have no way of knowing whether it prevailed against the storm.

I have all the archers here taking aim at Lord Dougal's men. We make a little sport of it, how many we can hit from a distance. After night falls, I might send some knights down to attack the camp. I've offered a reward of five thousand livres for the man who brings me Lord Dougal in chains.

—Claire de Murrow
Connaught Castle
The perilous siege

CHAPTER ELEVEN

The Argentine Prince

Longmont had evicted DeVaux's daughter from Ransom's room, and all Ransom's chests and clothes had been returned and configured the way he'd left them. So it surprised him to find Lady Léa pacing the corridor right outside his door when he returned, sweaty and dirty, from practicing in the courtyard. A maidservant stood nearby.

Ransom frowned when he saw her but did not slow.

"Ah, Lord Ransom," she said, giving him a nervous smile.

"Did you leave something behind?" he asked her. "The door was unlocked."

"I know, I tried it," she said, offering an apologetic look. "It was you I came to see. Please don't be cross with me, Lord Ransom. I was very rude to you, and I'm embarrassed by my conduct."

He arched his eyebrows. Was she being sincere or merely currying favor? He couldn't tell. "It's in the past," he said dismissively.

"That's kind of you, of course." She fidgeted with her hands. "I do remember you now. I was very young when you came to Roque Keep. You probably don't remember me."

"I don't," Ransom said. And it was true. He vaguely remembered DeVaux's wife but didn't recall taking any special notice of the man's children.

"I remember you limping," she said. "Your injuries looked very painful. I'm glad you are well now."

"Is that why you wanted to see me? To apologize?"

"Yes, for myself and for my father." She gave him an artful smile. "You're a powerful lord now. I beg your forgiveness."

He rubbed the thin scruff of beard on his chin. Had Lord DeVaux put her up to this little speech? It felt like it. He was the kind of man who would use his daughter to test whether a man was still an enemy.

"I thank you for the apology," he said. "Good day."

A disappointed wrinkle creased her brow, but she did a little curtsy and walked away to join her maid. Ransom opened the door, and as he shut it, he heard some tittering laughter behind him.

Léa DeVaux might be very young, but she was already far too cunning for a little girl.

X

It would take a while for Emiloh's messenger to get to the Isle of Korfe and back by ship, assuming the weather didn't interfere. Ransom worried about being away from Legault for that long, but he was confident in Claire's ability to handle any problems that arose. He'd sent messages to her, but fearing interception from the Espion, he'd kept them rather vague. He hadn't received a single missive from her.

On an afternoon a fortnight after his arrival in Kingfountain, he was sitting in the solar with Emiloh, telling her the story of Lord Tenthor's attempt to bribe him, when Longmont came rushing into the room with a feverish look.

Ransom sat up in his chair and looked at the justiciar with interest.

"You've found my son," the queen dowager said.

"Yes, how did you know?" Longmont said in surprise.

"By the nature of your rushed entrance. Speak, Damian. Where is he?"

"He was found in East Stowe," Longmont answered. "Duke Ashel is bringing him to Kingfountain immediately, accompanied by a hundred knights."

Emiloh and Ransom exchanged looks. That was a sizable show of force. It was a sign of distrust. A show of power.

"How far are they from Kingfountain?" Ransom asked.

"As you know, East Stowe is just north of here. They should arrive this evening. I was going to send two hundred men to take custody of him and tell Duke Ashel to return to East Stowe."

"That wouldn't be wise," Emiloh said. "What if he refuses to come with your men?"

Longmont frowned, looking offended. "I have the right to—"

"I'm not talking about your right, Damian. I'm talking about prudence. A hundred knights . . . Ashel is making a statement. What are your thoughts, Ransom?"

Duke Ashel was one of the Elder King's most loyal men. He was also one of the older leaders of the realm, one whose health had been precarious in the past.

"Ashel was loyal to your husband. He may have transferred that allegiance to Jon-Landon. I think he's felt slighted by his diminished role on the king's council."

Longmont huffed. "He should be grateful to be on the king's council at all!"

Emiloh rubbed her forehead, straining to exhibit patience. "Damian, most men don't accept a fall from grace with any degree of gratitude. Regardless of the reasons for it. You think he's resentful, then, Ransom?"

"I don't know him well, but he was often surly, even with Devon."

Emiloh gazed at him thoughtfully. "Ashel was rewarded with the duchy of East Stowe after Gervase relinquished the hollow crown. He has a son, whom he no doubt wishes to succeed him. Perhaps he has been given reason to doubt his son will inherit his title?" As she said this last part, her gaze shifted to Longmont, who scowled.

"By your own words, my lady, King Benedict has every right to name his own dukes."

"Has Ashel proven himself disloyal?"

"His present conduct is highly suspicious!"

"Stop being defensive and listen to me," Emiloh said. "Jon-Landon chose to return to Dundrennan. He's always favored James Wigant. They were boon companions, you might say. Then he went to Thorngate, which is also to the north, between Glosstyr and East Stowe. Another potential ally since Lady Deborah has also been treated unfavorably by you."

Longmont bristled again, but he didn't speak.

"Next, East Stowe. In just a few days, he's caused considerable damage. If he leads the northern duchies into rebellion, it could cause great harm."

Longmont looked flustered. "Are you saying it's my fault? I object, my lady. I have only acted in the king's best interest. I assure you, he has no love for Ashel or Wigant. But he didn't intend to depose either of them at this point."

Ransom was losing patience. "'At this point'? You've taken pains to stay in good standing with me. You've given me rewards I don't need."

"Are you ungrateful for them?" Longmont countered.

"What we're trying to help you see," Emiloh said, "is that you have contributed to the situation. And your instinct to send armed knights to collect Jon-Landon will likely not end well. If you pull too hard on a longbow, it will eventually snap and injure the archer."

Longmont began to tap his bottom lip as he started pacing. Her words had clearly upset him, but he was pondering what she'd said. He wasn't ignoring them. "Ashel wouldn't have dared to bring a hundred knights if Benedict were here," he said with resentment.

"You aren't Benedict," Ransom said.

"Indeed not," offered Emiloh.

The justiciar screwed up his face. "What do you suggest we do, then, my lady?"

"That we welcome Jon-Landon home in a manner befitting his rank. As a prince, not as a prisoner."

Longmont's eyebrows lifted high in shock. "You mean with trumpeters and flower petals and that sort of nonsense? He's broken his sworn word to remain in Atabyrion. You can have no illusions, madam, that he envisions himself sitting on Bennett's throne."

"Of course he does. I'm counting on it."

Ransom began to understand. "A ratcatcher uses bait to trick them into a trap. A wise hunter waits where the stag is going to drink."

Emiloh smiled at him and inclined her head.

Longmont saw it too. "He's expecting conflict. Instead of provoking a fight outside the city, we wait until he's inside and they're outnumbered."

"Exactly," Emiloh said. "Once he is separated from Ashel, I will speak with him about his intentions. He will likely complain about the grievances of North Cumbria, Thorngate, and East Stowe—all of which he couldn't care less about. He's a selfish boy. He doesn't know Ransom is here, or that the three of us have the authority to determine his fate. For now, I wouldn't trust him back in Atabyrion. Make his room ready, Damian. He'll likely be staying awhile."

Longmont's countenance fell.

The queen dowager sighed. "What is the problem?"

"That is where I put Lord DeVaux's daughter," he said sheepishly.

Ransom hid a smirk behind his hand.

They were bold today and suffered heavy losses. Even if I wanted to depart by sea, the tides are too dangerous. Our fate is bound with Connaught's. I have been tending to the wounded, offering them water to slake thirst and comfort to endure pain. The squires came tonight and begged me to let them fight on the morrow. They are the same lads who fought the pumpkins not long ago. Some are only twelve years old. I look at their faces, and my heart constricts. So young. So very young to die.

—Claire de Murrow, Queen of Suffering
Connaught Castle

CHAPTER TWELVE

Defiance

The prince arrived amidst a flurry of flower petals and the calls of trumpets. The scene wasn't pleasing to Ransom, but Jon-Landon had a smirk on his face, as if he were finally receiving his due . . . until he saw Ransom. Pure rage flashed in his eyes, but he offered no objection when Ransom led him and his companion, a rather sullen-looking Duke Ashel, into the great hall. The queen dowager sat in her council chair, her look impassive as she studied her youngest son. Longmont paced before the empty thrones, which conjured in Ransom's mind the images of twin ghosts—the two Devons he had served. Ransom turned to face them, hands clasped behind his back, his cheek twitching with controlled anger.

"You may go," Longmont said in a tone of rebuke to Ashel.

The duke bristled with offense. "Is my presence so irksome to you already, Lord Justiciar?"

"Need I remind you that my word is the king's?" Longmont said dangerously.

"You think I need *another* reminder?" Ashel scoffed.

"Please," Emiloh said before the tensions could escalate even further. "The hour grows late, Duke Ashel. I would speak with my son."

Her words mollified the surly duke, if only a little. Ransom wandered a few steps to the left, waiting to see whether he'd need to compel Ashel to obey.

"No harm will come to the prince," said Ashel in a tone that carried an obvious threat. "We came in good faith."

"I know you did," Emiloh said. "If you would give us a few moments?"

Ashel bowed his head to her, then did the same to Jon-Landon. From the look that passed between them, it was obvious they had indeed formed an alliance. How many others had Jon-Landon already rallied to his cause? The duke marched back to the doors and left the hall.

"If your intention, Mother, is to scold me into obedience, I'll save you the wasted time."

Ransom didn't like the superior air coming from Jon-Landon. He knew Devon Argentine, the Elder King, would have rebuked his son for such cheek.

Emiloh rose from her chair and approached Jon-Landon. As she drew nearer, his disdain began to waver. He looked discomfited by his mother's proximity.

"I'm glad to see you," she told Jon-Landon. He flinched.

"I hate to interrupt such a touching scene," Longmont said, coming forward. "You broke your sworn word that you'd abide in Atabyrion until your brother returned."

"Just as you broke your sworn word, Lord Justiciar, that you would defend the interests of my brother's realm. I came because of your outrageous offenses."

Longmont gaped at him. "My *offenses*? Are you impugning how I have performed my—"

"Yes," Jon-Landon snarled, cutting him off. "There is not a single drop of Argentine blood in your veins, sir. And yet you have all the pride. You've belittled and abused those who were loyal to my father.

You dress like a strutting peacock and act like a prince of the blood. I'm here to remind you that *I'm* a prince of the blood!"

Longmont's cheeks flushed with anger. Although the accusations were not unfounded, Ransom suspected Emiloh was right—Jon-Landon cared less about the damage done by Longmont than how he could use it to his advantage. Still, Ransom felt guilty he and Emiloh had not done more sooner to curb the lord chancellor's excesses.

"How dare you criticize me!" Longmont said with heat.

"How could I not?" the prince replied. "You've taxed the nobles heavily but some more heavily than others. That is not justice, it is corruption. How could I sit idly by in a foreign kingdom with all their *quaint* manners while you pillage my people?"

"Pillage?" Longmont declared hotly.

"Are you going to keep repeating everything I say? Defend yourself, man, if you can. I take by your silence, Lord Ransom and Mother, that you condone these actions?"

Ransom would not be drawn into the verbal brawl. He seethed in silence, but he admired Jon-Landon's ability to speak. He'd matured in many ways since his father's death—this was a bolder, more cunning boy than he'd known.

"You are an ungrateful—" Longmont started, but the queen dowager raised a hand to him to silence him.

"An admirable performance of outrage, Jon-Landon," she said. "It was very convincing. I'm not convinced, however, that your intentions for returning to Ceredigion were wholly moral ones."

"Madam, if I may defend myself from these false accusations?" Longmont demanded.

She gave him a withering look. "Everything my son has said is true, and you cannot deny it."

Jon-Landon smirked.

Longmont stared at her, dumbfounded.

Ransom stepped closer. "I agree," he said calmly, facing the prince. "You're not driven purely by good intentions. Your brother chose us to counteract any abuses of power."

"Which you haven't," the prince stated. "But then again, you've enjoyed the patronage Longmont has provided for you."

"What was your intention in returning?" Emiloh asked him pointedly. "Did you come to cause a rebellion?"

"Of course not!" Jon-Landon said sharply. "I came for one purpose, despite what you think. I want Longmont removed as high justiciar. I demand that he be replaced with someone else."

"You?" Ransom asked.

"No, of course not! I don't think my brother would trust me with that kind of authority. Give it to Duke Ashel, maybe. Or you can have it, Ransom, for all I care. But not *him*. Anyone but him."

Longmont was pale with rage. "Your brother should have punished you instead of forgiving you. Your treachery against your own father—"

Ransom sensed that Jon-Landon was about to fly at Longmont and pummel him. He quickly intervened and gripped the prince by the shoulder. "Not here, not now," he said in a low, dangerous voice.

"Get him out of my sight," Jon-Landon snarled, trembling with fury.

"I am the high justiciar," Longmont said in a quavering voice. His knees were trembling at the sudden threat of violence. "If you strike me, you'll be in . . . in chains . . . in the dungeon."

Ransom eased his grip on the prince. Jon-Landon didn't make any moves toward Longmont, but he stared at him with open hate. His haunted look was no act. No doubt the son had been plagued by his conscience at having betrayed his father at the end and then having it thrown in his face.

"I think we've heard enough for now," Emiloh said sternly. "Let's have his room made available and two knights assigned to guard him."

"Am I a prisoner, Mother?"

"I said your room. Not the tower. You're free to come and go, but you're confined to the palace grounds. No carousing in town."

Jon-Landon looked at her with loathing. "Did you ever prevent Devon or Bennett? But I'll obey because you are my mother, the Lady incarnate." Emiloh stiffened but didn't respond.

"Out," Longmont said to Jon-Landon, having regained some composure, although his knees still wobbled.

The prince bowed to his mother, gave Ransom a look of defiance, and then strode out of the chamber. Silence hung between the three who were left, broken by Longmont. "He is ungrateful for his brother's lenience," he said, not really addressing either of them. "Those who betrayed the Elder King at the end were not treated unfavorably, all things considered."

Ransom watched the queen dowager as she went back to her chair and sat. Her eyes were full of pain, one hand pressed to her chest as if to soothe her hurting heart.

"I don't think it would be wise to send him back to Atabyrion," Longmont continued in his ramble. "Did you hear how he criticized them? 'Quaint' indeed. They are a rather backwater people, but they're fearsome warriors, and until recently they ruled most of North Cumbria. He probably didn't find the king's daughter pleasing enough to look at. Ungrateful . . . he could have become King of Atabyrion!"

Ransom folded his arms. "I think he'd prefer to be King of Ceredigion."

Longmont looked at him worriedly. "Do you really think he'll rebel, Lord Ransom?"

"He already has," answered the queen with weariness.

"Are you suggesting we accuse him of treason now?" Longmont asked warily.

She shook her head. "Benedict could be gone for several years. If we accuse Jon-Landon of treachery, it may embolden his allies." She sighed. "Duke Ashel is ready for war now. As long as Benedict stays in power, his influence will continue to wane. We should have treated him with more dignity."

"Are you blaming me, Queen Dowager?" Longmont said defensively.

"I am speaking what's on my mind. Stop taking everything as a personal slight. If we try and coddle Ashel now, he'll see it as a sign of weakness."

"I agree," Ransom said. "We should order him back to East Stowe. Rebuke him for not sending word that Jon-Landon had come."

Emiloh nodded. "You do it, Ransom."

"I should be the one," Longmont said, coming in between them. "It is my role as—"

Ransom's and Emiloh's glares silenced him.

𝕏

"He's a puffed-up prig who's never wet his sword in battle," Ashel growled to Ransom as they walked along the docks leading to the river. The night was cold, and the fire from the torches whipped with the wind. The roar of the falls, which could be heard almost everywhere in Kingfountain, filled their ears.

"What you say is true," Ransom said, grateful the two of them were alone. "But you forget yourself. You're a duke of the realm. If Estian had sent an emissary to you to plot against the Elder King, would you have kept it to yourself? No, I know you. You would have told him immediately so as not to lose the king's trust."

"That's unfair," Ashel said angrily. "Estian is an enemy of the realm. Jon-Landon is Devon's son!"

"Aye, his favored son even. If Bennett believes Jon-Landon is a threat, do you think he'll forgive him a second time? Because I doubt that stripling can stand up to his brother."

Ashel scowled and turned away. "You're right. Bennett is ruthless enough to dispose of him."

"Is that what Devon would have wanted?"

"You've made your point, Ransom. Don't bludgeon me with it."

"Do you know why I'm here and not in Legault?"

Ashel turned his head, his eyebrows lifting. "Did the queen summon you?"

Ransom shook his head. "I'm here because Deborah sent for me the instant Jon-Landon arrived at Thorngate. And that is exactly what *you* should have done. Like it or no, Bennett is the king. If you don't show him the same loyalty you gave his father, you don't deserve your duchy."

The censure was a sour drink, and Ashel flinched at the taste. He had the good sense to at least look abashed. "You're right," he acknowledged. "I was angry at him for setting me aside so quickly. Felt I deserved a place on the council. And was jealous . . . perhaps . . ." He sniffed and then looked at Ransom with respect.

He put a hand on the older man's shoulder. "I think Jon-Landon knew that. He'll use anyone if it serves his ends. Be careful which master you serve."

"Aye," said Ashel. "We're not enemies, are we?"

Ransom shook his head. "I was hoping we'd stay on the same side," he answered. "Stay for a day or so, and then take your knights back to East Stowe. Send word if anyone else comes to you seeking to win your allegiance."

"I will. I promise." He thumped his chest with the edge of his hand, giving the familiar salute.

Ransom returned the gesture and watched as Ashel walked back to the castle. He felt his Fountain magic bubbling inside him, increasing his strength. His power had always been tied to acts of loyalty.

He lingered at the dock, staring out at the river and thinking about the bodies that he had seen sent down it. First King Gervase, then the Younger King. The Elder King had been put to rest in Westmarch.

So many Argentines had died. His mission from the Fountain was to protect them, yet the survivors were so far apart, so different, it felt nearly impossible.

There was always hope that Bennett and Portia would have a child during the campaign against the East Kingdoms. Another Argentine he could end up serving.

His mind turned back to Claire and the child they would have together. What was she doing right now? Writing a letter? Staring into a hearth fire and thinking of him? His heart ached from missing her. The last thing he wished to do was return to his empty room, so he continued to walk until the chill seeped in. Only then did he make his way back.

When he reached the landing, he entered the hall and found Léa DeVaux standing by his room again, talking to Jon-Landon. Staring at him with a gleam of speculative interest in her eyes.

Jon-Landon turned and saw Ransom. He bent down and whispered something to the girl, who gaped at him in astonishment and then giggled. Ransom didn't know what had been said, but he didn't like what he saw.

"Good night," Jon-Landon said to her, folding his arms and leaning back against the door of Ransom's room as she left. Her maid could be seen in the shadows farther down the hall.

Ransom couldn't help but give the prince a reproachful look.

"Where is your knight?" he asked Jon-Landon. The prince should not have been left alone so soon.

Jon-Landon shrugged. "I think he's lost. Or I am." He scratched the corner of his mouth where a little line of black stubble was growing into a goatee. "You've done well for yourself, Lord Ransom. You were rewarded for serving my father and even more so for serving Bennett."

"What do you want?" Ransom asked, cutting through the nonsense.

"I just want you to think about the future," said Jon-Landon evasively. "You've been to the East Kingdoms. From what I've heard, it's a dangerous place. The three kings are united in a common cause, for now, but you know as well as I do that when tempers flare and disaster strikes, even allies become enemies." He gave Ransom a meaningful look.

"I'm not your enemy."

"I wasn't suggesting you were. I hope we can be allies. I toss coins into the fountains each day that my brother returns safe and whole."

It felt like a lie. Ransom frowned.

"I'm only saying that if it comes down to a choice between a child and a man, I hope you'll choose wisely."

"That depends," Ransom said.

"On what?"

"On who Bennett chooses," he answered. "Good night."

The prince shrugged and ambled away, a little enigmatic smile on his mouth.

Ransom felt sick with dread as he opened the door to his room. A candle was already lit, and he saw a message with a wax seal on his bed. Frowning, he shut the door and walked over to it. It was Claire's seal, and it was slightly creased at one edge. It rankled him that someone in Longmont's Espion had read the message before he did.

He picked at the seal with his fingernail and then unfolded the paper, holding it to the light of the candle to read.

His heart sank and then began to pound with worry inside his chest.

Connaught was under siege.

𝔛

It is over. The rebellion has been put down. All was not so certain yesterday, but another armed band appeared up the road. It was Lord Tenthor. He went to Lord Dougal in deceit, offering to join him in exchange for being given a position, but when the two met, Lord Tenthor seized upon Dougal and held a knife to his neck while Tenthor's men scattered the others. Lord Tenthor then dragged Dougal behind his horse all the way up the hill to Connaught, where he turned him over to me for justice.

I asked Lord Tenthor why he did it. And he responded that he felt obligated because my husband had shown him clemency for his foolishness regarding the taxes. When he heard that Dougal had attacked, he came at once to our rescue. I thanked Lord Tenthor for his timely aid and promised rewards would soon follow, which he declined out of respect. I then asked him to seize Dougal's lands and hold them in the queen's name. He departed to fulfill my orders.

Lord Dougal was taken to the dungeon to await his condemnation. The knights who searched him found a strange stone in his pocket, which he violently protested surrendering. They brought it to me. It's a curious thing, about the size of an egg, made of white jasper. He refused to say what it was, but Sir Guivret recognized it. He said the Duchess of Brythonica has one just like it. They are called seering stones. They scry things that are hidden or secret. He warned me never to use it. And yet, I will admit it fascinates me. This must be how Dougal knew that Ransom was gone.

—Claire de Murrow
Connaught Castle
(costly victory)

CHAPTER THIRTEEN

Raging Storms

A vicious storm had broken out the previous night, and Emiloh had refused Ransom's request to set sail. The seas were raging, the journey too dangerous. He'd insisted on leaving come morning—if the storm had not passed, he and his knights would ride to Glosstyr on horseback—and she hadn't objected. The storm looked in no hurry to pass, so he ordered the men to prepare for a long, wet ride, then sought out Emiloh. She was in the solar meeting with Longmont, the conversation tense by the looks on their faces.

"I'm preparing to go," Ransom said as he joined them.

"It's miserable out there," Longmont objected. "Why not stay another day? There's little you can do about the situation anyway."

Emiloh shook her head. "Damian, please. He's right to be anxious. So am I, but I'm equally concerned about you getting into a shipwreck. Don't let your emotions rule your instincts, Ransom. Claire de Murrow will do what she can to fend off the attackers. Trust her."

It took an effort to relax his grip, but he did. "Thank you," he told her. "I'm hoping there will be more recent news when I reach Glosstyr."

He was about to leave, but Emiloh forestalled him. "Can I beg another moment from you, Ransom?"

He sighed and nodded.

"The Espion brought a report during the night that the Duke of North Cumbria is heading this way with a host of knights. You know James as well as anyone. What do you make of it?"

Ransom turned to Longmont. "How close is he to Kingfountain?"

"He should be here by this evening," said the justiciar. "You may encounter him on the road as you leave. I don't think he's foolish enough to attack."

"I know your opinion," said Emiloh patiently. "I'm seeking Ransom's."

He pursed his lips and looked at the queen dowager and then at Longmont. "I doubt Jon-Landon gave him any marching orders. It would take days for a message to get from East Stowe to Dundrennan then back. He might have realized that harboring your son without telling us could be viewed unfavorably." Ransom shrugged. "I think he's trying to protect his interests by making a show of strength."

"Wigant is a fool, and the king doesn't trust him," Longmont said. "Loyalty binds him to Jon-Landon. Mark my words."

"If you encounter him on the road," Emiloh said, "see if you can determine his intentions. I'd rather not have another duke making accusations like Ashel did. If he doesn't have a good reason for coming, send him back."

"Agreed," Longmont said, quick to assert his authority. "We'll send word to you at Connaught as soon as we hear back from the king."

"Thank you both," Ransom said, bowing his head. "I'll be off."

"Be careful," Emiloh told him, her eyes betraying her worry for him.

Ransom and his escort left Kingfountain amidst an unrelenting storm, water drenching them before they even cleared the city, and the hooves of their horses splashed in puddles on the cobblestones. The river and the falls had swollen, and the roar of the waterfall was deafening. Many of the townsfolk were keeping indoors, which was unusual for that time of day.

The rain slackened to an intermittent drizzle, but the road was a muddy mess, which slowed their progress considerably. After resting their mounts midday, they continued on the road toward Glosstyr. It was then they encountered James and his entourage on the road from the north. The duke of the North had about thirty knights with him, a sizeable force but not a menacing one. Ransom's Fountain magic did not alert him to any danger.

James wore his decorative armor, more showy than functional, and his hair was slicked down with rain. A sullen look crossed his face when he recognized Ransom was there to face him.

"You just coming from the palace?" James asked him as their horses stopped just shy of each other.

"Aye," Ransom answered. "Poor weather to be traveling in." He nodded to the knights accompanying James. "Why so many? Is something wrong?"

"For protection," answered James glumly.

"From what? These are the king's roads."

"Well, they used to be at any rate," James said with resentment. "We've been hunting some bandits who attacked Blackpool. I sent twenty men north to search for them. They've hit two villages so far, robbing all of the villagers and threatening them with arrows. I'm going to the palace to warn Longmont that he needs to increase patrols."

Ransom frowned. "Bandits?" He was surprised at James's amiable conversation. No barbed insults or condescending jests. Something had changed since they'd last met, and he wasn't sure what.

"These are strange times. The king is away, and folk are scared. One of the villagers I spoke to said the marauders spoke in a foreign tongue. Atabyrion, he thought. But they usually attack on the east, not the west. It's strange. Be careful."

It was one of the first conversations they'd had that didn't involve slights and insults. "Thanks for the warning," Ransom said. His brow furrowed. When he'd crossed from Legault, they'd been chased by brigands during the storm. Had they decided to hit the coast of Ceredigion instead? "What did these brigands look like?"

James thought a moment. "Like peasants, actually. Dressed in leathers and cloaks. They were using bows, not swords. Rogue knights wouldn't do that, I should think."

"Agreed," Ransom said. "Might the brigands be Gaultic, not Atabyrion? They speak in a foreign tongue."

James grinned. "Can't keep those heathens in line, Ransom? I jest. I don't know, to be honest. How is Lady Claire? Is she well?"

Ransom was not about to tell James about his own worries. "Well enough. Thanks again for the warning."

"You'd do the same for me, I hope. Oh—since you've been to the palace. Have there been any rumors about Jon-Landon returning?"

Ransom nearly smiled at the attempt to fish for information. "Rumors? Like what?"

"So you don't know?"

Ransom just gave him an expectant look and said nothing.

James scrubbed his hand through his hair. "Jon-Landon is back. He's plotting to get Longmont thrown out. I think he's with Ashel right now, seeking allies. Sounds like he doesn't intend to leave Ceredigion. I was going to tell the queen dowager myself."

"She already knows."

"Longmont is a fool," James said, chuckling. "An eejit, I should say. Farewell."

Ransom nodded, and the two parted ways. The encounter had surprised Ransom with its lack of animosity. James had almost treated him as an equal.

⋈

They camped for the night in a grove of pine, the mud having slowed their journey considerably. The next morning they heard rumblings about the marauders, but Ransom wouldn't let anything distract him from returning home. The weather had finally begun to improve by the time they turned onto the road to Glosstyr, which gave him hope they'd be able to sail out without delay. It was near dusk, Glosstyr visible in the distance, when it happened. He was struck by a forceful feeling of danger. Another summons from the Gradalis.

"No," he whispered. *Not now!*

Was the duchess trying to summon him? Or was the silver bowl being threatened again?

Ransom tugged on the reins and stopped his horse. The other knights followed suit and looked at him in surprise.

"Ride on to Glosstyr," he told them, the wrenching sensation in his gut making him miserable. He knew there was no denying it—he would be yanked away regardless of what he did—and there would be fewer questions if he was alone when it happened. "There is something I must do."

"My lord?" one of the knights asked in shock.

"Tell Sir Simon I'm coming," Ransom said. "Ride on."

"What about the brigands?" another said. "My lord, it isn't safe for you to be all alone."

"Do as I say!" he barked, driven to desperation. He could tell it would happen soon. Imminently.

The bark of command brought fear to their eyes. They were disturbed by his behavior, but it couldn't be helped. He had to protect the grove.

Still, they lingered, their eyes on him.

"Go," he demanded. They exchanged looks and then rode ahead while he watched them from his steed, wondering what news they'd bring Simon.

He breathed in gasps as he waited for the magic to take him away. Would it leave his horse behind or bring it as well? He didn't know. And that uncertainty made it all the more bewildering. His heart began racing. He gripped the saddle horn tightly and shut his eyes.

When the magic swept him away, he wanted to scream in anguish. But the pain ended in an instant, and he found himself back at the grove. Water dripped from the trees, fresh from an otherworldly storm. He blinked, realizing he was still on the horse. In the gloom of dusk, he saw men in armor, helmets and visors covering their faces. He looked around, his stomach lurching at the disproportionate odds. The knights were on foot, their armor dented. He sensed that some had been injured, but all were well enough to fight. Ten to one.

"It's Lord Ransom," said a voice in Occitanian. He recognized *that* voice. It was Chauvigny, one of the knights of Estian's mesnie. A quick glance assured him he was right—although the man's helmet covered his face, his armor was familiar. They'd fought in the siege of Dunmanis, the Elder King's last battle, and Ransom had taken the Occitanian knight captive briefly before he was saved by his fellows. It obviously still chafed, for his next words, spoken with contempt, were "Do you yield?"

Ransom drew his sword from the scabbard in answer. He wore a hauberk under his tunic, but he had no helmet. And he hadn't fought ten knights at once since Lord DeVaux's ambush on the road to Auxaunce. The Fountain magic began to bubble up inside of him.

"Encircle him," Chauvigny said to the others. "My lady will get her revenge at last."

Ransom kicked the horse's flank and charged the man closest to him, trying to break free before they fulfilled the command. The horse knocked the knight down easily, and he rolled to the side to avoid being trampled. But three others came up and thrust their swords at Ransom and his rouncy. He blocked and countered, feeling his desperation drown in a surge of defiance and determination. He kicked one man in the helmet and slammed his hilt onto another.

Someone grabbed Ransom from behind, and suddenly he was falling. The horse flailed its hooves, letting out a noisy whine as Ransom slammed onto his back. He felt a blade pierce his hauberk at his shoulder. Grimacing, he banged the flat of his blade against the man's helmet to stun him before he rolled to his knees and sliced the man's leg off in a single stroke.

He felt the pain in his shoulder but only vaguely. The Raven scabbard had already begun to glow, preventing any blood from flowing. Two more knights came at him, and he ducked a blow to the head that nicked his scalp. Undaunted, he charged forward, holding the flat of the blade and using his sword to push both men at once until they tripped and fell backward. Sensing danger behind him, he whirled around and blocked another attempt to club his unprotected head. He deflected it and skewered the knight, cleaving through his armor.

Then Chauvigny was advancing on him, swinging at him relentlessly. Ransom's advantage was not being encumbered by armor. It made him faster, but not fast enough—the odds were still overwhelmingly against him. Another cut to his arm made Ransom yell in anger and rush against Chauvigny, who deflected his hail of blows with expert form.

Ransom felt a blade slash his back. He didn't think it had pierced the links, but he couldn't be sure. He felt no pain, but weariness began to take its toll. His magic provided a defense, a way of discerning his opponents' weaknesses, but it wasn't unlimited. And Chauvigny didn't have any major weaknesses. Ransom broke off his attack and went after a more hapless foe, trying to reduce the numbers. His horse had ridden off, leaving him alone in his battle. How many were left? Six?

A sword pierced his injured leg, and he felt a thrum of pain shoot down to his foot. He grabbed the man by the collar of his breastplate and shoved him down, then drove his sword through a gap in the side of the man's armor. But another sword struck him, and his strength began to ebb, dizziness washing through him.

Panic began to quiver in his belly. Thoughts of Claire and her swelling abdomen filled his mind. He thought of the people of Legault and Glosstyr too—they looked to him and Claire as a hope for the future. Ransom bit down on his tongue until he tasted blood and lunged at the next man, begging the Fountain for strength to defeat his foes.

Chauvigny attacked him again. Ransom beat him back, but he wasn't able to penetrate the man's armor for a killing wound. Another stab to Ransom's side made him wheeze in pain. He spun around and took the man down. Sweat stung Ransom's eyes. His energy was flagging quickly. There were three of them left, including Chauvigny. He gazed at them, feeling drunk with determination and fatigue.

"Yield," Chauvigny growled, aiming his sword at Ransom's throat.

Ransom pushed the tip away and lunged forward, kicking him in the chest and knocking him down. He came at Chauvigny in savage fury, but the other two knights grappled with him. Before Ransom could process what had happened, he was on his back. He saw a blade sticking out from his stomach, yet he wasn't dead. He could barely even feel it. The knight pulled it out and backed away from Ransom. He lifted his visor, his face aghast with shock at seeing Ransom alive despite his grievous injuries. The next moment, he turned and ran away, screaming, into the woods.

Ransom rolled to his side and tried to stand, but Chauvigny kicked him back down. There were only two left. When Ransom lifted his arm to raise his sword, Chauvigny stomped on his wrist. He felt the bones break. His sword arm was useless now.

"He cannot be killed!" groaned the other knight in fear.

"He can," said Chauvigny. "Hold him down. I'll take off his head."

The other knight shoved Ransom onto his chest. Mud oozed against his face. Ransom reached with his left hand for the dagger he wore at his belt. The dagger he had saved from his first fight with Lady Alix. He stabbed the knight in the knee with it, causing a yowl of pain. Ransom rolled over, seeing Chauvigny rise above him, sword held in both hands to sweep down.

Ransom aimed for his visor and threw the dagger.

He heard a shriek of pain that rattled to his bones. Collapsing with exhaustion, Ransom waited to die, his final burst of energy gone. He breathed in gasps and gulps, his body afire with pain.

He knew what was coming next. The ground would suck in the dead and wounded.

Including him.

I went to the dungeon to ask questions of Purser Dougal myself. He is a dishonest man, conniving and sick in the mind. I asked him about the stone. There was a fevered look in his eyes when he answered me. He said it had belonged to my grandfather. Dougal had stolen it from the barrow mounds. He said my mother never knew of it.

He called it a seering stone. There was an avaricious look in his eyes as he spoke of it, a sickness that had gone deep. He asked me to kill him. He said he couldn't bear not having the stone. Losing it, he said, was worse than any pain he'd ever felt. Looking in my eyes, he said he'd kill me to get it back. It was a warning and a promise.

I held the stone in my hand. It felt like any other stone. But last night I had a dream unlike any other. It felt more like a vision. I saw Ransom in a bed. The Duchess of Brythonica sat beside him, leaning down to him. I've never felt such a horrible need for revenge. A jealousy so deep it hurts to the marrow. Is the stone affecting me already, just from touching it?

I had Dougal executed this morning.

—Claire de Murrow, Queen of the Stone
Connaught Castle

CHAPTER FOURTEEN

Broken Knight

The muddy ground sucked Ransom down, oozing into his mouth, his nostrils, and his ears, the choking feeling making him thrash in desperation. He reached for something to grab onto with his left hand, his right wrist still broken. But the tugging mud was inexorable, powerful, and determined to claim him. He wrestled against the wet, sinking grit as it pulled him into its embrace.

"Shhhh," soothed a woman's voice, breaking him free of the nightmare.

He awoke in a tangle of blankets, his arm throbbing, his body soaked with sweat. It was dark, deep into the night, he was confused, and his entire body ached from wounds. Dim light glowed from the Raven scabbard.

"Claire?" he whispered hoarsely, the fear still fresh in his mind.

He felt a soft hand smooth his brow. "You're in Ploemeur, Lord Ransom."

He blinked, confused. He could see Lady Constance's face in the dim glow of the room. She sat at his bedside, next to a small side table holding a basin of water and a single candle. The light came from both the candle and the scabbard glowing at his waist.

"How did I get here?" he croaked.

She removed her hand and reached for a rag hanging from the edge of the basin. After squeezing the excess water from it, she dabbed his brow and cheeks. "I summoned you," she said. "You were unconscious and terribly wounded. If not for the scabbard, you'd be dead right now."

"How did you know?" he asked, as weak as a kitten. His Fountain magic was spent, exhausted.

"How did I know what?" she asked, dipping the rag in the bowl again. "I've told you—I can sense the Gradalis's magic. I know when it is used."

"How did you know I'd failed?" he said.

"You didn't fail, Lord Ransom. You defended the Gradalis. It's still there."

That was a relief, but one he didn't understand.

"Who was it?" she asked. "Were they also from Bayree?"

Memories of the struggle were still fresh in his mind. "I don't know for sure," he said, stifling a groan. He felt the injuries in his back, his arms.

"We will talk in the morning," Constance said. "Rest, Lord Ransom. Let the scabbard heal you."

As he closed his eyes, he felt a powerful surge of jealousy and anguish . . . only they weren't his. He thought he sensed Claire's presence in the room. Guilt shot through him. He hadn't gone to Ploemeur willingly, yet he could not tell her about the summoning. Or about the wounds he now bore. He fell asleep fitfully, then sank into blissful oblivion.

$$\mathcal{K}$$

He awoke slowly, hearing cheerful chirps from the open window. The salty sea breeze welcomed him. For a moment, he thought he was still in Kingfountain, but then the pain made itself known. It was duller now, more of an allover ache than raw agony.

He heard the sound of wood knocking against wood, very lightly. When he opened his eyes, he saw a little boy, Drew, near the bedside, holding a carved wooden horse, which he was playing with as quietly as he could on the table. He brought the horse to the water bowl Constance had used during the night and lifted the horse up to drink from it as if from a trough.

The light shone in Drew's soft hair, and Ransom felt a swell of tenderness at the young boy's innocence. Then Drew turned the horse around and started it tip-tapping toward the edge of the table. He glanced at Ransom's face and then brightened when he saw he was awake.

"His name is Hengroen," said the boy. "He's a destrier."

"Is he hungry for some oats?" Ransom asked, trying not to groan.

"I think so," said the boy. He turned his full attention to Ransom. "You're very dirty. Were you playing in the mud? The blanket and sheets are messy. I hope you don't get scolded."

Ransom lifted his left arm and saw the mud caked into his fingernails and wrinkles of skin. He was a mess.

"Where is your mother?" Ransom asked.

"I don't know," the boy said, running the horse along the edge of Ransom's bed. "Are you going to be my father now?"

His words caused a jolt inside Ransom's heart. "No, lad. No, I'm not."

"Oh," he said innocently. "My papa is dead. He was trampled by a horse. I'm not afraid of horses."

"You have no need to be frightened of horses," said Constance, entering the room. "Thank you for tending to our guest. Go find Marie, and she will help you get something to eat."

The boy smiled and continued to maneuver his wooden horse to the edge of the bed. He walked across the room and waved to Ransom before he left. Ransom tried to sit up, but a stab of pain made him grimace. Constance hurried over and helped raise him, and although he felt nothing more than gratitude toward her, guilt washed through him.

She eyed his face and neck. "I'll have some servants help you bathe," she said. "It's hard to tell the damage through all this mud."

"I feel better," Ransom said, then stiffened with pain when he put too much weight on his wrist.

"I can tell," she said archly. "Are you hungry? I can have some food brought first."

"I need to get to Glosstyr," he said with urgency. "Can you send me back?"

She shook her head. "The magic can only send you back to the location from which it plucked you, and I called you here from the grove. Were you in Glosstyr when the Gradalis transported you?"

He shook his head. "Almost. I sent my knights on ahead. They'll be worried."

"The storm has died down, but you're in no state to travel. I can send a messenger, Lord Ransom. Tell them that you're safe."

He shut his eyes. "I don't want them knowing I'm here."

Constance was quiet for a while. "I see. Well, I won't detain you, then."

The anguish in his heart grew keener. "You truly cannot send me back?"

"I could only send you back to the grove, that is all." She sat on the edge of the bed. "I am grateful that you defended it again. Can you tell me what happened?"

He regarded her carefully but sensed no ill intention coming from her. Just concern. "I was summoned because they found it again. It was . . . Sir Chauvigny. He had at least ten knights with him."

"You fought that many?" she asked in wonder.

"It was not an even match. They were armored, and I had only a hauberk and my sword." He looked around. "Where is my sword?"

"Still in the grove, I'll wager," she said. "I sent knights there to hunt down any who survived. I expect they'll come back soon. Or others will."

Ransom sighed. "I did the best I could. One got away. I threw a dagger at Sir Chauvigny and may have killed him or wounded him enough that the grove finished him, but I don't know for certain."

"It was enough," she said, putting her hand on his. "So it was Sir Chauvigny, was it? He's been promised to Lady Alix of Bayree."

Ransom looked at her in surprise.

"I have certain informants in Pree," she said. "Following Dunmanis, he asked Estian for her hand and the duchy."

"He obviously didn't go to war with the king."

"No," she said. "He'd been injured during the fighting in Dunmanis, I believe. He needed to heal. But he asked the king for permission to marry her, and the king said yes. I don't think it has been celebrated yet. I suppose they are using the absence of Benedict and Estian to further their search for the Gradalis." She frowned. "And with the queen dowager away from the Vexin, they have an opportunity to do mischief. I cannot let these incursions go unpunished."

"What will you do?" he asked her.

She removed her hand from his. "I'll increase the border guard. I might send a raiding party into Bayree."

"That would break the truce between our realms."

"Haven't they broken it themselves?" she countered. "You were intended to be my *last* defense, Lord Ransom. Not my only one."

He sighed again. "You summoned me to Ploemeur last night. Can you tell me why? I'm not ungrateful, but you didn't do that last time. I thought the mud would claim me."

She looked away. "I knew you were in trouble."

He gave her a questioning look.

"Please don't ask me," she said.

"I fear I must. You saved my life, Constance. You knew I'd be injured?"

She nodded, still unable to meet his eyes.

"How did you know?" he asked softly.

She gave him a weary smile. "If I tell you, I must ask you to guard another secret."

Ransom flinched. There were already more secrets than he wanted between Claire and himself. But he saw Constance was in earnest and that the need was probably great. "I will, my lady," he said.

"Very well. I shall return in a moment." She rose from the bed and hurried out of the room. Her sudden departure confused him, but he was in no shape to follow her. His back groaned, and his wrist was painfully sore. The scabbard's magic had truly saved his life.

Constance returned shortly thereafter, holding something in her hand. When she drew near, she showed it to him. It was a marbled white stone, about the size of an egg, only flatter than one.

"What is it?" he asked her.

"It is one of the seering stones," she said. "They come in sets of two. One can see the present. The other, the future or the past. The one I'm holding is the kind that sees the future and the past."

"Where did you get it?"

"It's been handed down to the rulers of Brythonica since the flooding of Leoneyis. My grandfather told me that King Andrew the Ursus, the famous one, had both of them. They were given to him by the Wizr Myrddin." She looked down at the stone cupped in her hand. "Grandfather told me that they made him very powerful, for he could see his enemies before they attacked. He could spy on them and learn their secrets." She paused. "My grandfather said it was wrong of him to use them that way. They are very powerful, and to look at them when not commanded by the Fountain is a grievous sin."

He felt a shiver go down his spine and heard the shushing of the Fountain. This was a powerful artifact. Possibly the most powerful of them all other than the Gradalis.

"You said Sir Terencourt told you I would become the new guardian."

She nodded. "I did say that, Lord Ransom, in order to conceal the truth of the seering stone. I was the one who told *him* that you would replace him. The Fountain whispered to me to look into the stone last night after the Gradalis was activated. I wasn't going to. I'd assumed you would defeat the threat." She shrugged slightly. "That's how I knew what would happen to you."

"Do you know other things that will happen?" he asked.

"Of course you would ask me that," she said. "The answer is yes. Some things. But there is a warning about looking into the stone. The desire to peer at them becomes overpowering with time. It can drive one mad."

Ransom breathed out slowly. "You said there were two stones. Where is the other?"

"I've seen it," she said. "But I didn't recognize the man who has it. It could be the Atabyrion king or a noble. I don't know. I only know he uses it for a twisted purpose. It's safer to use the seering stones together. Their power helps balance each other."

Ransom gazed into her eyes. "Is your son going to become king?" he asked her.

She shuddered. "I've wanted to see that, Lord Ransom. But I dare not look for such a selfish thing. I've nearly done it, but each time I felt a warning not to." Her eyes locked on his. "I've learned to trust those warnings."

"Are you Fountain-blessed?" he asked her.

She shook her head. "No, although I've wished for it. Grandfather said anyone can use the stones. Knowing too much about the future is dangerous, though. Even knowledge of the present can be poisonous. There is . . ." She stopped suddenly, then shook her head.

"What?" Ransom pressed.

She looked at him again. "There is some fate that binds us, Lord Ransom. Often I have felt that you should have been . . . my husband. I don't understand these feelings. It's as if some fate was thwarted before we even knew each other."

He wanted to gasp at the audacity of her suggestion.

"You are safe from me," she said, seeing his reaction. "I would never come between you and Lady Claire. I want to look into this stone and see the future. To understand why I have these strange feelings." She sighed. "But I dare not. It's forbidden for a reason."

A long and awkward silence fell between them, his mind on Claire and her words about Constance. Had she picked up on something he hadn't?

"So you've seen the man who possesses the other stone, but you didn't recognize him," Ransom affirmed, drawing the conversation away from personal matters.

"He could be from Brugia," Constance said with a shrug. "The scabbard you wear also used to belong to King Andrew. It was more formidable than his famous sword, Firebos. Too much power in one man . . . that's what led to his downfall. All we have left are scraps of knowledge. And no Wizr to guide us."

I dreamed again last night. Ransom was arriving at Glosstyr by ship. A Brythonican ship. Are these visions the doing of the seering stone? Or is the babe in my womb causing all these fears and jealousy to surge within me? I threw up so violently this morning that splotches of color rose on my face and neck. I feared the spasms would do my child harm.

When I was trapped in the tower at Kingfountain, I felt misery and weakness. This feeling I have now, trapped in my own body, wary of my own husband, feels so much worse. If it is the stone that is causing me such anguish, then I need to be rid of it. Perhaps I should cast it into the sea, lest it claim my soul as it did Purser Dougal's. But how can a rock know my deepest fears? Am I just being a fool?

The storm has gone. The sea is clear. I will send a ship to Glosstyr to see if Ransom is there. So I may know whether these visions are true or false.

—Claire de Murrow
Connaught Castle
(sick of body, sick of heart)

CHAPTER FIFTEEN

The Still of the Deep

The storm that had battered the ship finally eased with the coming dawn. Ransom had barely slept that night, his healing wounds causing less discomfort than the tumultuous waves. When at last the deep surrendered its violence, he fell asleep, only to be wakened—what felt like moments later—at dawn with the pronouncement that they were nearing the harbor of Glosstyr.

He wore a new tunic the Duchess of Brythonica had provided for him. The mud was gone, but not the memories of the fight in the grove. A fight he'd nearly lost. Constance's men had retrieved his sword and Alix's dagger for him from the grove.

He rose from his bed and joined the captain up on deck, where he felt the cool morning breeze on his face. His heart swelled at the sight of Glosstyr.

"We'll be coming in with the tide by the look of it," said the captain. "Did you manage any sleep, my lord?"

Weariness blurred Ransom's eyes. "A bit. Thank you for getting me home safely."

"What the duchess commands, so I do," said the captain. "Have you any word on the East Kingdoms, my lord? How fares King Benedict?"

"He hasn't reached them yet. He'll winter on an island first."

"And it's true he's married the doge's daughter?"

"Aye. It's true."

"Our new queen and we don't even know her," said the captain. "Better than an Occitanian bride, I should say. There cannot be peace between us. We're like two brothers who can do naught but squabble."

It was well put. The conflict between Ceredigion and Occitania had dominated their history. The two kingdoms seemed destined to clash. But why? Had it all started because of a game on a magic Wizr board? To what purpose, and why had it gone on for so long?

After they docked, he thanked the captain again and tromped his way to the castle, where his sudden and unexpected arrival caused a storm of surprise. His bones and joints were weary, his Fountain magic still at ebb tide, but he made his way to his room without any assistance from the buzz of servants hustling nearby. He took off the Brythonican tunic and exchanged it for one of his own.

A knock sounded on the door, and Simon entered before Ransom could respond.

"By the Lady, Ransom—I've got a search party scouring the countryside for you!"

Ransom smiled wryly. "Call it off. I'm safe."

"There've been reports of marauders hitting north of here at Blackpool. You look terrible. Are you well?"

"I'm weary," Ransom said. "I had a private duty to attend to, so I sent the knights on ahead. I didn't realize I'd be so delayed by the storm."

"I'm just grateful you're alive. Lady Claire would have had my head if anything happened to you. Not to mention the queen dowager."

Ransom looked at Simon seriously. "What news of the siege? I feel urgency to return. Has the castle held?"

Simon laughed. "It's over. Lord Dougal was captured and executed. News of it arrived yesterday. She's safe, the rebellion is crushed. So what business did you have?"

Relieved by the tidings, Ransom shook his head. "I can't speak of it. I'm sorry. But I'm glad Claire is safe. When I got her message at Kingfountain, I was desperate with worry."

Simon smiled. "Yes, we were all relieved to get the message." He paused. "Is it true? Is Jon-Landon at Kingfountain now?"

"Yes, that's no secret. Thank you for summoning me. The prince is determined to overthrow Longmont. He aimed to cause an uproar, but I think we managed to quell it for now. Emiloh will stay at Kingfountain. I must get back to Legault."

"Now that the storm has ended at last, you can," Simon said. "But there are some matters we need to discuss before you leave. I'd like to discuss your income and the expense of repairing Connaught. Can you give me some time before you go?"

"Of course. But I'm too weary at the moment, Simon. I could use some rest."

Simon studied him with greater scrutiny. "Are you injured, Ransom? Shall I fetch a barber?"

"There is no need." The light shining from the Raven scabbard was dimming, its work nearly done. Ransom's wrist was tender, but it was whole again. His body felt like a hollow well, though, empty of power.

After Simon left, Ransom picked up the Brythonican tunic and folded it. Not sure what else to do with it, he took it to his closet and put it at the bottom of a chest. Being here, in this room he had shared with Claire, he missed her even more.

※

In the afternoon, Ransom went to the training yard to test out his body. As he practiced with his sword, he felt the gentle lapping of the

Fountain again, the soothing reassurance that the loss of power wasn't permanent. The confidence he felt with weapons returned, and he lost himself in the afternoon, unaware of the passage of time as he pushed himself and found solace in the routines of training.

A servant rushed into the training yard. "My lord, a ship has come from Connaught. Sir Dearley is here."

Ransom sheathed his sword, mopped sweat from his neck with a rag, and then followed the servant back into the castle. He met Dearley in the solar, and the two friends greeted each other warmly.

"You *are* here!" Dearley said with surprise. "I thought you'd still be in Kingfountain, but Lady Claire insisted I come here first."

"It's good to see you," Ransom said. "All is well?"

"Yes, now that Dougal is no more. Do you know how they execute traitors in Legault? They're burned alive! It's a horrid practice. He screamed for a good long while. I shudder at the memory. But he deserved what he got, the knave. He attacked as soon as you were gone."

"So I heard," Ransom said. "What's become of his family?"

"Lord Tenthor evicted them from the castle. It's now de Murrow land. The widow was given a cottage, I think. And their sons are being held by Tenthor. He saved the day, Ransom. His loyalty should be rewarded."

"I can't agree more," Ransom said. "When news of the siege came, I was beside myself."

"So were we," Dearley confided. "The danger was real. We lost many good knights and soldiers defending the castle. If Tenthor had turned against us, we would have lost." His voice became more somber as he spoke. "I did my best, Ransom, but . . . I'm not you."

It added to his guilt to hear how close it had come. He squeezed his hand into a fist, almost regretful that Dougal had already been executed. He wanted revenge, and now there was none to be had. At least Claire had been granted *her* revenge. "I'm glad you're all right. And so is she."

"I have some news of my own to share," Dearley said, his expression brightening. "Elodie is expecting as well. We're a little behind you and Claire, but we count ourselves blessed by the Fountain for such good news."

"Well done," Ransom said approvingly. "Have you warned her of the sickness?"

"I dare not," Dearley said. "I'm nervous, of course. But it's excellent news. A family! I had no one, growing up, and I couldn't be more chuffed. Shall we return to Connaught, then? The tide goes out before midnight. We could be there at dawn."

"We will," Ransom said, gripping Dearley's shoulder. "I'm so happy for you. Truly, you and Elodie deserve this."

Dearley grinned. "So what happened about Jon-Landon?"

"Let me tell you all of it," Ransom said, and he did.

The crossing to Legault was much calmer than the previous night's journey, and Ransom was able to sleep peacefully through the voyage. He awoke before dawn and went above deck, breathing in the salty air and gazing at the inky horizon, wishing for the sun to rise so that he might see his beloved's homeland.

The crew went about their work while he leaned against the railing. As the sky began to pale in the east, he glimpsed the coastline of Legault and felt a rush of relief. As it brightened, he could see Connaught castle in the distance.

Dearley came out of his room groggily, rubbing his eyes, then joined Ransom at the railing. "I wish we didn't have to ride the sea each time we left. But I can see why they call it the Fair Isle. It's beautiful. Has an ancient feel about it."

"Indeed it does," Ransom agreed, looking at the land. He wanted to explore the wonders of Legault with Claire, to learn more about her heritage and past.

"I heard you parted ways from the knights you were with on your return to Glosstyr," Dearley said. "Was there a reason?"

He felt a silent warning from the Fountain. "I cannot speak of it," he said softly, staring across the waters.

Dearley didn't press the matter. "I see. The knights were worried. They didn't understand why you'd left. I'll say no more about it."

"Thank you," Ransom said, grateful for his friend's trust but wearied by the secret.

His excitement and anxiety increased as the ship drew up to the docks behind the hill. The ships moored there had sustained some damage in the storm—a few had smashed planks, and one had a cracked support pillar—but his attention shifted to a small party gathered on the dock: Claire, her maid Keeva, and Guivret.

Claire looked eager to see him, and Ransom rushed down the gangplank as soon as it was fixed in place. The splotches on her cheeks, nose, and forehead gave her the appearance of someone with the pox. It startled him to see her in poor health, but his worries diminished when she smiled and came into his arms. He smelled her hair and held her close.

"I wasn't expecting you back so soon," she said.

He pulled back, caressing the side of her face. "Are you well?"

"It's the babe," she said regretfully. "I'm swollen and wretched, especially in the mornings. Sir Dearley!"

The young knight approached them on the dock. "I didn't have to go far to find him. He was at Glosstyr, just as you said."

"You knew I was at Glosstyr?" Ransom asked.

An unreadable look crossed her face. "Had you been there long?"

"No. I'd just arrived back . . . from Kingfountain."

"From Kingfountain?" she said, a little surprised. Was that worry in her eyes?

"I came back as soon as I could," he told her. She started to tremble. "Are you cold?"

"Yes," she said, her mood shifting again. "It feels like I'll never be warm. Let's go back to the castle."

She took his arm, and they walked down the planks. Dearley spoke to Keeva and asked how Elodie was doing.

"She's *sláintiúil*," said Keeva, mixing in some Gaultic.

"She's slain?" Dearley asked in confusion.

"*Sláintiúil*—healthy."

"Goodness," Dearley said. "I'm relieved to hear it!"

Claire smiled at the banter. There were shadow smudges under her eyes. She seemed to have difficulty with the steep stairs from the docks, so Ransom slowed down and went at her pace. When they reached the top and entered the castle grounds, he saw the workmen repairing the walls. It was a painful reminder that he hadn't been there when she needed him. Guilt wrenched at his heart.

When they got inside the castle, they went up to their room, alone at last. She stood by the hearth, rubbing her arms. He came up behind her and put his hands on her shoulders. She flinched.

"Are you all right?" he asked worriedly.

"I had a strange dream the other night," she said, looking into the flames. "I know it's silly. I dreamed you were at Ploemeur." Her voice held a throb of doubt. "But you wouldn't have gone there, Ransom. Not on purpose."

A feeling of darkness roiled through him. Something was wrong, but he didn't understand it. Nor did he know what to do about it. He'd been warned not to speak of the Gradalis, but he hated keeping such a big secret from Claire.

"Why would I go there?" he asked softly, trying not to lie to her directly.

"I don't know," she said, shaking her head. "Did you miss me?"

"Of course I did," he said sincerely. "You mean everything to me."

She bowed her head. "I don't feel it, though. Your duties to others have kept you away. I'm fat and sick and had to fight off a desperate attempt to murder me and my unborn child. *And you weren't here.*"

Pain burst in his heart. "I came as soon as I got your letter."

"Did you?" she asked, turning to look at him, accusation burning in her eyes.

A sour taste filled his mouth. He wouldn't lie, but lies of omission were still lies, were they not? He stepped toward her, anguish squeezing his chest. "I came as soon as I possibly could," he said sincerely, force-fully. "Jon-Landon nearly caused a revolt. And there's a madman plundering Blackpool and North Cumbria. I think he's the Gaultic brigand known as the Hood. He attacked our ship when I left Connaught."

"Truly?" Claire said in surprise. "Ryain Hood?"

"He shot an arrow at me," Ransom said. "I've not been rolling dice. It makes me sick that Dougal attacked you. I'm furious you had to worry about your safety for even a moment. But I have certain duties that I must perform. A loyalty to King Benedict Argentine that without . . . I wouldn't even be your husband. Forgive me for being gone. It couldn't be helped."

His words were sincere and passionate, and her look softened a little. But only a little. Perhaps her pregnancy made her feel unworthy of love.

He took a step closer. When he reached to brush his thumb across her cheek, she turned her head slightly, but she let him touch her.

"I'm *samhnasach*," she said.

"What?" he asked, teasing her hair with his finger.

"I'm loathsome. Disgusting. I'm hungry all the time yet cannot keep my food down. I get vomit in my hair."

He took a lock and pressed it to his lips.

She butted him in the stomach with her elbow. "I'm serious."

"You're the most beautiful thing in all the world."

"You almost sound as if you mean that," she said, her nostrils flaring.

"Claire," he said, shaking his head. "I do mean it. I'd be an eejit to want anyone else."

She closed her eyes as she started to weep and leaned her forehead against his chest. He stroked her hair as she nestled against him. Had the siege of Connaught been her first battlefield? How many had died? He held her, whispering softly, and finally she softened to his touch.

When she lifted her chin and kissed him, he could taste the salt from her tears.

⋈

It has been too long since I've last written, but today's sad news nudged me into lifting this quill once more. The castle is quiet now, the snow thick on the trees. Not long ago, there was a keening wail that made everyone weep. Lady Elodie lost her child ere it was born. A little boy, wrinkled and bloody. She nearly bled to death. Poor John Dearley was frantic, afraid of losing both wife and child on the same day. When I heard the news, I sent Dearley away and told Ransom to go to her and lay his scabbard on her breast. She was quite unconscious. He did it at once, and the bleeding stopped. When Dearley was told the bleeding had stopped and she would live, he wept in gratitude and grief. Poor man. Poor mother. My heart aches for them both as I write this.

This event has clouded my own feelings toward my coming confinement. I've been excited, but now I dread the worst. I thought this would be a daughter, but it must be a son. It feels as if I'm carrying a calf, not a child, all the wriggling and wrangling. My body aches all the time, and I've swollen more than even the midwife agrees is good. I love this child in me, and when he—and I say "he" because I'm all the more certain of it—is kicking and squirming, I take Ransom's hand and guide his palm to where he can feel it. He smiles and looks at me so lovingly.

I smile as well, knowing all the while that he lied to me. I forgave him, even though he does not know I did. The stone sees the present. That much I know for sure.

—Claire de Murrow
Connaught Castle
(on the stillbirth of Finnley Owen Dearley)

CHAPTER SIXTEEN

Silent Snow

Ransom had reached the top of the stairs, and still little clumps of snow were dropping from his cloak and sloughing from his boots. He opened the door to the bedroom and felt the heat from the brazier mix with the icy wind coming from the open window. Claire sat on a cushion at the window seat, a small round pillow at her back and a heavy book resting on her protruding belly.

She turned a page and then glanced up at him. "Did you enjoy your ride?"

He tugged off his gloves and set them on an end table. Keeva, who was tidying up the room, flashed him a smile in greeting.

"There was a herd of moose elk roaming through the frozen meadow," he said. "I wish I'd brought my bow, for I could have killed several before they charged away. The snow is very deep right now. We didn't go far."

"I imagine not," she said, still focused on the page. "Who went with you?"

"Dearley, Axien, and Guivret," he said. "I thought Dearley needed to get out of the castle for a while. The cold air did some good."

When he removed his coat, Keeva came and took it from him and hung it by the brazier to dry it out. Ransom approached the window seat and planted a kiss on Claire's beautiful hair. Things had been strained between them since he'd returned home from Ceredigion months before. He wondered if it was just the altering moods caused by her difficult pregnancy, but he feared it was more than that. He didn't understand what it could be, but she'd altered since his journey.

"What are you reading, my love?" he asked softly, toying with her hair.

"I'm going through the books Lord Tenthor found at Dougal's castle," she said. "He had quite a collection, ten books in all, which is considerable for such a man."

"Sir Bryon has twenty books, I think," Ransom said.

"Twenty-seven actually," Claire said, still not looking up. "Sir Dalian told me his father is a deep reader. This one is very interesting."

"Oh?"

"It's a record of King Andrew and Queen Genevieve. I've never seen this one before. It's not a translation from Occitanian, like others I've read. This one was written in Gaultic."

Ransom glanced at the page and could hardly recognize the script let alone the words. "How does it differ from the other legends?" he asked.

She looked up at him and then put a strip of ribbon in the pages to save her place and set the book down on the cushion. "If you rub my feet, I shall tell you. I warn you that my ankles are very swollen today."

Ransom nodded and sat down at her feet. He removed her slippers and began massaging her feet and ankles. She winced and pressed her lower back, clearly uncomfortable. Many nights she couldn't sleep at all and just wandered the room pacing and wretched while he slumbered. It wasn't fair, but there wasn't anything he could do about it other than offer little assistances whenever she asked.

"We both know the stories about Andrew's sword, Firebos, and the Ring Table his mesnie sat around at his palace because all of his men were Fountain-blessed and ranked equally. There were magical ravens in the story that came and attacked the soldiers. The book also speaks of the scabbard, which we both know is real. Dougal, or some other person, had marked a note in the margins about how much he coveted it. He made other defacements as well, which are curious. I won't bore you. But this Gaultic record says he had a special Wizr set, one with pieces that moved of their own accord."

Ransom listened keenly. "The one we've spoken of before."

"Yes. Andrew used to play Wizr against one of his bravest knights, Sir Owain. Did you know of that?"

"No," Ransom said. "I wonder if Estian took the set with him to the East Kingdoms?"

Claire shrugged. "The Wizr set is very powerful, according to the record. More so than we thought."

"It must be," Ransom agreed. "Knowing your enemy's position is a key part of war."

"No, more than just that. The book says the fate of kingdoms is determined by who wins the game. Leoneyis was drowned because of it. It is powerful magic, Ransom." Her eyes glittered with interest as she spoke. "I think the curse that banished the Aos Sí beneath the waves is connected to that Wizr set. Perhaps they were not cursed to live below the waters forever . . . only until a certain number of games were played."

A troubled feeling bloomed in his chest. "I'd hesitate to trust a book without knowing who wrote it and why." He picked it up and opened to a random page. The script was illegible to him. "Are you sure you read it right? I've studied the old speech, but this is nothing like it."

"Of course it isn't, you brainless badger," she teased, evoking feelings of their past banter. But the lightness faded quickly, gone too soon. "This isn't the old speech. It's ancient Gaultic."

"But how can you even read it?" he asked.

She looked down. "Practice, I guess. I just kept staring and staring at the words until they started to make sense."

She isn't telling the truth.

The subtle whisper in his mind only increased his worries. What did that prompting mean? How else could she have read the writings? He pressed his thumbs into her swollen feet, trying to ease her discomfort, yet he felt ill at ease and heartsick. Why had she lied about such a thing? And why had the Fountain seen fit to tell him?

"I'm impressed," he finally said. "But then you've always been clever."

She smiled at the compliment, her eyes still downcast.

"Where did King Andrew go? Did the record say?"

Her gaze lifted, and she looked him in the eye. "I'm not there yet. This book talks more about the Lady of the Fountain. It says she was Myrddin's lover. It's a very strange story. You see, Myrddin had two stones that helped him translate languages and see the past, future, and present. Before he was tricked into captivity by the Lady of the Fountain, he gave the stones to Andrew, who had them mounted into a breastplate."

As she spoke, he felt increasingly uneasy. He knew this story from the Duchess of Brythonica, although he couldn't reveal that to Claire.

"That's interesting," he said in a neutral voice.

"I thought so too," she said. "King Andrew had the Wizr set, the sword, the scabbard, and the stones. It made him a powerful king. But even still . . . his kingdom failed." Her nose twitched, her look of discomfort becoming more pronounced.

"Would you like me to massage your back?" he asked.

She shook her head. "Some cramps have been coming on," she said. "I could hardly sleep last night because of them. They go away but then return even stronger. I haven't felt this way before." She let out a whistling breath. He watched her, worried, and she reached for his hand. When he took it, she clenched it very hard, surprising him.

Keeva approached. "Are you unwell, my lady?"

"I've been unwell for many, many months," Claire answered. "There . . . it's passing. Your son is wriggling right now. I wish he'd go to sleep."

"Would you like something to drink?" Keeva asked. "Some spiced *fion* perhaps?"

Sometimes Keeva resorted to Gaultic words when she didn't know their counterpart in Ceredigic. She spoke both languages but typically stuck to Ceredigic to make Ransom comfortable.

"No, I'll be sick if I take even a sip," Claire said. "I just can't get comfortable."

"Maybe you should read some more?" Ransom suggested.

"I'm tired of reading. I'm tired of feeling like this!"

"I'm going to fetch the midwife," Keeva said urgently, starting for the door.

"What can she do?" Claire said with a little contempt. "It's not like I'm ready to give birth today."

Keeva gave her a small smile. "Actually, my lady, I think you are!"

Claire glanced up at Ransom in sudden fear.

He clenched her hand in return. "Is it time?" he wondered.

"I don't know," she said. "I've never done this before."

Ransom paced in the hall at the foot of the tower stairs. The cries of pain he heard from Claire tore at him. When she started swearing in Gaultic, he nearly ran up the stairs out of fear and concern. Dearley waited with him, sitting on a little bench by the wall, his head in his hands, his face pale with worry and awful memories. Even when Ransom told him to go, he refused to abandon the scene. Guivret stayed with them, pacing the hall restlessly, but many of the other knights had left them to their vigil.

The torture of waiting, of listening to the agony, made Ransom increasingly miserable. What if he lost Claire in childbirth? He had his sword and scabbard strapped to his belt, and he'd told Keeva to come for him if anything went wrong. Another pained cry rocked through the walls. Some of the servant girls, passing by, shared secret smiles as they watched the misery of the men. It went on for hours and hours. Out the window, silent snow fell from a pale sky that clouded the sun.

Ransom went to the window, closing his eyes as he pressed his forehead against the cool glass. *Please,* he prayed silently. *Let the Lady look after my wife. May you protect her life and the life of our child. I have done your will. I have kept your secrets. Please, if I merit any favor, let it be now. I would give my life for them.*

He'd already tossed four coins into the well of the castle, even though it wasn't a tradition in Legault. There was no reassurance or comfort to him. Just a brutal wait spent listening to his wife suffer.

The torment dragged on. He refused food and drink, his stomach too sour with dread and worry to accept any food. Her pained cries became weaker and less frequent. He kept looking at the door, wondering if he should force it open and march up the stairs. Surely Keeva would come for him if he were needed?

Dearley walked up to him and put a hand on Ransom's shoulder. "I didn't think it took this long," he said with a sigh.

"I can't even tell without the sun," Ransom answered. "Thank you for staying with me."

Dearley offered a sad smile. The two of them had become even closer after Dearley's son was lost.

"I saw some new birds yesterday," Dearley said. "I think it will be spring soon. I can't wait for this accursed snow to melt."

"Aye," Ransom said. And then he heard a shrill cry—this was no night bird, but a frightened, mewling thing.

Ransom's eyes popped wide in confusion. "What is that?"

Dearley brightened. "I think that's a babe squalling."

Moments later, Keeva burst into the hall, a grin on her face. "Come upstairs, my lord! Come and welcome your son!"

Dearley grinned and started to weep at the same time. He clapped Ransom on the back before the new father took to the stairs. He rushed up the flight and came to the room, finding Claire exhausted and plastered with sweat but smiling.

"I told you it was a boy," she said weakly.

The midwife, a stately Gaultic woman, grinned. "And a big un too, milord."

Claire caressed the babe's feathery head, crooning softly to him. She looked as if she would fall asleep, and Ransom's love for her took his breath away. He knelt by the rumpled sheets of the bed and stared, spellbound, at his child. He had a little pink nose, swollen eyes, and a budding mouth, which was rooting against Claire's throat. A feeling of gratitude filled him to bursting.

And then, suddenly, Claire arched her back and let out a moan of pain. Another Gaultic oath came from her mouth. "It's starting again! No . . . no . . . no . . ."

Keeva swooped the babe from her arms, and Ransom backed away, eyes bulging with fear and confusion.

"What's happening?" he demanded.

"I can't . . . not again . . . no . . . no . . ." Claire gasped, thrashing on the bed.

"It's all right, my lady," said the midwife. "The fight isn't over yet. You must rally. Come, my dear. Show your spirit!"

"I can't . . . I can't . . ."

"Is she dying?" Ransom said, choking with fear and doubt.

"It probably feels like it," said the midwife, giving him a sharp look. "Best go downstairs before you faint. I've not a moment to spare for you, milord."

"Why?" Claire panted. "Why?"

"Because you've got another wee bairn inside," said the midwife. "You've two instead of one."

Dizziness washed over Ransom, but he kept on his feet and remained in the room to watch in fascination and surprise as their second child—another boy—was born shortly after his elder brother.

Ransom held each child in turn, amazed by the enormity of the occasion. He was a father twice over already. The babes were both proclaimed hale and strong by the midwife, who praised Claire's fortitude for having carried them both for so long. He was struck by feelings he couldn't describe, feelings that made his own father's actions even more unfathomable to him. Ransom would never risk his boys' lives to make a point. He would have given every last drop of his blood to protect his family.

With that thought in his mind, he stared at Claire, who had fallen asleep. He brushed a kiss on her brow while Keeva and the midwife swaddled and tended to the infants. Although he needed to share the good news, he didn't want to leave the room, the place now hallowed by what had happened there. He saw, at the window seat, the small book that Claire wrote in to chronicle her memories. She'd never shared it with him. She said she never would, for they were private thoughts.

He felt the sudden compulsion to read it. If he knew her thoughts, he could span the last of the distance between them. She would likely never notice if he snatched it and brought it back later. A guilty feeling welled up in his heart for even thinking it.

In old Gaultic legends, having twinborns is either an omen of health, happiness, and prosperity or disease, death, and bad luck. Which is it to be, I wonder? I haven't written since the boys' birth because of how weary Ransom and I both are. These sons are voracious and growing so quickly. We agreed that I would name the eldest brother and Ransom would name the younger. I chose the name Willem after my mother's father. In Gaultic custom, he will choose his own last name, just as I chose mine. The younger brother is Devon, after the Younger King. Willem and Devon were boisterous inside my womb. They are even more so outside of it.

The snow has melted, and spring has come at last. Has the war with the East Kingdoms already begun? I've been hoarding our stocks of qinnamon as there is no guarantee we'll be able to locate more until the conflict ends. More and more ships from Genevar have been sailing past the Fair Isle to bring supplies to the armies assembled so far away. Now that the sea is safer to travel, I can expect another summons from Kingfountain, claiming my husband's time and devotion. I shall watch him from afar, yet he knows it not.

After the birth of our sons, he asked if he could read this little book. But how would that be fair? I cannot peer into his heart.

—Claire de Murrow
Connaught Castle
The tides of spring

CHAPTER SEVENTEEN

Lost

The yard was full of the familiar noise and commotion of knights preparing to ride. Ransom went back to the entrance of Connaught where Claire stood holding little Willem. Keeva stood next to her with Devon in her arms. He brushed his lips against the babes' scalps, and both lads squirmed.

"I wish I were coming to Atha Kleah as well," Claire said, tilting her head. "Try not to get into too much trouble."

"I'm going at your command, if I may remind you," Ransom said.

"I know, but that doesn't mean I can't be jealous. Still, the thought of riding a horse for that long makes me wince. Justice must be served, and who better to administer it than my own husband?"

"I'll return as quickly as I can," he said, hooking his hand around her neck. They touched foreheads, and he kissed her. She pulled away too soon, giving him a forlorn smile.

"Be safe," she said. "I'm glad we spoke of Dearley and Elodie returning to Josselin. I'll miss their company, but they need some time alone. Having two babes in the castle must be torture for her. One of them could have been hers."

Ransom nodded, feeling unsettled about leaving her. The children had not brought her much joy. If anything, her moods had darkened even more after their birth, and he felt helpless to understand the cause or what to do about it.

After kissing his children again, he mounted Dappled and prepared to leave. Guivret glanced back at the castle, a guilty look on his face.

"What's wrong, lad?" Ransom asked the young knight.

His eyes shifted to Ransom, and he shook his head. "The castle was ambushed the last time you left. I fear what might happen."

"There are fifty knights guarding Connaught. And the sea is calm. I have no doubt they'll be safe."

Guivret nodded to him. "If you say so, my lord." He turned away from the castle, but he had a brooding look.

They reached the coastal city in two days, and Ransom was pleased to see the port so busy with trading ships. Several of them bore the Raven banner. When he arrived at the fortress, Lord Toole greeted him, and they began discussing the cases they had been asked to decide on the next day. Lords with overdue taxes. Rivals who'd fought during the winter and were coming to appeal for justice. Both agreed it had the makings of a terrible day.

There was a celebratory feast that evening, and Ransom found himself mobbed by individuals seeking his favor. The deference and flattery felt false, and at the first opportunity he broke away to seek out Lord Toole.

The sheriff smiled as he approached. "Have you had enough deceitful smiles for one evening, Lord Ransom?" he asked with wizened eyes.

"I find the battlefield easier to parse than court politics."

"Courts are much the same regardless of which kingdom you live in," Toole said. "Just recognize that every man, woman, and child wants a favor from you. There's an old Gaultic saying. 'He who is not contented with what he has would not be contented with what he would like to have.'"

Ransom chuckled. "How very true. How long do you think the business will last?"

"It will last until the Aos Sí return, if you let it," said Toole. "It's best to set limits, Lord Ransom. Never be too available."

"Sound advice. What do you think we should do about Lady Dougal's request?"

"Ah, the grieving widow. I would encourage some leniency, my lord. But not too much. She may or may not be guilty of her husband's crimes. Even the best men cannot read another's heart. Her prospects are diminished regardless of what you decide. I don't see the harm in being a little merciful. Justice is like salt. Everyone only wants a little sprinkle of it for themselves."

Ransom noticed Guivret hovering nearby, looking agitated. He seemed to be waiting for a lull in the conversation. Ransom gestured for him to approach. "What's the matter?" he asked.

The younger man handed him a sealed letter. "This is for you. From one of Lady Constance's knights."

Ransom noticed the Raven seal.

"My lord," Guivret said, abashed. "He told me . . . my mother is unwell. May I beg leave to visit Ploemeur?"

"I'm sorry to hear that news." Ransom put his hand on the young man's shoulder. "Of course you should visit her. I saw some Brythonican ships in the harbor. Perhaps one of them could take you?"

A relieved look crossed Guivret's face. "I thought the same thing. Thank you, Lord Ransom. I hope to return soon." He bowed and walked off.

"Why do you think that young man looked so guilty?" Lord Toole asked.

"Pardon?"

"I cannot claim any ability to read hearts, but that young man looked troubled about more than his mother's ill health."

Ransom turned and watched as Guivret passed through the thick crowd. He had been assigned to protect Claire. Ransom hoped the young man hadn't developed feelings for the lady he served. It would explain his reluctance to leave the castle and why he'd been so agitated during her labor.

"I confess I don't know what ails him," said Ransom to Toole. "But I do remember being that young and having troubles of my own."

Toole grinned. "That is true. Still, I would keep an eye on that one. His conscience is troubling him. But that's a good sign. I worry more about the ones whose consciences don't trouble them enough."

"Lord Longmont comes to mind," Ransom mused, turning the note over in his hand.

"Oh? I thought you and the queen dowager had reined him in?"

"We tried. But it would take a rebuke from the king himself to make him cognizant of his affronts. I'm still not certain he believes he's done anything wrong."

Ransom broke the seal and unfolded the note. It was written in a woman's hand, and he saw Constance's signature at the bottom. It was a brief note.

King Rotbart is dead. Estian will return sooner than believed possible. Beware.

)(

The warning troubled Ransom's sleep. Had Rotbart been assassinated? The message provided no details, but either way, there would be trouble and unrest within Brugia. Constance's supposition that Estian would return was equally troubling. If Estian quit the field, leaving Benedict to face their enemies with the Genevese and Brugian troops who didn't know whose orders to follow, everything would be in peril. But why wouldn't it take Estian the same amount of time to return from the East Kingdoms as it took everyone else?

Even as the thought floated through his mind, he found himself thinking of Alix's magical ability to travel. Could her brother do the same? His soldiers would probably not be able to return with him, if he traveled that way, but perhaps he hadn't brought as many men as he'd promised. Some of them could be hidden away in Occitania's castles for all they knew. Estian had proven himself to be both wily and deceitful.

He thought about sailing to Brythonica for more news, but doing so would arouse his wife's suspicions. As he lay in bed that night, he wondered if he'd be summoned by the Gradalis, but the feeling never came, and eventually he fell into a fitful sleep.

The next morning, he and Lord Toole met to dispense justice and mercy, and he found it difficult to concentrate on the matters at hand. Should he send word to Emiloh about what he'd heard? But surely she'd want to know how he'd found out, and he couldn't compromise himself or the Duchess of Brythonica.

The next afternoon, one of his men came up to him and whispered that a ship with the banner of the Lion had been seen arriving in port. Ransom told Lord Toole to put a temporary halt to the session, expecting a messenger to arrive any minute. There was an outcry from those still awaiting judgment, but the hall soon began to clear. Ransom paced, his mind whirring uneasily, only to stop in his tracks. Sir Axien, one of the knights who'd stayed behind in Connaught, had walked into the chamber.

"Why are you here?" Ransom asked.

Axien looked worried. "The Queen of Legault sent me to you. She is furious."

"What's this?" Ransom asked in confusion.

"I hope you can make sense of it," Axien said, brandishing another sealed note. "I've never seen her so enraged. She ordered me to come to you at once. She . . . she wasn't in her right mind. It started after you left." He backed away as soon as Ransom took the note.

Ransom's heart clenched with dread as he stared at the note in his hand. Turning his back on Sir Axien, he broke the seal and quickly read Claire's message.

It's been stolen. If you took it, Ransom, I want you to bring it back at once. I think you read from my little book, even though I told you not to, and decided to take it before you left for Atha Kleah. You must bring it back, Husband. If it was not you, then it was one of your knights, who I know are more loyal to you than they are to me. If you truly have no knowledge of this theft, then search your men for a white stone. Do not return to Connaught without it. I am in earnest. It belongs to me. It belongs to my family.

> *Claire de Murrow*
> *Betrayed*

Ransom blinked and then realized he knew who had stolen the stone—and Guivret was already on his way to Brythonica. He pinched the bridge of his nose between his fingers. The line that had cut his heart the most was: *Do not return to Connaught without it.* He had never received such a rebuke before, and it angered him that she would say such a thing.

Guivret had served Sir Terencourt. Of all the knights, he alone knew about Ransom's role as guardian of Brythonica. Not only had Guivret betrayed Claire, but he had betrayed Ransom too. Had he done so at Constance's request? For he had a strong suspicion the stone Claire had described was the missing seering stone. Hadn't the duchess told him the two belonged together?

"Lord Ransom, can you hear me?"

He lifted his head and saw Lord Toole staring at him expectantly. Standing next to Toole was a knight wearing the badge of the Lion on his tunic. Ransom carefully folded the letter and then turned.

"I'm sorry," he apologized, trying to absorb the news without grimacing. He approached the two men. "Have you come from Kingfountain?"

"Aye, the queen dowager summons you," he said. "I went to Connaught first. The Duchess of Glosstyr received me quite coldly. She demanded to know the purpose before she'd tell me where you were. I did tell her, my lord. I was not wrong to do so?"

"No, you did right," Ransom said, his stomach flopping over. "What news do you bring?"

"King Rotbart is dead," said the knight. "Word just arrived at court through the Espion. The queen dowager asked me to bring you back to Kingfountain. Jon-Landon has gone missing as well."

Ransom stared at the young knight's face, remaining impassive as the news crashed into him like a violent surf against the rocks. "I will go," he said. He looked at Lord Toole. "You will hear the other cases."

"I'm afraid I cannot," said Lord Toole. "I'm the high sheriff, not a justiciar. I lack the authority to hear them. I'm only here to advise you."

Ransom closed his hand into a fist, the only betrayal of his feelings. He'd arranged to be in Atha Kleah for three days to hear cases, but it was impossible to delay his travel for that long. "Well then. Open the castle again. I'll hear cases until the morning tide leaves and I with it."

"As you wish, my lord," said Lord Toole. He immediately summoned the steward and relayed the instructions. The man gasped in shock at Ransom's decision. It meant they'd all be working through the night.

"I'll have the ship ready to take you with the tide," the knight said.

As the man turned to leave, Ransom grabbed a bit of his tunic. "We will stop in Ploemeur on the way back," he said. He wanted to grab Guivret by the neck and determine what, if anything, Constance knew about his thievery.

The knight gave Ransom a wary look. "If you say so, my lord."

Ransom bid a servant bring him a quill, ink, and paper, and the man returned with them as the room once again filled with people. He considered what he wanted to write. Although he was angered by Claire's accusation, he remembered what Constance had said about the seering stones. Those who used them without the Fountain's command risked madness. Things began to fall into place in his mind: Claire's altered mood since he'd returned from Glosstyr. Had she seen him in Ploemeur?

Pain stabbed at his heart, and he hurriedly scrawled a letter back to Claire.

> *Dearest,*
>
> *I know you are angry. Sir Axien just arrived with your rebuke. I knew nothing of it. Guivret was acting guilty when we left and after we arrived. Before your letter came, he begged leave to return to Brythonica. I let him go, for he persuaded me that his mother was unwell. You know I have received a command to return to Kingfountain. It is my intention to go to Ploemeur first and demand an accounting from Guivret. I'm ashamed of his trickery and deception. Let me try and recover the stone and fulfill my duty as Lord Protector of Ceredigion. Estian, I've learned, is also returning. No doubt he will wage war on us.*
>
> *We have much to talk about when I return. There are secrets that I cannot tell you, but I will confess all that I can.*
>
> *With devotion,*
> *Ransom*

The seering stone is gone. It was missing the day Ransom left for Atha Kleah. There's a Gaultic saying I've never understood until now. "No war is more bitter than the war of friends." I've done my best to forgive and trust Ransom. But if he truly stole the stone from me, without a whisper of apology, I will find it hard to move past it. I sent Sir Axien with a letter and await its return. My anger frightens me. It is so very cold.

—Claire de Murrow, Queen of Legault
Connaught Castle

CHAPTER EIGHTEEN

Into the Snare

When Ransom reached the docks in Brythonica, he was given a horse to make the journey to the palace. He rode swiftly up the switchbacks, his gaze fixed on the fortress atop the massive rock outcropping. A flash of memory came upon him—he'd ridden this route once with Devon the Younger's wife, Noemie. The memory was not a pleasant one.

When he reached the top of the hill, he rode to the elegant gates and left his horse with a waiting groom with instructions to keep the horse there until he returned for it. He did not intend to stay long.

"Good day, my lord," greeted one of the servants. "The duchess is expecting you."

Ransom nodded and followed the man down the polished corridor. His anger toward Guivret still simmered in his chest. Whether or not the young knight was at the palace, Ransom had decided it best to seek out Constance and find out what she knew. Even though he had told his wife where he was going, he felt uncomfortable being in Ploemeur.

The servant paused at the doorway to the solar and bowed to him, allowing Ransom to enter first. He did and found Constance standing by the window, gazing out at the sea. She turned to him, her expression one of deep concern.

"I knew you'd come," she said.

"Do you know why I've come?" he asked.

"Why don't you tell me," she said calmly.

"One of the knights of my mesnie used to work for Sir Terencourt. Has he returned?"

Constance nodded. "He has. He's here." She gestured to something behind him, and he turned to see Guivret pressed against the wall, a look of guilt and misery on his face.

Ransom glared at him before turning back toward Constance. "I've been put in a very difficult position."

"Indeed," she answered. "And it's not fair to ask more of you."

"More?"

The duchess walked to a chair and rubbed her palm against the plush cushion. "Guivret has also been struggling with divided loyalties. Loyalty to you and loyalty to the Fountain."

"Or do you mean loyalty to *you*, Duchess?" Ransom asked her.

"You must decide that for yourself, of course," she said. "Perhaps it would be best if he explained himself. I did not order him to do what he did. It was his decision. He must face the consequences."

Ransom sighed and turned back to Guivret. The young knight approached, his eyes roiling with guilt and regret. He dropped to one knee before Ransom. "I plead with you to hear me out, my lord, before condemning me. I will accept any punishment you can devise."

"Stand," Ransom said. "Come on, lad. On your feet."

Guivret did so, but he couldn't meet Ransom's eyes. He was harrowed by his emotions. Wringing his hands, he tried to speak. "When Lord Dougal was captured, he had with him a white stone. I recognized it from Lady Constance's stories. She'd seen it in a vision. I tried to warn the queen, Lady Claire, about using it, but she ignored my warnings." His lip trembled. "I've seen it change her, Lord Ransom, and not for the better."

"How so?" he asked, although he'd seen signs of alteration himself.

Guivret rubbed his mouth. "How to describe it? A darkness has fallen over her. She's more quick to distrust. More suspicious. I've seen her scold Keeva more sharply than usual for no reason at all." He flushed when he said the maid's name.

"Have you an attachment to the maid?" Ransom asked.

Guivret nodded guiltily. "She . . . confides in me," he stammered. "She's seen the changes in her mistress as well. We thought it was the pregnancy at first. Bearing children is a difficult task, and she's borne two. But it started when she began using the stone . . . and everything got worse after she started reading that ancient book. It's done her harm. She's fixed on learning its secrets. It's even altered how she feels about you, my lord."

Ransom stared at the young knight. "And you know this . . . how?"

"Lady Claire has a little book she's kept for many years. She writes her heart in it. She won't let anyone else read it. But Keeva has. And she told me what she learned."

Ransom rubbed his eyes. How had he missed what was going on in his own home?

"Lord Dougal raved like a madman when he lost the stone. We couldn't bear to see the same thing happen to Lady Claire. That's why I asked you if I could go home. I lied to you, my lord. I freely admit it. Keeva knew where the stone was hidden, and I stole it ere we left. I brought it here because the Duchess of Brythonica, whom I know to be wise and unselfish, has the other half. Your wife believes in other traditions. She doesn't trust the Fountain is real."

Ransom struggled with his feelings, but he put his hand on Guivret's shoulder. "Thank you for telling me. You betrayed your mistress, but your intentions were honorable. That leaves us in a pickling jar, though."

"Indeed it does, my lord," Guivret said. He straightened his shoulders. "Whatever comes, I will take the blame. I'd not have Keeva suffer, if possible."

Ransom frowned. "Let me think on it, lad."

"Ransom," Constance said. "I felt a strong direction to use my seering stone as well. That is why I sent you the message that I did. Estian is coming back, and he intends to start a war. He won't have all of his men with them—some will take their time returning—but he'll have more than we do. But that is not all that I learned."

"Tell me," he said.

"The book that Claire has, the one that was found in Dougal's library, is extremely dangerous. *The Hidden Vulgate* was copied by the Black Wizr in a previous age in another world. Even without the seering stone, that book will corrupt Claire. From what Guivret's told me, I suspect it has already started."

A trickle of Fountain magic inside him confirmed the words. He squeezed his hand into a fist. "Are you saying I must steal it from her? Destroy it?"

"It cannot be destroyed," Constance said. "It must be hidden, safeguarded. Once it is taken away from her, its power over her will begin to dwindle. I'm sorry to give you these ill tidings, Ransom. After she first used the stone, she had a vision of you when you were here and wounded. She believes we are lovers. We both know that is not true."

"Some of the knights in the mesnie believe something is amiss as well," said Guivret darkly. "It didn't go unnoticed that you returned from Brythonica by ship after disappearing on the road to Glosstyr."

"Who spoke of it?" Ransom demanded.

"Axien," Guivret said. "Some of your actions have been misconstrued, my lord. Like when you left your knights and went off alone. As soon as I heard the story, I understood why you'd done it, but the others gossip about you. When someone told Dearley about the talk, he rebuked them and said they'd be dismissed from your service if they ever besmirched your good name again. He doesn't believe any of it."

"Why hasn't he told me?" Ransom asked, surprised by the news.

"He knows you have heavy enough burdens to bear. He says you have your reasons, and that is good enough for him."

Ransom's gratitude for Dearley's loyalty throbbed inside him. "I thank you for telling me. He should have . . . he should have told me as well. I could have put his mind at ease."

"His mind is already at ease," Guivret insisted. "He knows you'd not do anything to dishonor yourself or Lady Claire."

"I try not to, anyway," Ransom said with another heaving sigh. "Claire sent me a letter when I was in Atha Kleah." He turned to Constance. "She said not to bother returning if I don't bring the stone back."

Guivret shook his head in dismay. "I'm sorry, my lord."

"Her feelings may soften in time," Constance said. "But only after she stops reading that book." She stepped around the chair and approached him. "Do not open its pages. It will corrupt anyone who tries to read it."

Ransom nodded, grateful he'd put it down so quickly. "Is that the other secret I must keep? The one you mentioned before?"

Constance shook her head. "No, it is not. Before you go to Kingfountain, there is something else you must do. Something you *both* must do," she added, glancing at Guivret.

Ransom furrowed his brow. "Part of your vision?"

She nodded. "In my vision, I saw you both in Pree. Before Estian returns. And he is on his way now."

Her words felt like a rope cinching across Ransom's chest. "I am not welcome in Pree, my lady," he said, remembering his last visit there. "I was told never to return, on pain of death." He'd threatened Estian's life in front of his nobles and advisors.

"I know," she said. "I'm telling you what I saw. In the palace of Pree, there are many fountains. The king's private chapel is on the west side of the fortress. You'll know it from the three enormous chandeliers that hang down the aisle. I saw you both in there. Ransom, you reached into the fountain and withdrew a wooden box containing a Wizr set. It is one of the relics of King Andrew's reign. You took it before Estian could return and stop you." Her eyes narrowed as she looked at Ransom. "If Estian wins the game that is being played on the board, then the Deep Fathoms will engulf Ceredigion in a flood. Ransom, so much is at stake here. More than just your marriage."

He raked his fingers through his hair. Her words made him shudder, for he realized, through the Fountain, that she was speaking the truth.

"But Emiloh has summoned me," he said, conflicted.

"Send word that you're delayed. From here you can be in Pree in two days' time. You have to get there before Estian returns. You speak Occitanian as a local, Ransom. Those years you spent in Chessy will serve you well."

"If I'm captured . . ." Ransom said, shaking his head, unable to finish the thought. Would Claire even attempt to buy his freedom?

"You must succeed," Constance said, touching his arm.

"I am to go as well?" Guivret said eagerly.

"Yes, I saw you both there."

"Can we not send a warning to Benedict?" Ransom said. "Or have you already seen his fate?"

Constance looked down. "It would take too long to reach him, even if we sent it now. And I cannot look into the stone to find out where he will be in the future. I only dare use it when the Fountain bids me do so. Benedict is headstrong and reckless. He's capable of any number of choices that could affect how things turn out. I've heard from several Genevese traders that he's offended both the Brugians and the Occitanians during this conflict. With Rotbart dead—"

"How did he die?" Ransom asked.

"They were crossing a river, and he fell from his horse and drowned before they could save him. The war is not popular anyway, and this could make people believe the Fountain is against it. The Brugians have already started to pull back. Estian, as I've seen in my vision, will forsake the conflict and return early, leaving Benedict and the Genevese to bear the brunt of it. The alliance has already fallen apart, and spring has just begun. Benedict is stubborn, though. He'll still try to reclaim the oasis, which will delay his return."

"And you don't know if he will succeed?" Ransom asked.

Constance shook her head. "I don't. What I *do* know is that we'll be fighting Estian soon. The voyage should take a year, but he will be here much sooner. Without the Wizr board, we cannot win."

Guivret gave Ransom an encouraging look. "I'm with you to the end, my lord."

Ransom rubbed his forehead vigorously. "I'll need to send a message to Emiloh, but the Espion keeps intercepting them. I'll have to be careful with the wording."

"I will send a trusted knight to deliver it in person," Constance said.

"I do not like keeping secrets from her either," Ransom said. "There is information I know that would be helpful to her."

"It would be fatal if revealed," the duchess countered. "Longmont's Espion have tried to infiltrate Ploemeur. They pay well for information." A thoughtful look came to her eyes, and her expression softened. "Secrets squirm inside of us. Like a chick wanting to be free of its egg. Or a moth quivering inside a seed. They *want* to be told. That is why the rumors about you persist, Ransom. Not because they are true, but because some thoughts itch to be shared. And then shared again." She shook her head. "It is given to some to know the mysteries of the Fountain, but if we wish to know more of them, we must respect the gifts we've been given. I've found that if I heed the Fountain's commands, I'm granted more information. I don't ask for more. I accept what is freely given and act on it."

Ransom admired her wisdom. *Like a chick wanting to be free of its egg. Or a moth quivering inside a seed.* The words sounded hauntingly familiar to him, but if he'd heard them before, he couldn't remember when.

He looked at Guivret.

"I am ready to go," the young knight said with determination.

"So am I. Yet it feels like we're going like rabbits to a snare," Ransom said.

Sir Axien returned with a letter from Ransom. The seal was marred, but it was written in Ransom's hand. He says there are secrets between us. Worse, he claims Guivret fled to Brythonica. I cannot help but suspect it is a ruse, another stolen opportunity to visit the precious duchess. I wish I still had the stone, to see with my own eyes what sort of betrayal this is. I want to believe my husband. But many wives have been blind to the depravities of men.

If there is a war, if Estian truly does return soon, I may not see Ransom for a long time. Perhaps it is better this way. Perhaps I trusted too much in an unsteady nature.

Why would Guivret have stolen the stone? Was his allegiance also to another duchess? Trust is like glass, so easily broken.

—*Claire de Murrow*
Connaught Castle

CHAPTER NINETEEN

Threat

The barber stepped back, wiping a streak of lather from his hands with a towel. The man had a plain face and an appraising arch to his eyebrows.

"You do look more Occitanian now, my lord," he said. "In fact, you look like another man."

"He does," agreed Constance, coming around and holding out a hand mirror. When Ransom took it from her, he almost dropped it. His locks had been shorn in the Occitanian style, his beard completely shaved off. He barely recognized himself. The razor had revealed a little scar on his chin and another on the edge of his jaw. He didn't even remember when he'd earned them or how, but it had likely happened in the training yard. He handed the mirror back to Constance.

"I think it a fine job, I must say," said the barber, bowing to the duchess. "An odd request for a knight of Ceredigion to be clean-shaven."

"And one you must keep quiet, Matthew," said the duchess. "Tell no one of this."

"As you command, my lady," said the barber, bowing again. He gave Ransom another scrutinizing look. "I bid you good day," he said before leaving.

Guivret had already had his own shave and stood with a hand on his sword hilt. "Shall we go?"

"Two horses have been prepared for you," said Constance. "But one thing more." A servant had brought in a leather chest earlier, and she walked over and opened it. Inside were two black tunics.

"The color is not popular here in Ploemeur," she said, taking them out. She handed one to Guivret and the other to Ransom. "The garments are not Occitanian, but it was the best I could do under the circumstances. Put them on."

Ransom tugged off his tunic and struggled to put on the other, which was smaller than the one he wore. Guivret did the same.

"Maman," said a child's voice at the doorway. "Who are these knights come to visit?"

Constance smiled and sank down to one knee as the boy came and embraced her. She pressed a kiss to his forehead. "It is Lord Ransom and Sir Guivret, darling. Don't you recognize them?"

The boy looked at Ransom with confusion. "Are you sure, Maman?"

"I'm quite sure," she said, squeezing him. Then she rose. "Go swiftly," she said, looking into Ransom's eyes. Although she smiled, he saw something in her gaze that disturbed him. It reminded him of what she'd said about their fates being intertwined. He didn't believe it, but she hadn't asked him what he thought. So he just gritted his teeth in discomfort and bowed slightly.

"I will send your letter to the queen dowager with one of my trusted knights," she said.

"I plan to return directly to Kingfountain after I've claimed the Wizr set," Ransom said.

"I know." She looked down and then forced another smile. "Farewell."

Ransom and Guivret took their leave and rode their horses down the trail. Many of the Brythonicans they passed looked at them with curious stares, no doubt wondering what two knights of the Black Watch were doing in Ploemeur.

As they rode, Ransom's heart darkened at the awful task ahead of them. If not for the duchess's vision through the seering stones, he would never have imagined he'd voluntarily intrude on enemy territory with the goal of stealing a treasure from another king. What would happen if they were caught? He thought of Claire and his sons. He wanted more than anything to return to them and watch the boys grow.

"What's to become of me, Lord Ransom?" Guivret said after they'd ridden for some time. "I've betrayed Lady Claire, but not out of any ill intention. If I am banished from Legault, I could bear it. But my heart would pine for Keeva."

"And she returns your affection?" Ransom asked.

"Aye. By looks more than words. There is so much we say to each other with our eyes."

Ransom could appreciate the feeling. "I hate seeing two people in love and unable to act on it. I understand that particular torment personally, from my long separation from Claire."

Guivret sighed again. "You waited for her, and I'd do the same. It would be hard, but I would bear it."

"We bear what we must," Ransom said, eyes fixed on the road.

When they entered Occitanian territory, the feeling of dread and gloom increased. They passed Occitanian travelers on occasion. They greeted them in passing, and Ransom replied in kind, keeping his words brief so as not to arouse suspicion with his accent. It had been several years since he'd lived in this kingdom. But the words came easily, and he felt the throb of his Fountain magic guiding him.

They camped for the night in a small copse of trees off the main road, not wanting to arouse attention or risk suspicion by staying at a tavern. The next day, they continued riding, moving past hamlets and villages that had sprung up since Ransom's last visit. The businesses were bustling and cheerful, and the people seemed completely unaware they were a nation at war.

Just after midday, they encountered a band of armed knights heading toward them. Ransom's stomach sank, and Guivret whistled softly under his breath.

"Keep your eyes on the road," Ransom said to him. "Don't answer. Let me speak."

"I have no intention of doing otherwise," the younger man confessed.

As the other knights drew closer, the lead one tapped his chest in a knightly salute. Ransom reciprocated and slowed when the other man did. He didn't recognize the fellow, thankfully.

"Have you word on the king's arrival?" asked the knight. "Has he reached landfall yet?"

"I know not," Ransom said with a shrug. "I was heading to Chessy."

"For the tournament?"

Ransom hadn't heard there would be one. "Aye."

"Don't count on winning anything," said the knight with a chuckle. "The tournament is a pretext for our knights to gather. We're riding to war against the dogs of Ceredigion."

Ransom wrinkled his brow. "When?"

"Soon. Enjoy the delights of the market at Chessy. But you'll not be there long."

"Thanks for the news," Ransom said, bowing his head. The two groups parted, and Ransom breathed a sigh of relief that he hadn't been discovered.

Guivret grinned at him. "We could have taken them, Lord Ransom. I wasn't afraid."

The bold declaration made Ransom shake his head.

As they drew near Chessy, the road was thronged with travelers coming for the tournament. Memories of Ransom's younger days crowded his mind. He was tempted to stop by a certain market stall and buy some penuche for Claire, but he didn't want to risk even the smallest chance of being recognized. As they passed other knights, his stomach felt sick with worry. He quickly glanced from face to face, trying to beware any who would recognize him.

And as they reached the thickest part of the road, moving at a slow clop, he sensed the vague presence of Lady Alix for the first time since the Elder King had died. His eyes shut with dread.

"We must hurry," he muttered to Guivret. Had she sensed him as well? He'd felt just the slightest tremor in his Fountain magic—a warning that another with the power was nearby. Fear bloomed in his chest.

He urged his horse forward, forcing his way through the crowd. Some cried out in anger at being bypassed, but he didn't slow or halt, and neither did Guivret. The feeling of her presence began to fade, and it dissipated altogether as soon as they left the crowd.

There were so many people around them. Was it even Alix he had felt? Was it possible there was another Fountain-blessed who served Estian? He wasn't completely sure.

They reached Pree as the sun sank in the western sky. The city gates were open, streams of traffic coming in and out. The walls surrounding the city were massive and defended by a battalion of sentries. Pennants bearing the Fleur-de-Lis of Occitania fluttered in the breeze from spire spokes. The city shone with splendor, but it was a dark glory. It felt unnatural being there, as if he were trudging through a slimy bog, unseen but keenly felt.

When they reached the gate, they were waved through by the guards on duty without even a comment. One look at their black tunics had been enough.

They rode side by side on the crowded street.

"How will we get inside the palace?" Guivret asked softly.

"We are not at war currently," he said in response, not wanting their foreign tongue to be overheard. "We might not even be challenged."

"But if we are?"

"Then I'll say we have news of the king. It seems he's expected."

"By the Lady, I hope he doesn't come while we're here," Guivret said nervously.

Ransom agreed.

He was able to guide them to the palace, but they stopped before approaching the building. Guards in black tunics patrolled it, and no travelers were going in or out.

"What do we do?" Guivret asked.

Ransom remembered the fish-shaped charm he had taken from one of the knights of Bayree. Perhaps it would get them through.

"I have an idea," he said, then tied a little knot in the broken chain and slipped it around his neck. He let the emblem fall on the breast of his tunic.

"What is that?" Guivret asked him.

"The symbol of the Fisher Kings," Ransom answered. He looked up at the silver spires of the palace, glinting in the sun. "It may help us get past the guards."

Guivret nodded, and the two of them approached. The sound of shushing water filled Ransom's ears. Part of him thought they were risking too much, that this gambit was utter madness, yet he also felt a strange confidence that he'd succeed.

As they rode across the drawbridge to the gate, the knights on duty barred the way. They both reined in, and Ransom stared down at the man who approached them.

"It is forbidden to enter or—" he paused, his eyes going to the charm on Ransom's chest.

"I come with a message," Ransom said.

The guard nodded curtly and waved them both in. As they reached the portcullis, he saw the vicious spiked teeth of it and remembered a story Alix favored about a Fountain-blessed knight whose horse was cut in half. A shiver went down his spine.

They rode into the yard and left their horses with a stable boy. Ransom gave him a livre as a reward, with the charge to keep their mounts ready if he wanted another.

Guivret looked a little greensick as they marched toward the palace doors. Ransom gripped the hilt of his bastard sword, ready for anything, but two servants opened the doors for them. No one attempted to speak with them, the servants continuing with their work as they passed by. There didn't appear to be other visitors, which made sense because of the coming tournament at Chessy.

Ransom led them through the shadow-dappled passageways, guiding them toward the chapel Constance had told them about. As they turned down the hall, he saw a single knight standing on duty at the door. A tingle of warning went down his neck as they approached the man. His magic informed him the man was highly skilled.

"This corridor is off-limits," the knight said as they approached. "Away with you."

Ransom didn't slow his pace. "Is this the king's private chapel?"

"It is, and turn back before I sound the alarm," repeated the knight. His hand dropped to his sword hilt.

"I wanted to toss a coin in the fountain as a prayer for the king," Ransom said. "I've heard he will return soon."

"There are other fountains in the castle. Are you daft, man? Did you not—?"

Ransom lunged for him and slammed his forearm into the man's throat. The knight, caught off guard, tried to push Ransom back, but Guivret slammed the man in the temple with the hilt of his dagger. The knight sagged against Ransom, unconscious, and Guivret opened the door, allowing Ransom to drag the body into the chapel.

"What's going on?" asked another man on the inside. By his robes, Ransom took him to be the sexton, not a deconeus.

"He fainted," Ransom said, setting the body on the ground. He looked at Guivret and nodded to the sexton. Guivret marched toward him.

The sexton paled and then fled out a side door. Guivret charged after him, but by the time he reached the door, it was locked. Guivret pounded his fist against it in frustration.

"We don't have time," Ransom said. He hurried to the fountain, its waters placid, and knelt before it. He felt a powerful sense of Fountain magic emanating from the waters.

"I don't see anything in there but coins," Guivret said worriedly after joining him.

Ransom's stomach twisted. Even though he couldn't see anything, he *felt* a presence. Taking off his glove, he dipped his hand into the water. It was cool to the touch. Memories of the oasis came to him, and he recalled how he had found his scabbard in the well. By touch, not sight. He plunged his hand into the water and felt a box or case of some kind. Groping his hand across the surface, he discovered a handle. He tugged with all his might, and a box emerged from the waters. Guivret gazed at it in shock.

"Blessed Lady," he murmured.

Ransom stood with the box, which was surprisingly heavy, then unlatched it and peered inside. A sigh escaped him. It was the Wizr set they sought, but how were they going to get it out of the palace before the sexton raised the alarm? He latched it shut again.

"Come on," Ransom said, and they walked back to the chapel door. The knight they'd left just inside was already groaning, struggling to rise. Guivret hit him again, and they left the chapel—closing the door behind them—and started down the corridor. Ransom's heart thundered in his chest. If they could get off the palace grounds quickly, it would be easier to escape the city. But it was still a long ride to the border, and he expected to be chased.

A prickle of awareness went down his back as they reached the end of the corridor. He felt Alix's presence in the chapel behind him, appearing out of nothingness. Although he didn't understand how she did it, she had the power to travel long distances through the waters. He had a strong sense of her presence, and he was keenly aware that she could sense him too.

"What is it?" Guivret asked in concern.

"Run!" Ransom barked.

I spent most of the morning today striking targets with my bow. My arms and fingers hurt from the strain, but it felt good to be outside again and away from the squalling children. They are often so sweet tempered, but every now and then they choose to raise an unholy storm. The exercise did some good. There is some satisfaction to be gained from piercing a hay bale at fifty paces. Yet even the splendor of archery couldn't dispel the dark mood that continues to plague me. I'm angry that what was mine was stolen. My anger frightens me. It runs very, very deep.

—Claire de Murrow, Daughter of Richard Archer
Connaught Castle

CHAPTER TWENTY

The Poisoner

Almost as soon as he sensed the presence of Lady Alix, he felt the first pangs of a summons from the Gradalis. He had never been able to stop it before, and he realized with frustration that he and Guivret would soon be separated.

They both turned the corner and rushed down the corridor, but the smell of cooking food wafting down the hallway told him he'd gone the wrong way.

"This isn't the right passage," he said, halting. Guivret stopped with him, and they doubled back to the corridor they'd left. They were running, but it didn't feel fast enough. "I feel the summons, Guivret. I think the duchess is trying to draw me out."

Guivret blanched. "That means I won't be going with you."

Could he bring him if they were touching? Ransom had been able to bring his horse, so it was possible he could take another man. And yet . . . if he tried and failed, the result would be deadly for Guivret. It was too great a risk. His mind tumbled with thoughts and fears as they reached the junction of the corridor. Ransom heard the sound of racing footsteps, and when he looked down the corridor as they passed it, he saw Alix coming toward them at a dead run, a dagger in her hand. She raised her arm to throw it, but they made it across the gap.

They put on a burst of speed, but so did Alix, and he sensed her getting closer with every stride. He needed to get her away from Guivret. If he lured her into one of the towers, Guivret might have time to escape through the palace gardens.

Ransom didn't have time to convince him—he just raced toward the tower he knew best, the one where Devon the Younger had once stayed. Slowing as they reached it, he gripped Guivret by the shoulder forcefully, his other hand clenched around the handle of the chest with the Wizr set. Sweat trickled down his cheek, and his breath came fast.

"Go that way," he said, nodding down the hallway. "There's a door at the end that leads out to the palace gardens. Hide there and try to escape the island."

"I'll not abandon you until I know you're safe," Guivret said, shaking his head.

"The duchess is summoning me. I'll be able to escape. I fear for you—"

Lady Alix was about to turn the corner.

"Go!" Ransom said, propelling the young knight ahead. He grabbed the handle of the door, and when it didn't immediately open, Ransom smashed his shoulder into it. He ducked inside just as a dagger thunked into the wooden frame. He heard Guivret's boots pounding down the corridor.

Ransom gritted his teeth, holding the chest close, and started running up the stone stairs. Light beamed in from arrow slits along the wall. He took the steps two at a time, hoping his longer stride would increase the gap between them. The stairs wound around in a circle, which would make it harder for her to hit him.

A dagger hit the back of his leg, sinking into his muscle. A tingle of pain shot up his back, and he slumped forward, nearly dropping the box. He caught himself on his forearm, the stone biting into him. He grunted in pain. And he soon felt the poison begin to weave through his blood.

"How did you know it was there?" Alix demanded, huffing as she climbed the steps. He saw her draw another dagger. The look of cunning and rage on her face made his stomach turn. His leg and buttock grew numb. He rolled onto his back and plucked out the dagger from his leg.

"You were foolish to come here," she said, drawing closer. "But I have questions you must answer. I can make you tell me things, Ransom. I can make you confess your secrets."

He tried to stand up, but his one leg was useless. He threw the dagger back at her, but she sidestepped it, and the blade clattered uselessly against the wall and then tumbled down the stairs. He felt the tingle of the summons increase, but the magic didn't sweep him away. Would it happen too late? He tightened his grip on the handle of the chest.

She lunged at him then, knocking him back against the steps, and brought the dagger to his throat. "Don't think I will show you any mercy," she said, nicking him with the blade. Then she looked down at his neck, her eyes widening with surprise. "You're not bleeding."

Her eyes shot down to the glowing Raven scabbard.

Ransom punched her in the ribs as hard as he could. He heard her gasp in pain, and then she was stabbing him, the knife coming down again and again. Pain bloomed from a gash on his cheek, then another on his forearm as he raised it to block the blows. Then his chest. Her face was a twisted mask of hatred and revenge as she plunged her dagger into him again and again.

Guivret tackled her into the wall, and the two bodies became entangled. Ransom didn't know why the knight hadn't used his sword on her, but it was still in the scabbard. Pain had made his thoughts sluggish, and he watched as Alix elbowed Guivret in the nose, grabbed his wrist, and torqued his arm so hard the young man shrieked in pain before going face-first into the wall and then slumping down.

Ransom rocked forward, trying to support himself with his good leg despite the numbing, paralyzing poison that was stripping him of his strength. He hefted the chest, prepared to swing it around and hit Alix with it.

And then he was plummeting, the magic taking him away just as Alix turned to look at him. Her shriek of rage mingled with the rush of the falls and the terrifying sensation of falling.

He collapsed on a polished stone floor, still gripping the chest. The blue light from the scabbard flared even brighter as his vision blurred. The poison had incapacitated him. Suddenly Constance was there, tugging on his arm, trying to help him stand, but his strength failed.

His last thought before he lost consciousness was that Guivret was in the poisoner's hands now.

And there wasn't anything Ransom could do to save him.

𝕏

When consciousness returned, it was sluggish and fleeting. He tried to force himself to move, but only managed to rip a blanket away before falling again on the bed.

"He's waking, my lady," said a familiar voice. The barber, he realized. Matthew.

"Ransom? Can you hear me?" Constance asked.

He tried to speak, but his mouth was dry. When he tried to sit up again, he felt her warm hand against the bare skin of his chest, pushing him back down. "Don't struggle, Ransom. Let it happen gradually. Your wounds were very deep."

He tried to summon some moisture in his mouth and failed. His eyes opened, and he saw the barber's and the duchess's faces hovering over him.

"Would you like something to drink?" she asked.

He nodded, and she fetched a cup, propping his neck a little so he could drink. It was morning, and he heard birds chirping outside. He'd slept through the night. He felt some of the liquid spill down the side of his neck, but Constance mopped it with her sleeve.

"Guivret," he managed to say. "Did you know?"

"Yes." Her voice was soft, her tone sad.

He shut his eyes again, wanting to swear in anger. He clenched his fists instead. They'd removed his hauberk and his shirt, leaving his pants and boots on, as well as his scabbard. He felt his body healing from the magic, but the soreness of the cuts still troubled him.

When he opened his eyes again, he saw the barber looking at him with pity. "I bandaged your wounds as well as I could," he said. "The lady bid me not stitch them. She said they'd heal on their own, although they were severe. That's all I can do, my lady."

"You've done enough," Constance said and nodded for him to go. She sat at the bedside.

When the barber was gone, Ransom turned his neck and looked at her. "Why? Why did you send Guivret if you knew he'd be captured?"

"It wasn't my choice, Ransom."

"Wasn't it? If I had gone alone . . ."

She lowered her head with sadness. "The Fountain had a reason for him to be there. I don't know what purpose, but I knew he would not come back. If I told you, you would not have taken him."

"She could kill him!" Ransom said, his emotions trembling on the verge of rage.

Constance traced her finger along his neck. "As she tried to kill you. I know what she's capable of, Ransom . . . and that this pains you even more because you know what it's like to be a hostage. I *am* sorry."

Her words cut him to the quick. Yes, he knew those feelings. And he didn't want Guivret or anyone else to suffer as he had. He was the lord of a mesnie. It was his duty to safeguard his knights. Yet he knew some would fall in battle serving him. It was a heavy burden to carry.

He felt a shiver start. "Where is my shirt?"

She rose from the bed and started toward a little table, where he saw his clothes. "We took it off, as well as your armor, to see to your wounds. There's one on your leg as well, but . . . I thought it prudent to leave that one for the scabbard alone to heal. The wounds are all nearly closed."

He sat up, feeling dizzy, but didn't collapse again. He swung his legs over the side of the bed, and she handed his shirt to him. He saw a bandage tied around his arm and felt another one wrapped around his chest. Grimacing, he pulled on the shirt and noticed Constance wincing as she looked at him. She had sent him to Pree knowing he'd be hurt. But she'd endured that knowledge just as she was now enduring the sight of his pain. If she could bear it, so could he.

Ransom rubbed the back of his neck. "Where is the chest?" he asked in a gentle tone.

"Over here," she said. "Can you stand? I can bring it to you."

He came to his feet and felt a throb of pain run the length of his injured thigh. Still, he managed to limp to the chest, which Constance had set on a small round table near a couch. Looking around, he didn't recognize the room . . . and then he realized why. She'd had him brought to her private chamber. The curtains were open, revealing an incredible view of the cove. He massaged his throbbing forearm. Why had she brought him here?

Constance unlatched the chest and opened the lid. The Wizr set was inside, each piece intricately carved and unique, playing on a board made of polished stone with alternating colors of dark and light. He sensed the power of the Fountain radiating from it. The pieces were already in play, as if a game were in progress.

"Let me share what I've learned so far," she said. "The pieces are welded to the board somehow. I've tried to move them, but they won't budge. See for yourself."

Ransom tried one of the smaller pawns and discovered she was right. He nodded in agreement.

"The pieces represent Occitania and Ceredigion. I think this is you," she said, pointing to a knight piece near one of the edges of the board. "The square you're on is halfway between the two sides. I think this part of the board represents Brythonica, and the piece next to yours is mine." The piece she indicated was the same color as the knight piece, but he didn't recognize the shape. "This is Alix," she said, pointing to one of the opposing team's pieces, "and I think this is where Pree is on the board. Here is Emiloh on the other side. I don't know if I'm right, but I think so. Notice that both of the kings are gone from the board. When Estian returns, I think his piece will show up again. The same with Bennett. The board represents real people, the state of the game being played." She touched the knight piece, the one that represented him.

Ransom stared at the board. "Claire has been reading the book you warned me of. *The Hidden Vulgate*. She said she read a passage about this Wizr set. It plays itself, she said. She believed the Aos Sí were trapped by it, that after so many games were played, it would unlock the gates of their prison."

Constance tilted her head slightly. "Tell me more of the Aos Sí. I'm not as familiar with their legends as I am with the Fountain."

Ransom thought a moment and then told her the stories Claire had shared with him about the Aos Sí's war with the Wizrs. How they'd tried to drive them into submission with various magical artifacts. How the war had ended with the Aos Sí "winning" half the world . . . the half beneath the sea.

She listened patiently, asking few questions, until he was done.

"Ransom," Constance said, "is it not possible the Black Wizr himself spawned these legends in *The Hidden Vulgate*? The book has been in Legault all this time." She paused. "He was a dangerous foe, full of power and cunning. I don't believe any 'truths' revealed in that book."

"It's hard to understand what is true, my lady," he said. "If I were raised in Legault, I would have believed the legends just as they do."

"Of course. The world is full of strange things. Things that have no explanation because the source has been lost to time."

"Indeed," he agreed. "When I first arrived, Claire took me to the barrow mounds. It is where they bury the bones of their ancestors. There was a stone with a face carved—" He stopped when he saw the startled look on her face. "Do you know of it?"

"There is something like that here in Brythonica," she said softly. "It is a great secret."

He wrinkled his brow. "What is it?"

She glanced down at the board again, not meeting his eyes. "Our beach is known for the glass beads that wash ashore. When Leoneyis succumbed to the Deep Fathoms, the palace windows shattered, and the relentless waves have crushed and polished the glass into smaller gems. But there are other secrets on that beach. One of the stones you described is hidden within a sea cave, and its power has protected Brythonica from drowning too. I must go there at certain intervals to bolster the protections. It is a secret handed down for generations." She glanced up at him. "Until now, I had only shared this with my husband."

"So Goff knew of it?"

She nodded. "He never told anyone. Not even his father. That I risk telling you shows my trust in you, Ransom."

The door opened, and her son, Drew, ambled inside. "Maman! Maman!" He started when he saw Ransom and then smiled. "Hello!"

Ransom felt uncomfortable being in her private chamber, but Constance didn't seem bothered. She turned to her son with an open, loving expression. "What is it?"

As the two spoke, Ransom studied the board. He saw several pieces that he assumed represented the different dukes of the realm. But there was a mottled white piece near the ones representing Constance and him. Who might it be, and what did the square represent? Averanche, perhaps? It lay near Brythonica.

"Yes, Drew, we can go down to Glass Beach this afternoon. You can show me what you found."

She held the boy's little hand and turned to Ransom, her forced smile revealing the heaviness of her heart. "I'm sorry for what you've endured, Ransom. Truly. As I said before, I do not control the visions. The Fountain has a wider vision than any of us can understand."

"I can see that," Ransom agreed. "This piece here? Do you know what it is?" He pointed to the one.

"The location is probably Averanche," she said. "I think that's Jon-Landon."

"My uncle?" asked Drew innocently. He looked in the box with eager eyes.

"Yes." Constance pointed to the piece she'd indicated earlier. "This is Ransom." Shifting her finger, she added, "And this is Jon-Landon, your uncle."

The boy touched the piece that represented Ransom, and it felt like an invisible hand had clutched his heart. Something inside him lurched as the boy effortlessly moved the piece across the board. A sound filled his ears, although it was not that of the Fountain but the dissonance of stone grinding on stone. Dizziness washed over him. The feeling left as quickly as it had come, but it made him feel sick inside.

And he remembered that he had experienced that feeling before. With Noemie at the sanctuary of Our Lady of Toussan.

※

My hand trembles as I write this. Keeva is dead. A ship arrived this morning with knights from the Vexin on board. We were told they were escorting Emiloh back to her duchy. It was an unexpected boon, or so I thought. My stomach . . . I'm going to be ill.

It wasn't Emiloh. She looked like her. She even sounded like her. But something was amiss. Her mannerisms were different. I thought it strange that her knights remained on the ship. Then Emiloh asked if I knew where Ransom was. The question surprised me because he had been summoned to court. Shouldn't he be with her? Then she asked to see my baby. Didn't she know I'd had two? Keeva went to fetch the twins, but all the while I felt unsettled, confused.

She found the book at the window seat, almost as if it had led her to it. Even before I knew who she was, I feared she would take it. I don't know why. I asked her why she had come, and it was then she revealed herself. It was Alix in disguise. While she tucked the book into her leather satchel, much too calm for a thief, she told me that Ransom has betrayed me. That he and Constance have been lovers before and since my wedding. She insisted she would take my son back to Bayree with her and hold him there until Ransom came for him and returned something he'd stolen from her.

My mind went black with fear and panic and then anger. This woman had killed my father, and now she wanted my sons. Then Keeva arrived holding one of the babes. Just one. I told her to run, but the poisoner struck her down. I grabbed my bow, which I had restrung earlier to practice with, and sent an arrow at the poisoner.

She vanished before the bolt could strike her. I screamed for my knights, and they came. The babe, little Willem, was safe in my maid's arms. But Keeva is dead. The ship from the Vexin was already gone when I sent the knights to seize it.

I'm convinced that what the poisoner said about Ransom was true. He has betrayed me. That thought burns in my mind like a white-hot spike.

—*Claire de Murrow*
Connaught Castle
(blood and revenge)

CHAPTER TWENTY-ONE

Averanche

"You look pale," Constance said.

The feeling of dizziness had subsided, but the memory still tickled inside Ransom's mind. "He moved the piece," he said, looking at Drew's face.

"I saw that," said the duchess. "That means the Wizr game can be manipulated. It doesn't just reveal where the pieces are."

Ransom felt a strong compulsion to go to Averanche and bring Jon-Landon back to the palace. The conviction of it surprised him.

"I must go," he said to her.

"You still need to heal, Ransom."

He shook his head, trying to understand his surging feelings. "When the piece was moved, I felt it in my soul. Now I feel that I need to go to Averanche and bring Jon-Landon back to the palace."

She looked at him curiously.

"Did I do something wrong, Maman?" asked the boy. "Should I move the piece back?"

She tousled his hair. "Why did you move the piece there?"

"It felt right," said the boy simply. He looked at Ransom. "He's supposed to go."

The board had created a compulsion too strong to be denied. He rubbed his mouth, thinking again of Noemie. "I've felt this way before," he said, glancing at Constance.

"When?" she asked.

"It happened here in Brythonica," he said, "at my last tournament with Devon. I'd gone to visit the Sanctuary of Our Lady."

"I remember that day," she said. "So do many." It was the time he had defeated Sir Terencourt.

"I spoke to the deconeus, and he told me to visit St. Penryn. I found Noemie kneeling before the waters of one of the fountains. I had the same feeling then that I had just now. Like one of the Wizr pieces had been dragged across the board. Noemie tried to convince me to meet with her that night, at one of the fountains here in your palace."

Constance studied him. "That *is* strange. So you think Estian used the Wizr board against you?"

"He must have. His sister tried to . . . seduce me."

Constance gave him an approving smile. "But you did not fall, Ransom. The pieces may create a powerful compulsion, but it cannot supersede a person's free will."

Ransom snapped his fingers. "Alix told me Estian has some sort of power over her, and while I don't believe anything she says, I suspect he has the ability to recall her whenever he wishes. This Wizr set is powerful indeed. It must be brought to the king." He gave her a significant look. "If the king's posterity can use it, that includes Jon-Landon as well as your son."

"Take it with you," she said. "They will not let such a prize go easily. Some people have the ability to travel through fountains, so there's no knowing how quickly they will come for it. I don't quite understand how it works, but many cities are built where the Fountain's power is strongest."

"Alix has that ability," Ransom said.

"All the more reason for you to take it," Constance said. "The Fountain-blessed can hide relics in water, Ransom. You must hide the set, and it would be better if I didn't know where you kept it. I will assign patrols to guard each of the fountains in the palace."

"I need a horse," he said. "Averanche isn't far, but I'll stop by Josselin on the way and bring some knights with me. I need my armor as well. Jon-Landon may not come willingly."

"Are you sure you've recovered enough, Ransom? Your injuries were severe."

"The scabbard will continue to heal me on the journey."

She gave him a pained look. "Be careful." She pulled her son close, stroking his hair, but her eyes were fixed on Ransom.

"Thank you for helping me," he told her. "Have you seen what happens next, Constance?"

She nodded but said nothing, which only added to his alarm.

"Will they kill Guivret?" he asked.

"Don't ask me that," she said. "Don't ask me anything about the future. I will tell you what I can when I can. Know this: if you hadn't gone to Pree to get the Wizr set, we would have lost."

The scabbard continued to restore Ransom's health as he rode from Ploemeur alone, heading to Josselin. In addition to his hauberk, Constance had given him a new tunic and cloak. The injuries he'd sustained throbbed, but the pain lessened as the day wore on. His castle at Josselin was on the border of Brythonica, protected on one side by a river. The townsfolk mostly dealt with sheep and traded in wool and candles. When he came down the road, people looked at him without recognition. His hair was shorn, his beard gone, and he looked like a foreigner to them.

When he arrived at the castle gates, he dismounted and was soon met by his steward, Westin.

"Welcome, traveler," he said. "Where do you hail from? Did you bring a message?"

"It's me, Westin," Ransom said and smiled as his steward did a double take.

"By the Fountain! Lord Ransom, what are you . . . ? Why didn't you send a message you were coming?"

"There was not time. Is Dearley here?"

"He is. I hardly recognize you!"

Ransom detached the large saddlebag that contained the chest with the Wizr set. He flung the bag over his shoulder and followed Westin into the castle. Elodie had updated the decorations, and he was pleased to see everything was clean and orderly.

"Send Dearley to my room," Ransom said, eager to sit down and rest. Westin agreed and departed to obey, while Ransom mounted the stairs and went to his personal chamber. It smelled musty from lack of use, the windows closed and barred. He set the saddlebag down on a table and then sank into his favorite chair.

His mind was afflicted by worries, and he found himself brooding about what he should write to Claire. He hadn't recovered the stone, nor did he intend to now that he knew what it had been doing to her. They needed to open their hearts to each other, to talk privately and sincerely. But he was bound by his secrets and worried that the conversation might strain things further. Still, he needed to save her from the book. Angry as she was, she was unlikely to heed a warning from him, but he needed to deliver one, nonetheless. And if that didn't work . . . should he hire someone to steal it? He hated the thought—it was underhanded and wrong—and yet Constance's warnings rang through his mind. He could not let Claire fall victim to the dark magic. He would save her even if she hated him for it.

The sound of approaching footsteps prompted him to look up as Dearley and Elodie arrived. The expression on his first knight's face showed his astonishment.

"Westin said I wouldn't know you, Ransom, and he wasn't lying."

Lady Elodie smiled at him, but a certain sadness underlay the gesture. The grief of losing her unborn child had hit her hard, something he understood keenly now that he was a father. He felt a pang of longing for his sons, for Claire.

Ransom gestured for them to come closer because his body ached so much. He winced as he sat up.

"Are you injured?" Elodie asked in concern. She and Dearley held hands as they approached. It was just a small gesture, but it heightened his longing for his family.

"I'm well enough," he said. "It's good to see you again. Any news?"

"Not really," Dearley said. "Things are quiet here. That's been good for us." He gave his wife a fond smile.

"I'm sorry to disrupt the quietude." He glanced at Dearley. "How many knights are guarding the castle?"

"Twenty," said Dearley.

"We'll take half of them. We need to ride to Averanche immediately. King Rotbart is dead, Estian is coming back to start a war, and Jon-Landon has fled the palace."

"Goodness!" Dearley gasped.

Elodie's eyes filled with worry, and he was sorry to have put it there.

"I've learned that the prince is in Averanche. I'm going to take him back to Kingfountain whether he wants to go or not. I hope to surprise him with my sudden arrival. I don't want to give him a chance to flee."

"Of course. Let me decide who will come."

"I'll have some provisions prepared," Elodie said. She left first, Dearley lingering behind.

The young knight's hesitation showed he was ill at ease. He shook his head and was about to depart, but Ransom stopped him.

"What is it?" he said.

Dearley turned. "It's not my place to question you, Ransom."

"But as my friend, you are worried by what you see."

"I have to say that I am. There have been rumors, but I've quashed them—"

"And I appreciate it," Ransom said. He grunted as he rose from the chair. "Power is beguiling to some. I've risen very high very quickly, but I'm still the same man I ever was. I cut my hair and shaved because I had a mission in Occitania. It is done. I was injured . . . seriously."

"You did seem unwell," Dearley said. "But then you've always recovered rather miraculously."

"It is a blessing of the Fountain," Ransom said. "I came by way of Brythonica. I've spoken to the duchess. I know that Claire . . ." Here he paused, his heart aching with the torment of his secrets. He sighed, struggling with his emotions. "I know the situation is strange, but it's not what it seems. You have my word. My duty requires that I say no more."

Any appearance of unease or doubt disappeared from Dearley's eyes. He gripped Ransom by the shoulder. "You are the last man I would ever accuse of being untrustworthy. Thank you, all the same. It bolsters my confidence in you." He tapped his hand against his chest in a knightly salute, and Ransom reciprocated.

"How is Elodie?"

Dearley shrugged. "Some pains take time to heal. Our grief has not yet passed. I don't know why it happened. Sometimes life is not just."

"It is not," Ransom agreed. "I worry for you both."

"We'll endure our trial. Now, let me fulfill your commands as is *my* duty."

"Thank you. I need you to send a knight to Claire at once. I've learned that a book in her possession contains dangerous magic. It's written in ancient Gaultic. Please . . . she must be warned to get rid of it. I cannot rest until she's freed from its thrall. If she won't part with it freely, he must try to find it."

Dearley's eyes widened with surprise, but he nodded somberly. "I'll send someone before we go."

As they rode into Averanche, Ransom felt the grip of his memories. Training with Lord Kinghorn. Bunking with James. Learning to be a knight.

"You trained as a boy here," said Dearley as they rode side by side. Ten knights accompanied them, and they'd ridden all night to get there by dawn. "Wasn't Lord Kinghorn the one who took you in?"

"Yes, he's my kinsman on my mother's side," Ransom said. "My father had nothing to offer me, but my mother sent me with a message to Sir Bryon." He smirked. "James Wigant and I were particular friends back then."

"Oh, I've heard about your *friendship*," Dearley said with a drawl. "It's a beautiful castle. Pleasant day too."

The morning was a glorious one, the sun knifing over the eastern mountains and bathing the valley in buttery light that illuminated the pasture grass, sparse woodlands, and smoke rising from chimneys in the village below the castle.

They entered town and cantered up the road to the castle gate, which was shut.

"Who do you be?" said a sullen guard from the upper wall.

"Open the gate," said Dearley in a tone of command. "This is the Duke of Glosstyr! Are you blind, man?"

The knight on duty scrambled into action. Some barks of command were given, and the gate began to squeal as it opened.

The knight came forward apologetically. "I had no news you were comin', my lord," he said in apology. "Why have you come?" He gave one of his compatriots a nervous look. All of them appeared nervous now.

Ransom said nothing and tapped the flanks of his horse, leading the way into the courtyard. He saw one sentry creeping toward the inner doorway.

"Halt!" Ransom shouted, freezing the man. "Back to the gate." When the sentry returned to his post with a stricken expression, Ransom dismounted from his horse. He checked the saddlebag with the Wizr set and patted it to make sure it was secured. "Watch my horse," he told Dearley. "Don't let anyone touch it but yourself."

Dearley nodded and maintained an imperious pose. He directed the other knights to fan out around him and stand guard.

Ransom walked to the doors alone. He knew the castle well, its corridors intimately familiar to him after the years he'd spent there. He tugged open a door and was greeted by the alluring scent of cooking meat and bread. Only a few paces down the hall, he happened upon a servant who looked at him in confusion.

"Who are you?" he asked Ransom.

"Where is Jon-Landon?" Ransom asked.

The man started. "Pardon?"

He heard some steps and turned to see Lord DeVaux approaching him with purpose. The sight of him tightened Ransom's gut.

"I saw you ride into the yard," said Lord DeVaux. "What are you doing here, my lord duke?"

"I find your presence here troubling," Ransom answered tightly. "When did you leave Kingfountain?"

"Not long ago," said DeVaux. "We're going back to the Vexin, so we decided to rest here along the way. We have permission. With Estian returning from the East, I thought it . . . wise . . . to safeguard my own territory. Since the duchess cannot."

Ransom did not trust the man in the least.

"Where is Jon-Landon?" Ransom asked.

A slight tightening of the eyes was the only betrayal of emotion. "Isn't he still in Kingfountain, my lord?"

"Would I be here if that were true?"

Lord DeVaux scratched his neck. "I suppose not."

"Take me to him."

"I would like to do that, my lord, but—"

Ransom stepped closer in a threatening way. DeVaux edged back. "Best to get this over with. Follow me."

He brought Ransom out the rear of the castle and led him to the outer steps to the beach. Gulls cried out, and the crashing of the surf became louder.

As they descended the steps, Ransom saw two people walking hand in hand along the beach. Even from a distance, he recognized the young man as Jon-Landon. His companion was DeVaux's daughter, Léa.

When Ransom and DeVaux reached the bottom of the cliff, their boots crunched into the sand. Stray bits of seaweed littered the shore.

Ransom breathed out his dissatisfaction.

"I know what you're thinking," DeVaux said. "The two were much thrown together in Kingfountain. Can a man not desire a good station for his daughter?"

"I thought Longmont was interested in her," Ransom quipped.

"That attachment was entirely one-sided," said DeVaux with a cunning smile. The young couple noticed their approach and came toward them. Léa smiled cheerfully and waved at her father. Jon-Landon frowned when he saw Ransom but didn't seem to recognize him.

"What is it?" Jon-Landon asked DeVaux, ignoring Ransom as a lesser man, a servant. "Did the Espion find out? Do I need to hide?"

"No, Jon-Landon. You have bigger troubles than that," said DeVaux. He gestured to Ransom but said nothing.

The prince looked at Ransom's face in confusion, and then the realization struck him like a thunderclap.

"Hello, Lord Ransom," said the prince with a greensick sort of look. "This is a surprise."

The bright smile on Léa's face wilted, and her eyes shot wide with recognition and sudden embarrassment. But she clutched Jon-Landon's hand and arm more fiercely, as if claiming him for herself.

"Isn't it, though?" Ransom answered, countering Jon-Landon's queasy look with a disapproving one of his own.

I feel unsafe in my own castle. The surprise visit of the poisoner has ruined the semblance of security I once had. The rooms were all cleaned, everything wiped down and tended to, yet still we worry Lady Alix may have done some additional mischief on her visit.

Today I ordered the funeral rites for Keeva. She was so young, so faithful. I will seek justice from the Duchess of Bayree. I sent a letter to Emiloh to inform her of what happened here. I don't even know where Ransom is right now. My heart grows more conflicted day by day. War is coming, one way or another.

At least my little ones are safe. I kiss them and worry for them. This intrusion must not go unpunished.

—Claire de Murrow
Connaught Castle
(weighing and considering risks)

CHAPTER
TWENTY-TWO

The Espion's Reach

hen they reached the streets of Kingfountain, people waved and shouted at Jon-Landon, showering him with coins as if he were a living fountain. Jon-Landon smiled with triumph, acting the part of the exultant prince even though he was returning in disgrace.

After they crossed the bridge, passing the sanctuary of Our Lady, they were met by twenty knights on horseback wearing the Lion badge of Benedict Argentine.

The lead knight, a man named Sir Bettencourt, reined in before them, looking confused as his eyes shot from face to face.

"Lord Ransom . . . is that you?" he asked at last.

"Aye, just bringing the lost prince home."

"I chose to return," Jon-Landon said, shifting in the saddle. "I'm not under arrest."

"We were alerted to a riot happening in town," said Bettencourt. "Well, my lord prince. At least the lost has been found. Go ahead to the palace. I have orders from Lord Longmont to clear the streets." He said the last with a menacing tone.

Jon-Landon chuckled.

"Go easy, Sir Bettencourt," Ransom said. "No use stirring trouble where there is none."

"Oh, there is," said the knight, giving the prince a hard look.

The knights passed them, and Ransom continued up the hillside to the palace. When they reached the fortress, they left their horses with the stable hands, but Ransom slung the saddlebag with the Wizr set over his shoulder. He noticed the prince was still smirking as they approached the palace on foot. Sir Iain met them, blinking with surprise when he recognized them.

"I'm home, Sir Iain," said Jon-Landon. "I hope my absence didn't cause much of a fuss."

"I don't know what surprises me more, lad. Seeing you or seeing you *with* Lord Ransom."

"Where is Emiloh?" Ransom asked, shifting the burden on his shoulder. His wounds had completely healed, and the scabbard's glow had finally faded.

"It's a warm afternoon. She was walking in the cistern garden. There was a rabble forming in the streets, so we heard, but now I understand what caused the fuss."

"I'll meet her there," Ransom said. "Keep your eye on the prince lest he try and slip away again."

"Yes, never take your eyes off a serpent," Jon-Landon said with an air of self-importance that made Ransom want to cuff him on the back of the head.

He turned to Dearley, who'd come in behind them. "I'll meet you later."

"Of course," replied his first knight.

As Ransom walked through the palace corridors, he saw that even more decorations had been added since his last visit. The effect was distasteful, especially considering the country was still at war, and it proved Longmont had done little to change his ways. It took a moment for the knight standing guard to recognize him, but then he nodded.

"The queen dowager is there. She'll be happy to see you, Lord Ransom."

"Thank you."

Ransom passed through the door and entered the garden where he used to visit Claire and Emiloh during their confinement. The memories reminded him of his estrangement from his wife and how powerless he felt to do anything about it. But he had a duty to fulfill. He ventured into the space and immediately saw Emiloh walking along one of the walls, running her hand through the ivy. She heard the sound of his approach and turned, her expression startled.

"My goodness, Ransom. You've changed."

He couldn't wait for his hair to grow out again. His cheeks and chin already bristled with new growth. He gave her a little bow.

"There was some disturbance in the city. Was that you?" she asked.

"I'm the cause, yes. I brought Jon-Landon with me."

Her eyes widened. "Longmont's Espion failed to find the prince, both times, and yet you've found him twice in a row. Who told you where he was this time?"

"In a way, the Duchess of Brythonica," Ransom said. He unslung the saddlebag from his shoulder. There was a little stone wall, more of a bench, with rows of flowers growing in the rich soil. He walked over to it and sat down, lowering the saddlebag, and Emiloh joined him.

"After I received your warning about Estian's return, I took a gamble. Remember the Wizr set that Bennett mentioned seeing in Pree? The one with magical properties?"

"I do. You told me that Devon knew of it as well. You schemed to retrieve it for him."

"I did try to trick Lady Alix into giving it to me. I'm not sure your husband fully believed in its power, but we both thought it was worth a try. Well, while I was in Brythonica, I had a . . . revelation from the Fountain to seize it." He needed to be careful about what he revealed.

Although he considered Emiloh trustworthy, he couldn't tell her any more than he could Claire or Dearley.

She looked at the saddlebag. "I'm assuming you found it."

"I did," he said, unhooking the clasp on the saddlebag. He widened the opening and dragged out the Wizr set by the handle. He hoisted it onto his lap, arranging it so the hinges faced the door he'd come through. She sidled closer to him as he opened the latch and raised the top of the set. The pieces were all there. They had changed since he'd last looked at it. The two pieces representing him and Jon-Landon were now back at Kingfountain.

And, to his dread, he saw the Black King was back in play. Not in Pree, but on the edge of the board. Even with Constance's warning, he hadn't thought the Occitanian king would make it back so soon. The time it would take Benedict to return . . .

"How do you know it is magical?" Emiloh asked him softly.

"Because the pieces move of their own accord. If I understand things properly, only someone from the house of Vertus can move the black pieces—Estian, Noemie, and possibly Alix herself. I believe any of them can control their pieces. If you or I try, the pieces are fixed in place. They do not move."

"That would mean the Argentines can manipulate the white pieces," she said. "Bennett, Jon-Landon, or my grandson, Drew."

"Exactly," Ransom said. "I found Jon-Landon by using this board. He was in Averanche."

"We sent people there," the queen said.

"He had time to hide from them. I surprised him. Lord DeVaux and his daughter were also there."

Emiloh's thoughtful look grew worried. She massaged her temples.

"It's as you suspect," Ransom said. "He was holding her hand on the beach when I arrived with her father."

"I'd heard reports that they'd struck up a friendship of sorts," Emiloh said with exasperation. "That's why I sent DeVaux back to the

Vexin." She dropped her hands to her lap and then clenched her fists in anger. "No doubt DeVaux has encouraged the tryst."

"It would seem Jon-Landon has found himself another ally. I suspect he intends to lay claim to your duchy as well."

"Perhaps he does, but I'm afraid we have bigger problems." Reaching out, she touched him on the arm. "I sent for you because of Estian's return but also because I need you here. Word came from Bennett that I haven't shared with Longmont yet."

Ransom swallowed, feeling a plummeting sensation in his stomach. "What news?"

"You know that the Brugian king is dead. Some of his force has abandoned the war. But some, fearing to displease the Genevese, have stayed and accepted Bennett's command. Estian has withdrawn to wage war on us." She sighed. "Bennett is going to retake the oasis anyway. He's charged us—you and I—to defend Ceredigion against Estian while he battles the East Kingdoms alone."

It felt like a hand gripped his heart and squeezed. He lowered his eyes. That was not the news he'd wanted to hear.

"I've received Bennett's permission to remove Longmont if I feel it appropriate." She squeezed his wrist. "The time has come to strip him of his rank as justiciar," she continued. "He has no military experience, and he'd only get in the way. The man we need is *you*."

The burden on Ransom's shoulders felt crushing. He had served kings before, but he had never been in charge of a war effort. The decisions would be his to make. His own inexperience troubled him, yet . . . he did know strategy and tactics, and there were capable men for him to call on for guidance, men like Duke Ashel.

"It was the Fountain's will that I take this," Ransom said, running his hand along the outside edge of the box. "I see that now."

"It will help us wage this war while our troops are so few." She studied him for a moment. "Still, stealing it was very dangerous. I would have forbidden it if I'd known."

"That's why I didn't tell you," he said. "I lost one of my knights there. He's been captured."

"Dearley?" the queen asked in concern.

"No, Guivret."

"He was a favorite of Claire's, I think. I'm sorry to hear it. Have they asked for a ransom for him yet?"

"No, but I would be willing to pay any price. Well, except returning this."

Emiloh nodded. "We must hide the Wizr set well, somewhere even the Espion cannot find it."

"Leave that to me," Ransom said.

"Once Longmont is forced out, we'll have another problem to solve. He controls the Espion right now. All news, all information—as poor as it is—comes through him. While much of the information is inaccurate, some of it has been very helpful. I'd hate to lose the whole network, but I don't trust Longmont to control them after we depose him. We need someone whom we can trust, someone who would be loyal to Benedict and to us."

Ransom thought a moment. "What about Sir Simon of Holmberg?"

Emiloh's expression turned thoughtful. "I hadn't considered him, but I recall he was in my son's mesnie, with you, before he joined my husband's council."

"He's in Glosstyr right now," Ransom said. "I don't know who else I'd recommend. Simon has proven himself trustworthy."

"By all means, summon him," Emiloh said.

The door leading to the cistern garden opened, and Longmont strode out with urgent steps. Ransom quickly shut the lid on the chest and set it down.

"Jon-Landon has returned!" said Longmont in astonishment. He paced like a caged animal, pausing only to look at Ransom. "I like how your barber cut your hair," he said as an aside. "I can't believe he's hidden under our noses in Averanche all this time. I wonder, my lady, if you'd be opposed to him spending a few days in the dungeon. Just to frighten him. Or maybe the tower?"

Ransom watched the queen dowager's nostrils flare. "I don't think that would do," she said.

"I don't trust him," Longmont said, shaking his head vehemently. He continued to pace before them, his black velvet hat slightly too large on his small head. His decorative gloves went up to his elbows. "With Estian about to return, we need Jon-Landon on a short leash. It would be a prime opportunity for him to try to claim the throne for himself. I cannot allow that."

Ransom glanced at Emiloh again. He nodded to her.

"Damian—" Emiloh said, but he wasn't even paying attention.

"It's good that you're here, Lord Ransom. I think Estian may attack us through Westmarch. I'd like you to take an army to Beestone castle and prepare to defend our borders."

"Damian," Emiloh said again, more firmly.

"What is it?" he said, looking at her with a hint of annoyance. "We need to discuss war preparations. I will summon the king's council."

"You will not," she told him, rising from the bench seat. Ransom rose also, towering over the other man, who looked at them with growing confusion.

"Why not?" he asked.

"Because I received a letter from the king that you've been removed from your position as high justiciar. He's ordered the Duke of Glosstyr to prepare for war, not you."

Longmont's jaw dropped open.

"You've been heavy-handed, Damian," Emiloh continued. "You've made Jon-Landon seem like a sensible alternative, and that won't do. I would like you to stay at the palace until Sir Simon of Holmberg arrives to replace you as overseer of the Espion."

"B-but *I'm* the one who created it!"

"Yes, but its purpose was to serve the king's interests, not yours. I've shielded you from many of the complaints. But you've lost the confidence of the nobles of Ceredigion. You haven't heeded my suggestions as you should have."

His cheeks had grown pale. "My lady, but the . . . I thought . . ." His voice trailed off. His shoulders slumped.

"Your services will no longer be needed," Emiloh said. "You'll return to Auxaunce when it is time."

"If you'd just give me another chance," pleaded Longmont desperately.

For a brief moment, Ransom felt sorry for the man. Not because he deserved sympathy—he didn't—but because he knew how much it chafed to be dismissed from a duty. It had happened to him twice.

"That is all," Ransom said, joining his voice to Emiloh's.

Longmont looked at them both, opening his mouth to speak, but he must not have trusted the right words to come out. He turned slowly, then walked off and left them, slamming the door behind him.

Ransom sighed.

"I don't think we've seen the last of him," Emiloh said. "He's not a man to take disappointment gracefully."

I received a letter back from Emiloh. She was distraught at the news, yet she asked me why I hadn't written to Ransom about our misfortunes. Why should I bother my husband with news he can neither act on nor sympathize with? Ransom sent a man to remove the book from me—the cheek of it— although there was naught for him to take. The knight carried a honeyed note that did not sway me, fresh as I am from Alix's attack. The knight looked like he didn't believe me when I said the book had been taken, and after he left, I found my things had been rummaged through.

I do not have my husband's loyalty or trust. His devotion has always been, and ever will be, to the hollow crown. How can I tell Emiloh that when I married, I wed but half a man?

Emiloh said the king himself has put Ransom in charge of the defense of Ceredigion. Well, I have a revenge of my own to plot.

Maybe, when Benedict returns, Ransom will be allowed to come back. I will not go back to Ceredigion. It is a mire that sucks in everything.

I still miss Ransom sometimes, but I'm learning it's possible to live alone.

—*Claire de Murrow*
Atha Kleah
(preparing for war)

CHAPTER
TWENTY-THREE

Return of the Tide

Ransom snapped the quill in his hand and slammed his fist on the paper, smearing his attempts to put his raging thoughts down in ink. He shoved away from the desk and marched out of his bedroom at the palace and down the stone steps of the stairwell.

A man he didn't recognize tried to stop him. "My lord Ransom, if you have a moment, I'd like to—"

"Not now!" he barked at the man, silencing the request before it was offered. He made his way to the training yard. Already the day was hot. He'd commanded the knights to get into peak condition, and several of them were practicing in the courtyard. Ransom summoned three to attend him and immediately began to pummel them with a relentless fury.

Emiloh had shown him the letter she'd received from Claire. The guilt and anger it had unleashed in him made his insides feel like a storm at sea. The book was gone, at least, but at what price? Keeva was dead. Willem had almost been kidnapped. And it had all happened because he'd stolen the Wizr set from Pree. It had never occurred to him that Alix would attack his family. It went against every tenet of the knightly code . . . but it had been a foolish oversight on his part. When had the Occitanians ever adhered to the ideals of Virtus? He'd assumed her travel was limited to the fountains, and there were none in Legault, but he'd gotten that wrong too.

Worse, Claire had contacted him about none of it. He'd tried, unsuccessfully, to write her a letter of reconciliation, yet every time he started, he began to accuse her for her silence. Had she but told him, he would have sent a hundred soldiers from Glosstyr to defend her and the boys at Connaught. Even though he would need every last one of them to defend Ceredigion.

His mood was bleak, and the three knights he'd charged with defeating him were beaten back without gaining any advantage on him. One nursed a swollen wrist from the violence of Ransom's counterstroke, which made him chide himself. These men needed to be ready for war.

After the bout ended, he dismissed the other two and sent the injured man for aid. Sweat trickled down his cheeks, and when he rubbed it away, he felt the stiff bristles of his returning beard. Hot, miserable, and still raging inside, he went to a bucket for a drink and ladled some water down his neck and back.

Claire should have told him what had happened to her. *Someone* should have at any rate. He thought about Guivret rotting in some Occitanian dungeon . . . likely at Kerjean. Did he know about Keeva's fate? The thought tore at Ransom's heart. But how was he to help Guivret when no one had contacted him about a ransom?

The sun breached the walls of the training yard, and Ransom started to march away, feeling miserable but slightly less angry.

Before he reached the door, he met Jon-Landon coming into the training yard.

"You're leaving already?" the prince asked in confusion.

"There is much I must do today," Ransom answered. He was about to walk past the prince, but he noticed the young man's supplicating hand.

"I was hoping, Lord Ransom, you'd spend a moment teaching me."

He wrinkled his brow and looked at the prince with surprise. Jon-Landon had never expressed an interest in training.

"I'm not Bennett," the prince admitted. "Frankly, I don't enjoy the training yard. But if we're going into a war with Occitania, I'd feel more comfortable knowing enough to survive in battle."

It was a sensible sentiment. Ransom didn't want to stay but felt he should.

"All right," he answered with a sigh. He nodded back to the training yard. "What weapon do you prefer?"

"A trebuchet," the prince said with a smirk. It was a powerful siege engine, one that could be used at a great distance. "I've been partial to using a sword and dagger in close combat. One for each hand."

"It's a good combination," Ransom said as they walked back. The noise of the training yard filled in around them, but he could feel eyes on them. No one was accustomed to seeing Jon-Landon in the training yard. "You can deflect your enemy's weapon with the sword and then use the dagger to stab through a gap in the armor. Let's see how well you do."

Ransom watched as the prince drew his weapons, which looked too shiny and decorative to have spilled any blood. He stared at the young man, his Fountain magic already supplying him with information about the prince's prowess. He had some skill. But it wasn't anything compared to Bennett's ferocity with a blade.

"Attack me," Ransom said, gesturing for him to advance.

"You haven't drawn your sword."

"I know," Ransom answered.

And he didn't. He waited for the prince to attack and immediately trapped Jon-Landon's sword arm against his hip. The dagger came up, but Ransom blocked it and wrested it away. He held the dagger against Jon-Landon's throat.

Jon-Landon's eyes bulged at how quickly he'd been disarmed.

"Now is where the teaching begins," Ransom said, face-to-face with the prince. "You've just been disarmed. Put your leg behind mine and twist your hips. If you do it right, you'll lever a man down on his back. Try it."

Jon-Landon did, but he wasn't strong enough to move Ransom. He strained, the dagger still at his throat, as he tried to comply.

"Harder. Put your spine into it. Try to throw me down."

"I am trying!" Jon-Landon said with clenched teeth.

"Harder!"

X

When Ransom left, the prince was gasping for breath, with sweat streaming down his face and a look of exhaustion reminiscent of young squires at age twelve or thirteen. The prince had never worked so hard or been pressed to continue even after he'd decided to quit. Ransom had tested Jon-Landon's patience and perseverance and found both equally lacking, yet . . . by the time he'd called an end to the practice, he'd sensed a little spark of pride in the prince.

Jon-Landon should have been sent to live with another duke, someone surly like Duke Ashel, who wouldn't have given a care for his royal blood and certainly wouldn't have allowed him to get this far without any real show of effort. It was the Elder King's fault for depriving his son of good mentors, ones who didn't brook excuses or allow privileges of rank to ease the work.

He went up to his room to change, but when he opened the door, he was startled to see a young woman he didn't recognize.

"Goodness, you startled me!" said the lass, hand on her breast as she turned toward the door. "S-Sir Ransom? Sorry for intruding."

"Who are you?" Ransom demanded. She wore the dress of a serving maid, a simple gown and girdle.

"I saw you . . . in the training yard," she said, unable to meet his face. "You were so fierce . . . so angry."

He saw smudges of ink on her fingertips, and some of his discarded letters to Claire lay on the floor.

A sensation of wrongness surged within him, and he noticed the girl was holding one of her hands behind her back. He searched her with his Fountain magic and learned she had skill with weapons and intrigue. This was no serving maid. In fact, her words of flattery had been a deliberate trick to put him off his guard.

He stepped toward her quickly, and she backed up until she hit the wall. Her nostrils flared with fear at his sudden closeness. He grabbed the arm tucked behind her and wrestled it forward until she opened her hand and revealed a crisply folded piece of paper.

Her eyes blazed with worry, and when he released her arm, she rubbed her wrist. She tried to slip around him, but he blocked her.

"Not yet," he said to her angrily. "Stay where you are."

After unfolding the note, he saw that she'd copied some of his words down in her own hand. She hadn't stolen his letters . . . only tried to duplicate them. A queasy look came over her face as she realized she'd been caught in the act.

"You're one of the Espion?" he murmured to her. He folded the sheet of paper and stuffed it into his pocket.

"Yes," she answered flatly, sweat beading on her brow.

He sighed. "Longmont sent you, did he?"

She met his gaze. "No."

"You are already in serious trouble. Be honest with me, or it will get worse."

"I was being honest with you, Lord Ransom."

"If not Longmont, who?"

"Jon-Landon," she answered. "He said he was going to distract you in the training yard. I was to learn what I could from your room."

His anger grew even hotter. "Were you looking for something?"

"Nothing specific," she said. "He just wanted to know more about you. He asked me to go through your letters. Learn if you had a mistress."

Her words felt honest enough, although he didn't like hearing them.

"I have none," he answered. "Nor will I." The knowledge that the prince had so easily duped him only made him angrier. His own good nature had been used against him.

"So you are part of the Espion, but you serve Jon-Landon."

"Indeed," she said. "There are many of us who are paid by both men."

"Do you know which ones?"

"Some of them," she said. A sly smile came over her pretty mouth. "I could work for you as well, my lord."

"I respectfully decline your offer of treachery," he said blandly. "Get out of my room. And tell your fellows that anyone who's caught in here in the future will find themselves in irons in the dungeon until King Benedict returns from the East Kingdoms. That might be a very, very long time. Am I clear?"

She swallowed, the sly smile turning into a worried one. "Quite clear, my lord. I beg your pardon. May I go now?"

He looked her in the eye. "If you're a smart lass, you'll reveal nothing of what you read. My personal business is of no concern to the prince, Longmont, or anyone else." He gave her a hard look, one that conveyed his displeasure.

"I understand you, my lord," she said meekly. "I'll not say a word. I promise."

He didn't trust her. But he let her go and then burned the letters one by one.

Emiloh had already finished her breakfast when he arrived in the solar. His own stomach growled with hunger, but he denied her offer to send for more food. He was still upset after the incident with the Espion girl.

After he revealed everything to Emiloh, she shook her head and sighed. "My youngest son may be clever, but he's also reckless. Why would he deliberately make an enemy of you? Did he trust that he wouldn't be caught? His conniving is certainly ill-timed."

"Which leads us back to the discussion we've had before on whether I should take the Wizr set with me when Estian starts his war." Ransom raked his fingers through his shortened hair.

"Having the set with you would be an advantage," Emiloh said. "But I see an even greater one in keeping it at the palace. Jon-Landon could move the pieces."

"Jon-Landon could *steal* it," rejoined Ransom. "For all we know, he heard whispers about it and paid the girl to try and find it. Your son has betrayed us to the Occitanians before."

"She didn't say she was looking for the set," Emiloh pointed out.

"She could have stayed silent out of loyalty. Or maybe she didn't know, specifically, what she was looking for. It's hidden for the moment, but if I draw it out of the waters, you won't be able to put it back."

"I see your point, Ransom, but could you do any better safeguarding it yourself? You'll be in a tent. Estian kept it at his palace, and I think it should stay here. If I can see the game as it plays out, I can tell you where to go next to challenge Estian. And if the situation grows desperate, Jon-Landon can move your piece to respond to any threat."

"Yet, I don't trust him."

"He's given you no reason to," said the queen dowager. "But he is still my son. He is still an Argentine."

"What about Drew?" Ransom said. "Why not summon Constance to Kingfountain and ask her to bring her son?" He knew she would not want to come, but the situation was desperate.

"It's a possibility," the queen acknowledged. "But I'm loath to use a child in war. And knowing Constance as I do, she would not wish to leave her duchy unprotected."

No, indeed. From what she'd told him about the rites at the beach, he suspected she wouldn't want to be away for long.

A knock sounded on the door, and Sir Iain entered. "Sir Simon of Holmberg has arrived from Glosstyr."

"Send him in," said Emiloh.

When Simon entered, he acknowledged Ransom with a friendly nod, but he looked uncomfortable. Something had happened.

"It's good to see you, Sir Simon," Emiloh said to him.

"I'm thankful to be back at the palace," he said as Sir Iain left and shut the door behind him. The man would guard the room from the passageway. "I came as soon as I could after receiving your message. What is this about?"

"I've called you here on Ransom's advice. We would like you to take control of the Espion. There are many messages that come in from all quarters of the kingdom. Your role will be to seek out the information we need, to pay men . . . and women . . . to provide this information, and to report the pertinent details to us. Estian is returning early from war with the East Kingdoms. Your service is needed, Sir Simon."

She didn't ask if he would accept the post. It was a command.

Sir Simon bowed his head. "I shall do my best to live up to your confidence in me," he said simply, looking a little greensick.

"Good. Seek out Lord Longmont and have him educate you on how things work. When you are confident you can handle the reins, let me know so I may send him back to the Vexin. We will also accommodate your family here at the palace. Bring them from Glosstyr whenever you are ready."

"As you command, Your Highness," Simon replied. "Thank you."

Emiloh glanced at Ransom. "Get some food. I don't think I want to upset things with Brythonica at this point. But I will think on what you said. We can speak about it later."

"Very well," Ransom said. He nodded to her and then suggested that Simon join him in the kitchen.

"Thank you," said his friend.

As they started down the corridor together, Ransom put his arm around Simon's shoulders. "You seem concerned. What is it, old friend?"

"The new position suits me, I suppose. Information has always had a way of finding me. I don't seek it out . . . it just comes."

"Do you have news?" Ransom asked.

He nodded, his eyes wide with worry. "Your wife is preparing to attack the duchy of Bayree."

This is no game. I do not treat it as such. I have nothing but cold determination to punish our foes.

A Genevese trader arriving in Atha Kleah said Occitanian warships have been ordered to defend the coast. I've also heard that Estian is back in Pree and has summoned his knights and dukes to attend him. No one knows how he accomplished it, but he did. There are whispers that it was some sort of black magic, and some of his men were left behind, but there is no way of knowing. War is coming regardless of what we do, but I will not wait for it to come to us.

A letter came from Ransom. Does he believe fair words will placate me? Will not the hornet sting when its nest is troubled?

—Claire de Murrow
Atha Kleah
(the reed song is sung)

CHAPTER
TWENTY-FOUR

Moving Pieces

eary from another restless night, Ransom walked into the main hall in his riding armor. The hall was full and brimming with the noise and smells of the morning meal—oat bread, cabbage, carrots, and fruit. Soon the men who were gathered here would ride off to war. They were just awaiting orders—*his* orders—about where to go. If only the Wizr board showed what Estian was planning rather than what he was currently doing.

"Lord Ransom, a ship arrived from Atha Kleah this morning," said a servant. He handed a letter to Ransom, who instantly recognized his estranged wife's handwriting. How many days had it been since he left Legault? The days had begun to swim together, but each letter he'd received from Claire had heightened his concern about their fraying relationship.

He thanked the servant and was about to lift the wax seal when James Wigant approached him. Ransom's stomach soured. He was in no mood to suffer the man's disrespectful attitude.

"The supply wagons heading to Glosstyr were attacked last night," James said by way of greeting. "That Fountain-cursed rogue with a hood killed four men and made off with two of the wagons in the dark."

"I haven't even had breakfast yet, James. You've ruined my appetite."

"I thought you should know, of course, but I want your permission to gather two hundred men to hunt that coddling moth down and squish him beneath my boot. This has gone on long enough!"

Ransom sighed. "I don't have two hundred men to spare," he said. "Nor do I need you off hunting a man you've been trying to capture for so long already. How did he get away with wagons? Surely a rider could outrun them?"

"The wagons were emptied and then pushed into the river and found downstream, dashed against the rocks. They were worth more than the cargo they carried, food and weapons for the upcoming war. He's growing bolder with his attacks. Give me two hundred—"

"I don't have two hundred!" Ransom snapped, barely able to keep his temper in check. "Take fifty. But I can't spare you for more than a fortnight. I need your army from Dundrennan down in Blackpool as agreed."

"And leave Dundrennan defenseless?"

"Surely you left a garrison," Ransom said, exasperated.

"I did, but I'm worried those knaves from Atabyrion will take advantage of the situation while I'm gone. I don't want to have to win that castle back like my father did."

Ransom wondered whether the request to hunt Ryain Hood was merely an excuse for James to straddle the fence of loyalty. To give him a cause to be away when his soldiers were needed most.

Ransom held his gaze. "You'll have them at Blackpool as agreed. No excuses."

"Of course—I'm no fool to counter the mighty will of Duke Barton. One thing more and you can get your breakfast." He dropped his voice lower. "Master Hawkes continues to remind me that my land

and title are at risk of going to the crown because I have no heir. As if I needed his somber assessment of my situation. When the king returns from the East, I intend to ask him for Lady Constance of Brythonica."

It sickened Ransom to think of such a match, but he didn't let the feeling show on his face. "Why are you telling me this?" he asked.

"Obviously because I don't want you to thwart it," he said. "Surely you won't begrudge me the chance of marrying someone of my own rank. We're not enemies anymore, Ransom."

Ransom looked him in the eye. "Prove it. Have your men at Blackpool as agreed."

James gave him a hopeful look. "And you'd take that as a sign of my sincerity?"

"I would indeed."

"And you wouldn't block me from asking for Lady Constance?"

Again he felt the wrongness of such a match. "I'm not the one you'd need to convince."

James nodded and walked away. Ransom maneuvered through the crowd for the food trays and helped himself to some cheese and bread. He noticed that there was a slight depression in the wax seal of Claire's letter. Had it been tampered with? He opened the letter in frustration and read the short message quickly.

> Lord husband,
> Do not censure me for my course of action. I am the right-ful ruler of Legault, and it is my decision to make. You've made it clear your loyalties are tied to the fate of the court of Kingfountain. I have a duty to my own people. There is a saying in the Fair Isle. "Reverence ceases once blood is spilled." I will avenge Keeva's death and the threat made against our sons. It shall be blood for blood.
> Written on High Day,
> Claire de Murrow, Queen of Legault

He almost crumpled the letter in his fist out of pure frustration, but he managed to keep his temper in check. Eyes were everywhere in the palace, and the last thing he wished to do was gain the attention of one of the Espion. He took some more bread from one of the serving tables, glancing around the room full of strangers, and his eyes briefly landed on the Espion woman he'd caught in his room.

Simon approached him. "Can we talk, Ransom? Away from the noise?"

Ransom nodded and took the plate with him, grabbing a cluster of grapes too. He followed Simon down to the room Longmont had established as the palace headquarters of the Espion. The fashionable lord from the Vexin had used a master stonecutter to carve stars into the ceiling and then named the room the Star Chamber. There were no windows, so it was lit by lamps, and a small brazier kept it warm.

Simon locked the door behind them. He looked as if he'd aged several years in the short time since he'd been called to run the Espion. The desk was a jumbled mess of papers and scrolls.

"I've never been so weary in all my life," Simon lamented. "And you look worse."

Ransom smiled and sat down in a stuffed chair across from the desk, setting his plate on an end table near it. Simon picked up a letter, scanned it, then tossed it into another pile. "The supply wagons to Glosstyr were attacked last night," he said with a sigh. "They destroyed the wagons after they made off with the cargo. The brigand is becoming more brazen, and they've plenty of arrows now. I think you should send more men to hunt him down."

"I told James he could take fifty men," Ransom said. "He told me first."

"You think fifty is enough? From what I'm hearing, he's convinced some rogue knights to join him. There could be fifty of them by now. And with all the arrows they've stolen . . . they could be quite a threat."

"I need to have a large enough force to hold off Estian. What news from Pree?"

"Nothing you don't already know," said Simon, massaging the bridge of his nose. "The Espion we have in Occitania give conflicting reports, but all agree that the king is preparing to invade us. Do you want my honest opinion?"

"Would I ask for anything less?"

"No, I don't think so. I think Claire is waiting on Estian to attack before she launches a raid against Bayree. I have a source in Legault who says that's her intention."

Ransom looked at his friend. "Do your sources intercept messages? I just got a letter from her this morning when a ship arrived. The seal looked a bit . . . off."

Simon shook his head no and frowned. "I've forbidden that, although I understand it was a common practice under Longmont's orders. He has special men who know some tricks about wax. Half of the messages on this table are about our nobles. Longmont seemed to delight in prying secrets out of his peers." His nose wrinkled in disgust. "I've said I won't pay for it, that I'm only interested in intelligence about Occitania."

"Bad habits are difficult to unlearn," Ransom said with a sigh. "Have you found out anything about the girl who was in my room spying for Jon-Landon? I saw her in the great hall not long ago."

"Not yet. I'm reading messages night and day. It's all a jumbled mess, but the quality of intelligence has been improving now that I'm only paying for what I want. I don't want to shock you, but Longmont spent a veritable fortune on intelligence. He had people spying on DeVaux's daughter constantly. There was so much . . . I just started burning them all."

Ransom shook his head. "He fancied her. But I don't think she would have appreciated knowing his interest in her was so relentless."

"And disgusting," Simon added. "Estian's army is still gathering at Pree. His forces are less limited than one would think, given he had to leave some behind." He paused, giving Ransom a look. "And since I didn't pay anyone to give me word about Claire's letter, I don't know what she wrote to you."

Ransom fished the letter from his pocket and handed it to Simon. He ate some grapes in the meantime.

Simon lowered the letter after he was done and then handed it back. "So things are still estranged between the two of you?"

"Unfortunately. More than anything, I want to get back to Connaught or the fortress at Atha Kleah to try and reconcile with her. And I won't rest until I see my sons with my own eyes. It horrifies me to think of what could have happened. She's furious about Alix's attack, and she has every right to feel that way."

"She's not unreasonable," Simon suggested. "Give her time."

That was not what worried him. She wasn't unreasonable, no, but the stone had changed her, and then that book . . . *The Hidden Vulgate* had twisted her heart against him. It was gone now, and he hoped its effect on her would fade, but perhaps the damage had been done.

Ransom held up his hands. "Preparations for war are taking up all my time. Before I know it, the ocean storms will start up again. What if I can't get back to Legault before then? What if we're trapped apart during the winter?" He rubbed his forehead. "We haven't even been married that long, Simon. I didn't think it would be this difficult."

"Nor did I at first," said Simon. "It takes time to understand each other. I have no advice for you other than . . . be patient. Give it time."

Ransom didn't like that suggestion, but there wasn't anything else he could do.

"I would say your marriage seems happier than Benedict's at any rate. A note that I received yesterday . . . or was it . . . ? I can't even remember now. Portia decided to return to Genevar instead of making her home in Kingfountain."

"Do you know why?"

"Nothing solid. The knights escorting her were stunned by the sudden change in plans. Everyone believed she was pregnant, but apparently that might have been a ruse. One of the knights had the presence of mind to send Longmont a note . . . not realizing of course that he'd been replaced. I did pay for that news. The Queen of Ceredigion still hasn't set foot on our soil, nor does she intend to."

A knock sounded on the door. Ransom grunted. They hadn't been given much of a chance to speak privately. Simon went to the door and unlocked it, opening it to reveal Sir Iain.

"The queen dowager wishes to see you both," he said.

Ransom took a bite of bread and left the dish in the room. They went to Emiloh's chambers and found her sitting in front of the Wizr board. Ransom had brought it from the cistern waters so that they could track Estian's pieces, which had been congregating around Pree.

She had a wizened look to her eyes as she greeted them. Sir Iain departed and shut the door, leaving the three of them alone in the room. Warm sunlight spilled in from the gauzy curtains over the balcony window.

"Has he started moving?" Ransom asked with interest.

"See for yourself," answered the queen dowager.

Ransom and Simon approached the board. Other than Sir Iain, they were the only ones privy to the secret of the Wizr set.

Looking down at the board, Ransom saw the king's piece had moved diagonally. He gazed down at the board, feeling a sense of giddiness that it had finally started. Another piece, a knight, had gone in another direction. And a third piece, a castle piece, had gone in a third direction.

Ransom looked up at Emiloh. "He's dividing his army."

"Apparently so."

Simon studied the board. "His piece is headed toward Brythonica. Do you suppose he's going to attack the duchess?"

"I don't think so," said the queen dowager. "It's possible, of course, but I'd be surprised. I think he's going after Josselin castle."

Ransom blinked. There was no piece on the board to represent it, but his castle was located along the border between Brythonica and Ceredigion.

"Josselin is a strategic castle," said Simon. "Not just for its position but because it is Ransom's."

"I sent Dearley there two days ago," Ransom said. "Better send a courier to him."

"I'll write the letter myself," said Simon. "If that is Estian's target, we have plenty of time to get there first. I'll also alert the castellan of Beestone. But there's something we ought to consider." He paused. "Estian knows we have the board. He knows we can see his movements."

"Yes, and that should concern us," said Emiloh. "We still don't know the motives behind his actions. We have to discern them, just like in the game." She looked at Ransom. "With Estian dividing his army, it is imperative that the Wizr stay here in Kingfountain. I will use Jon-Landon to control the board and move the pieces as needed. I need you to focus on defending the realm, Ransom. Let me maneuver the pieces."

Ransom felt a tugging at his heart. As they stared at the board, his gaze was drawn to the piece representing Alix. So he saw it glide from Pree to the spot marking Ploemeur.

Ransom's stomach dropped sharply in his gut. He stared at the pieces, one representing Lady Constance and the other representing Lady Alix. Dread quivered down his spine.

He had no way of warning his friend of what was about to happen.

Merchants fleeing Brythonica came to Atha Kleah with the news that King Estian has begun his invasion of Ceredigion. They also brought an unexpected report that the Duchess of Brythonica has declared neutrality in exchange for more sovereign rights. They say Brythonica will stand independent, its own kingdom once more, paying homage to neither side. The Occitanians are marching on the borderlands between the kingdoms, putting them directly in the path of Ransom's land.
  I care not.

—Claire de Murrow
Atha Kleah
It begins

CHAPTER
TWENTY-FIVE

The Siege of Josselin Castle

A ship was sent from Kingfountain to warn the Duchess of Brythonica of Alix's movements, and the queen dowager dispatched Ransom to face the brunt of Estian's army while warnings were sent to Duke Rainor at Southport and Duke Ashel at East Stowe to defend against the forces coming against them. The garrison at Beestone would join Ransom's force.

During the journey back to Josselin, Ransom wondered if Constance would summon him as she had in the past. He rode ahead of the army with just a handful of trusted knights in case it happened. But it didn't, and he couldn't understand why not. He hoped Constance had foreseen Alix's arrival in Ploemeur through the seering stones, but there was no way of knowing for certain.

When he arrived at Josselin, he found the townsfolk hunkering down within the walls of the castle. A warning had been sent to Dearley to prepare for a siege, and Ransom was grateful to see the command had been taken seriously. The absence of carts and noisy sheep made it feel like a different place.

The inner bailey was crowded with animals and carts, and little tents had been put up in the gardens for families. Ransom observed the chaos of the scene and then dismounted when he saw his steward, Westin, approaching, crumpled hat in hand.

"These are sorry circumstances, my lord," he said. "But we're relieved to see you all the same."

"It's good to see you," Ransom replied. "Have we enough room for the soldiers on their way?"

"We'll make room. The shepherds moved the flocks out of town to prevent them from being seized by the Occitanian army. Their knights have been scouting and foraging already, making no attempt to disguise their movements. We've also warned families to depart before the siege happens. If they have loved ones elsewhere to stay with, now is the time to escape."

"Good to hear. Where is Dearley?"

His answer arrived in person, wearing armor, and they greeted each other with a knightly salute followed by an embrace.

"I'm glad you came so quickly," Dearley confessed.

"What news from your scouts?" Ransom asked.

"An army is headed this way, should be here on the morrow. I was worried you wouldn't get here in time. We have the river as a defense, but after seeing what Estian did to the river at Dunmanis, it's no protection at all. How many did you bring with you?"

"About three thousand, but more are coming from Beestone."

"Thank the Lady," Dearley sighed. "I sent Elodie back to her estate at Namur. Didn't want her being here when the fighting started."

Ransom smiled, but he couldn't help thinking Claire wouldn't have left in the face of battle—she'd have run straight into it. His heart constricted with pain at her indifference to his plight. He'd poured his heart out in his letters—his sorrow about the attack and their estrangement, his worry for her and his sons, his need for help in the coming war—and yet her replies had been perfunctory and stony. It was *his* war, she'd told him, and she had her own to wage. While they might share an enemy, they needn't share a strategy.

"Let's go inside the castle," Dearley said, clapping him on the back. "I'm expecting scouts to return with a report. It's still early in the afternoon. We have time before they arrive."

Ransom followed him in. He wouldn't remove his armor, not with the Occitanian force so near. As they walked through the castle, a strong feeling of protectiveness surged in his breast. If he remembered right, it had not been attacked since the days of King Gervase. The humble town was about to see the grim desolation of war once more.

The interior halls were crowded with soldiers and knights coming and going. Pallets were stretched along the halls, mostly empty, though a few had snoozing soldiers on them.

"How are the defenses?" Ransom asked.

"There are no weaknesses that I know of. We have buckets ready atop the walls to douse flames if they try to burn us out. Spears and hooks to repel scaling ladders. And every villager who can use a bow was pressed into service to defend the keep. Josselin will not be an easy target."

"And Estian knows it," Ransom said with a frown. "It might be a feint. He might come here and then pivot and strike elsewhere." He thought again of the Wizr board. Estian knew they had it. Would he really allow his movements to be so easily interpreted?

The scouts returned within the hour, led by Sir Dawson, one of the knights in Ransom's mesnie. The young man found them in the solar, and Ransom, who hadn't seen him in several months, greeted him with a salute. Although he'd always liked Dawson, he didn't feel as strong a connection with him as he did with some of the other men. There was something impetuous about Dawson, hotheaded almost.

"Lord Ransom, welcome back," said Dawson with a broad smile.

"The day is waning, what have you seen?" Ransom asked.

"They're coming in force. Five thousand by my estimation. They're using the main road on the other side of the river, so there can be no doubt as to their target. They're coming here. I can't wait."

"How far off are they?" Dearley asked in concern.

"If they don't stop for the night, they'll be here by midnight." Dawson said it with no small amount of eagerness. He'd always been hungry for a fight.

"Which fords and bridges lie between here and there?" Ransom queried.

"There's a ford to the north at Applewell, but we both know they don't need bridges or fords to cross."

"They do not," Ransom agreed. "Any word from Brythonica?"

"No," Dearley said, shaking his head. "Not even a whisper."

Ransom curled his hand into a fist and turned to Dearley. "Prepare the night watch. We want to be ready when they arrive."

The Occitanians did arrive at midnight, and they wasted no time in crossing the river. Ransom felt the magic at work, the familiar feeling slithering down his back. He rode Dappled to the front line of his men, along the shore, and thought he recognized Estian astride a coal-black destrier amidst the parted waters.

The clash of arms began immediately, but Estian didn't lead the charge himself. Row after row of enemy soldiers pressed in, mostly on foot, using spears to drive the knights back. Ransom's blood sang with the passion of battle, his Fountain-blessed instincts reaching a peak as he led his men.

But the enemy marched onward relentlessly, each fallen man replaced by three fresh ones. He saw his own lines begin to bend. Arrows whistled down from the walls, but the darkness hindered the archers' aim. Cries of pain and shouts of anger filled the air around him.

He saw Dawson on horseback, chopping down an enemy knight with a battle axe. It was a skillful blow, and he was proud of his young knight.

Ransom deflected a spear thrust up at him and countered by nudging Dappled forward and then slamming his pommel against the soldier's helmet, dropping him.

The feeling of grating stone jolted him to attention. His pulse began to race as he realized the intention of the order. The piece representing him had moved, and he felt a strong compulsion to abandon Josselin and go to Glosstyr. It made no sense to him, and in the thick of the fighting, he rebelled against the instinct. It was his castle, given to him by the Elder King. Could he forsake it so quickly? They hadn't even tried to defend it for long!

"Retreat to the castle!" Ransom shouted, a taste of bitterness in his mouth. Soldiers continued to pile into the gaps in the line, pressing his men back, squeezing them. If they didn't flee soon, they'd be overrun.

It took time for his command to go down the ranks. He led the rear guard himself, holding off the attackers so his knights could escape. The glow of blue started from his scabbard before he even realized he'd been struck. They gave ground slowly, but the gristmill continued to grind against them. Finally, he cried out the final order to retreat, and they rode back to the castle gates, which were hurriedly closed and barred. Archers rained arrows down at the attackers.

With sweat trickling down his neck, he thought of the command he'd been given through the Wizr board. Something had changed. Something he couldn't see. He had to trust Emiloh's judgment.

After dismounting Dappled, he climbed up to the battlement walls, where Dearley was leading the defenders. The twang of bowstrings sounded again and again. Dearley strode up and down the wall, his gaze intense. When Ransom caught up to him, he stopped moving but continued to tap one heel.

"They keep coming and coming," Dearley said, shaking his head. "I've heard many are taking shelter in the villagers' homes. Tomorrow will be a dangerous day. There are so many. How long before the men from Beestone get here?"

Ransom shook his head. "It doesn't matter. I have orders to abandon Josselin."

Dearley swallowed, his eyes wide with shock. "Whose orders?"

"The queen dowager."

"When did they arrive? I've seen no courier."

"I have the orders all the same. We must prepare to leave."

The look of disappointment on Dearley's face was powerful. In some ways, the castle had become his home. His wife had made a mark on it, and it was where they had first met. "If you say so, Ransom. But I think we can hold it."

"I know we can," Ransom said. "But there is more at stake here than one castle. We'll leave men to defend it."

"How many?"

"A hundred. No more. We're going to Glosstyr."

His words had clearly gutted Dearley, but his friend, ever faithful, merely nodded. "I'll rouse the men. Better if we leave before dawn." He seemed on the verge of saying something else, but then he shook his head and started giving orders.

Ransom was grateful for Dearley's trust in him, particularly when Dawson strode up to him in a fury not long afterward.

"We're abandoning the castle already? My lord, I don't understand!"

Ransom tried to keep his patience. "I have orders from the queen dowager. We're going to Glosstyr."

"This is *your* castle. Why let Estian have it?"

"I'm not giving it to him, lad. I'm following orders."

"It's folly!" Dawson nearly shouted at him.

Ransom gave him an icy stare. "I'm not looking for your approval. If you're a true knight, you will obey your orders."

Dawson threw up his hands and stormed away.

It took the rest of the night to prepare to withdraw. The rear gate was in constant use as knights, soldiers, and villagers fled into the darkness. More than one accusing look was sent his way. His forces began their march to the fortress of Glosstyr, but he remained behind to consult with Dearley on the evacuation.

Westin approached him, wringing his hands. "My lord, if I may?"

"What is it?" Ransom asked. The darkness was beginning to lift, the night nearly over. A few morning birds had begun tweeting.

"I wish to remain behind with the defenders."

Ransom studied him. "If the castle falls, you'll be held for ransom."

"I know, my lord. It would break my heart to leave, though. Let me stand with the defenders until there is no longer hope."

Dearley had overheard the conversation and approached them. "I've given Sir Trent command of the defense," he said. "There's no need to stay, Westin."

"I know, my lord." He continued to wring his hands. "But it's my home."

Ransom clapped Westin's shoulder. "If you are taken hostage, I'll pay your ransom."

"I'll do my best to keep that from happening," Westin said, relieved.

Ransom turned to face the knights who'd been left to defend the stronghold. "I know you've been put in a difficult situation. Josselin has never fallen to the Occitanians. I'd like you to keep it that way. I don't expect you to fight to the last man, but I do expect you to make the siege costly for them. Get away if you can and leave nothing of value behind. Then ride and catch up with us."

A few determined nods came in reply. With that, Dearley and Ransom mounted their horses and followed the last of his troops out the back gate. They rode through forests meant for hunting, following the only available road. Sunlight slit through the branches, and the thump of hooves against the recently trampled dirt brought an earthy smell to his nose. The woods were thick and imposing and quickly blocked the castle from sight. His heart ached at the thought of leaving his castle behind for Estian to try to pluck. How he wished he could have faced Estian in single combat in the river.

After riding the breadth of the woods, they finally caught up with the main force of the army snaking its way to Glosstyr. Dawson sat atop his charger, a chagrined look on his face.

"What's the matter?" Ransom asked, reining in near him.

Dearley reined in as well.

Dawson hesitated. "When we emerged from the woods, we encountered Occitanian knights riding toward us."

Dearley gasped in surprise. "On this side?"

"Aye," Dawson responded. "We outnumbered them, of course, and they fled, but we took one of them prisoner. I asked him how they got there, and he said they'd been ordered to cross at the ford at Applewell. They had axes and were planning to barricade the road to prevent us from escaping. If we'd stayed another day, we'd have been trapped in Josselin. I was wrong to doubt you, my lord. It won't happen again."

"Ride on to Glosstyr, Dawson. Tell them we're coming."

"I will." Dawson spurred his charger and began galloping across the plains alongside the marching army.

Dearley gave Ransom a quizzical look. "How did the queen dowager know they were flanking us?"

"Always trust a queen's intuition," he said, smiling. Would Estian follow him to Glosstyr? It was the largest city on the western coast. Hopefully, Duke James would be standing by at Blackpool as promised. This would be a decisive battle.

One that could change the fate of kingdoms.

The harbor in Atha Kleah is tangled with so many ships. I await the fair tide to give the men the order to sail and confront the enemies of Legault. The flagship will lead the way, setting the direction of the assault. I've instructed the captains to keep the destination secret in order to surprise our foes. The Duchess of Bayree will regret her trespasses.

Another letter arrived from Ransom this morning, asking me to send support to Glosstyr. I cannot afford to divert a single ship. He chose his loyalty already. I've chosen mine.

He wants to reconcile, and perhaps we shall someday. But not until I've had my revenge.

—Claire de Murrow
Atha Kleah
(fair weather—foul intentions)

CHAPTER
TWENTY-SIX

The Black Banners

ear and terror wriggled inside Ransom as he grappled with Alix on a bed, gripping her wrist to keep the dagger from plunging into his bare chest. His sword and scabbard were gone, so he faced her unprotected and disarmed. Claire was screaming his name over and over.

He awoke from the dream with a start, panting, covered in sweat, echoes of his wife's screams still ringing in his mind. At first he thought it was the middle of the night, but as he looked at the open window, the curtains rustling with a breeze, he saw the pale colors of coming day. His stomach twisted with anguish. It was his bedroom in the fortress of Glosstyr. There was no Claire, no poisoner. And he knew that the Occitanian army would be arriving that day.

Tossing aside the sheets, he swung his legs over the edge of the bed. His sword and scabbard were still where he'd left them—in the middle of the bed, within easy reach. He'd slept in his hauberk, wanting to be prepared for anything, and his body now smelled of sour sweat. But he thought he detected a hint of lilac too. Alix's scent. A chill went down his spine. Had she been in his room during the night? Uncertainty raged within him.

Grabbing his sword, he strapped it to his waist and then washed his face in the basin. A knock sounded on the door.

"Enter," he said in a voice still rough from sleep.

It was Dearley, who looked weary as well. And worried.

"Why do I have the feeling you're bringing bad news?" Ransom asked.

"Because you're perceptive. The Duke of North Cumbria left Blackpool yesterday. He's gone, and so is his army. The scout you sent didn't encounter them on the road."

Disappointment thudded inside Ransom's skull. James's final words to him had vouched for his trustworthiness. And Ransom had dared to believe him.

"No one knows where he went?" Ransom asked, struggling to keep his emotions under control. The desire to smash James's face into a pulp sizzled beneath the surface.

"The knight returned after finding Blackpool abandoned. The citizenry wondered if you were coming to their defense. Everyone is fearful with that outlaw on the loose."

Ransom stared at the floor for a moment. How was he to defend Glosstyr from Estian with only one army? He'd sent another letter to Claire, pleading for reinforcements, but her previous cold responses made him believe help would not be forthcoming. The anguish of their estrangement broke through his dread for a moment.

Dearley handed him a sealed letter. "This arrived for you during the night."

Ransom recognized the palace seal. He took it slowly, dreading the possibility of more ill news. The seal looked intact. After peeling it loose, he unfolded the letter and recognized Simon's handwriting.

Lord Ransom,

I've received information from multiple sources confirming the Duchess of Brythonica has made a truce with Occitania. She has declared herself independent of allegiance to either Occitania or Ceredigion and has invoked her rights of sovereignty. I was shocked by the original news, but it has come from too many witnesses for me to doubt its veracity. The queen dowager is concerned, but she did not seem surprised and indicated that you might not be either. Of course, I've shared all of this with her. We look to you and the Duke of North Cumbria to hold off the invasion. The Occitanians have launched an attack on the Duchy of Southport by sea and by land, led by the Duke of Garrone. Duke Ashel is defending Kingfountain, though I have some Espion reports that he might try to seize the palace for Jon-Landon. I don't know what to believe, but we've decided to keep his forces outside the city for now in case it's true.

Do your best, Ransom. If Glosstyr falls, I don't need to tell you that we would not hold out for long. A messenger has been dispatched to inform King Benedict of our situation, though there will obviously be a long delay in learning his will or what is happening in the East.

I wish I had better news to give you, my friend. If there is anyone Estian fears, it is you. I've put a coin in the fountain here at the palace for you.

I look forward to news of your victory.
Simon of Holmberg,
Master of the Espion

Ransom rubbed his mouth and then looked at Dearley, who was staring at him solemnly, waiting for news. He handed his friend the letter to read for himself and then poured himself a cup of water from a nearby pitcher.

"We're alone," Dearley murmured softly. He handed the letter back.

"So it seems."

"What are you going to do, Ransom? It won't be easy to besiege Glosstyr. We could last for some time. Maybe long enough for the king to return."

"I think that's what Estian wants. He wants us to hunker down and wait for deliverance. But no deliverance will come. He'll bottle up the harbor and trap us in here while he ravages the kingdom with his army." He sniffed and shook his head. "I must face him."

Dearley's eyes widened. "We're outnumbered on all counts."

"I know. But if I'm going to die, I'm taking Estian to the Deep Fathoms with me."

⋈

Ransom walked along an outside corridor, one with arched windows open to the view of the bay of Glosstyr. The town had walls around it, but the fortress was situated on a hilltop at the shore. He paused to look out one of the arches, watching the sun glisten on the waters. From where he stood, he could see the sanctuary of Our Lady where he and Claire had been married. It felt like a lifetime ago, and the memory brought a wave of sadness and despair.

He paused for a moment, letting himself dwell on the feelings, then continued up to the defensive towers, which would offer a wider view. Several sentries stood watch, and they greeted him with forced smiles.

"Any sign of ships coming?" he asked them. The harbor seemed relatively empty, but the tide wouldn't come in until just before nightfall.

"Not even a merchant vessel," said one of the men. "But we'll keep watch, my lord. Those Occitanian knaves won't take us by surprise, by the Lady."

Ransom gazed down at the plains where his army was camped. He saw the tents and pavilions, the knights practicing with their lances. The bulk of the army was situated on higher ground, facing the direction in which Estian's force would arrive. They were close enough to the castle walls to retreat, if necessary. But Ransom was determined to bloody his sword before that happened. He'd left Dawson in charge of the camp and Dearley in charge of defending the fortress and securing the supplies they needed. Scouts had gone out earlier and returned with news that the enemy army was not far off. They'd be in sight of each other before nightfall.

As he made his way around the tower, surveying the scene from all angles, he noticed a cluster of knights riding toward Glosstyr from the southeast. Who were they?

Ransom pointed the group out to the sentries before heading back to his room to put on his armor. After he suited up, he walked down to the bailey and discovered, to his surprise and delight, that reinforcements had come. It was his brother and the knights of the Heath.

"Well met, Marcus!" Ransom said with excitement.

His brother had already dismounted, and the two embraced. It had been too long since they'd come together.

"I heard Estian was headed this way. I couldn't let you have all the glory for yourself, little brother."

Ransom gazed at the knights, many of whom he recognized from previous conflicts. Some he didn't recognize at all.

"Your mesnie has grown, Marcus."

"They're not all mine. Some are from Thorngate castle. Lady Deborah sent help as well. I see you've arrayed troops in front of the city. You're going to fight, aren't you?"

"It seems a reasonable course," Ransom answered. "A lot can happen on the battlefield."

"And Estian knows it," said Marcus with a bold stare. "Where should I gather my knights?"

"Report to Sir Dawson at the command pavilion. You'll be leading one of the forces."

"I'd hoped you'd say that!"

The brothers embraced again, Ransom beyond grateful for Marcus's support, even if the men he brought were too few to make a difference in the outcome. Their sister, Maeg, was still under ward in one of Benedict's castles far away. That left their mother defending the Heath, but she was up to the task.

Ransom asked for Dappled to be brought. He gave his final orders to Dearley, then headed down to his command tent to meet with Marcus, a few of his key knights, and his battle commanders. Two of them, Sir Thatcher and Sir Harrold, had served the Elder King during his wars, yet Ransom would have felt better if someone like Lord Kinghorn had been there to lend his wisdom and years of experience.

The tent was lit by several lanterns and furnished with a pallet to sleep on, several chests, and a table outfitted with a large map of the city and the surroundings. Ransom nodded to his knights and went to the table.

"How far off is Estian's army?" he asked.

Dawson pointed to a spot on the map. "Here. And they're bringing siege engines. At least three trebuchets were lumbering down the road behind them, drawn by horses. There is a line of wagons going back to Josselin."

That wasn't good news, but Ransom had expected it. "The trebuchets will be of no use during the battle we'll be fighting. Have they spied us yet? Do they know we're waiting for them?"

Sir Harrold spoke up. "We've seen their scouts at a distance, like flies hovering over a pile of stink. They know we're here."

Ransom nodded and planted his palms on the tabletop. "It's just us, lads. They have the advantage of greater numbers, but we have the advantage of higher ground. There are no rivers between us, so no tricks can be performed. This is where they test our mettle. This is where they'll find what true knights are made of."

All the kings he'd served had been better at rousing speeches than he was. But it didn't seem to matter. They beheld him with respect, knowing he'd be fighting in the thickest part of that battle.

A squire barged into the tent.

"Excuse me, my lord! Come quickly!"

Ransom straightened. "What is it?"

"There's another army coming! Our scouts just spotted them."

"Where?" Ransom barked.

"From the north! It's Duke Wigant!"

Ransom ordered one of his men to collect fifty knights, determined to ride out himself to learn the truth. The sun was about to go down, and the tide was already coming in. Merchants would be arriving soon, hopefully with news from Kingfountain, and the timing of James's arrival was highly suspicious.

Dawson fell in next to him as he approached Dappled.

"Do you think it's an ambush?" the other knight asked. They both knew James could be fickle. Ransom had led a group of knights, including Dawson, on a mission to Dundrennan for Devon the Elder, only to be attacked by the new duke—James Wigant—who'd shifted his allegiance to Benedict.

"It might be," Ransom said. He didn't feel any warning from the Fountain. But the warnings weren't always predictable or timely.

They mounted and rode north. Just as the squire had informed them, there was an army riding toward them, some foot soldiers too. Ransom took up a position and waited, seeing the banner of the North fluttering in the breeze. The army came toward them purposefully, led by a knight whose flashy armor revealed him. As they got closer, James detached from the bulk of the group with four knights and rode ahead to meet them. He lifted his visor as he approached, glancing at Ransom's escort as if silently counting them.

"I'm here, Ransom," he said with a wary voice. "I disobeyed the queen dowager's order, but I made a promise to you, and I've kept it. Now why does it look like you're going to arrest me?"

"What order?" Ransom demanded. "I asked you to wait at Blackpool."

"I did," James said. "Then I got a message that I was to withdraw to defend Kingfountain. I left Blackpool and started east, but I kept feeling this nagging sensation that I was going the wrong way. The order didn't make sense to me. I couldn't imagine why the queen would want you to face Estian alone."

Relief came like a cool drink. "Let me see the order," Ransom said.

James reached into his saddlebag and produced a letter and seal. The handwriting was similar to the queen's, but Ransom thought he saw differences in the style.

"It's a forgery, I think," he said to James. "Who brought it to you?"

"One of those Espion types," James said. "Truly? They've compromised our messengers this badly? This did not come from Emiloh?"

"Definitely not. You were supposed to be here. I'm relieved you came."

James glanced back at the men Ransom had brought, then gave him a surprised smile. "You thought I'd betrayed you."

"It's happened before."

"True," James admitted. "But if you go down, Ransom, we *all* go down. Where would you like my army?"

Ransom couldn't help the smile. It felt good to smile at last. "I'd like you to lead the left flank."

"You're taking the vanguard?"

"Of course. I'm assuming Estian will lead his."

"That suits me," James said. "Based on what you've told me, Occitanians have infiltrated the Espion."

"That's evident, yes. But I don't think they were counting on you keeping your promises."

"Don't get used to it," James shot back with a grin.

They rode back to the command tent together, side by side. But they didn't make it all the way before Sir Thatcher came riding up to them quickly, eyes blazing.

"What is it?" Ransom demanded.

"Ships," he said, out of breath. "Word just came from . . . Sir Dearley."

"Friends of yours?" James drawled to Ransom.

"The tide is coming in," Ransom explained. "I've been expecting more bad news all day. A blockade. How many Occitanian ships, Sir Thatcher?"

"No," gasped Sir Thatcher. "They're Gaultic ones. Sir Dearley said to come at once. So many ships. It's . . . it's your wife! She's returned to Glosstyr!"

We sail into Glosstyr Harbor with the coming of the tide. Thank the Aos Sí the trick worked, and they did not know we were coming. I did not wish to deceive my husband—deceit feels wrong, even when it serves a greater purpose—but I knew there were traitors among us who were stealing our messages. And someone had riffled through the pages of this little book. Now, at last, we can confront each other and discuss the matters that have plagued our marriage. No more will I need to write lies. Let the previous pages be a testament to the dark times in which we live, to the need for dissembling when your enemies are as manipulative as King Estian and his sister.

I wonder what Ransom will say when he learns I've come with an army to help him face Estian? That the coolness I expressed in my letters belied what I really felt? I've missed him. I've missed him so very much.

—*Claire de Murrow*
Glosstyr Harbor

CHAPTER
TWENTY-SEVEN

The Breach

Ransom urged Dappled to greater speed as he raced back to the fortress of Glosstyr, his heart afire with the news of Claire's unexpected arrival. Sir Thatcher rode alongside him, the two of them charging down the road with a handful of other knights who'd been summoned as impromptu bodyguards. Before they reached the castle, Ransom saw men in Gaultic armor carrying the banners of war.

After closing the distance, he reined in, signaling his group to do the same, surprised to find Lord Tenthor of Legault approaching him on a massive black-and-gray destrier with streaks of white war paint across its neck and withers.

"Aye, Lord Ransom it is!" cried Tenthor when they drew near. "I'd heard of your ugly brute of a horse. But nothing can match the hideousness of mine!" He laughed, and the beast tossed its mane as if disagreeing with its rider's sentiment.

"You've come at a perilous hour," Ransom said. "I'm grateful for it."

"I'm ready to bash in some Occitanian heads," said Tenthor with a grunt. A wicked-looking hammer hung from his saddle strap. "Just point the way."

"How many came?"

"The queen sent five thousand of us," said Tenthor with a proud smile. "We'll make short work of Estian's rabble. Where would you like us on the field, my lord?"

A thrill filled Ransom's chest. "Words fail me right now, Lord Tenthor."

Tenthor nodded. "I've not forgotten the service you did me, Lord Ransom. Now get thee to the castle and greet your wife. Just tell me where I should assemble."

"The duke of the North is on the left flank. You've got the right," Ransom said. "Wait for orders in my command tent atop the hill."

"I will do so," said Tenthor. He looked around the landscape in the fading light with an appraising eye. "I've not been to Ceredigion since I was a boy." He grinned. "You can keep it."

Ransom gave him a salute and rode through the man's ranks until he reached the castle proper. The heaviness that had pressed on him for days lifted. It felt like he could breathe freely again. His brooding worry about Claire had shifted to hope, like a dull rock overturned to reveal a shiny surface.

After dismounting in the bailey, he was met by a page who told him Claire had gone up to their room with Dearley, and the two were awaiting his arrival. Ransom thanked the boy and told Sir Thatcher to stand ready. His sense of anticipation was almost painful as he marched through the halls. The castle was still churning with life, and the late arrivals had changed the mood drastically. Soldiers smiled and shared the news with each other as Ransom passed them. He jogged up the stairs, and not even the weight of his armor could slow him down.

When he reached his room, the door was already open. The mood in the room seemed perfectly congenial, Dearley and Claire talking as friends would. That boded well.

When he appeared in the doorframe, Claire turned, and his heart stuttered in his chest at her beauty. The torchlight from the wall sconces illuminated flashes of red in her hair and cast flickering light on her expression—wary but not upset. She, too, was nervous about this meeting.

"My lady, I'll bid you farewell," Dearley said. "You've saved us. I'll put the prisoner down in a cell in the dungeon for now."

"Thank you, Dearley. It's good to see you again." Claire's soft accent made Ransom's throat go dry. He could only gaze at her, rendered silent by the crashing surf of feelings inside him.

As Dearley passed, he gave Ransom a hopeful smile and said, "I'll give you as much time as possible," then left and shut the door quietly behind him.

For a moment, Claire just studied Ransom, as if he were a puzzle she wished to solve, and then she rushed forward, and they embraced. He couldn't believe he was touching her again. She trembled, and he wished the barrier of armor weren't between them. He wanted to be vulnerable at that moment. Not a knight on the brink of war.

She looked into his eyes and lifted a hand to touch his jaw. "Your beard is trimmed and *scáthanna!* What did you do to your hair!" Her fingers swept back to graze his neck. He'd almost forgotten his brief trip to Pree. "You look a different person, Ransom. How am I supposed to take that?"

"None of that matters," he said. "What truly matters has not changed." And because he needed to touch *her* hair, those brown-and-red strands that had always delighted him, he reached behind her neck and ran his fingers through it.

She let him toy with her hair for a moment before pulling away. "Are you surprised that I came?"

"I'm astonished," he said. "I thought you were attacking Bayree."

"That's what I wanted everyone to think. I came to help you fight Estian, that miserable wretch. Glosstyr is mine as well as yours. I will defend it." She looked him in the eyes again, a bracing look that showed her worry. "Will you be honest with me? I can bear the hurt so long as I know you're being honest."

Worry trembled inside him. Would she ask for truths the Fountain had bid him not reveal?

"I will . . . if I can," he said.

"Have you been having an affair with the Duchess of Brythonica all along?" He saw her hands clench, but not in a combative way. She was preparing to be devastated.

"No, Claire. Never."

She closed her eyes slowly and opened them again, searching his face. "Honestly? There is no need to lie to me. I can bear the truth. Although I don't trust Lady Alix's words, they had a feeling of unshakable truth when she spoke them. The more I've thought on it, the less I've believed it, and yet . . ."

He stepped closer. "I swear it by the Lady of the Fountain. I am faithful to you."

"But there is something between you. A loyalty that binds you."

"Yes, but it is not what you fear. I swore an oath to protect her son. To protect Brythonica. But I cannot say much more about that without violating it."

She expelled a slow breath. "Your eyes tell me you're being sincere. I struggle with trust, but I know you have no reason to lie to me. I believe you, Ransom. And I know you only sent a knight to take that book out of worry for me. You were right. There was something strange and uncanny about it. I'm glad she took it."

He couldn't express how much her words meant to him. "I don't ever want to be estranged from you, like Devon and Emiloh were."

Claire gave him a sad smile. "Neither do I."

"And the boys? They're safe?"

"They are being guarded at the hunting lodge," she said. "The poisoner can get into and out of my family castle rather easily, it seems, but it is guarded more strictly now. Still, I thought they'd be safer at the lodge."

Gratitude and relief surged within him, waves washing over a parched shore.

She came to him again, enfolding him in her arms and leaning up to kiss him. The pressure of her lips against his awoke memories that stirred his blood and nearly made him weep. He clutched her to him, amazed that she was there. The broken world felt like it could be fixed at last. And he kissed her harder, more urgently.

"I've missed you," she breathed in his ear.

The gentle sound of the crashing surf came from the open window. The torches had burned low, but candles now brightened the dark room. The night was still young, but there was much to speak about, much to share.

"How did you figure out our letters were compromised?" Ransom asked, offering her a drink of wine from the pitcher that had been brought in by servants along with their shared meal.

"I kept noticing the disturbed seals," she answered, accepting the goblet and sipping from it before setting it down. Her hair was a little tousled, and he liked it that way. "I began to suspect that one of your mesnie had betrayed us. Someone besides Guivret. I told Lord Toole about my suspicions, and he said it would be useful to find out who it was by placing misinformation inside our letters. I also suspected that my journal had been compromised. Those were the only two places where I shared information that could be stolen."

"So who was it?" Ransom asked.

"Sir Axien," she answered with a sad smile.

Ransom started. "Are you certain?" Axien, one of the Elder King's men, had joined his mesnie following the king's death. He'd never demonstrated signs of disloyalty before, but perhaps the promise of extra pay had enticed him.

"Lord Toole had him followed, discreetly of course, and found him to be in correspondence with an Espion assigned to Atha Kleah. There was another one, a lesser servant, in Connaught. Lord Toole was going to arrest them both after we left, but I confronted Sir Axien myself with the evidence." She sighed. "And he confessed it all. He was paid handsomely for his information by none other than Lord Longmont."

"Did he know Longmont was replaced?"

"Yes, but he still meddles in things. There are some Espion who have stayed loyal to him. Still others have been paid by Occitanian livres. Hence my deception. I wanted Estian to think I was attacking Bayree. No doubt he has ships anchored there waiting to 'surprise' us." She gave him a very fetching smile.

"Sir Axien," Ransom said, shaking his head in disbelief. "He was loyal to the king."

"To Devon, maybe. But not Benedict. He's been playing you for a fool. Playing us both. I'll let you divine a suitable punishment for him once this conflict ends. He's still on the boat we sailed in on."

Ransom's thoughts darkened at the prospect. He wanted revenge.

"I've also heard the news," Claire continued, "that the Duchess of Brythonica has forged her independence from both kingdoms. Did you hear the same?"

"Yes, the news reached us as well. But there is more to the story." He quickly told her about stealing the Wizr set, the very one they'd spoken about some months ago, and how Guivret had been captured during their escape. He didn't reveal that the duchess could summon him at will.

"That was a foolhardy mission, Ransom," she said. "What if you'd been captured as well? I can't believe Emiloh condoned it."

"She didn't," Ransom said, cringing at her rebuke. But she was right—the danger had been real. If not for Constance's vision, he wouldn't have gone. Nor would he have risked it had he known what would happen to his family. "I took advantage of Estian's absence. That is why Alix came to you. By kidnapping one of our sons, she no doubt hoped to force us to return it." What an unbearable thought. He felt a pulse of longing for the boys, but it was better that they were safe at home than here, on the cusp of war.

"I still mourn Keeva. She was so brave and loyal."

Ransom nodded solemnly. "Guivret will be heartbroken. The two of them had feelings for each other."

Claire looked at him in surprise. "Did they?"

He took a hasty bite from the roast fowl. His hunger was ravenous now. "They both thought the seering stone was harming you, so they conspired to take it away. Used indiscriminately, it's as dangerous as the book Alix took. Was it through that stone that you began to suspect I was unfaithful to you? Or did it happen sooner?"

Claire's gaze fell. "Yes, but my fears sprung to life before that, I confess. You hadn't done anything wrong, Ransom. It's just . . . as I've said before, I had this strange sense of a connection between you and the duchess, almost as if . . . It feels foolish to say it, but it felt like if fate had twisted a different way, you might have chosen to marry her and not me. The stone only confused me more."

Her words caused a jolt in his heart. Constance had expressed a similar sentiment. He didn't understand what it meant, but it was curious that Claire should feel the same way. Perhaps it was similar to the way he sometimes felt a strange place or person was familiar. Either way, there was no knowing the cause.

"The seering stones serve a purpose," he declared. "One must be commanded by the Fountain to use them."

She tilted her head. "You know I don't believe in all that. If you'd been raised in Legault, under different beliefs, you might feel the same way."

"It wouldn't have made a difference, Claire." He looked away for a moment, trying to find the words, then gazed into her eyes. "The Fountain *speaks* to me. It warns me of danger." He pressed his fist to his heart. "Lord Bryon told me that very few people can hear the Fountain's voice. He's spent his whole life hoping to be one of them. But to me . . . it came easily. The Fountain-blessed aren't just a myth. I'm one of them. My gifts for war started young and aren't entirely natural. I sense things that others cannot. I foresee dangers other people do not."

Conviction swelled in his chest as he spoke, and something in Claire's eyes changed.

"Oh, Ransom," she said. "I—"

A firm knock sounded on the door and startled them both. Ransom rose from the floor, where they'd spread a blanket to share the meal. He walked to the door and opened it and found Dearley waiting there expectantly.

"I gave you as much time as I dared," he whispered. "Estian's army has arrived. They are setting up camp across the meadow and have sent scouts to investigate our position."

"He might attack tonight," Ransom said with conviction.

Claire had risen from the floor and sidled up next to him. She gripped Ransom's arm. "Then you should attack him first."

"I would highly recommend he get his armor back on first," Dearley said with a meaningful look. "I'll assist you."

Claire helped too, and having her there, knowing all was well with them and their boys, gave him a feeling of confidence and determination that bolstered his strength and doubled his courage. Every layer of armor increased his confidence that he could defeat Estian.

As Ransom helped Claire tighten the strap on his arm bracer, he looked at Dearley. "Make sure there are sentries posted in the castle at all times. If Alix tries to sneak in, I want her apprehended or killed. I can sense her if she's near, and I intend to find out whether she's with Estian's army tonight."

"She may be waiting in Bayree," Claire said. "They believed I would attack there."

"True, but she can travel great distances quickly. She could be in both places tonight."

Claire nodded. "The book she stole from me speaks of such things. Of ley lines and words of power. I'm grateful it's gone, but I fear she might learn some new tricks from it."

Ransom flexed his arm and twisted his elbow to ensure the fit was right. "That book is dangerous for anyone to read. It corrupts."

"It is true. I hadn't realized it at the time, but I felt lighter as soon as she took it."

Their eyes shot to the door as one at the sound of rushing steps. Dearley hurriedly fit on another piece of Ransom's armor while Claire went to the door.

"Message from the palace," said the page, handing the note to her.

"Read it to me," Ransom said, forced to stand still while Dearley knelt to fix on his leg armor.

Claire opened the seal and started to read. It was from Emiloh.

"'Lord Ransom, I felt I should send these tidings straightaway. Jon-Landon has fled the palace through the Espion tunnels and joined with Duke Ashel's army.'" Claire grunted. "The carp-faced eejit! Sorry, let me continue. 'We are defenseless now, save the warriors who have sworn to hold Kingfountain with their lives. I know you face terrible odds, but if you can spare any men to come to our aid, I will bless your name. If you cannot spare them, I understand. We can hold out for several days. But the people are beginning to clamor for a new king.'"

Claire lowered the letter and shook her head in disbelief. "They want a brainless badger as their king? A pox on them all for so utterly lacking in sense!"

"Read on," Ransom said, feeling the tension return.

Claire lifted the page. "'I also received word today that Lord Kinghorn . . .'" Her voice caught. She swallowed and then read more slowly, sadly. "'. . . succumbed to an illness brought on during the campaign. Benedict requested . . . and was given permission . . . for him to visit the inside of the oasis before he died. He was buried there, by one of the fountains since it's forbidden to bury in water in that land. My heart grieves for his son.'"

Claire's voice trailed off, and she regarded Ransom with warmth and empathy.

He stared at her, stunned. She knew how much he admired Lord Kinghorn. And to hear this news on the eve of battle was a terrible, terrible blow. His first battle as a knight had been fought alongside Sir Bryon. And it was on that very eve that he had knighted Ransom.

"I'm so sorry," Claire said, coming to him, her voice throbbing with sadness.

"At least he got to see the oasis before the end," Ransom whispered hoarsely.

The King of Occitania must have learned that Glosstyr was well defended. Instead of attacking during the night, he began to withdraw his forces. He left behind a contingent of knights to hold the retreat. Ransom promptly attacked them, and he's since been chasing the Occitanians all day. I'm still at Glosstyr, awaiting news of the outcome. Another message arrived from Emi today, saying that she's heard Benedict has had some early success in the East Kingdoms, although we doubt whether the rumors can be true. It takes so long for messages to cross between us, however, that the conflict may be over by now. If he is successful, Benedict will be returning home sooner than we thought. It is a relief that help will be coming, even if it is far away.

I am still grieved by the news of Lord Kinghorn's death. His son, Sir Dalian, was a friend to me while I was in the queen's tower. Lord Kinghorn was to become the Duke of Westmarch once we reclaimed the duchy from Estian. Will the promise be honored, as Ransom's was? Or will the king decide to reward someone else from the oasis campaign with such a privilege?

   Will he keep his word?

—*Claire de Murrow*
Glosstyr
(turning the advantage in our favor)

CHAPTER
TWENTY-EIGHT

The Loss of Josselin

A throb of warning from the Fountain alerted Ransom moments before a group of knights emerged from a thicket of trees on a hilltop. Sunlight flashed off their dark armor and shields as they raised their lances and began to charge into Ransom's cohort.

Dappled's strength had been tested that day as Ransom set a punishing pace to try to overtake Estian's army before it reached Josselin. They'd captured many abandoned supply wagons and faced a number of brief skirmishes, all of which had yielded prisoners and provisions. The attacks had worked their intention, however: they'd slowed down Ransom's advance guard.

"My lord!" shouted Dawson, pointing at the charging enemy.

Gripping a fresh lance, Ransom gestured for his knights to engage the foes. The thunder of hooves grew louder as the much smaller force charged toward them. Ransom's own soldiers were spread out for nearly a league behind him, some escorting wagons full of prisoners back to Glosstyr, others seeking out Occitanian stragglers who had fled to the hills.

His concentration focused as he prepared to exchange blows with the Occitanians. He lowered his lance, homing in on the lead knight, sizing him up for weaknesses. The man headed straight for him, lance aimed at his heart, but Ransom sensed the knight would lower the tip of the lance at the last moment in an attempt to skewer Dappled instead. He veered to the side in anticipation, and the two rode past each other without either of them making a hit. Another knight was suddenly in Ransom's path, and he took aim with his lance and unhorsed the fellow with a solid blow that sent him crashing down to the meadow.

Dappled snorted in apparent satisfaction. With a quick tap of his spurs, Ransom engaged another knight and unhorsed him as well. He sensed danger from behind and turned in the saddle, realizing the lead knight had come after him again. There wasn't enough time to gather speed for a charge, so Ransom tossed down his lance and unsheathed his bastard sword. The other knight tossed his lance down as well and brought out a chained flail with spikes protruding from the balls. They clashed in close quarters, and the chained flail snared Ransom's sword.

Leaning back against the saddle cantle, Ransom twisted his waist and wrenched the sword hard. The flail was ripped from the other knight's hands, but rather than yield, the knight spurred his horse and came at Ransom from his blind side.

The man leaped out of his saddle to grapple with him, the sudden weight jolting him. Dappled nickered in anger and took a bite out of the fellow's horse. Ransom felt his balance shift, and he toppled off the edge of his horse, the other knight landing atop him.

The knight pinned Ransom's sword arm to the ground and drew a dagger, which he tried to plunge into Ransom's visor. A blow from Ransom's elbow deflected it, and he managed to roll and throw the other knight to the ground.

Ransom's blood boiled with rage, and he raised his sword to stab through the gap between the helmet and breastplate.

"I yield!" exclaimed his foe, dropping his dagger and holding up his hands, palms facing Ransom.

Caught up in the maelstrom of battle, Ransom felt his inner nature compel him to finish the knight. There had always been a murderous corner inside Ransom's heart, and it took him a moment to conquer the savage instincts.

"I said I yield!" the knight repeated desperately.

Ransom stood and kept the tip of his sword pointed at the weak spot in the man's armor. He glanced around through his visor and saw his knights had once again won the skirmish. The Occitanians had known they wouldn't win. These men had been sacrificed so that Estian could escape.

"Where's the king?" Ransom barked at his subdued opponent.

"I don't know," answered the knight. "I serve the Duke of La Marche."

"I've not heard of that," Ransom snapped. "Where is it?"

"It is the duchy you call Westmarch. He's fleeing back to Tatton Grange. We were sent to slow you. Are you going to kill me?"

Ransom lowered his sword. "You were captured and yielded. I will hold you ransom to the duke."

"He will pay for my release," said the knight with a tone of relief.

One of Ransom's knights rode up to them. "My lord, Lord Tenthor is coming."

Ransom turned and saw another company of warriors riding in, wearing Gaultic armor. "How many survivors?"

"Most of them," said the knight. "After the first charge, they started to quit."

Ransom found Dappled nearby. He sheathed his sword, picked up a fallen lance, and mounted. By the time he was situated in the saddle, Lord Tenthor came. His helmet was more open than the ones of Ceredigion and Occitanian make, with a sculpted nose guard coming down the middle.

"You didn't save any for me, Lord Ransom?" demanded Tenthor.

"I was saving the King of Occitania for you, but he got away," Ransom said in jest. "I'm glad you finally caught up."

"Your army is strung along for a league behind you," Tenthor said. "I overtook Duke James as he was taking supply wagons back. He said you were riding ahead of everyone else like a crazed fool."

"Will you join me?" Ransom asked.

"That's why I hurried. Let's hunt this king down!"

Dawson rode up to them, a smile on his face. "I captured Sir Begret," he said. "He was a tournament champion, I think. I give him to you."

Ransom was proud of the young man. It was a mark of respect, giving your best hostage to the leader of the mesnie. "No, Dawson, he's yours. You earned it."

Dawson's grin spread wider. "Are we riding still?"

"Of course. Disarm the hostages and have them escorted back to Glosstyr. You're riding with us to Josselin."

"Aye, my lord!" Dawson said with enthusiasm. "We're not far behind them. If we ride hard—"

"Quit jabbering, and let's go!" Tenthor shouted.

The chase continued.

⋊⋉

They reached Josselin castle before all Estian's army could get safely inside. Several more skirmishes had stalled them, but with Tenthor's men they'd made quick work of the defenders. More and more knights continued to bolster Ransom's ranks as they caught up, and by the time he was within sight of the walls, he had about a thousand men with him, all mounted and ready for conflict.

The Occitanian foot soldiers were rushing to get back into the castle through the rear gate, but Ransom's arrival threatened to forestall them. His heart filled with fury at the sight of Estian's flag fluttering from a parapet.

As he led his men forward, he heard the Occitanians cry out in terror and flood toward the gate in a panic. If they didn't close it, then Ransom's men would be able to force their way inside, allowing him to seize his castle back.

The sun was starting to fade, and Ransom was weary from the hard ride and constant fighting, but he'd done it. They'd made it back to Josselin again.

"Like pigs for the slaughter," Tenthor said next to him, gesturing to the helpless soldiers spread out before him.

A familiar presence tingled down Ransom's spine as they drew nearer. Lady Alix was there at the castle. In fact, he thought he sensed her on the battlement walls.

The groan of the portcullis sounded as it began to lower, causing a shriek of despair from soldiers who hadn't made it through. Estian was trapping part of his army outside. He had no other choice. There was nowhere he could run.

Ransom turned to his knights. "Ready!"

Tenthor grunted in anticipation.

What would Alix do? Did she have her crossbow again? Was it her intention to kill him? There was utter chaos outside the castle walls as the portcullis slammed shut.

Ransom knew Estian had made it to the castle. He was probably the first to have set foot inside it. How the situation had turned because of Claire's timely arrival and her brilliant deception. He wanted to capture Estian before Bennett returned, to end the conflict and restore Ceredigion's borders. He was so close . . . so very close to achieving his goal.

"Line up," Ransom ordered his men. They all held lances, and they assembled into a long horizontal line as the first shadows of evening began to fall.

When they were in order, Ransom began to ride forward. Occitanian soldiers huddled together against the walls, some wailing in fear. As Ransom and his host drew near, he saw a hooded figure on the battlement walls, surrounded by knights. It was Alix, her golden hair slipping from the hood she wore. She stood by Estian. What advice was she giving?

When they were within earshot of the walls, Ransom held up his hand to order a halt. He gazed up at the figures standing atop the walls, then at the miserable mass quaking in front of them gripping spears with shaking hands.

"Well done, Lord Ransom!" shouted Estian from above. "You've always been a notable adversary. Are you ready to discuss terms?"

"I would be glad to discuss your surrender," Ransom said. "By morning we'll have the castle surrounded and begin to lay siege. So yes, by all means, let's discuss terms."

A brief silence ensued as Estian considered his words. "I'm not trapped here, Ransom, as you well know. I was merely going to barter for the lives of my soldiers trapped outside. Withdraw your force so I can bring them in safely."

Tenthor snorted with disgust and said in an undertone, "Not bloody likely."

"And why would I want to do that?" Ransom asked. "If they lay down arms, I'll not slaughter them."

"I know you won't," said Estian. "But more than their lives are at stake. We captured many of your townsfolk hiding in the woods. Your steward is here as well. You recognize him, don't you? He has very distinctive hair."

A knight shoved Westin to the edge of the wall. A sense of dread crept into Ransom's stomach at the sight of the steward's shock of pumpkin-colored hair.

"Withdraw so my soldiers can come inside. Or I will start hanging them, one by one, from the wall. Within view of your men. There are women and *children* here, Lord Ransom. They are your people, and it is your duty to protect them. We'll start with your steward, just so you know I'm serious."

Ransom watched in horror as some of Estian's knights put a rope around Westin's neck. His hands were bound behind him.

"That is against the order of Virtus!" Ransom shouted, his voice trembling with pent-up fury.

"This isn't a tournament," Estian spat in disdain. "This is war. I think we both know that I don't make empty threats. Let my soldiers in, or he dangles from the wall. And the others, one by one."

Ransom's stomach felt ill as memories from his childhood came charging back. A castle under siege. The castle of the Heath. King Gervase had been asked to sacrifice a child's life to prove his mettle, and now Ransom was being faced with a similar test. This was deliberate. Lady Alix had known exactly what would wound him most.

How many of the townsfolk had been captured?

"Can he truly escape?" Tenthor asked in a low voice. "If the castle is surrounded . . ."

"He can escape," Ransom answered just as softly. He suspected Alix's magic would allow it. He might not be able to bring his army back with him, but before he left he could take his revenge on Ransom's people.

"You're hesitating," Estian said. "I think you doubt my sincerity. Throw him over the wall."

"Wait!" Ransom barked before they obeyed.

"Don't try my patience," Estian warned. "Retreat now so I can draw my soldiers inside."

Ransom felt impotent and furious. Was Estian bluffing? How many townsfolk had been captured? He had no way of knowing. The only question he could ask himself was whether Estian would murder the innocent. And yes, he believed Estian would.

"We will retreat," Ransom said. "But I warn you. Whatever you do here tonight, whether you show mercy or murder, it will be done back to you at Pree."

"You are just a pawn in a game of Wizr, Ransom. I don't fear your threats."

Ransom remembered when Alix had given him the chance to slay Estian, to stab him in an act of murder. How might things have gone differently if he'd gone through with it? The thought of killing Estian quivered inside him. He motioned for his knights to lower their arms, and they began to back up their horses.

He heard the portcullis groan and saw it begin to lift. One by one, the soldiers skulked back into *his* castle, protected by the walls. What would Benedict have done if he'd been there? Would he have persisted with the siege? Was the price worth the cost?

As he watched the soldiers slip one by one into the castle, he stared at them bleakly, the exhilaration he'd felt snuffed out. He'd come so close to catching Estian. To be thwarted now, his efforts foiled by his own mercy, was a sour brew. It wasn't fair. But war wasn't fair.

"What would you have done, Tenthor?" Ransom asked.

"If it had been *my* castle, *my* people? The same as you. You did order the villagers to flee, didn't you?"

"I did," Ransom answered. "But some wouldn't go, it seems. I don't know how many."

"The Occitanian king has a heart as black as his tunic," said Tenthor. "All that chuff he and his father made about Virtus. It's just smoke. Nothing more."

"It seems so."

Another prickle went down Ransom's spine. Dread quickly followed it—this was the feeling of warning that signaled he was about to be summoned to Brythonica.

Not now!

He could still feel Alix staring down at him. Was she smiling at his weakness? But the more he thought about his decision, the more certain he was he'd made the right choice. The only choice. It was like the ghost of Gervase had told him. The murder of innocents was against the order of the Deep Fathoms. His heart recoiled from it.

Ransom needed to find a way to escape his soldiers. The duchess's summons would sweep him away regardless of where he was or who could see him.

We have captured many Occitanian knights in this war so far, and they've been brought to Glosstyr for confinement until this is over. Still no word from my husband on his pursuit of Estian, but surely he could not have made it all the way back to his borders by now. The lack of news is worrisome. I must endure it as best I can. As the Gaultic saying goes, "Misfortune might follow you for the rest of your life, but may it never catch up."

I am not a prisoner in a tower any longer. If word does not come from him today, I'm taking my bow and a horse, and riding hard after him. I'm not proud of my traitorous thoughts, but I had a dream last night of Ransom and Constance sitting together on a balcony, hand in hand.

—Claire de Murrow
Glosstyr
(the worries of war)

CHAPTER TWENTY-NINE

Twilight in Ploemeur

need some time to think," Ransom told Lord Tenthor in a low voice. "I'm going to send a rider back to Glosstyr to inform my wife of the situation. Remain here and keep watch over the castle from afar."

"And where are you going to be?" Tenthor asked with concern.

"The woods, over there," Ransom said, pointing to the darkening forest. "If I'm not back within the hour, return to Glosstyr." Anxiety coiled within him. He feared he was about to vanish in front of the others, thus revealing his peculiar duty, but he was also concerned about what would happen to his army, and to the people held captive by Estian. He could still sense Alix's presence in the castle.

"Do what you must," Tenthor said.

Ransom gave orders to send word to Claire about the situation at Josselin. Then he mounted Dappled and rode a short distance away. He continued until he could no longer feel Alix's presence—knowing that she, in turn, could no longer feel him. Then he dismounted and found a small spot in a grove of trees, where he lashed Dappled's reins to a branch so his destrier wouldn't wander off. Dappled offered a noisy grunt, and Ransom patted the beast's neck, grateful for his immense stamina. Stars had begun to appear in the sky overhead, their glow visible through the curtain of tree limbs. His stomach squeezed unpleasantly as he anticipated the final rush of summoning magic.

It came while he was staring at a bit of starlight.

The sensation of plummeting roiled inside him, and he found himself back in the city of Ploemeur. He turned around slowly, taking in the salty sea air, and found himself on a balcony in the palace. A night bird sang from atop one of the stone ravens along the rim, and he saw a harbor full of ships, the tall masts void of sails.

The door opened, and Constance joined him on the balcony, her arms folded, her eyes downcast. She looked weighed down.

"I didn't want to summon you, Ransom," she said, her voice thick. "But I had no choice."

From the doorway, he recognized her bedchamber, where he had recovered from his previous injuries. He felt a tightness in his chest. It felt wrong to be here, especially now, when he was so needed by his army.

"Why did you bring me here now, and not before, when Alix came?"

Constance stiffened at the mention of the poisoner's name. She still didn't look at him. "There was nothing you could have done," she said. "I'm meant to use the visions from the seering stones to help others, not myself." There was so much pain in her voice that he felt the stirring of compassion.

"What happened?"

"I didn't call you here to share my woes, Ransom." Her gaze lifted to his face. There was a yearning in her eyes that whispered of more than just friendship. His stomach clenched. He stared at her, waiting for her to speak but dreading it at the same time.

"Benedict is going to be captured," she said, her voice calm and deliberate.

She might as well have struck him with a battering ram. "What? How?"

Constance walked to the edge of the balcony, resting her hands on the smooth stone. "The messages you receive from him don't always arrive in the right order," she said. "I've seen a vision of what's to come. A truce at the oasis will happen soon. Benedict will learn that Estian has abandoned him and plans to invade Ceredigion, so he will come home as swiftly as he can . . . and that means leaving his army behind."

Ransom winced. "That is terribly reckless."

"Indeed. He's also worried about Jon-Landon seizing the throne, as he should be. He will be traveling with a small group of knights pretending to be mercenaries." She turned away again, gazing down at the bay of Ploemeur. "They'll find passage on a Genevese ship headed to Brugia. When they get there, a Brugian duke will apprehend them, and Benedict will be held prisoner until his ransom is paid. All of this will happen months from now, but I've seen it as if it happened this very day. And I cannot hope to warn him because there is no way of knowing where he will land." She shot a look at him. "It's not the Fountain's will that I intervene. Only that I tell you so he can be saved."

Her words plunged like knives into Ransom's chest. "Do you know which duke will capture him?" he asked urgently.

Constance nodded. "The vision was clear on that. His name is Gotz the Iron Hand, and he is master of the Wartburg in Brugia. That is where you will find your king. And that is why I summoned you. Many people will be interested in buying him, Ransom, and Estian will be among them. You must win the negotiation. The duke is irascible. It won't be easy. And there will be other . . . complications."

So Benedict wouldn't be returning to save them—rather, he would need saving. The disappointment was a terrible blow, especially on the heels of Lord Kinghorn's death. Benedict had always had impetuous tendencies, and if the Duke of Westmarch had lived, he would have kindly but firmly dissuaded him from such a course of action. The cost of the ransom would be a burden on the people, especially after the steep expenses of the war with the East Kingdoms and Longmont's profligate spending. They could send for help from Genevar, but hadn't the queen, Portia, returned to her father's house? What did that imply?

"This is hard news," Ransom said, shaking his head. "Do we prevail?"

Constance had tears in her eyes. She wiped them on her sleeve. "Eventually," she said softly.

Seeing her pain made his heart ache. "What is it?"

She patted the stone railing and let out a deep sigh. "She took my son." As if admitting it aloud had made it real, she finally gave in to her grief, clenching her hands into fists and letting her shoulders quake. Sinking to her knees at the edge of the balcony, she pressed her cheek against her forearms, her face turned away from him.

Ransom didn't know what to do. Drew was gone? Now he understood why Brythonica had claimed independence. Her hand had been forced.

"Where is Drew now?" he asked her. His promise to protect the boy struck his heart like a bell.

"I've no idea," she gasped. "Do you know how hard it is, Ransom? I could find out this very instant. But I *cannot* use the seering stones for myself. I cannot . . . I cannot . . ." She began to gasp for breath and then wept piteously.

Ransom's heart twisted in shared pain. Alix had come for his sons too. And Keeva had lost her life protecting one of them. It made his stomach turn to think of Drew, so innocent and good-natured, in the grips of Alix and Estian.

"If he harms your child . . ." Ransom said, his voice throbbing with anger.

When Constance turned her face toward him, her cheeks were still wet with tears. "No, Ransom, don't even think it! She . . . she said he wants Drew to be named Benedict's heir. That he will allow him to claim the throne in Kingfountain."

"But you cannot trust a word he says," Ransom countered. "He's willing to murder children. He threatened it just now at my castle in Josselin."

"I know his character," Constance answered. "But I couldn't stop her from taking him away. I don't know where he is, and the uncertainty is torturing me."

"Let me look at the seering stones," Ransom insisted.

Constance shook her head. "It would be the same as if I used them, Ransom. Neither of us have been commanded by the Fountain. I dare not risk it."

Ransom wanted to bury his face in his hands. Instead, he dropped to one knee in front of her. "Then let us petition the Fountain. Let us at least *ask*."

"I have asked," she whispered.

"And?"

"Only silence." She wiped a tear from her cheek. "It's been very hard. I didn't mean to burden you with my cares."

"Who else could you have shared it with?" Ransom asked.

She smiled and looked away. "Sir Terencourt advised my father. I used to confide in him. He became like a second father to me."

"I understand. My own father never cared much for me, but King Gervase was like a father to me, and so was Lord Kinghorn." He was silent for a moment, then added, "Lord Kinghorn is dead."

Constance met his gaze, her eyes full of sadness. "I'm so sorry. I didn't know. Although I didn't see him in the vision of Benedict, I assumed he'd been ordered to bring the soldiers back. He was so kind, so in tune with the Fountain."

Ransom sat down, his back against the balcony wall. He rested his arm on a bent knee, grief rising within him like a tidal wave. It felt like his moorings had come undone and he was drifting in an endless sea.

Then he felt Constance touch his gauntlet. He looked at her, feeling utterly miserable.

"I think you're right," she said. "Let us petition the Fountain together. Shall we not try, at least?"

"I have a coin, I think," Ransom said. "Is there a fountain nearby? There is, isn't there?"

She smiled and shook her head. "It's not like that, Ransom. The Fountain hears our prayers without coins. Let me . . . let me teach you." Kneeling next to him, she placed both of her soft hands atop his gauntleted ones. Then she bowed her head, an act of submission and reverence. "Oh, please help us in this dark hour," she pleaded gently. "Ransom and I have chosen to serve. To do your will. But the path that lies ahead is masked with shadows, and we cannot see our way. We need guidance."

As she spoke, Ransom felt the Fountain magic within him ripple. Her words were doing it. It wasn't just her words, though. It was her meekness, her quiet strength, her character.

"I feel you," she went on, her voice thick with emotion. "Please be a comfort to my poor son too. He's in a strange place, so far away from us who love him. Watch over him. And, if you would, please help this brave knight endure what he must. Let . . . let the weight fall on me, not on him." She sobbed as she said it, and Ransom felt his heart stretch into an unfamiliar shape. Tears trickled down his cheeks as he listened to her petition the Fountain on his behalf when her pain was the greater one. "If ever I did anything worthy in your sight, let that be my reward. I would be willing to give up any blessing in the Deep Fathoms for this man's sake."

He sat there, dumbfounded. The worry and despair that had festered in him had been checked by a greater power, and the sense of peace he felt was indescribable. Her hands, atop his, had become an anchor.

Ransom stared at her and could have sworn the stars made her face glow. She looked into his eyes, weeping softly, and then lifted his gauntlet to her lips and kissed the metal.

"How did you . . . do that?" he asked her, still feeling the settled peace of the Fountain within his heart. It continued long after her prayer was done.

"It's not what I was intending to say," she answered. "It's what needed to be said. Sometimes the voice of the Fountain teaches us the right words. What we *should* ask for." She kissed his hand again. "Never forget this moment, Ransom. Never doubt that we both felt the presence of the Fountain here."

"But your son . . ." he started to say.

"I've prayed for him. That's all I can do. I must trust in the Fountain's blessings. And so must you."

She cupped one of her hands atop his. "If we never see each other again, I want you to make me a promise. If you see Drew before I do, remind him of me. And stand by him until we meet again, even if it's in the Deep Fathoms. And I promise thee, Ransom Barton, that if I see him first, I'll remind him that you were his protector, and we will watch for you constantly until you come."

Her words seemed to come from a source deeper inside herself. It filled him with foreboding. "Will we not see each other again?"

She looked him in the eye. "I don't know. I said what I felt."

Slowly, she rose to her feet and helped, in her small way, for him to rise as well.

"I see now why I was supposed to summon you tonight," she said. "We both needed comfort and strength. I couldn't ask for you earlier because Emiloh has kept vigilant watch on the Wizr board. I didn't want her to see you come here and then ask you questions you could not truthfully answer. I'll send you back now. The news will be coming soon. Be ready for it. You are the one who will secure Benedict's release." She shook her head slowly. "But at great cost. Stay faithful to him. I believe in you."

The peace was still in his heart. He swallowed and nodded to her.

She released his hands and whispered, "Farewell."

When the magic struck him and sent him flying away, he landed in the spot he'd left, with Dappled still nickering softly by the tree. His strength nearly failed him, and he slumped down to his knees again, breathing fast and hard.

And realized that he would never see the Duchess of Brythonica again.

X

I have not written in this book in over a year. I do not seek to make excuses, but the babe squirming inside me has made me sicker this time if that were possible. The leaves have turned a bright red, and storms brew in the sea. I shall need to leave Glosstyr soon, for I wish all my children to be born on the Fair Isle.

Our lads have visited several times, in the lulls between battles. As much as we wish to have them with us constantly, their safety must be our primary concern. They're not old enough to understand another babe is growing inside me, but both are fascinated by my growing belly. Soon it will be unsafe to travel back and forth like this. The only question remaining is whether my sons' father will be coming with us for the winter.

Word has reached us of King Benedict's truce with the East Kingdoms, although no knights have returned yet. He departed before them, in secret, to defend his realm. But there has been no word. Some at court fear he was shipwrecked. Others say he was captured. Ransom feels in his heart that the king was likely captured and is being held prisoner somewhere, but Jon-Landon is insistent his brother is dead and that he should be made king. Estian backs up that claim, but he insists Andrew Argentine, the Elder King's grandson, be named king. This, he says, is why he attacks Ceredigion.

Thus three rival factions disrupt the peace in Ceredigion. Jon-Landon from East Stowe is trying to win support as king, although he has not yet openly rebelled. Estian attacks us from Westmarch and constantly raids our lands. And Ransom is caught in the middle, trying to hold the kingdom together to buy time for Benedict. His castle in Josselin is lost, but he negotiated the release of the villagers in exchange for the knights they'd captured. A man and his family for one knight. Estian accepted and those released were brought to shelter in Glosstyr.

I am in charge of the defense of Glosstyr, with Dearley's help, and we've had to send forces to block further incursions set loose on us from Josselin. When Ransom isn't here, he writes me often, more so than he used to. We no longer care if our letters are intercepted. The situation changes constantly because of Estian's determination to seize more land.

I no longer have premonitions about Ransom and the Duchess of Brythonica. Those ended with that strange dream of them on a balcony. The duchess has promised to marry an Occitanian nobleman, Lord de Montfort. He will be her lord consort, not Duke of Brythonica, and the protector of the duchy. Their marriage will seal the independence of Brythonica as its own sovereign duchy. Maybe it is because of the marriage that my worries concerning her have lessened.

—Claire de Murrow
Glosstyr
(A winter in peace?)

✕

CHAPTER THIRTY

The Intrigues of Men

G et down, Ransom!" Marcus barked, squatting beneath the protection of the wall. Smoke slithered through the field below them, blotting out the tents and Occitanian banners. The ominous row of trebuchets were being fitted, one by one, with massive stones that their enemies had dragged by cart and horse to be hurled at the fortress of Beestone castle.

Ransom planted his hands against the wall and leaned forward slightly, watching with unconcealed wonder as the trebuchet was triggered. The massive beam swung down, and the net holding the boulder flipped, the counterweight hurling it toward the castle. A few lucky shots had managed to reach the castle. But it was on high enough ground that the trebuchets hit it only sporadically.

He watched the boulder arc through the sky and felt no warning from his Fountain magic that he was in any real danger. It landed in the rubble of the destroyed village at the base of the hill. The Occitanian soldiers would have to fetch it back again, putting them at risk from the archers who perched in wait.

"It didn't even come close," Ransom said to his cowering brother.

Marcus lifted his head warily, rising a bit higher, and then came to stand next to him. He had smudges of soot on his face and smelled terrible. But so did all of them. "I have a fear of being crushed by stone. I've always worried about it, but this siege . . . it's made it so much worse."

Ransom gazed down through the smoke and haze. He believed they kept things burning perpetually to make it harder for the archers to shoot at them from above. Ransom wished the notorious robbing archer, Ryain Hood, had been captured and put to work defending a castle instead of plundering them. With a marksman like that, they could do some real damage. But the bandit was elusive and continued to steal from their supply lines. Every attempt to capture him and bring him to justice had failed.

But they could ill afford to send soldiers to hunt a small group of bandits when there were so many conflicts throughout Ceredigion. News of Benedict's capture still had not come, and Ransom strained with agitation, knowing what would happen but not knowing exactly when. It was a difficult secret to keep, especially from Emiloh, who worried over her son's failure to arrive and watched the Wizr board daily for a sign of his appearance. Ransom wanted to tell her, to put her mind at ease—if only a little—but he kept silent to guard the secrets he'd learned in Brythonica.

"I wouldn't worry, Brother," Ransom said calmly. "You're more likely to die of the bloody bowels than a boulder."

"Is that supposed to comfort me?"

"We've lost more to that disease than we have to Occitanian blades. Or boulders."

"Aye. And Estian justifies his attack by claiming he fights for a young lad's right to inherit his uncle's kingdom. I don't think the people would accept the boy now."

Ransom watched as another trebuchet was loaded. He began to walk along the battlement wall, observing the mood of the defenders. They were weary from the long siege, but their courage hadn't faltered. Although the Occitanians outnumbered them, especially now that

Estian's remaining men had returned home from the East Kingdoms, they didn't have enough men to surround the castle and cut off supplies. Ransom would just as soon attack them and be done with it, but there were too many troubles elsewhere in the kingdom to justify the risk. Without Jon-Landon or Drew to move the pieces of the Wizr set, all Emiloh could do was watch the danger unfold and send orders from the palace.

A knight ran up the stone stairs leading to the battlements, ducking as a precaution when he reached the top, and then quickly strode toward them.

"Lord Ransom, a supply convoy was spotted coming from the east."

"That's good news and ahead of schedule," Ransom said, giving Marcus an appreciative look. "Let's send some soldiers out to greet and escort them."

"They have soldiers with them," said the knight. "Reinforcements carrying the Lion banner."

Marcus grinned. "Another detachment has returned from the East. Good. They might be enough to drive these Occitanian wolves away."

"I hope so," Ransom agreed.

The sound of a trebuchet chain cut through the air, and Marcus flinched and ducked down again. So did the knight. Ransom stood, hands on hips, and watched the stone wing its way toward the fortress. It exploded against the rocky hillside, the impact pulverizing the boulder.

"At least they won't be able to use that one again," he said with a chuckle.

He and Marcus followed the knight down the steps to the bailey, which was crowded with soldiers, most of them bored and playing dice, awaiting their turn to guard the ramparts. Ransom recognized the captain of the detachment on sight—it was Captain Baldwin, the grizzled old instructor who'd trained Ransom as a lad in Averanche and come to DeVaux's castle to pay for his release.

"Baldwin!" Ransom said with enthusiasm. He gave the graying man a knightly salute.

Baldwin smiled through his graying beard and tapped his own chest. "After getting back from the oasis, I asked if there was a nice quiet place an old knight could rest his bones. And the queen dowager sent us here to relieve a siege. Well met, lad. Well met!"

The two embraced, and Ransom introduced his brother.

Baldwin nodded and spat on the stones. "How many are against us?"

"We think about four thousand."

"Pfah, you could have driven out twice as many, boy."

"We have a thousand men," Ransom countered.

"Now you have two thousand. I brought some young lads, fresh from their travels in the East. While they're more used to skewering desert rats for dinner, I'm sure we can make quick work of these fools." He reached into his tunic and withdrew a sealed letter. "This is for you. Unfortunately, our reunion will be brief. You're needed back at the palace. It's almost as if you were someone important now."

Ransom took the letter, smiling at the jesting words, then quickly opened and read it.

"Has the king been found? Is he dead?" Marcus asked.

"The king isn't dead," Ransom said, betraying no emotion. He'd learned the news months ago. "He's being held hostage by the Brugians."

"That might be worse than death," Baldwin said with an expression of distaste. "I knew he shouldn't have left on his own like that. If Lord Kinghorn had been alive . . ." His look darkened.

Ransom nodded to Baldwin, sharing the sentiment. "We cannot change what's happened. Only what will happen. Have Dappled saddled. I need to ride back to Kingfountain."

"Remember how much the queen paid for your release?" Baldwin said. "I imagine they will squeeze her for every livre she has left. Is he even worth it?" This last comment was whispered under his breath.

Ransom felt a throb of anger at the sign of disloyalty. His own duty was clear. He'd sworn an oath to Benedict, who had fulfilled his father's promises to Ransom. It felt wrong to repay him with even a ghost of contempt.

"He's our king," Ransom said firmly. "And I know what it's like to be held captive by an enemy. I wouldn't wish it on any man."

"I might wish it on Estian," Marcus suggested.

"I could be persuaded," Ransom said. "Although I'd rather just kill him."

Baldwin nodded with respect. As the other men hurried to prepare Dappled and an escort of knights for the journey to the palace, Baldwin hooked his meaty arm around Ransom's neck and walked with him toward the well in the center of the courtyard.

"I wish you'd been with us," Baldwin said. "Sir Bryon also regretted your absence. I'm not being disloyal when I say that Benedict was foolhardy on many occasions. He was so determined to prove himself, like he was competing with your shadow. 'Reckless'—that's the word that comes to mind. But he has the Lady's favor, for even though he did some foolish things, no harm came to him." He shook his head regretfully. "I think that only made him willing to take more risks."

"He's still our king," Ransom said.

"I know that. But you can feel the wind blowing in your face, even if you cannot see it. What if he dies in captivity? He's worth a hefty ransom, no doubt, but to some, he's worth more dead. If he's out of the playing field, whose side will you be on?"

"Why are you asking me this?"

Baldwin lowered his arm and turned to face Ransom. "Because I have no one to serve, and I wish to serve you."

"What about Sir Dalian?"

Baldwin sniffed and shook his head. "I like the lad. But he will never be Duke of Westmarch. Or La Marche, as I've heard it called these days. Benedict won't give it to him, even after he's reclaimed it. He'll reward his own men, those who journeyed with him to Chandleer. It'll likely go to one of the knights in his mesnie— Kiskaddon maybe. He's a good chap. Still, I can't see myself serving another Duke of Westmarch after losing Sir Bryon. But I'd willingly serve you. I'd be grateful even."

Ransom clapped Baldwin on the shoulder. "I'll have you."

"Good. You have two sons. I can make sure they become men."

"They are babes still. And another is on the way. You can't grow old on me yet."

"I won't if you let me train the rascals."

"Well, I wasn't planning on sending them to Dundrennan," Ransom answered.

Baldwin laughed. "Still that rivalry between the two of you?"

"Not as much anymore. He did me a service when Estian attacked Glosstyr."

"It must be one of the Lady's miracles," joked Baldwin. "Get riding, lad. I'll keep your brother in line."

⚔

The journey from Kingfountain to Beestone took a day, and Ransom and his escort were exhausted by the time they arrived because of skirmishes they faced along the way. It was after midnight, so the queen dowager was abed, and Ransom went to see Simon in the Star Chamber. The room was crowded with correspondence, but it was all neatly organized now, and Simon sat in his chair writing a note.

"I was expecting you earlier. It's only a day's ride."

"It can take longer with raiding parties roaming about," Ransom responded. "I need some sleep right now. I just wanted to let you know I'm here."

"Thank the Fountain. I'll notify Emiloh in the morning. You'll have a chance to sleep on the ship when we send you to Marq."

Ransom's brow wrinkled. Constance had named the place where Benedict was being kept, and it wasn't the Brugian capital.

"When did you find out about Benedict?"

"The same day we sent reinforcements to you. It's a . . . strange story. But you need your rest. I can tell you in the morning."

Ransom leaned against the wall and folded his arms. "Tell me now."

"Longmont's under house arrest, but he's still pulling strings. He found out about Bennett before we did and tried to sneak away from the palace. Do you remember the Espion lass you caught in your room?"

"I do."

"She's my chief informant," Simon said. "Everyone seems to trust her, but she is loyal to the throne. Longmont stole one of her dresses and a cloak and tried to leave the palace disguised as her."

"You are joking."

"I'm not. He made it as far as the docks when a . . . rather drunk sailor took him for a lady he could woo. By the time the night watch arrived, his humiliation was complete. I interrogated him, and that's when the story about Benedict came out. Longmont insisted he was going to share the information after he left, and he proved his words by producing a letter he had written before disguising himself. He was hoping to earn favor by rescuing the king himself, or at least negotiating the ransom."

Ransom massaged the bridge of his nose. "And you think we can trust the girl?"

"I do," Simon said. "She reported her missing dress immediately, which helped us put it together. I've even considered sending her to Pisan for training. It costs twenty thousand livres, though, and we don't have enough to spare, not when we'll have to pay for the king's ransom."

"Do we have Espion in Marq?"

"Of course!" Simon said, pretending to be offended. "What kind of spymaster do you take me for? I've heard that Estian has already put in a bid. There is someone from the East Kingdoms who also bid on him. He made enemies there, as you know. Get some sleep. You won't be staying in the palace for long."

"I imagined I wouldn't be. Tomorrow, then."

"It's good to see you, Ransom," Simon said with a broad smile. "I think we would have lost the kingdom by now if you hadn't been here to protect it. Estian is hitting us hard. He knows if Benedict returns, he's a dead man."

Ransom nodded and left, but the sentiment gave him little comfort. As he walked the darkened halls, his mind shifted to Claire. He had a powerful longing to see her again—to press his hand against her belly and feel the fluttering kicks she'd written him about. At least their separation had not been long. Since she was in Glosstyr, they were able to meet periodically, and they could send and receive letters more quickly than if she'd been in Legault. He'd written her before leaving Beestone to let her know the king was a hostage. It had been a relief to finally share the knowledge that had festered in his mind these last months.

He climbed the steps and started down the corridor toward his room, his Fountain magic alerting him to a presence within. The person who lurked there was dangerous, yet he sensed they weren't a danger to *him*. Nor were they Fountain-blessed. He saw a dim light, probably a candle, shining from beneath the door.

Ransom gripped his dagger and slowly turned the handle. When he opened the door, he saw a woman pacing inside. He recognized her at once. The Espion girl.

She turned as he pushed the door open.

"I can't stay long," she said. "But I had news that couldn't wait."

He looked at her guardedly and then entered and shut the door, leaning back against it.

"What is your name?"

"I have many names, Lord Ransom."

Her hair was darker than he remembered it. He waited for her to continue, saying nothing.

"I have a message for you from Jon-Landon."

X

News from court arrived today, sent by Ransom, who is now at Kingfountain. Benedict was captured on his return from the oasis and is being held prisoner in the kingdom of Brugia. Estian will attack Ceredigion again with all his might in order to win before Benedict can be released. I think it is not unreasonable to believe that Occitania has more in its treasury than we do. Only a loan from the Genevese could tilt the scales, but will they grant it with such ill humor between Benedict and Portia? This news will embolden Jon-Landon further. He hasn't resorted to violence yet, but I believe he will if he doesn't get his way. We cannot afford to fight a war from within while fighting one from without. The only reason we have survived so far is because Ransom knows where the Occitanians' attacks are coming in advance, thanks to the Wizr board, and has been able to counter them with minimal loss of life.

I wonder who Emiloh will trust to negotiate for her son's freedom. It should be Ransom, but if he leaves Ceredigion,

*there will be no stopping Estian the Black. But who else could
be trusted in such a dangerous mission?*

—Claire de Murrow
Glosstyr
(a king's ransom to be paid)

CHAPTER
THIRTY-ONE

Secret Embassy

Before you deliver your message, give me your name," Ransom demanded of the Espion woman. "Your birth name. What duchy are you from?"

She gave Ransom a quizzical look and twirled a strand of hair around her finger. "Cecily of Yuork, my lord."

"You don't have a North Cumbrian accent," Ransom said.

"I donna mean to disappoint thee, milord, but thou sayest wrong."

Ransom smiled at the deftness of her ability to conceal her native accent. "You have other names?"

"Depending on where I am or where I need to be from. I have a gift for languages. Can I deliver my message?"

"By all means, Cecily. What does Jon-Landon want?"

She stopped twirling her hair. "Your support if he becomes king. If Benedict is ransomed, it will impoverish the kingdom. It will make us vulnerable to Estian. Jon-Landon will continue to spread the rumor that Benedict is dead, with witnesses to back him up, and try to seize the throne in the uncertainty."

Ransom felt his anger stir. "That won't help anything."

"It will, my lord. It gives Ceredigion someone to fight for against Estian. If Benedict returns, Jon-Landon will step down. If he doesn't, at least there's a king to keep fighting for. He's not asking you to betray Benedict."

"It sounds like a betrayal to me."

Cecily shrugged. "I've delivered my message. Do you want my advice?"

Ransom wrinkled his brow. "Can I trust it?"

"You'll have to decide that for yourself. I'm not like you, Lord Ransom. I have no loyalty except to my own interests. I've been watching you for a long time. I've heard conflicting things about you, but I've learned to sift the chaff from the wheat."

"And what have you concluded?"

She gave him a knowing smile. "That you're a man of principles. I let you catch me in your room that day, you know. I wanted to see how you would react. A man with less honor might have threatened or abused me. In short, I'm on *your* side. I serve Sir Simon because I know he's loyal to you. If you want Benedict released from his Brugian prison, I'll help you."

"How?"

"Longmont knows where the king is being kept, and it isn't Marq. He hasn't told anyone because he desperately wants to be the man who rescues the king. It's the only way he can regain his lost status. He's blind to anything but his own ambition and helping his master. If I come with you, I can make sure you succeed. Everyone trusts me because I've managed to balance these conflicting interests."

Her words were convincing, but Ransom was still doubtful of her motives. "You openly admit that you deceive everyone around you. How am I supposed to believe that I'm the exception?"

"What I've told you has compromised me completely," Cecily said. "But I trust you. I want to help rescue the king because, as flawed as he is, he would make a much better king than Jon-Landon, who schemes with Lord DeVaux and his daughter to steal his own mother's duchy. Although he'll only be content when he sits on his brother's throne. But I do believe it is in your own best interest, and Benedict's, not to publicly refuse his claim. Give the kingdom an Argentine to rally around. It will take time to secure Benedict's release. Time you do not have."

"I will speak with the queen dowager," Ransom said. "I'm going to tell her about you."

Cecily nodded. "I knew you would. I've delivered my message and my warning."

She started toward the door, and Ransom stepped aside. She paused, her hand hesitating above the handle. The look she gave him didn't reveal much, but he sensed she was worried she had compromised herself too much.

"Thank you," Ransom told her.

A relieved smile flashed on her mouth. "I'm naught but a poor waif from North Cumbria, milord."

"Do you speak Brugian?"

"Aye, milord. I do."

The following morning, Ransom joined the queen dowager at her breakfast and explained what he'd learned. He noticed the age lines around Emiloh's eyes, the additional streaks of gray in her hair. The pressure of her worries had increased. She'd always been a strong woman, tall and imposing, but she looked weighed down by the realm's troubles.

After listening to his account, she rose from the couch in her personal chamber and began pacing, arms folded tightly, her head slightly bowed. A memory teased him of when they'd first met in secret in Lord Rakestraw's tent. It seemed like several lifetimes ago.

"So Longmont has lied again," she said with consternation. "Bennett isn't in Marq?"

"No, I don't think he is. But the news probably came from Marq, so he may just have neglected to impart the full information."

"That's the same as lying," Emiloh said bitterly. "And Jon-Landon wants the Vexin. This is quite a morning you've given me, Ransom. Our situation could not be more desperate. It feels like . . ." She stopped herself, shaking her head.

"Go on," Ransom said.

She sighed. "It feels similar to the time before Devon died. So much of power is a precarious balancing act. I'm just trying to keep it all from shattering."

"I will go and bring back your son," Ransom said determinedly.

Emiloh gave him a heartfelt smile. "There is no one I'd trust more. But if Jon-Landon rises in revolt, I need you *here*. Maybe the best option is to let Longmont have his moment of glory."

Ransom knew he needed to go, but he couldn't mention Constance's vision. Perhaps he didn't need to. "If he were the most capable person, I'd welcome it. Look how he's bungled the Espion. Can you trust Bennett's deliverance to someone like him?"

Emiloh's shoulders sagged. "No. Not really."

"Then heed my counsel. I will go and bring Cecily with me. Longmont will come with us so I can keep an eye on him and prevent him from doing more damage here. We'll find the king and negotiate his freedom."

Emiloh met his gaze and held it. "And what do we do while you're gone? Jon-Landon won't sit still. And we can't afford to let him access the Wizr set."

"I agree. A taste of power will only make him hungry for more, and Cecily is correct in her assessment. I fear he would make a poor king."

"Devon spoiled him too much," Emiloh said. "I cannot undo that."

"No. We just need to keep his ambition in check. Here is my suggestion. Estian has spies in court. We must use them to our advantage."

"How?"

Ransom gave her a thoughtful look. "Make him believe I'm still here. One of my knights could wear my armor and ride my horse. Dappled is distinctive. It would encourage the deception. I could be in Marq in three days."

Emiloh brightened. "Who would impersonate you?"

"One of my knights is young and headstrong. Sir Dawson. He could act the part. Send him to Glosstyr first, to tell Claire of our plans. Then he can ride after the bandit and try to put a stop to his pillaging. Or some other highly visible mission. Whatever it takes to convince Estian that I'm still in Ceredigion."

"Once you get to Brugia, the game will be over," Emiloh said. "Estian's spies will inform him of your arrival."

"Unless they don't know. If I wear a tunic with the Lion badge, no one will look twice at me. Knights are invisible. I won't reveal myself until I find out where Bennett is being kept."

Emiloh pursed her lips. "I want to hear Simon's take on this. Your strategy is sound, Ransom. But if Estian learns you are gone . . ."

"That's why we need to keep him guessing," Ransom said. "Beestone castle was just reinforced, so it will not easily fall. Claire is holding Glosstyr. James holds the North."

"That still leaves Jon-Landon as a source of trouble."

"But you can trust him to act in his own self-interest. All we need is to delay him awhile."

Emiloh shook her head. "But how long can I hold him off? You have to hurry, Ransom. If this drags on, he could usurp the throne."

Ransom frowned. "If he does, he will contend with *me*."

The sunlight was beginning to fade, and Ransom knew he needed to be aboard the ship before Longmont arrived there. He walked down the palace corridor, illuminated by torchlight, and found no one paid him much attention in his tunic and cloak. He'd written a letter to Claire explaining the decisions they'd made and pleading with her not to depart for Legault until he returned. Her presence in Glosstyr would be a strong deterrent against Estian's ambitions. But the change in seasons was coming, which left Ransom only a little time to succeed in his mission. She would leave soon, and if he didn't go with her, he would be parted from her and the children for months, a thought that pained him keenly, especially since he would miss the birth of their youngest child.

He arrived at the queen's chamber and was promptly admitted by her guards. Once inside, Ransom experienced the strange sensation of staring at himself from behind. Dawson was clad in his armor, and Simon had even arranged for a scabbard to be crafted with the raven-head insignia on it. It wasn't exactly the same, but it was a convincing substitute. Simon and the queen dowager stood on either side of him.

Dawson turned when Ransom arrived, and he had a look that exuded too much confidence. He'd been overjoyed with the assignment to impersonate a duke. Ransom worried that overconfidence might ultimately get him caught, but Dawson was the only man in his mesnie who had the build to play the part.

"We're just waiting for the sun to set," Dawson told him. "Then I'll ride out to Glosstyr. I can't wait to see Dearley's face when we get there."

Ransom gave him a pointed look. "Don't let it go to your head. Here, this letter is for Lady Claire. Do not let it out of your possession for any reason."

"I won't," Dawson said, showing a little flash of offense. "I'm not a fool."

He felt another pang of misgiving. He had enemies, and Dawson would have to face them. Would he be up to it?

"I see that you're worried," Dawson told him in a low voice. "I can do this, master. I won't let you down."

"I know you can," Ransom said, putting his hand on the knight's armored shoulder. "That's why I chose you." The words were intended to instill confidence, but his worries had not abated. Dawson's confidence always made him seem older, but Ransom remembered that he was only nineteen.

Dawson glanced out the window. "I think it's time."

Ransom offered one more encouraging nod and then tapped his breast in a knightly salute. Dawson reciprocated and donned the helmet that would finish the disguise. "I hope Dappled won't balk," he said, his voice sounding strange from beneath the helm.

"He knows you," Ransom said. "Ride on."

Dawson dipped the pommel of his bastard sword and then bowed to Emiloh and Simon and departed.

"I trust Claire's instincts more than his," Emiloh said to Ransom, frank as ever. "But you were once so ready to serve. Look at you now."

"Yes, a humble knight in service to the queen dowager," Simon said with a wry smile. "Let's get you on your ship. I have several Espion disguised as crew members. We told Longmont he's bringing four guardsmen with him for protection, chosen by the queen dowager."

"And he doesn't know I'm coming?"

Emiloh shook her head. "No, and he won't find out until you are underway. Right now, he believes he's been entrusted with this mission. You'll take command after the ship leaves, when it's too late for him to send word to anyone."

They heard steps moving down the corridor, heading their way. Simon turned to Ransom. "That might be Longmont. Time for you to disappear. We'll take the Espion tunnels."

He opened a triggered latch, and the wall grated open quietly, revealing the dark, tomb-like passage. Ransom went in first, and Simon grabbed a candle from the table before joining him. It cast barely enough light for them to see, and the musty smell of the dank corridor filled Ransom with apprehension. He much preferred the wide halls of the palace to skulking around in these narrow passages. A bead of sweat trickled down the side of his face as they walked, Simon leading the way.

After going down some narrow steps and passing through various twists and turns, they saw another dim light ahead. Simon held his candle up higher as they approached, the glow revealing Cecily in a hooded cloak.

"She'll take you the rest of the way," Simon said. He turned and gripped Ransom's arm. "As I told you before, they'll ask for a steep ransom. It may even be as high as a hundred thousand livres. If we squeeze all the duchies, we can get seventy thousand. That means we'd need a loan of thirty thousand from the Genevese. Do your best to get it down. But I recognize you'll be competing against Estian. He has the means to outbid you." Simon sighed. "Do your best, Ransom. Make them *want* to accept your offer."

Ransom nodded to Simon, and the two embraced in the passageway. When would they see each other again? Would it be under better circumstances?

Simon took the candle with him, leaving only Cecily's light. She wore an interesting gown—the fabric darker than was fashionable in Ceredigion, the sleeves a little tighter, the whole thing dotted with little dark beads that glistened in the candlelight.

"Are you ready for this, my lord?" she asked with a Brugian accent. He'd heard the Brugian tongue before, with its harsh, throaty sounds.

"To the ship," Ransom said with a nod.

At the end of the dark passageway, she led him down another set of stairs. He could smell a hint of perfume coming from her, reminding him of the lilac scent Alix wore. It gave him a shudder of misgiving. No one he was leaving behind would have any protection against the poisoner. Only another Fountain-blessed could sense her presence.

The queen has the board, Ransom reminded himself. *And Alix does not.*

They reached a closed stone portal. Cecily touched a spot in the shadows, and the portal opened, bringing in the scent of wet stone and the sound of lapping water. In the distance, he could hear the river and the falls.

Impulsively, he gripped her arm. "Where are we?" he asked, unable to subdue the sudden feeling of terror.

Cecily held up the candle, its glow reflecting on a vast expanse of water. Arches crisscrossed the ceiling overhead. It felt like they were in the very depths of the castle.

"This is the cistern," she whispered. "The water is pretty low right now since we've had a dry year. Are you afraid of water, Lord Ransom?"

A strange feeling tingled down his spine as he stared at it. He had never been there before, but it felt as if he had.

"Lead the way," he whispered, and she stepped into the dark void.

You can imagine my shock when I was told Ransom had returned to Glosstyr without sending word of his arrival, only to discover it was Sir Dawson in disguise, riding that ugly brute Dappled. Dearley joined us in the confidence, so at least I'm not the only one burdened with the information of what is being risked to free King Benedict from a Brugian prison.

Fool, fool eejit. This is a secret that cannot be kept for long. Surely Estian or Alix will learn of the deception. I want to go back to Legault, but now I cannot. There is too much at stake here.

—*Claire de Murrow*
Glosstyr
(on the intrigues of brainless badgers)

CHAPTER THIRTY-TWO

Callait

Ransom walked into the dark vault of the cistern, led by the Espion woman and her fragile candle. There was a small ledge around the cistern, a pathway that allowed them to circumnavigate the chamber. The stone arches supporting the castle's bulk overhead were reflected in the calm water. Drips and plops echoed through the vast stone area. The strange sensation of familiarity did not lessen.

Cecily slowly brought them around the circumference. A set of stairs led up to a wider platform, but she went past it.

"Where does that lead?" he asked her, then quieted when his voice carried farther than he'd wanted.

Cecily stopped and raised the candle higher, chasing some of the shadows away. The ceiling, speckled with dark stains, had a hole cut into it. "There is a garden up there," she whispered. "It's one of the openings that fills the cistern when it rains."

Ransom recognized the shape of the hole. It was in the gardens he'd been to several times to visit with Emiloh and Claire. Was that why the cistern had felt so familiar?

"I know that place," he answered.

A strong premonition struck him as he looked at Cecily. He heard two children splashing in the cistern waters, their laughter echoing down the long tunnel. Then a grating sound came, and he sensed the waters of the cistern had begun to drain toward the river and the falls. A feeling of panic entered his chest, making him put his hand to the wall to steady himself. He couldn't explain himself, but he feared for the life of the children.

Cecily touched his arm, a look of concern in her eyes. "Are you unwell?"

He looked down into the black hall of the cistern, hearing the children's cries of terror. It was obvious only he could hear them. It baffled him, but he felt a strong connection to the pair, as if he were the boy and Claire the girl. But it wasn't a memory—he was certain they'd never come down here before. What was happening to him?

"I'm all right," he said as the premonition began to fade. His knees strengthened again, and the fear ebbed.

"Some people cannot abide enclosed places," she said. "Come with me. We'll be out soon." She lightly tugged on his arm, and the two went around the ledge until they reached the other side of the cistern. Another tripped latch opened a door into a different dark tunnel.

The sound of the river grew louder as they walked down a twisted series of stairs. They passed through another stone door and stepped into a warehouse full of crates, illuminated by light shining in from the upper arched windows.

"Where are we?" he asked her.

"We're above the king's docks," she answered. "The rest of the journey will be out in the open. But at least no one saw us come this far."

They made their way out onto the cobbled street full of carts and horses that had brought goods from the docks. The roar of the falls could be plainly heard now, and he saw the spike of the sanctuary of Our Lady rising from its island in the center of the falls, connected to the land on each bank of the river by stone bridges. Ransom felt more confident amidst the familiar surroundings. He glanced back at the castle atop the hill and noticed a number of stars had appeared in the sky.

No one paid them any notice as they passed the sailors and merchants attending to the arrived goods. After they descended the stairs to the docks, Cecily led him to the ship that would take them to Brugia.

"Our first destination is Callait," she informed him. "We'll arrive there before dawn. It has a deep harbor, so we won't need to wait for the tide. From there, we're supposed to ride to Marq under escort, but I suspect Longmont will have a man waiting for us there with additional news."

They approached the ship and quickly boarded it. One of the sailors made a hand gesture to Cecily, and she responded with one of her own. The sailor then looked at Ransom and gave a subtle nod. He had to be one of the Espion that Simon had sent with them.

"Let's get you out of sight for now," Cecily said. She brought him belowdecks to one of the main cabins.

"Once Longmont's here, I won't be as friendly with you," she said. "But trust that I'm on your side, whatever you may hear me say."

"I want to trust you," he replied, looking at her. "Don't give me any reasons not to."

She nodded and slipped away. As Ransom sat waiting, his thoughts strayed to Brugia. The Brugian king had died, and an heir had not yet been chosen. The situation they were going into was unstable.

Ransom heard Longmont's grating voice as he descended the steps toward the stateroom. The walls were thin enough that he could only make out a few words, but the tone was familiar. He was already giving orders, one of which included the command to "make way."

The ship was shoved from the dock by mooring staves, and soon the creaking noises and swaying increased as they left the harbor of Kingfountain. Having felt he'd waited long enough, Ransom left his room and walked the few steps to the stateroom. He twisted the handle and pushed it open.

Longmont wore a wide velvet hat, expensive furs, and a costly gold chain around his neck. He had his arms folded imperiously as he spoke to several men gathered before him, including two more knights wearing the Lion badge.

"I cannot overstate the importance of our mission," Longmont was in the middle of saying. "The very fate of Ceredigion hangs . . ." His voice trailed off as his eyes met Ransom's. Recognition battled with intense and sudden terror.

"Lord Ransom!" he gasped in shock. "What are you doing here?"

"Did you really believe the Duchess of Vexin would entrust you alone to rescue her son?" Ransom asked pointedly.

Longmont blanched, and his hands began to tremble. "I . . . I thought . . . oh dear."

"Where are the Brugians keeping the king?" Ransom demanded. He saw a smirk on one of the knight's faces. The two others looked abashed.

"I h-heard it was Marq," Longmont said.

"We both know that isn't true," Ransom countered. "Do you know where he is?"

Longmont had totally been caught off guard. He swallowed and groped for the edge of the nearest chair and sat down in it. "The duchess sent you?"

"Answer me," Ransom demanded.

"I don't know where he is," Longmont said. "I have a man awaiting us in Callait who will tell me. I assure you, Lord Ransom, that—"

"I don't think there's anything you could say that would reassure me," Ransom interjected. "If King Estian finds out I've left Ceredigion, then he'll unleash his full fury on our realm. It is imperative that we get to Benedict swiftly to negotiate a ransom. I think we both agree that is our mission."

"Yes, my lord," Longmont said meekly.

"Good. Now get out of my room. Let me know when we get to Callait."

Longmont rose from the chair, swallowed nervously, and then nodded in submission. Ransom caught the flash of anger and humiliation in his eyes, but he met the look with one of indifference. After the room had been vacated of the entourage, there was a small tap on the door. Cecily entered and shut the door behind her.

"Well done," she told him. "He's going to try and slip away in Callait. He's not thinking clearly right now. He's a fool."

Ransom folded his arms. "Have him watched."

"That's already done," she answered. Nodding to him, she turned and slipped away.

The fortress of Callait overlooked the harbor, and men with torches patrolled the ramparts even in the middle of the night. Being a port city, Callait was constantly under threat by sea, but it had strong armaments and walls. The town was quiet, but the port was open, and they made berth quickly.

They waited on deck until an officer from the harbor came to inquire. He had a thick accent and a sour expression. Ransom let Longmont do the talking.

"You came in ze middle of ze night," said the officer. "The inns are crowded. Where do you hail from?"

"My name is Longmont, I am the high justiciar of Ceredigion. Awaken the castellan of the fortress and tell him we have arrived to negotiate for the release of our king."

The officer looked at him, his brows furrowing, and then burst out laughing. "I'm a lowly harbormaster, and even *I've* heard of you, Master Longmont. I'll not waken the castellan, for he deeply resents such intrusions on his sleep. Come in the morning, and you'll be seen. Hah! High justiciar indeed."

Longmont's face went crimson with anger. "Do you mock me, sir?"

"I mock your pretense. You cannot give orders here. You are in our kingdom now."

"I demand an audience with the castellan now," Longmont insisted.

The harbor officer spat on Longmont's shoe and walked away.

Although Ransom had no fondness for Longmont, he had the urge to hoist the harbormaster off his feet and thrust him into the water. Still, he suspected that might not be the wisest course of action. After he'd witnessed enough of the man's humiliation, he took him aside.

"We'll go to the fortress at first light," he said. "But arrange for horses so we can be on our way immediately."

"What about a carriage? I could arrange for two of those."

Ransom shook his head. "Horses. We'll make better time."

Longmont clenched his fists and squared his jaw. "If you say so, Lord Ransom. One of my men can make the arrangements in the morning. We can ride the horses to the fortress too."

Ransom nodded. "But try not to tug on the reins too hard, Damian. Neither horses nor men care to be yanked around."

"I see," Longmont said with a curled lip. "I'm going to rest in my room for a while."

Ransom continued to walk above deck, waiting and watching, until the sun began to brighten the eastern sky. Additional ships floated into the harbor, chasing away the silence of night. Ransom saw Longmont climb the steps leading to the helmsman's post. He stood there, conversing with the man, hands on his hips. A little while later, another man jogged down the planks to enter the city to make the arrangements.

As the noise on the dock increased, Ransom felt the uneasy sensation that all was not as it should be. Another man from the crew walked down the gangway. Then another. Ransom marched to the helmsman's ladder and quickly climbed it. Longmont had his back to him, the thick velvet hat bedecked with a single ostentatious ostrich feather.

"Too many of your men are leaving," Ransom said. "I thought you were sending one."

"I did send one," replied a voice that wasn't Longmont's, although it tried to be.

Ransom grabbed the man's shoulder and spun him around. It was someone else, wearing Longmont's clothes. The man's eyes blazed with fear at Ransom's sudden look of anger.

"When did he go?" Ransom demanded.

"He was the first to leave. I'm sorry, my lord! I'm sorry!"

Ransom whirled around to look at the wharf. But it was crowded with people, and it would be impossible to discern which were Longmont's men.

"Do you know where he went?"

The man shook his head. "He wouldn't tell me."

Ransom went to one of the other knights. "Go get us some horses. We need to ride."

"Aye, my lord," said the knight.

Ransom looked around the deck for Cecily, but there was no sign of her. He was angry he'd been duped, especially since the trick Longmont had played on him was the same one he was attempting to play on Estian.

He went to his room and wrote a letter to Emiloh, informing her of Longmont's treachery, but he halted before sealing it. His intention had been to write to Claire too, to inform her of his safe arrival. But if he sent the ship back to Kingfountain, one of the sailors might reveal Ransom's presence in Brugia. Time was also a critical issue. He couldn't wait for a response—he had to get to the king quickly, especially with Longmont running about, potentially causing trouble. Thankfully, because of Constance, he already knew where the king was being kept. So he might as well head straight there.

A knock landed on the door before he could dispose of the letter, and Cecily entered with a hard expression.

"Did you know?" he asked her.

"No. Or I would have warned you. I think Longmont suspected me because I hadn't told him about you."

"We can't stay here."

"I know. A message just arrived from Longmont." She handed him a letter, and he quickly unfolded it.

> *Lord Ransom,*
>
> *I mean no disrespect, but I've decided to go ahead and try and rescue the king. While you are a capable soldier and warrior, your skills of negotiation are untested for such an important mission. I bear you no resentment for deceiving me and hope you will return the favor. I've learned that the king is being kept at Schveriner castle in the middle of Schveriner Lake. It's the least I could do to at least help you on your journey. But if you would hearken to my advice, since you so freely dispense it yourself, I suggest you return to Kingfountain and do what you do best and counter Estian's invasion. Protect our people.*
>
> *Courteously,*
> *Damian Longmont,*
> *High Justiciar of Ceredigion*

"Did he say where he was going?" Cecily asked him.

Ransom nodded and ripped the paper to pieces, throwing them into the bin. "And either he was misled, or he's misleading us again. I think I'm going to wring his neck."

"I can contact the Espion here in Callait to see if anyone knows where he went," she suggested. "I need some time, though."

"I know where we're going," Ransom said. "We're riding for the Wartburg."

Her eyes widened with surprise and recognition.

"Did you know the king was there?" Ransom asked.

"No. The master of that castle has a reputation. His name is Lord Gotz. The Iron Hand."

"What do you know about him?"

"He lost his hand during the war with us many years ago. The iron one is prosthetic. He *hates* Ceredigion."

Ransom's heart sank at the news. He was still furious at Longmont for escaping. But that wouldn't stop him. He would try anyway. He had to.

⋈

I have not heard from Ransom since he arrived in Callait several days ago. I know he is deep inside Brugia right now—but where? I don't know enough about the Brugians, their language, or their customs. Are they an honorable people? They do not worship the Lady of the Fountain, although I understand they have permitted a few sanctuaries to exist for foreigners. Since their king died, they have experienced great turmoil within, with different factions vying for control. Unlike Occitania and Ceredigion, there is no hereditary right to rule. The strongest warlords prevail, but few are strong enough to pass power down to the next generation.

Sir Dawson stayed in Glosstyr for a day and then rode to Beestone castle. After the reinforcements arrived, the Occitanians besieging the city lost heart. They continue to launch against the walls but not with the same intensity. Sir Dawson will test the defenses of Josselin next to see if the castle is still heavily guarded.

Jon-Landon has declared that his brother is dead, and he is the rightful king. Duke Ashel supports him. Duke James is wavering, trying to hold off on making a decision. If Benedict returns, those who rally to Jon-Landon will be punished. If he does not, then those who didn't support Jon-Landon will be considered traitors. There are many in Kingfountain who want the stability of a king—one who's here—and they do not know Benedict lives. If they rise up in revolt, then Emiloh will be forced to abandon the city. Everything teeters on a knife-point as we await news from my dear husband. Every day without a message adds to my worries. And every day the babe in my belly squirms more strongly. I think she's a girl. I don't know why. But how I want him to be home before she comes.

—*Claire de Murrow*
Glosstyr
Perilous days

CHAPTER
THIRTY-THREE

The Wartburg

It was a three-day ride to the Wartburg in the hinterlands of Brugia. Ransom was accompanied by two knights, Cecily, and a "servant" named Terric who was actually part of the Espion in Brugia. Cecily wore the gown of a noblewoman, something that had allowed them to continue the ruse Ransom was just a regular castle guard. Ransom pushed their horses hard, trying to overtake Longmont and his allies, but there was no sign of them on the road, and he realized his determination to catch up with them was exceeded by theirs to arrive first. Presuming, of course, Longmont had correctly learned where the king was being held.

Because Cecily and Terric could speak the language, they did the communicating along the journey. Even though Ransom couldn't follow what was being said, he'd detected a certain air of distrust toward outsiders. A small band of rogue knights had accosted Ransom's group once along the way, trying to demand payment to pass. He'd sensed their evil intention through his Fountain magic and was on his guard as they approached. When Cecily revealed the threat, he drew his bastard sword and pressed forward to attack. The knights had backed off and departed in haste. The language of violence was recognized everywhere.

The Wartburg was built on a promontory overlooking the village of Eisen. They reached the village in late afternoon on the third day, and after resting their horses a bit and eating some Brugian food—breaded slices of meat bedecked with herbs and boiled in fat, which Ransom particularly liked—they mounted again and began the ride up the mountainside to the castle high above town.

The entire area was heavily wooded, which created ample opportunities for ambush, so Ransom kept his instincts sharp for any traps. A steep trail wound its way up the side of the mountain, making their horses grunt with the strain. As they climbed higher, the trees became sparser, giving them a better view of the fortress—a long, narrow structure that occupied the bulk of the promontory. Strong battlements rose above the sparse tree line. The central square tower had a spiked roof and a banner waving from it, but from the height it was impossible to see the design of the standard.

Judging by the height and the windows, the main structure had at least three levels. Smoke drifted lazily from the many chimneys on the eastern side. From what Ransom could see, the castle looked about half the size of Kingfountain. As they reached the top of the promontory, a great cleft in the mountainside loomed in front of them, spanned by a drawbridge. Breaching such a castle by force would be a daunting task. The rock cleft, the steepness of the road, and the dense woods were all natural protections that would inhibit invaders. It was more of a prison than a fortress, and if Benedict were there—as he expected—there would be no easy way to free him without a ransom.

A squad of four knights guarded the drawbridge with pikes. They each wore hauberks, blue tunics, and carried shields. Their helmets were vastly different in design from what Ransom remembered from his previous encounters with Brugian soldiers. Shaped like bells, they fanned out in a full circle from the top of the head. Their chainmail didn't just cover the neck but also the chin and the bottom half of the face.

One of the men challenged them in Ceredigion, his Brugian accent sharp.

"Welcome, host! Welcome to the Vartburg. Whom do ye seek?"

Cecily, playing the role of the noblewoman, said, "We seek audience with Lord Gotz."

The knight gave her a probing look. "The eventide is nigh. Have you come to barter for your king?"

"Yes," Cecily said.

The knight gave her a cunning smile. "Then enter. The great lord of the Vartburg is in the hall vith his guests. You are welcome to bring your veapons, but do not use them. Drawing a blade in the Vartburg is punishable by death."

Cecily nodded and gestured for her companions to follow her. As they rode past, the knights stared at them with savage eyes. Ransom felt their animosity, their desire to provoke a conflict, but he kept his eyes fixed on Cecily's horse as they crossed the massive drawbridge.

Beyond it lay an extensive gatehouse. It was wide enough to rally defenders to protect the drawbridge, although only a fool would consider making such a crossing. Any attempt to arrange a makeshift bridge would be met with a hailstorm of arrows. Gotz could defend such a castle with only fifty men.

After passing a stone arch, they rode through a long courtyard that became wider the farther they went. Now that they were closer to the castle, he could see a few buildings that had previously been concealed due to the height of the rampart walls. Another gate with a portcullis lay at the end of the courtyard. When they reached it, they were greeted by grooms who cared for their weary horses.

Ransom felt a pulse of warning in his heart as he dismounted. He glanced around, anticipating an ambush, but there were only a few knights milling about. Joining the others, he continued through the portcullis, which opened to another massive courtyard. A single cottage sat to his right, servants passing in and out of it, and the palace loomed to his left. A huge well lay partway across the wide-open space, and servants were drawing water from the cistern waters below. The huge square tower was impressive, but Ransom's attention was drawn to another tower, a shorter one, off by itself at the farthest point of the building. Covered walkways led to it, and he felt a whisper from the Fountain confirming that Benedict was being kept there. He stared at the small windows, at the thick stone walls. Gripping the pommel of his sword, he fought the urge to charge the structure and rescue Benedict himself. He knew in his heart that such an attempt would be folly.

A messenger approached them after the grooms had taken their horses. The man spoke to Cecily in Brugian at first and then, once he realized where they were from, he changed his language.

"Velcome, honored guests. Follow me, please."

He led them toward the castle, and as they approached the looming structure, Ransom felt a throb of Fountain magic coming from within. It was the presence of another who had Fountain magic . . . but it wasn't Alix. This magic had an unnatural element to it—like a stagnant pond instead of a cool rush of water. It felt wrong, twisted, and it made him instantly uneasy at what they would find within the keep.

They were escorted up a twisting set of stairs within a tower well until they reached a higher level, whereupon they were brought through several rooms, each one richly furnished. The interior passageways were narrow and short and very dark, and Ransom had to duck to change rooms on occasion. His feelings of dread intensified the deeper they went. In his mind, he cast a silent plea to the Fountain for help.

When they reached the main hall, the sense of splendor rivaled anything Ransom had seen in Kingfountain or Pree. The space boasted a vaulted ceiling, and the walls were covered in rich wainscoting stained a rich chestnut. Four chandeliers hung from elaborate chains, bathing the hall in warm light. There were windows on the left side, which he'd seen on the ride up, but inside, they were framed with stone embossed with gold. The floor was also polished wood but fixed in an elaborate herringbone pattern, the strips of wood alternating in color and stain. Padded benches framed the area to his right, with wooden chairs filling in the open space. There were easily a hundred people crowded into the room, the guests representing a variety of stations and kingdoms. The feeling of Fountain magic was coming from the other end of the hall. He looked for Longmont but didn't see him.

An elaborate golden facade decorated the far end of the hall, with a few shields bedecked with the crest of a gauntleted fist arranged amidst a swooping design. The metal reflected light from the four chandeliers, giving the impression the facade was on fire. Two rows of chairs, perpendicular to the rest, stretched across that side of the room. The guests who sat there were more expensively appointed than the rest.

The servant led them down a gap between the benches and the chairs on the right side of the hall and brought them closer. A velvet curtain hung between a triple archway in the facade and there, at the base, sat a man who was undoubtedly the master of the castle.

Gotz was an older man with thinning hair streaked with gray and a bushy goatee covering his mouth. Even though he was in the middle of his own castle, he wore armor. Ransom wondered whether he was always on his guard. The iron hand was fixed to his arm like a gauntlet, the fingers folded into a fist except for the extended index finger. As they drew nearer, Ransom noticed the man's bloodshot blue eyes, one of them milkier than the other. Scars mottled his face—burn marks by the look of them. He ignored the commotion of the hall, his gaze fixed on them as they approached.

But the sense of power didn't come from him. No, the power emanated from one of the noble ladies who sat near him. Ransom was taken aback by her appearance. She wore a mask of polished silver, with openings only for the eyes and nostrils and a thin slit for the mouth. It was fashioned into a nose and lips and was so reflective it, too, seemed to burn. Even her hair was concealed beneath a hood fashioned of gold that was sculpted to look like hair. A golden crown had been designed into it. He felt power radiating from the woman—at least, he assumed it was a woman beneath the garb.

The lady leaned in and said something to Gotz as they were brought to stand in front of them, but the noise obscured her words.

Ransom felt his nerves twinge with unease. He looked at the masked face of the lady, trying to understand the source of her power. Her whole countenance was otherworldly and strange.

"Velcome to the Vartburg," said Gotz in a ragged voice. He looked at each of them in turn before his gaze came to rest on Ransom. "Velcome, Duke of Ceredigion. You come garbed as a common knight. But you are not common. No, our ancient foes send their best varrior. How fitting."

Cecily seemed taken aback by how quickly they'd been discovered. She looked at Ransom for what to do next.

Ransom stepped forward. "Greetings, Lord Gotz. I've come to bargain—"

The iron fist rose. "I know vhy you've come, Lord Ransom. You seek Benedict the Unfortunate. He is here."

Ransom glanced at those seated closest to the duke. He recognized Estian's steward, whom he'd met before, and a Genevese man, identifiable by his vest and jerkin. Was he here to save Benedict or murder him, freeing Portia to marry again?

"May I see him?" he asked through the tightness in his throat, which suddenly felt as dry as the sand in the oasis.

"Of course!" said Gotz. "But I am doubtful you can match the highest price offered." With his normal hand, he tapped on a button on the knuckle of the iron one, and the fist sprung open, the fingers splayed wide. The contraption was startling. The iron hand gestured to the lady with the silver mask. "Von hundred fifty thousand livres. Bid by a combination from the East Kingdoms. I vould be a fool to refuse such a generous offer." He glowered at Ransom. "And I am no fool."

A hundred and fifty thousand livres? The East Kingdoms would pay that amount for revenge against Benedict? The cost was so overpowering that Ransom felt his knees weaken. Ceredigion couldn't afford to match it, let alone surpass it.

A hundred and fifty thousand. The sum lingered in the air, an impossible amount. Ransom glanced at the woman in the silver mask. No emotion could be seen in that carefully crafted face, but he felt a feeling of gloating and revenge that was not his own. Another mystery. If it was from the masked lady, he didn't understand why he'd sensed it.

"I may see him, then?" Ransom said after wrenching his gaze from the strange mask.

"I am a man of my vord," said Gotz. "I do not suffer fools, Lord Ransom. If you attempt to rescue him, I vill fix your head to a spike on the tallest tower. Make no mistake. I mean to have my prize."

"May we have lodging?" Ransom continued.

Gotz shrugged. "Of course." He looked to his steward. "Take him there. Only him."

Once they left the dazzling hall, Ransom's heart began to quiet. Another servant took Cecily and the others in another direction, leaving him alone with the steward.

"Is he cared for?" Ransom asked.

"Lord Gotz is generous to his noble prisoners," answered the steward in an offended tone.

They went through a series of walkways and passages, enough to thoroughly confuse Ransom. But he recognized the covered walkway where they finished their journey—it was the very one he'd noticed from the courtyard below. When they reached the walled fortress, which was guarded by several men, one of them unlocked the iron door. The room had a stone floor and sparse furnishings—a small cot, a writing desk, and a single chair—and the only warmth came from a small brazier.

A man sat huddled in the chair with a blanket over his shoulders, back facing them, warming his hands at the brazier.

Benedict looked forsaken and haggard and utterly depressed. His beard was long and matted. So was his hair. The royal tunic had holes in it, and from the condition of his boots, they likely did too.

"Leave the food on the desk," Benedict said dispassionately, gazing at the brazier.

Ransom knew how it felt to be a prisoner. And his heart softened with compassion for the king. Benedict's mother had been trapped in a tower, but at least her accommodations had been comfortable.

"I'm here, my lord," Ransom said, his voice suddenly thick.

The chafing hands stopped their movement. Benedict turned his head slightly until he saw Ransom filling the doorway.

A look of hope and misery wrestled in his expression. "You've come! Blessed Lady, you came! Ransom!"

Then the king surged from the chair and rushed forward to clutch him in a fierce embrace.

Word just arrived that the city of Kingfountain has pronounced Jon-Landon as the rightful king of Ceredigion. He will be welcomed into the city, but the palace remains loyal to Benedict. A confrontation between Emiloh and her son is coming. We've heard Jon-Landon is in East Stowe with Duke Ashel, but it's said they will come forward to claim their prize soon. No word from Ransom on whether he has found Benedict, but such news would certainly shift events.

The force I sent to Josselin was attacked by Estian's men. There was a skirmish between the knights, and we lost several good men in the conflict. Dearley led the knights back to Glosstyr. He was disappointed they hadn't routed the Occitanian knights, but he bloodied his sword. Sir Dawson is returning from Beestone in case they bring the attack here next.

I miss my sons. I yearn to be back at Legault. Not much time remains before winter. I'm worried. I must admit it. All we've worked for could fall if Ransom fails. I plead with the Aos Sí to watch over him and my children. But perhaps they *cannot hear my pleas because I have been away from the Fair Isle for too long.*

—*Claire de Murrow*
Glosstyr
(on the death of certain knights)

CHAPTER
THIRTY-FOUR

The Silver Lady

Benedict withdrew from the embrace, his face awash with emotion, but the hope seemed more predominant now.

"How is it that you are even here?" Benedict asked in astonishment. "I should not question what I see before my eyes, but I must. You are here, in the flesh."

Ransom gripped Benedict's shoulder. "Has Longmont arrived?"

"Damian? Is he coming? I've heard nothing—*nothing!*—from home since I was brought here. What a mess I've made of things." He shook his head and began to pace and prowl like the lion on the badge Ransom wore. His brief burst of joy was muted by thick despair. "I've demanded Gotz send word to Kingfountain to negotiate for my release, but he's a strange fellow. What is the state of things, Ransom? I'm nearly delirious with happiness right now and can bear some bad news."

"The situation at home is dire, my lord," Ransom said without pretense. "Estian has invaded. Your brother tries to claim the throne."

"Of course." He sighed, shaking his head. "My father's final curse still rings in my ears. Like a fool, I fell under Estian's sway as my brother did before me. And now Jon-Landon, no doubt, thinks to use Estian to his own advantage as well. He'll be tricked just as we were."

"You were not deceived so much as influenced by a stronger power," Ransom said, speaking of Lady Alix. "You could have left the oasis when Estian did."

"True. I could have. But I believed in our mission, not just to secure trade routes but to protect our people. It was a calamity from the start, but I don't begrudge going there. I curse my own folly in how I was caught." Benedict squeezed his hands into fists and shook them. Then he walked to the wall and planted a fist on the barren stone.

"Were you betrayed by one of your men?" Ransom asked with concern.

"No, I betrayed myself," Benedict said. "I traveled in disguise as a common knight. But I forgot to remove my royal ring before we reached Brugia. A serving lass saw it and told the innkeeper, who sent for the guard. We were rounded up before we had a chance to draw our swords."

Ransom shook his head. "I'm sorry, my lord. Sometimes it is the small details that can save or sink us."

"Don't I know it. I'm grateful you are here, Ransom, but I worry about what will happen in your absence. Estian's Wizr set will show him your piece is no longer on the board. Who else can better defend my realm from treachery?"

Ransom smiled. "He doesn't have it."

Benedict turned his head to Ransom, giving him a quizzical look. "What do you mean? Not even his privy council knows where he keeps it hidden."

"I went to Pree with one of my knights and retrieved it. His poisoner kept it in a place only another Fountain-blessed could reach. I was led there by the Fountain, although I lost my knight as a hostage."

The king's jaw dropped. "That was entirely reckless, Ransom, but who am I to condemn you for the very sin that landed me here?" He grinned and stroked his unkempt beard. "He is furious, I am sure. So we have the board?"

"Your mother, specifically. Jon-Landon was apprised of it—"

"To what purpose?" Benedict snarled.

Ransom held up his hands. "The pieces can only be used by one of the heirs on either side, or so it seems. I can't budge the pieces, although I can look at them and glean information from where they're positioned. That leaves you, your nephew, and your brother as the only ones who can influence the game directly on our side."

"Then why not use Drew? I would much rather trust Constance's loyalty than my brother's."

"That wasn't an option, Bennett. Estian abducted the boy shortly after he returned to Occitania. He is using the child to claim your throne at the moment and has given Brythonica independence of fealty from either side so long as the duchess remains neutral."

Benedict's cheeks flushed. He turned and slammed his fist into the wall, which made Ransom wince.

"I'm sorry. I said I could bear bad news. We've lost Brythonica. What of the Vexin? Please tell me my duchy is still loyal to me?"

Ransom sighed, and the king's eyebrows lifted.

"It gets worse and worse," the king muttered. "Go on. Say it."

"Your mother has been fighting to keep your kingdom intact, but DeVaux has formed an alliance with Jon-Landon. His daughter—"

"Isn't she but a child?"

Ransom paused. He saw the Argentine temper showing through. Of all the Elder King's sons, Benedict was the most similar to him in temperament. Only he was far less shrewd.

"I'm sorry," Benedict said. "Go on."

"Because we had the Wizr board, I knew where Jon-Landon went when he escaped confinement. Lord DeVaux had stopped at Averanche on the way back to the Vexin. He'd met with the prince in secret, and I found the two young people walking hand in hand by the surf."

"He's trying to steal the Vexin from me as well," Benedict said, his voice throbbing with wrath. Ransom was too circumspect to remind him that he'd given control of the duchy back to his mother. Like Devon, he had trouble relinquishing power.

"DeVaux is trying to steal it," Ransom said. "And your kingdom, as well, through his daughter. I've never liked the man."

The king chuckled darkly. "No, I didn't imagine you would." He leaned back against the wall and thumped his skull against it. "I've thought of you, Ransom, while I've been in here. I was but a lad when you were captured by DeVaux and held for . . . for ransom, obviously. One that my mother willingly paid to free you, once she learned you were alive. I thought of your injuries, your shattered leg, and how you were forced to bandage it yourself, nearly bleeding to death in the process." He shook his head. "Your story has given me strength. It's helped me go on when my doubts threatened to unman me. Surely this confinement," he said, gesturing toward the room, "is not as harsh as what you endured for so many months. And yet . . ." He hung his head and fell silent.

Ransom hadn't expected such a confession. He saw the shadows of anguish in Benedict's soul. The confinement had impacted him deeply. It had given him a new depth of character.

A sense of deep conviction burned through Ransom's very soul: he had to free Benedict from this prison. The loyalty he felt to the king stoked the Fountain magic inside him to new heights.

Benedict turned and looked at the brazier. "I've realized I'm not as strong as I once thought. When I consider what my mother suffered, being confined to that tower for years, my courage falters. I'd rather throw myself off this mountain instead of enduring such a long confinement. I regret . . ." He paused, his voice thickening. Ransom watched his lips twitch as the emotions he felt for his mother consumed him. "I regret not doing more for her," he ended in a near whisper. "If my suffering is only a tithe compared to what she endured, I don't know how she bore it for so long."

Ransom agreed. Emiloh was a force to be reckoned with. So was Claire, who'd borne the captivity beside her. "She has an indomitable will, my lord. Her own suffering, in her youth, helped her endure it."

The king blinked and brushed away a tear. "You speak of King Lewis . . . what he did to her. You're right. I'd neglected to reflect on that aspect. Her character was forged in a hot furnace."

"You are made of the same stock," Ransom said reassuringly.

Benedict let out a heavy sigh. "I hope so." He turned and gave Ransom a fierce look. "Get me out of here. Whatever the cost. How much is Gotz asking for now?"

Ransom looked abashed. "Someone has come from the East Kingdoms. A woman with a silver mask."

The king blanched. "So it is not just Estian who is bidding for me? I know many from that court shield their faces. It is said their beauty drives men mad, but those are just rumors . . . boasts."

"The lady has offered to pay a hundred and fifty thousand livres for you."

For a moment, the king was stunned silent. "You mean fifty thousand?"

"No. I'm afraid I meant what I said."

"I am . . . astonished," Benedict said. "Who but someone from the East Kingdoms could afford to pay such a ransom? Surely not even Estian would match it, and he's the wealthiest of us all."

"Would not your father-in-law contribute?"

Benedict's shoulders slumped. "Possibly? Lady Portia and I . . . it has not been easy for either of us. We didn't even meet before the wedding. It was a strategic match, and I trusted my mother's instincts. But there is no feeling between us." He shook his head in disappointment. "Did she even return to Kingfountain?" When Ransom shook his head no, the king nodded glumly. "I'm not surprised. The doge would contribute, I think, but not to such a ghastly sum." Benedict began stroking his beard again and leaned back against the stone wall. "It's a strange thing, Ransom. They have such beautiful things over there—spices, gemstones, and cloth dyed in such a way the colors don't bleed or fade. Everyone wants something they produce. But they only want our gold and our silver. I've heard the palaces in some of the larger cities are so inlaid with gold they shine like the sun. They melt down our gold and silver into jewelry that they wear. Necklaces, bracelets, crowns, anklets, earrings, navel rings—I jest not. Yes, they can afford a hundred and fifty thousand livres."

"So if I attempt to offer more, they can exceed it."

"Yes," Benedict said blackly.

"Then I need to offer something other than golden livres. I need to make Gotz see that having you as a friend is worth more than money."

Benedict looked at Ransom thoughtfully. "He's abrupt and ill-tempered but not unreasonable."

"He wants to be king," Ransom said. "I think he intends to use the ransom to pay for it."

"It would be a start," Benedict said. Then he straightened. "I trust you, Ransom Barton. See if you can entice him to agree to a lesser amount, one that we can afford, and promise an alliance that would truly be in his interest."

"I shall do my best, my lord."

Benedict approached and embraced him again. "I'm counting on you."

Ж

At the conclusion of his visit with the king, Ransom was escorted to the room that had been arranged for him and his party. It was not a large room, given the size of the castle, but the window overlooked the town of Eisen far below.

Cecily and Terric asked about his visit to the king, and he quickly related a few details. He'd not been there for long before a knock sounded at the door. Cecily answered it and then stepped aside to allow the visitor to enter.

The stranger wore a colorful outfit that reminded Ransom of the oasis. He had jeweled earrings, expensive necklaces, and a shaved head.

"My lady of Chandigarl wishes to meet you, honorable knight of Kingfountain," said the man is a resonant voice that carried a slight accent. "Tales of your prowess have traveled great distances."

Cecily gave Ransom a hopeful look.

"I will go," he said. He felt a flash of worry in his gut.

He left the others behind and followed the man down the hall to a door. It opened and revealed a stairwell leading up to one of the towers of the fortress. Obviously, the lady was entitled to greater status. As he climbed the stairs, he felt the stirrings of Fountain magic. Worry welled in the pit of his stomach. Was the woman Fountain-blessed? Or had she recovered one of the lost relics of the Deep Fathoms?

After a quick climb, they reached the top of the stairs. Two servants stood outside the door, each with a curved saber fixed to his belt. The one guiding Ransom opened the door and let him in.

He was struck by the spicy perfume that hung in the air. Standing at the far side of the room was the woman in the mask of silver and gold.

"*Iss kamare se chale jao,*" said the woman with a flick of her fingers.

The servant dropped to his knees and stretched out flat on the floor before rising and leaving the room. Alone in the masked woman's presence, Ransom sensed the depth and range of the power she wielded. It was so immense his own magic trembled in its presence.

"I do not speak your language," Ransom said.

"I speak yours," she answered curtly. Her Occitanian accent caught him off guard. He could see her eyes through the mask, but the other things that gave a person away—her mouth, her nose, the crease between her brows—were all hidden. It put him at a decided disadvantage.

"Why did you summon me?" he asked her.

She stared at him, the mask showing nothing. He felt a foreign surge of emotions again, as he had earlier, and noticed her eyes had begun to flash silver behind the mask. A twisting sensation gripped his stomach. He realized she was *making* him feel uncomfortable.

"Who are you?" he asked, bothered by the intrusion into his feelings. Something about it felt familiar. He didn't understand why, but he felt he'd been in this situation before. He was about to turn and head for the door when she reached up and lifted the mask from her face.

It was Noemie Vertus, Estian the Black's sister.

Ⅺ

Once again, I have a deep foreboding about Ransom. Not that he's unfaithful but that he is in grave danger. I despise the voice that whispers worries into my ear in the dark, moonless night. Ransom is so far away from me. I hold my swollen belly and fear my husband will not come home, that the child in my womb will not know its father. These troubling thoughts often come in the still of night, when the work of the day cannot distract me from them. The voice whispers that it all will end badly, that the Brugians are capricious and so is fate. That Ransom may be a warrior like no other, but he is still just a man.

Jon-Landon has taken the city of Kingfountain. There is to be a marriage between him and DeVaux's daughter at the sanctuary of Our Lady. Some say he will turn the wedding into a coronation. The hollow crown is locked in a vault in the palace. Yet he just may have another forged in its stead. Winter is coming. This is the chance he's been waiting for.

Léa DeVaux is so young. Does she realize how capricious Jon-Landon is?

—Claire de Murrow
Glosstyr
(sleepless, anxious, restless)

CHAPTER
THIRTY-FIVE

A Fact of Loyalty

ave you missed me, Ransom?" Noemie asked. Her tone lacked any intonation, and he couldn't tell if she was trying to be playful or vengeful. A storm of memories broke over him, causing him to relive some of the darkest hours of his life. This was the woman he'd been accused of seducing, when in truth she was the one who'd attempted—and failed—to seduce *him*. More than once.

He ignored her question. "There were rumors you'd gone to the East Kingdoms," he said warily, shaking his head.

Another surge of feeling struck his chest—her feelings, he realized, or ones she was compelling him to experience—accompanied by a rush of tainted Fountain magic. Dark thoughts began to swirl in his mind, unbidden.

"Yes, if I couldn't be Queen of Ceredigion, I decided I'd rule elsewhere. The people in the East Kingdoms are less . . . sanctimonious. Power is what they crave. And they brook no rivals. It is an ancient land." Her eyes continued to glow silver, which gave her an otherworldly aspect that made him inwardly cringe. This was magic he did not understand and felt powerless against.

"Were you behind this war?" he asked.

A knowing smile came to her beautiful mouth. "I will answer all your questions, Ransom, but not now. You will come to me at midnight, as you refused to do before. If you want best to serve your king, you will do exactly as I say."

She had demanded this of him before, and in the past, he'd refused. This time, his knees felt weak, and he nearly gasped as another spasm of emotion tore through him. His will was bending.

The look on Noemie's face was one of triumph. She knew the sway she held over him, and she gloated in it. "Midnight, Ransom. You will come at midnight."

He tried to deny her, to say the words of refusal he knew he should utter. But then he heard a whisper in his mind. It was so soft, it couldn't have been louder than a breath.

Go at midnight.

He didn't understand what was being asked of him, but the gentle guidance came from a different source from the hurricane of emotions emanating from Noemie.

The voice had spoken to him.

"I will," he heard himself say, and then he felt tears prick his eyes. Tears of shame.

With a satisfied toss of her head, she dismissed him.

He staggered down the stairwell before he came to his senses again, sweat dripping down his ribs and trickling down his cheeks. Guilt and terror battled inside his chest. Was he utterly mad? What if the voice he'd heard—the one that had bid him go to her—had been hers after all?

Returning to see her in the middle of the night would go against every principle he'd sworn to uphold when he became a knight. He almost turned around and marched back up the stairs, but he feared the power she wielded against his emotions. He paused to rest on the stairwell, his feelings galloping like a runaway destrier without any reins or bridle.

When he returned to his room, he walked straight past the others, poured some water in the basin, and splashed his face with it. They could clearly sense his agitation and held silent until he had mastered himself enough to speak. Grabbing a towel, he wiped his face and then his neck.

"I take it the meeting didn't go well," Cecily said.

He turned and leaned back against the table, resting his hands against the flat wood top. The basin quivered, the water inside trembling.

"The emissary from the East Kingdoms is Noemie Vertus," he said flatly.

Cecily's eyebrows rose. "The king's sister?"

The other Espion, Terric, looked confused, but one of the knights whistled softly and shook his head.

Ransom grabbed the towel and then flung it onto the floor. "We cannot outbid them," he said, despairing. "Even with Genevar's help, were they willing to give it."

"Is that what she told you?" Cecily asked.

"No," he said. "But it's implied. Leave me alone for a while. I need to think." He sat on the edge of the bed, which was short and cramped compared to his own at Glosstyr.

What would he do to save his king? Anguish spread through him. He shuddered to think on it.

From the corner of his eye, he watched the knights leave, followed by Terric, but Cecily waited at the door. When the others were gone, she came back and knelt by the edge of the bed.

"Tell me," she said.

"I'd rather not," he muttered. But he was grateful for the kind look she gave him.

"You know of her. I've heard stories, Lord Ransom. But I've also heard that they aren't true. And for all the people who still speak of your temporary disgrace, there are more who admire you for the loyalty you showed Devon the Younger even after he shamed and dismissed you."

Ransom remembered watching Devon die at Beestone castle. His suffering had been terrible to behold. Noemie hadn't been there to experience it—she'd left him after seducing another knight in his mesnie. Sir Robert Tregoss, who'd met his fate in a meadow in Brythonica.

Ransom touched his hand, and the invisible ring he wore on his finger. He thought on Constance and the secret duty he held to the lady. Had she known about Noemie's role in the ransom auction? There had been no hint of that, only a warning that there would be other interested parties.

Yes, he decided. She'd known . . . and she'd insisted Ransom would win the negotiation. It wouldn't be easy, she'd said, but he would win. What did it mean?

He gazed at Cecily's face. "I must see her again," he said softly. "She told me to return at midnight."

"I would advise against it," Cecily said, her look worried. "It's most likely a trap to get you out of the way."

"I know," Ransom said with a chuckle. "Yet I must go. The Fountain commanded me."

"Are you sure?" Cecily asked, her voice dripping with doubt.

Although he'd questioned it after leaving her room, overcome by the horror of what he'd agreed to, he couldn't deny what he knew in his heart. "I know the difference," he said. "I don't want to do it. But I must."

"Is there anything I can do to help you?" she asked.

He shook his head. "I need some time to think."

Cecily rose, touched him lightly on the shoulder—a gesture of comfort—and departed from the room, leaving Ransom alone with his demons.

X

A banquet was held in the great hall. The food was plentiful, but the noise and clatter of dishes grated on Ransom's fraying nerves. Noemie sat there in her silver mask, her plate untouched. Gotz speared strips of meat with a two-tined fork and ate it voraciously, grease dripping into his graying beard. He glared at his guests—or at least that was how Ransom interpreted the look.

Following the meal, minstrels came to entertain the guests with music and small feats of acrobatics. Applause rocked through the overcrowded room. Ransom kept glancing at Noemie, but she was impassive behind that mask. Still, he felt that strange power radiating from her, sickening him to his core. It made him question, again, the directive to go to her. Then he thought of Benedict, alone in his prison, probably hearing the sound of the laughter and merriment from the open windows. He needed to save him.

The feast ended after dark when Gotz burped loudly, rose from his chair, and left the hall. Servants immediately began to clear up the dishes and half-eaten food. Ransom rose from his chair to leave, only for an Occitanian to bump into him. The man offered a mocking apology, and Ransom gritted his teeth to keep from punching the man in the jaw.

The stranglehold on his emotions began to lessen, and he looked up to see Noemie leaving the hall. She paused at the doorway, turning back, the silver mask flashing in the torchlight, and looked straight at him. A throb of desire chafed inside of him. It was completely unbidden, and it made him feel awful. He looked away, and then she was gone through the doorway.

Cecily approached him through the throng. "I have some news. Can we talk in one of the alcoves, where we won't be overheard?"

He nodded in agreement. The other guests had started filing out, but they seemed in no hurry to leave. When Ransom and Cecily reached a small alcove, he gave her a look that bid her speak.

"I overheard an Occitanian knight during dinner," she said. "This afternoon the emissary ordered one of them to return to Pree and tell Estian you're here. He was joking that they'd carve up Ceredigion like a meat pie."

"That's to be expected," Ransom said with a snort.

She shook her head. "The other knight butted him with his arm. He had a concerned look. He said that they'd best be careful to leave an heir. Or everyone in Ceredigion would drown."

Ransom creased his eyebrows.

"I assume he was referring to the old legends of King Andrew. But he seemed in earnest. He thought it could really happen."

It matched the stories Constance and Claire had told him. "After Benedict, there are two heirs left. Jon-Landon and the Duchess of Brythonica's son, Andrew. The younger is held hostage in Pree."

Cecily looked confused. "I don't understand. Is it true? If Benedict and his brother die, does the fate of our realm hang on the life of a child?"

When she put it that way, it made his heart clench with dread. Alix could easily kill both Argentine brothers. Which would put the fate of the kingdom on Drew's shoulders. Drew, who was in Estian's custody. Maybe the plan was not merely to defeat Ceredigion but to destroy it.

A prickle of warning went down his back. There was more at stake than just Benedict's life. Countless lives were at stake. Claire's life was at stake, presuming she'd stayed in Glosstyr.

Come to me at midnight. I will tell you all.

That was the offer Noemie had made before.

"I thought those were only legends," Cecily said, her face pinched with concern.

Ransom shook his head. "They aren't. That's all I can say. But that is why we must keep Benedict safe. This isn't just about him."

Something shifted on Cecily's face, determination overtaking her confusion, and he knew she believed him. "Do what you must, Lord Ransom."

He wasn't sure what the Fountain expected of him. But he trusted the Fountain, as Constance had bid him, and he was willing to do whatever it took. After the bulk of the guests departed, Ransom bid Cecily good night and went down the stairs to the inner courtyard to be alone and watch the stars until midnight. He could see candles burning in the windows of the castle as he paced in the center of the courtyard near the huge cistern opening he'd noticed on the way to the palace. There were guards stationed on the ramparts on the castle heights, but it soon became so dark they couldn't see him. One by one the candles began to go out.

The mouth of the cistern was wide—it would probably take thirty men to encircle it—and a set of stairs led up to it from either side of the low stone wall forming the lip. He walked in a circuit around it, repeatedly going up and down the steps. For a castle on a hill, having a cistern was imperative, especially during a siege. Reaching into his pocket, he withdrew a coin. There was no moon yet, so the metal looked dull in his hand. The cistern waters were dark and gloomy.

Ransom bowed his head and tossed the coin into the waters. It landed with a small splash. He turned and sat down, his back against the upper wall of the cistern, and listened to the breeze and the sound of the guards talking to each other in Brugian. He imagined his coin had sunk until it settled on the bottom of the cistern floor. How long would it stay there? Would it ever be found? Would tarnish eventually dissolve it? How long would that unspoken prayer last?

He sat like that for a long time, waiting in the quiet of the courtyard, one of the shadows, one with the dark. He could hear the lapping of the water far below, and it brought him a modicum of peace.

As time sped by and he watched the swirl of stars shift and change position, he knew it was nearly midnight. Ransom was about to rise, but then he stopped and stayed on his knees. He remembered how Constance had shown him another way to pray to the Fountain. What he needed was help and wisdom. And, more importantly, the determination to do whatever was asked of him, even if it was something he loathed.

Bowing his head, he spoke within his heart.

I am here. I have done what I was asked to do. Give me strength to do this task. To do the will of the Fountain.

He remembered how Constance, suffering from the agony of missing her child, had prayed for him. The memory made him tremble with emotion.

Bless the Duchess of Brythonica. Bless her in her grief. Bless my wife, Claire. Bless our children, Willem and Devon. Bless the child who has not yet been born.

As he thought about all the people who held his loyalty, his heart swelled, and he felt the magic of the Fountain seep inside him, making him stronger, more determined.

Bless Bennett in his prison. Bless Emiloh with wisdom and understanding.

The power grew stronger. He could feel his stores of Fountain magic increasing, as if the cistern inside his chest were growing larger. He remembered when he'd seen the shade of Gervase in Kingfountain. He pressed his hand to the edge of the cistern wall. It seemed as if he heard a whisper.

Go, my boy. All is well.

Gripping the edge of the wall, he rose to his feet, full of new power and strength. He walked across the courtyard, his tread soft. When he reached the doorway, he opened it and started up the stairs until he reached the second level. Then he went to the door leading to Noemie's tower and opened it. It was unlocked.

He climbed the steps in the dark shaft, feeling the uncomfortable press of her power, but he was stronger now. Even though the shaft was dark, he felt light pulsing inside of him, through him.

When he reached her door, he saw dim light emanating from beneath it. Candlelight. He opened the door and stepped inside.

Noemie wore a pale white chemise. The mask was gone, the golden headdress as well. The first buttons of the chemise were undone, revealing a golden necklace and some ink stains on her breastbone, forming a design of some kind. He looked up into her glowing silver eyes.

"I knew you'd come," she said with a victorious smile. "You are mine now, heart and soul. Give yourself to me, Ransom. You know that you want to. It is the only way you can save your king."

He sensed the lie as it passed her beautiful mouth. She was exultant, relishing her power. Understanding flooded him—her power came from the curious medallion she wore around her neck.

Feelings battered him like howling winds attempting to rip down a sturdy oak. He felt his roots straining against the savage torrent. There had ever existed a darkness in his soul. His proclivity for violence had always frightened him, which was why he'd invariably sought to put his talents to good use rather than selfish purposes. But that inner darkness—the thrill of battle and plunder and war—swelled inside him now, making him stare at her with hunger.

"Come, Ransom," she breathed. "Come and take me. You've always wanted it."

Take the medallion.

The whisper cut through the storm, sharp as a blade.

Before his determination could melt in the heat of desire, he closed the gap between them. Her breath came in heady gasps as she reached for him.

His fingers grazed her skin as he felt for the edges of the chain. Then he grasped the medallion between his fingers and jerked hard. The golden strand snapped effortlessly.

The silver in her eyes vanished, and the calamitous feelings rushed from the room so violently the silk curtains began to flail. He held the source of the magic in his hand, a howling windstorm of power, while the broken chain dangled from his clenched fist. The presence of magic vanished, leaving both of them suddenly gasping.

"What have you done!" Noemie accused.

Holding it tightly, he turned and walked away.

"Come back here! I order you to come back here!" she began to shriek. "Give it to me!"

He reached for the door handle and twisted it, looking back at her. A sudden insight took hold of him, driving out any remaining influence of the medallion. "You were never going to pay for Benedict's release. And neither was Estian. You just wanted to prevent anyone else from claiming him. It's over, Noemie. Go back to Chandigarl. You have no power here anymore." He squeezed the medallion until its edges hurt his hand.

"Give it to me!" she pleaded desperately.

He saw the truth in her face. She had tried seducing him to the dark side of the Wizr board before. To shift his allegiance and make him one of Estian's pieces. Her intent had been the same this time, and she'd had new tools to help her succeed. But he knew about the medallions now. He would not fall prey to one again.

She rushed at him, her eyes wild with determination, but he slipped out the door and wrenched the handle with all his strength. It came off, and he left it on the floor. He heard a rattling sound on the other side and then her small fists pounding against the wooden door, but she was incapable of breaking it down. Ransom hurried down the steps, gripping the medallion still, and went out to the courtyard again.

Standing at the edge of the cistern, he raised the medallion to his lips as if it were a coin meant for an offering. In the darkness, he dropped it into the waters, listening to the little plunk it made when it entered the pool.

As if in answer, the moon rose above the wall of the castle, its silver light blinding him. He thought of Claire, back in Glosstyr, and wondered if she was awake too, watching the same moonrise. He hoped so.

Gratitude and joy filled him until he felt almost giddy. And then, as he stood by the cistern, he realized someone else was awake that night. He could almost feel Constance's eyes on him through the seering stones.

And he could see her smiling in satisfaction that he'd faced his challenge and won.

✕

Sir Dawson's force was attacked by surprise. It was a bloody conflict with many lost on each side. But Sir Dawson won the day and returned to Glosstyr with eleven hostages from the Occitanian ranks. It was a much-needed victory.

Duke Ashel has arrayed his knights on the bridge spanning the waterfall. The wedding will happen this week, and then Jon-Landon will, no doubt, try to seize the castle. The eejit is taking a great risk. If Benedict returns, he would be guilty of treason. Word from the North is Lord James is holding out for as long as he can, but he will go where the wind blows. Everything can turn one way or the other. Still no word from Brugia.

And yet, I feel hopeful that Ransom will succeed. Last night, I couldn't sleep, but when the moon rose, I felt confidence fill me. If anyone can right this ship, it is my Ransom. A storm is coming. Let it come.

—Claire de Murrow
Glosstyr
(determined)

✕

CHAPTER THIRTY-SIX

The King's Ransom

The following morning, Ransom was summoned to Lord Gotz's private chamber to share breakfast with him. When he arrived, the mottle-cheeked lord was chewing furiously on a meal of steak and glazed potatoes. The fork he used was attached to his iron hand. He glanced up when Ransom was announced but went on with his noisy meal.

Ransom was directed to a wooden chair opposite Lord Gotz, and a servant poured wine into his goblet and gestured to the spread of steaks, hams, eggs, the breaded meat dish he'd enjoyed before, and some melon with orange flesh. Gotz took a quick slurp from his goblet.

"Sit! Eat!" came the hasty command.

Ransom seated himself, stabbed some of the food, and placed it onto his own plate.

"Ah, you like the schnitzel," said Gotz after Ransom took a piece of the breaded meat. "You are Brugian at heart, I think."

It was strange being alone with the lord of the castle. Gone was the sense of dread he'd felt the previous day. So much of it had arisen from the medallion's power over him.

"Thank you for your hospitality," Ransom said.

"First eat. Then talk. Try the sauce on the schnitzel. Very good." He picked up his knife and gestured to a golden vessel.

Ransom complied and rather enjoyed the heavy meal. A large wolfhound sauntered up, and Gotz tossed it a bone from his steak and chortled as the hound began gnawing on it.

After a tirade of slurps, loud chewing, and clattering, Gotz finally stopped eating and leaned back in his chair. He pressed a button on the knuckle of his iron hand, and it released the fork, which dropped heavily to the table. Frowning, he arranged the gauntlet again, using another series of buttons to close it into a fist.

"That's remarkable," Ransom said after wiping his mouth on a napkin.

Gotz burped loudly. "Genevese-made. Supple enough to lift porcelain and strong enough to break your jaw. I like it." He fidgeted in his chair a bit and then rested his hands on his belly. "Are you ready to make me an offer, Lord Ransom?"

"Yes. I come on the queen dowager's authority and my own as lord protector of Ceredigion."

Gotz sniffed and inclined his head. "It must be a good offer. Don't waste my time."

Ransom saw the cunning look in Gotz's eyes. He didn't believe Ransom could best the offers he'd been given, but he was willing to let him try.

"I wouldn't dream of it, my lord," Ransom said. "Nor would I seek to fool you as the previous emissaries have."

Gotz frowned. "Fool? You take me for a fool?"

"I do not, no. I think you will do what is in your own best interest."

"But you said I was a fool."

Ransom leaned forward. "The emissary from the East Kingdoms. The woman with the silver mask."

Gotz's gaze narrowed. "What of her? She has offered one hundred fifty thousand livres. Can you best it?"

"I don't need to," Ransom answered, meeting the gaze calmly. "She will not pay it."

"How do you know zis?" His accent, which he'd ably concealed, slipped a little.

"Because I know the woman behind the mask."

Gotz snorted and leered at him. "How could you possibly know her? She does not show her face to anyone, although I long to see if the rumors are true. You convinced her to remove it, eh?"

"She removed it herself," Ransom said. "She is Noemie Vertus, King Estian's younger sister."

Gotz blinked, the wrinkles on his face deepening. "That makes no sense. The lady has been bidding against Occitania."

"To what purpose, do you think?" Ransom asked mildly.

Realization came swiftly. Gotz thumped his iron hand on the table. "To deceive me?"

Ransom offered a slight shrug. "The riches of Chandigarl have blinded you, my lord. A hundred fifty thousand livres. Who would have believed even a king to be worth so much? Occitania's ambassador never expected to win. They drove the price as high as they could to ensure no one does. You won't get the money, Lord Gotz. They've both played you for a fool." He reached out and took a small sip from his goblet.

"Zis is an outrage! Alpert! Alpert!"

"Yes, my lord?" answered a tall, thin man, scurrying from his position by the wall.

"Tell the emissary from Chandigarl to come at once. I demand to speak with her."

"M-my lord?" asked the man.

Gotz began to curse at him in Brugian, and the man replied hesitantly and with confusion. The duke slammed the table harder with his iron hand, rattling the dishes.

"What is it?" Ransom asked after the servant strode away.

"She's already *left*," Gotz said, his cheek twitching with outrage. "I've ordered my servants to give chase. I will get my revenge!"

Ransom was grateful for his rage. It would make him more amenable to discussion. "What did Occitania offer?"

Gotz, still upset, jostled the table again. "One hundred twenty thousand."

"They will not pay it, Lord Gotz," Ransom said, shaking his head.

"Why not? Everyone knows Benedict and Estian are enemies now."

Ransom leaned forward. "Estian has a poisoner, trained in Pisan. Why pay a fortune if he could have his enemy killed for free? He offered you that sum as a ruse so you'd keep Benedict a prisoner. If you agreed to release him to us, Estian would send his poisoner to kill him. He pays nothing in the end, and you get the blame for killing a king. Threat and mate."

His words had rattled the Brugian. Ransom could tell the man was considering the situation carefully. He waited, letting him absorb the information, test it against what he already knew.

"You know this . . . poisoner?"

Ransom nodded.

"Who is she?"

"Lady Alix, Duchess of Bayree. The king's half sister."

Gotz let out a sharp breath. "The spawn of King Lewis?"

"Indeed. My lord, Estian has tried to deceive you. What better revenge can you accomplish than by letting us pay our king's ransom? I assure you, Estian will be punished."

Gotz sniffed and couldn't refrain from showing his annoyance. "No poisoner will kill him here. I've one of my own to keep her away. A hundred fifty thousand livres."

"My lord?" Ransom asked with confusion.

"Give me a hundred fifty thousand livres, and he's yours."

Ransom felt sweat begin to gather on his brow. "We do not have such a sum, your greatness. I could offer you—"

"One hundred . . . fifty . . . thousand!" Gotz said, banging his iron hand on the table three times to emphasize his words. His look of fury increased. The sum was fixed in his mind—even if it had been a scheme, he was determined to have it still. Ransom saw little purpose in bargaining with Gotz when he was so distraught.

"Thank you for hearing me out," Ransom said, pushing away from the table.

"Get me vhat I vant, Lord Ransom," Gotz said with a dangerous look. "Or your king vill never leave the Vartburg alive."

Ransom wandered the grounds of the castle, admiring the sturdy walls. He'd been to the king already to relay the news. The amount Gotz had demanded was well beyond what Emiloh had authorized him to offer. And yet, he suspected she would have agreed to any cost.

As he passed a small well in the tiny front courtyard, he heard the sounds of hoofbeats coming from beyond the gate. He walked over, expecting to find Gotz's guards with Noemie and her retainers, but it wasn't them. It was Damian Longmont and his Espion.

The guard at the gate questioned him.

"I am the high justiciar of Ceredigion, come from the court of Kingfountain to negotiate for the release of our king," Longmont said with great bravado.

"Vat is zis?" asked the guard. "Emissaries from Kingfountain are already here."

"They are imposters, surely," said Longmont. "I am the high justiciar. The king will vouch for my identity. Bring me to him at once."

Ransom continued his approach and then leaned against the gatehouse wall, folding his arms.

"You are in no position to give me orders!" exclaimed the guard with offense.

"Take me to him at once, or I will see that you are punished for defying me!"

Ransom coughed into his fist, drawing the notice of one of Longmont's Espion.

"It is you who vill be punished if you persist!" said the guard. "Avay vit you! Begone!"

The Espion nudged his horse closer to Longmont and addressed him in an undertone.

"I don't have time for this," Longmont said, trying to wave the man away. "I demand to see Lord Gitz!"

Ransom shuddered at the offense being caused. The Brugians were a proud people, and they would not take it well to hear their lord's name mispronounced.

"What is it?" Longmont thundered, railing on the Espion who was still trying to get his attention by pointing at Ransom.

Longmont followed his arm and then saw Ransom leaning against the gate. He went pale with dread.

Ransom approached. "These men are from Kingfountain," he told the guard placatingly. "They were sent to prepare our lodgings but clearly got lost in the woods on the way. Damian, if you say another word, I'll knock you off that horse."

Longmont's jaw slowly closed, and a flush of humiliation made his pale cheeks turn crimson. Some of the Espion snorted, earning daggered looks from Longmont as he dismounted.

Meekly, the king's ex-justiciar approached Ransom. "Have you seen him?" he asked in a subdued tone.

Ransom nodded. "I'll take you to him."

"Have you already negotiated, then? When did you arrive?"

"Yesterday," Ransom said. "We must have passed you without realizing it."

"Some bandits tried to attack us," Longmont said. "We had to ride for our lives into the woods and . . . were delayed. How did you know to come here, Lord Ransom?"

Putting his arm around the smaller man's shoulder, Ransom answered, "I knew he was here before we came. You'll be spending the winter here. It's best you start getting used to it."

"The winter?" Longmont stammered. "I don't understand."

"Gotz wants a hundred fifty thousand livres."

"By the Lady's legs, you can't be serious?"

Ransom gave him a reproving look. "I'm very serious. I'll explain as we walk. It will take us quite a while to gather that sum. Months, actually. I don't see Benedict being released until the spring. He needs a companion, someone to keep him company. You."

"Ah," Longmont said, nodding. "I understand. The castle seems formidable. I've heard Lord Gotz is a very wealthy man."

"He is."

"Then the accommodations cannot be too uncomfortable. Very well. I will help as I can. You know I have the king's greatest interest at heart."

"You've certainly proven *that*," Ransom said, trying not to sound too amused.

⚹

By the middle of the next day, Ransom had secured an official agreement with Lord Gotz for a ransom of one hundred fifty thousand livres. Gotz had sworn on his honor as a knight that he would accept no other offer, even if a greater one was offered. They had until the spring solstice to deliver the money to the Wartburg, upon which the king would be freed.

Ransom went to the king's prison to deliver the news. When he arrived, he found Longmont lying on a straw pallet on the floor, looking uncomfortable and miserable, although he quickly got up. The king, who had been pacing the whole time, rushed up to Ransom.

"Did he accept?"

"He did, my lord. There was a last-ditch effort from the Occitanian ambassador to counter the offer, but Gotz was persuaded that ours would actually be paid. I'm sorry you will spend the winter here, my lord. But they were the best terms I could arrange."

Benedict clapped Ransom on the back. "If my mother could endure so many years in captivity, then I can endure a Brugian winter. A hundred and fifty thousand. It'll take all winter to gather that much."

"I could help," Longmont suggested. "If you let me return, I could secure additional loans . . . raise taxes?"

The king looked at his former justiciar with disappointment.

Ransom intervened. "You're staying here to protect the king and look after his interests. Someone else might come. The poisoner, for example. Have your men at the ready in case anyone tries to harm the king. It's important you stay here, Damian."

"I agree," offered the king. "You'll do more good here."

And less harm at home, Ransom thought, but he kept it to himself.

"And, if I heard the gossip correctly," the king added, "Gotz has claimed the poisoner who used to work for Rotbart. That might dissuade Estian's poisoner from meddling in person."

"He admitted as much," Ransom confirmed.

Benedict stepped to the window and gazed outside. "I see storm clouds coming on the horizon. You'd better hurry, though the storm may still overtake you. You need to get back to Kingfountain before the seas become too treacherous to cross. I pray to the Lady you're not already too late."

"I will cross," Ransom promised. "Callait is a narrow gap. I'll swim it if I have to."

"No, not that," laughed the king. "A rowboat at the least."

The two men exchanged a look, and Ransom felt a strong surge of loyalty in his chest. "I'll hold off Estian until you return, Bennett."

"Do," said the king. Then he gave Ransom a fierce embrace. "Tell my mother I'm grateful she defended me . . . and that I'm sorry I didn't do more to get her released. I'm in her debt. I'm in all of your debt. You are the richest man in Ceredigion, Ransom. Your share of the burden weighs heavily on me."

Ransom felt a stab of sympathy. He gripped the king's shoulder. "Were it not for you, I wouldn't have had any of that wealth to begin with. Or my love."

Had Claire already returned to Legault? Would they have to spend the winter apart? He chafed inside to get moving.

"You could have killed me outside Dunmanis," said the king. "I think I still owe you in the end. We will take back what we've lost. And believe me, Pree has plenty of gold. Estian will end up paying the ransom one way or another. Off with you." He jostled Ransom with his elbow in a friendly manner.

Ransom left the tower and hastily crossed the courtyard. Cecily was waiting near the gate, already astride her horse. One of the knights sat on a horse next to her, holding the reins for Ransom's mount. The other knight they'd brought would be staying to help protect Benedict, and Terric had already left to make sure their boat was still ready for them.

"Looks like it's going to storm," said Cecily, the wind blowing hair in her face as she gazed up at the sky.

"The real storm is coming," said Ransom after he mounted his horse. "We're not stopping until we reach Kingfountain."

"Lead on, my lord," said Cecily with a smile.

The storm will be here soon, and the last ship to Legault is ready to sail. The captain said if we leave now, we'll have a better chance of arriving safely in Connaught than if we delay even one more day. The air is cold, and the wind has been scouring the streets. The gulls are thick in the sky, some unable to fly because the wind is pressing on them so hard. This is our last chance to depart. Still no word from Ransom or court.

If I leave now, I'll lose contact with what is happening. I'll also lose the chance of seeing Ransom for many months. I'm torn between what I want to do and what may be the wisest course. Part of me yearns for the seering stone and the answers it would bring, yet I'm grateful to be free of its hold over me. I remember the way Sir Dougal Purser ranted and raved at the end.

Instead, I must make my choice the way most of us do: blindly. If I go, my child will be born in my homeland, and I'll be reunited with my sons. If I stay, perhaps there is some *little good I could do. The Aos Sí must be mocking me right now. Either choice means stepping into the dark.*

I've decided.

—Claire de Murrow
Glosstyr
The changing of the season

CHAPTER
THIRTY-SEVEN

Friend or Foe

The seas were too rough to approach the king's docks. The crossing from Callait had been a heart-pounding affair, the ship pitching and tossing from start to finish. Ransom stayed above deck, clutching the ropes until his arms ached as the spray stung his face and soaked him through. On a clear day, it was possible to see the coast of one kingdom from the other, but the raging water and furious winds concealed what lay ahead until they were halfway across.

Unable to do anything but throw down an anchor and ride out the blast, they lingered outside the harbor, rocking back and forth, until one of the shipmates cried out suddenly.

"A longboat!"

Ransom squinted and wiped moisture from his eyes, and sure enough, he saw the longboat rowing hard against the surf to reach them. Hope and weariness warred within Ransom's chest. There had been no rest, no sleep, since leaving the Wartburg. They'd nearly killed their horses getting to Callait in the storm.

The captain pulled his way toward Ransom, moving from rope to rope. "She'll be able to get close to us, but boarding her will be treacherous, my lord. Shouldn't we wait?"

Ransom shook his head. Emiloh must have been watching the Wizr board for his movements. She knew he was home, and no doubt she was the one who'd dispatched the longboat. His mission wasn't over yet, and he was determined to fulfill it.

Cecily stumbled toward him, her cloak drenched and her wet hair clinging to her forehead and cheeks. When she reached him, she looked over the side at the advancing longboat fighting the waves.

"This is where we part ways, my lord," she said to Ransom, nearly shouting to be heard over the wind. "I'm fearful of drowning."

He nodded to her, then took off his cloak and handed it to her.

"Wait, be reasonable," said the captain. "Let's at least tie a rope around you. The queen dowager will have my head if you drown before you make it back."

Ransom agreed, and a sailor quickly provided one.

"You should remove your hauberk," said the captain. "If you fall into the waters, it'll pull you straight down to the Deep Fathoms."

Ransom remembered the siege of Dunmanis. The Elder King had removed his armor prior to exiting the castle gates and nearly died for his error. He shook his head. "I'm keeping it, Captain. Just don't let go of your end until I make it to the boat."

"You're mad, my lord."

"I also outrank you. Do it."

They wrapped the rope once around his chest and then tied a quick sailor's knot. The longboat drew nearer, but it couldn't get too close because of all the waves slamming against the ship. Ransom would not be delayed. He went to the edge and then climbed over the side. They gave enough slack for him to make it over and then slowly began lowering him toward the waves. Another round of spray struck him in the face, and he started spinning on the rope, losing his sense of direction.

"Over here!" cried the sailors on the longboat.

The sailors lowering him down gave the rope more slack until he was submerged in the ocean. Ransom started swimming, but he felt the weight of his armor and sword dragging him down. He clenched his jaw and fought the sensation as he swam toward the longboat. One sailor held out an oar, but he missed it on the first reach and dunked beneath the waves.

And that's when he saw it.

Submerged, he opened his eyes despite the sting of the salty water. A vision of sorts unfurled, and he saw what seemed to be the ocean floor, littered with casks of jewels, chests of coins, and ancient weapons and armor. He saw dead men's bones within the armor, knights who had drowned during the crossing between Callait and Kingfountain. The raven's head on his scabbard shone like a bright star on a clear night. He didn't think he was injured—was it merely reacting to the sight of the treasure buried in the deep? He longed to swim down to it, but the oar jammed against his shoulder, rousing him from the trancelike state. He grasped it, and then the sailors were gripping his arms and pulling him aboard. The longboat tilted, bringing in water, but they dragged him on board and whistled in joy that they'd saved him.

"It's him," said one of the men, a knight with the badge of the Lion on his tabard. Ransom recognized the face, but he was so waterlogged and groggy he forgot the man's name. "It's Lord Ransom!"

"Come on, lads," said one of the sailors. "Put your backs into it. Let's get him home! Pull! Pull!"

Ransom was still dripping when he reached the palace walls. The weariness was terrible to endure, but he pressed on, marching through the torchlit halls of Kingfountain, leaving a trail of wet in his wake. Servants ushered him to the great hall. When he entered, he saw Simon, of course, pacing nervously. James Wigant, duke of the North, was also present, and he gave Ransom a look that suggested he looked half drowned. Emiloh had been sitting on one of the council chairs, leaving the two thrones vacant, but she leaped to her feet and approached him.

"Look at you, Ransom," she said, her voice full of worry. "You're sopping."

"I came as swiftly as I could."

"There has been no news, none at all. Does my son still live?"

Ransom nodded, and Emiloh clutched her breast and groped for a nearby bench. She slowly sat down.

"There hasn't been news on my side either," Ransom said. "What is going on?"

Simon stepped forward. "Jon-Landon is at the sanctuary of Our Lady at this moment, marrying DeVaux's daughter. Some are already proclaiming him king and her queen. But you've seen Benedict with your own eyes. You know he's alive?"

"Yes, and we've agreed on a ransom payment with Lord Gotz of the Wartburg. It will take months to gather it, I'm afraid, but he's very much alive."

"It is enough," Emiloh said, giving him a blinding smile. "I feared . . . that no longer matters. It is enough. You succeeded, Ransom. In spite of this storm. In spite of all the treachery and greed and misinformation. *Thank you.*"

James rose from his council chair and sauntered over. "I suppose it would be timely and appropriate for us to disrupt the nuptials? We may be too late to stop the wedding, but at least we could stop the coronation."

"Yes," Emiloh said, rising from the bench. "That would be the proper course. Will you act on my behalf?"

"Of course, my lady. Although I do think Ransom should come. Jon-Landon doesn't fear me, but I know he fears the Duke of Glosstyr."

"Take thirty knights from the guard with you," Emiloh said. "Ransom, I know you are fatigued, but I must ask—"

"I will go," Ransom said, interrupting her. He was a little surprised that James had remained loyal. In the past, he'd gone to great lengths to make a friend of Jon-Landon, and Ransom had always taken him for a man who'd exploit unrest to serve his own interests.

"Hurry," Emiloh said with an encouraging smile.

Simon approached Ransom and asked in a low voice. "How much did you promise the Brugians?"

Ransom gave him a weary look. He said it loud enough for them all to hear. "A hundred fifty thousand livres."

Silence fell—Simon standing dumbfounded while the others gaped at them. Not that Ransom was surprised. It was an unimaginable ransom.

Ransom clapped Simon on the back. "I'll tell you the story later. It was the only way to secure his release."

Emiloh lowered her gaze. "Thank you, Ransom. With all my heart."

Ransom nodded to her, and then he and James left the great hall and headed toward the main gates. He glanced at his old training companion.

"Admit it, you're surprised I'm here," James said with a mischievous grin.

"To be honest, yes."

"I shouldn't always be predictable. That would be boring."

"I'm sure you have your reasons. Loyalty probably isn't one of them."

James snorted. "Never. Farthest thing from my mind." He chuckled. "I've bet against you before, Ransom, and lost every throw. I'll admit that switching sides to Jon-Landon would seem, on the surface, to be to my own advantage. And now that I've heard you've squandered a hundred fifty thousand livres, I'm more right than I knew. That's a fortune, Ransom. Thankfully, paying it may not be as difficult as you think."

Ransom glanced at James in surprise.

"Remember that brigand who has been stealing from everyone?"

"Ryain Hood?"

"Yes, that rascal. Well, I finally caught him. I've spared his life so far because he has, or so he's promised, close to fifty thousand livres hidden away in various caches. Some here and others in Legault. He's in irons in Dundrennan right now. I haven't even told the queen dowager yet."

"I'm surprised you're telling me," Ransom said with a feeling of wonder. He'd feared the time they'd been allotted might not be enough for them to secure the appropriate loans. This news was truly a miracle worthy of the Fountain.

"I'm not your enemy, Ransom. I hope this proves it." He smiled wryly. "I would have told you as much months ago, but I knew my word would mean less than nothing. So instead I tried to show you. Once again, you've dodged death, overcome storms, and managed to arrive when you were needed most. If you are truly Fountain-blessed, then I want to be on your side. Or at least not against you."

Ransom remembered his past encounters with James. He still didn't fully trust him, and there'd been many occasions when he would have gladly throttled him. But having the North on his side was not an unwelcome proposition.

"I have enemies enough. If we both support Benedict, we can bring peace to Ceredigion that might actually last."

"A truce, then, if you will," said James. "I'll take it. I suppose now isn't the best time to tell you that I might be marrying your sister?"

The news was so sudden that Ransom wondered if he'd heard correctly. "How did this come about? She's the king's ward, and he's been absent for over two years."

"Ah, yes. I see by your expression you aren't entirely thrilled with the prospect, but hear me out. It was your brother's idea, actually. While you were gone and Jon-Landon began his treason, Marcus thought it might be beneficial to secure my allegiance through . . . *softer* means. I am unmarried still, and while I respect Lady Deborah, she's a bit too old for me. Many of the other heiresses are too young. Maeg is not displeasing to the eye, and as I understand it, she is available."

Ransom knew her heart was set on marrying Sir Kace, and Ransom himself had encouraged the match. The thought of James marrying his sister made him agitated. But he also saw the possible benefits.

"I know she's the king's ward and all," James continued in an off-handed manner, but Ransom could tell he was serious. He wanted this. "He could say no and give her to someone else, like Sir Kiskaddon. But . . . he might feel more inclined to be agreeable if I were to provide a substantial part of the ransom that liberates him. I'll let you think on it anyway. Let's upset this wedding. That should be fun."

He smiled in response, and they made their way into the courtyard, where rain continued to pelt the beasts and splash on the cobblestones and puddles. The knights who'd been ordered to accompany them were already congregating. Once their small host was assembled, they left the palace at a gallop and rode down the hillside to the bridge gate. The order was given to open it, and the portcullis was raised with a loud clacking of winches and cranks. Soldiers heaved against the doors to open them, and the knights rode across the bridge.

A huge crowd had gathered, mostly onlookers to the event, and they parted as the horsemen approached them, many looking fearfully at the knights as if expecting them to draw swords.

When they reached the gate of the sanctuary, they were met by a rain-spattered knight wearing a tunic with Duke Ashel's badge. Several other knights joined him, and they all blocked the way forward.

"Ho, there!" the knight said angrily. "What's this about? You can't come in."

"And you're going to stop us?" James said over the noise of the storm and the violence of the falls. "Don't you recognize us? This is

Lord Ransom, the high protector! I'm the duke of the North. Stand aside, you fool."

The knight turned and looked up at Ransom and then did a double take. "M-my lord!"

Ransom didn't even speak to him but nudged his horse forward, and the knights quickly backed off to let them through. Water gushed from the spouts of the sanctuary, coming down like waterfalls so that the entire structure seemed an extension of the massive falls thundering beyond the bridge.

They rode their horses onto the sanctuary grounds, beyond the pools of the fountains, which leaped with agitation as they were struck by the rain. Some onlookers had gathered on the steps of the sanctuary, but the doors were shut. Ransom and James and their knights dismounted and then strode up the steps.

When they reached the top, Ransom and James pulled the double doors open, one on each side. Warmth from the interior came rushing out to greet them, along with the smell of candles and torch smoke. Many nobles and dignitaries had gathered for the ceremony.

Jon-Landon and Léa DeVaux stood at the far end of the sanctuary, the deconeus between them. All faces had turned at the intrusion, and Ransom and James walked in steadily, their clothes dripping and their boots making little squeals as the leather brushed the polished marble of the black and white squares. Murmurs began immediately when they were recognized.

Jon-Landon's face went dark with bridled rage, while Léa took his hand and sidled closer. A quick glance at the front row of guests revealed Lord DeVaux, his face blanched with terror. Lord Ashel was also present, wearing a rich tunic and fur-lined cape. He gave Ransom a wary look.

The deconeus gathered himself. "Lord Ransom? What is the meaning of this?"

"What is the meaning of *this?*" Ransom shot back with anger in his voice.

"I've just solemnized a marriage between these two young people and was about to start the coronation."

"Why is there to be a coronation when there is still a king?"

More murmurs and whispers skittered through the hall.

"The king is dead," Jon-Landon said, gazing hotly at Ransom. "I am his heir."

"My prince, you are deceived or misinformed. I left the king's presence not two days ago, and he was very much alive and in good health. He is a prisoner to the Brugians. But he is still the King of Ceredigion."

The deconeus's eyes widened. He turned to Jon-Landon in accusation. "You assured me, my lord, that you had proof of your brother's death. The letter you showed me, from King Estian—"

"Is false," James added curtly. "Of course he would say that. As always, he sows dissension in our realm. That will change."

The deconeus began to tremble. "My lords, I swear on the Lady that I knew nothing of this plot." He backed away from the young couple. "Your word is trusted, Lord Ransom. If you say the king lives, that you've seen him yourself, then I believe you. I was given to understand you couldn't come to the wedding because you were fighting Estian's army."

Ransom looked Jon-Landon in the eye. "It's over, lad. Step down."

Jon-Landon's cheek muscles twitched with rage. "You know my father wanted me to have the throne. You cannot deny this. He trusted you to give it to me. How could you betray him?"

Ransom walked closer, his hand dropping to the pommel of his sword. "I never betrayed your father. I was with him until the end when he learned that you had switched sides. Don't mock his memory. Your brother is the true king. You'll answer to him for your presumption."

Tears were streaming down Léa's cheeks, but she clutched Jon-Landon's arm protectively, as if fearing for his life.

Jon-Landon's plan had been thwarted, but he didn't give any ground. "The kingdom will be mine," he said in a low, firm voice. "This day or another. I swear it." Then he gave James a black look, one that promised revenge.

"Lord Ashel, Lord DeVaux—you are under arrest," Ransom said sharply. "The king will decide on your fate for conspiring against him. You will go with Lord James to the palace and submit to the terms of imprisonment."

"I did not knowingly betray the king," Ashel said, his hand dropping to his sword.

"Gentlemen," said the deconeus in a quavering voice. "It is sacrilege to spill blood in the Lady's sanctuary! I adjure you, forbear! There are dire consequences for violating the terms of sanctuary."

"You will be tried, my lord," Ransom said. "You may provide evidence of your innocence. But until the king returns, I am your judge. Or you may rot here in the sanctuary and be presumed guilty."

Ashel's look softened. "I submit to your honor and justice." His shoulders sagged, and he released his weapon.

Lord DeVaux wrung his hands. "What of my daughter? What will you do with her?"

Ransom glanced at Léa and Jon-Landon. He could separate the two, await Benedict's release, and let the king decide whether he would honor the marriage. But it was obvious there was real feeling between them.

"Return to the castle," Ransom said to both of them. "The queen dowager will decide your fate." Then he glared at Lord DeVaux. "I will show you more mercy than you showed me, but do not try my patience again, my lord. It will not go well for you."

The celebrants were dispersed, and Ransom watched as his orders were obeyed. The deconeus tried to speak to him, to plead his innocence in the affair, but Ransom had no patience for the man. Weariness had begun to crush down on him, and by the time the great audience hall of the sanctuary was cleared, he wanted nothing more than to drag himself to his room to collapse in a heap on the bed.

After returning to the palace, he did just that and fell asleep still wearing his armor and wet clothing. He was awakened by a firm knock on the door. The room was pitch-black, and it took him a moment to place his surroundings. It was still nighttime. He opened the door and found Dearley standing outside, holding a lantern.

Ransom squinted at the sudden blaze of light.

"I'm sorry I woke you," Dearley apologized. "But she ordered me to bring this to you, wherever I found you."

"Who?" Ransom asked, his stomach plunging when he saw the ink-stained letter gripped in Dearley's glove.

"Lady Claire," he said. "I've ridden long and hard. I had no idea you'd be here at the palace, but they said you'd just returned, and in time to halt the coronation. Here, my lord. She so wanted you to know."

His heart sank. She'd wanted to be reunited with their sons, and to have their next child at home. Disappointment raked his heart as he prepared for the news that she'd already left. After hazarding the short sea crossing from Callait, he knew it would be much too dangerous to cross to Connaught now.

With Dearley holding the light so he could read, he broke the seal and unfolded the paper.

Dearest—Come home to Glosstyr. I'm waiting for you.
Is breá liom an iomarca duit.

—Claire

※

It has been a short winter. The snow in the mountains is still thick, but it has started melting on the roads, and the merchant ships are beginning to arrive at Glosstyr harbor. One of them was a ship from Connaught. Our two lads are hale and driving Dame Roisin desperate for help. She says they climb everything, and the younger likes to sit in a pot on the kitchen floor and spin until he's dizzy. The other took a huge spoonful of qinnamon and stuffed it in his mouth before she could stop him. He nearly choked and spewed dust. That made me laugh, but I miss my sons desperately and cannot wait to depart. It pains me to have missed so much. We risked one winter voyage during an especially calm spell and made it safely to Connaught and back within the month.

I should also mention that our babe was born, a girl—a lass we named Sibyl after Ransom's mother. Lady Sibyl, the grandmother, spent the winter with us here at Glosstyr. She's a fine woman, and I'm grateful to know her better now. It fascinated me to hear the story, from her perspective, of when Ransom was nearly executed by King Gervase. Pain and suffering are something we all share in this life.

During the winter, Ransom arranged to collect the funds to free King Benedict. The bandit Ryain Hood bartered his treasures for his life and will earn his freedom once he delivers the last of his ill-gotten fortune. He demanded to barter directly with Ransom, for he knows him to be a man of honor. The story of Ransom's dealings with Lord Tenthor are apparently more well known than we even realized. Because of the mildness of the winter, we were able to bring back much of the hidden treasure, and it was where he'd concealed it.

The fighting quieted a bit this winter, as it always does with the changing of the season, but once Bennett returns, a war of retribution against Occitania will begin in earnest, the goal being to reclaim the duchy of Westmarch and thus restore the Elder King's empire. The king has written many messages to his council. Duke Ashel was replaced by Sir Kiskaddon as Duke of East Stowe. Sir Dalian, my erstwhile friend and captor, is heir to Lord Kinghorn's power and has been promised Westmarch if we reclaim it. Many of the Gaultic lords are interested in joining the fight against Occitania. There are prizes and honors to be had if we prevail.

It will be sad parting from Ransom again, but we've had a good winter together. A chance to heal wounds of the heart. He says our separation will only motivate him to be a scourge to the Occitanians. That way, he can return to me all the sooner.

I'd like that.

—Claire de Murrow
Glosstyr
(the robins are nesting again)

CHAPTER
THIRTY-EIGHT

The Coming of the Rightful Monarch

From the window, there was a trace of pink in the sky, revealing the coming of dawn. The sound of the surf crashing against the lower rocks was soothing. Ransom sat in a large stuffed chair, his baby daughter lying in his arms, her small rosebud mouth yawning now and then, making him smile with wonder. Her feathery hair was as soft as down. Cradling her in his arms, he felt like the luckiest man in all the world.

The door creaked open, and when he turned his neck, he saw Claire enter, wearing a thick robe over her nightgown. Claire approached them and then bent down and kissed Ransom's neck.

"I love seeing you holding her," she said, dropping to her knees and grazing the babe's nose with her fingertip. Claire rested her cheek on her arm, gazing at the infant. Her hair fanned out, unkempt and wild, and a feeling of loss swelled in Ransom's heart. They'd be parted soon, and he wasn't ready. He'd never be ready.

"I wanted to savor each moment," Ransom said softly. "She's such a little thing."

"But how quickly they grow. The boys will love to torture her. I have no doubt of it. Like poor Maeg, having two brutes as older brothers." She gave Ransom a teasing smile.

"Poor Maeg indeed," Ransom echoed. When the king returned, there would be a push for her to marry James. Ransom knew that his sister wasn't keen on the match. Not only did her heart belong elsewhere, but the duke of the North was a known carouser. Ransom himself had told her plenty of stories about his old companion that had likely inclined her against him. But he couldn't deny James had changed a great deal. He'd been steadfast to King Benedict during Jon-Landon's revolt, which had kept things just unbalanced enough for Ransom to return. The man had matured into a more decent fellow, but their past interactions still were cause for worry. Would he remain faithful or slip back into his old ways?

"I'll be lonely without you in Legault," Claire said, her head still tilted sideways. "Promise me you won't drag this war on needlessly." She reached out and stroked his chin, then his neck.

"Now that the king is returning and the season has changed, we'll cripple Estian's army, then lay siege to Pree," Ransom answered.

"You talk of Pree, but you need to take Tatton Grange first. It's a formidable castle."

"So was Dunmanis," Ransom answered. "And yet it fell in a day. Once we've reclaimed Westmarch, we'll go straight to Pree." He felt the desire to punish Estian. Truthfully, he was looking forward to it.

Little Sibyl was disturbed by their talking and yawned again and began to gurgle and make noises.

"She'll be hungry soon," Claire said, stroking the babe's nose again. "Give her to me. I didn't even hear her awaken. Was she fussing?"

"Only a little," Ransom said. "I wanted you to sleep."

Claire kissed him and scooped Sibyl into her arms. The warmth and love in her eyes made Ransom's heart swell. "I should go to the training yard."

"Very well. We can breakfast together afterward."

Ransom rose from the chair. "I would like that."

As he was about to go to the door, she stopped him.

"Do you love me, Ransom Barton?"

He looked at her in concern. "You know I do. I love you too much."

"I know." She smiled. "But I like hearing it all the same."

He'd told her about the strange medallion Noemie had worn, which he'd been prompted to tear off her neck and throw in the cistern. Yet there was, on occasion, a look in her eyes that showed she worried still. Worried that his heart might be entangled elsewhere.

He walked up to her and cupped her cheeks between his hands and kissed her fiercely. Her breath quickened, and so did his.

"I am loyal to you," he told her, looking deep into her eyes. "And I always will be. And I deeply, deeply love you, Claire de Murrow."

"Now I believe you," she said with a cocked grin. "Go make war."

※

Ransom and many of the nobles were gathered at the king's docks, watching the royal ship as it approached the harbor. Emiloh had personally delivered the final portion of the ransom payment to Lord Gotz in the Wartburg. She had left the Wizr set in Ransom's care, and he had watched the board anxiously until the king's white piece appeared again on the edge.

When the ship bearing the banner of the Lion docked in the tranquil waters, Ransom heard a swelling cheer rise up from the populace of Kingfountain. Then the king strode down the gangplank, one hand stretched out to bring his mother safely down, and Ransom felt a throb of relief. He had dreaded an unexpected turn of events. A last-ditch effort from Estian to undermine the rescue. The dockworkers broke into cheers as the king raised his fist into the air and waved to the crowd.

Horses were brought, and the king and his mother began to ride up to the palace.

James leaned toward Ransom, pitching his voice loudly enough to be heard over the commotion. "I don't see Portia with them. Is she still in Genevar?"

Simon, who stood on the other side of Ransom, answered, "She decided to stay. She's waiting for the king to come to her and woo her."

"That won't happen anytime soon," James chuffed. "He'll want to bloody Estian's nose first. I think it peculiar she didn't come."

"There is estrangement between them," Simon said. "Not all marriages are as happy as Ransom's." He butted his friend with an elbow.

But the jest didn't land well. It wasn't so long ago that Ransom had worried whether his own marriage would survive.

The king and the queen dowager soon arrived at the upper landing, where Ransom and the others awaited. Emiloh looked radiant astride her stallion, and Ransom gave her a respectful smile and nod, which she returned.

The king wore a velvet tunic with a glistering chain hauberk beneath it and the hollow crown atop his head. The tunic was as red as blood, the threads of the lion a startling gold. His beard and hair had been trimmed and groomed, and he looked every bit the part of a king. Benedict nodded in greeting to the various nobles, then swung off his horse and embraced Ransom like a brother.

Grinning with ferocity, the king proceeded to look up at the palace. "I thank thee, Lady of the Fountain, for delivering me home again," he murmured.

Amid the swelling cheers, they returned to the palace together and assembled for the first king's council since the war with the East Kingdoms had begun. Some of the faces in the room had changed. But Ransom's seat of prominence had not, nor had the queen dowager's. There was a palpable sense of power in the room, a strange energy that buzzed inside Ransom's chest. He felt his Fountain magic fill to bursting.

"Our first matter of discussion," said the king in a formal tone, "is what to do with my brother, Jon-Landon, to punish his rebellion against me. I would hear your views."

The discussion was a familiar one, but the nobles repeated their arguments, some pleading for leniency and others for punishment. The king listened patiently to each member of his council, but Ransom already knew what he planned to do. Emiloh had told him that her son had learned from his father's mistakes. He was willing to forgive his brother if he apologized. But would Jon-Landon bend the knee to a brother he hated?

"Lord Ransom, you've been thoughtful. What is your view?" the king asked.

"There is a long history in your family," Ransom answered, feeling the eyes on him, "of brothers vying for control of the hollow crown. He grew up watching his elder brothers do it, so can we not see reason behind what he did? Would you not have considered it yourself, my lord, in his place?"

The king nodded. "You make a strong case, Lord Ransom."

"You've shown forbearance with him thus far, my lord. I think mercy would be appropriate considering we're about to go to war. Give him an opportunity to prove his loyalty to you. Give him men to command and a duty to fulfill. His actions will prove his heart in the end."

From his side vision, Ransom saw a few of the other nobles nodding in agreement with what he'd said. He'd given the king the opportunity to follow counsel and not just decide on his own.

Benedict looked to Simon. "Bring him in."

Simon bowed. Ransom watched a look pass between mother and son. They were both hoping Jon-Landon wouldn't react in a way that would make it difficult to rationalize pardoning him. Wisdom dictated a prudent response, but Jon-Landon wasn't known for his discretion.

When Simon returned, Jon-Landon in tow, the two approached the council. Jon-Landon's eyes revealed nothing of his intentions, but when he met Ransom's gaze, something dark and vengeful flashed between them.

Once he reached the front of the audience hall, Jon-Landon gazed up at the double throne installed there. He smirked a little as he beheld the empty chair next to his brother. Some at court had been disgusted by Jon-Landon's marriage to a bride who was little more than a girl. But no one who saw them together could doubt the two were devoted to each other. The king had delivered his judgment by letter: he'd decided not to dissolve their marriage since it was sanctioned by the deconeus. The younger man should be grateful, but instead he seemed disdainful of the less happy circumstances of his brother's marriage. Emiloh's eyes tightened, and she leaned forward, giving her youngest son a warning look.

Jon-Landon opened his arms and knelt before his brother. An audible gasp of relief came from someone in the hall. Ransom kept his eyes fixed on the young prince.

"My lord king, Brother, I submit to your authority and confess my guilt before this hall and the peers of the realm. I conspired against you, my liege, and for this horrid crime, I beg your pardon and forgiveness." The prince's head was bowed low, so he said the words to the floor rather than his brother's face. Although he'd spoken in a proper manner, the words lacked conviction and feeling.

Perhaps Benedict sensed the same. His face became inscrutable as he gazed down at his youngest brother.

"What you did was wrong," Benedict said. "Your lies nearly ruined the kingdom of Ceredigion."

"I admit it freely," Jon-Landon said, still bowing. "I accept any punishment you would devise. If my death must wash away my wrongs, so be it. Send me over the falls."

Was Jon-Landon goading his brother? By demanding the worst, was he revealing the king lacked the courage to execute him? The uneasy feeling in Ransom's stomach grew worse.

"I'll not kill you, Brother, if that is what you fear. Rise. We are reconciled." The king opened his palm and gestured.

Jon-Landon stood. "Thank you. Brother." His final word was said with just a hint of disdain.

"Take your seat at this council," Benedict said, gesturing to the only vacant spot, the one next to Lord Kiskaddon. The new duke shot Jon-Landon a look of disgust.

Jon-Landon bowed his head and started toward the chair. But he paused before sitting, turning around and facing the council. "I know many of you may believe my repentance is insincere," he said in a formal tone. "But I assure you that it is not. Many months have passed, allowing me to consider my ways. What I risked. I hope my past actions have not jeopardized the future rights of my posterity."

He let the words hang deliberately over the hall. Then, with a triumphant smile, he turned to Benedict. "My wife is expecting. Soon, in a few months, there shall be *another* Argentine."

From the look on Emiloh's face, she was just as surprised by the news as the others in the chamber. Benedict glared at his brother in unspoken rage, realizing that he'd been caught unaware. Yes, Jon-Landon had asked for forgiveness. But he was even more anxious to claim the throne now, especially since his brother had failed to produce an heir.

In the surging emotions that followed the abrupt declaration, Ransom heard a whisper in the stillness of his heart.

The scion of King Andrew will be reborn through an heir of the Argentines. They will try to kill him. You are all that stands in the way.

And he realized, to his horror, that the voice was speaking of Jon-Landon's son, not Constance's.

I just received word from Ransom. The siege of Josselin hasn't yielded any benefits yet. The Occitanians are determined to hold on to their possessions. Benedict is leading the siege against Tatton Grange himself, while Lord Kiskaddon has been ransacking the Occitanian countryside, trying to draw off forces from the castles to defend their lands. Sometimes we can even see smoke rising from Ceredigion. The land is at war. It is midsummer, and Occitania's fields of grain have been trampled or torched. Something must give, or they will both continue to suffer.

Things are much calmer in Legault. The three children keep our nursery in constant chaos. I miss Keeva. Still no word about Guivret, who is dead or languishing in an Occitanian prison. No word has come. No answer can be given.

Some things must be determined by the sword.

—Claire de Murrow
Connaught Castle, the Fair Isle

EPILOGUE

The Poisoner

The air reeked of smoke, and the heat of the late afternoon had continued into evening. Benedict Argentine was dripping with sweat. Many men had collapsed that day from the strain caused to their bodies. Water was being carted in barrels from the nearby river, and some of the knights were stripping off their armor and plunging into the flow to cool themselves down.

Another messenger arrived from Lord Kiskaddon, wearing the symbol of the buck with massive antlers. Kiskaddon was an able man, and they'd become close during the war with the East Kingdoms. A war that now seemed more like a ruse than a proper conquest. Benedict had once enjoyed, or so he believed, the confidence of Estian. But it had all been a sham, a ploy to weaken Ceredigion so it could be plucked.

"What news?" Benedict asked, wiping the sweat from his face.

"We torched another grain field, one that was plump and ripe, my lord," said the courier, handing over the letter. "I swear there will be no bread in Pree this winter. The people will starve."

"Let them starve," Benedict growled impatiently. He broke the seal and quickly read the letter, which ended with a request for permission to attack the duchy of Garrone and lay siege to Castillon. That duchy lay due south of Pree, and if Benedict and Ransom succeeded in reclaiming both Westmarch and Josselin, it would enable them to attack the Occitanian capital on three sides. But it was risky. If Kiskaddon overextended himself, he could get cut off, and that would be a disaster. No . . . it would be more prudent to wait until Westmarch had been reclaimed before they moved onward.

"It's too hot, and I don't have time to write a proper response," Benedict said. "I need to ride with the patrol to see what damage we did today. Tell your lord to keep roving with his knights. Terrorize the villages. Be unexpected. When it's time to attack Castillon, I will order it, but not until then."

"Very well, my lord," said the knight, giving him a salute.

Benedict returned it, and the knight left. After he was gone, Benedict pulled off his tunic and fought to get out of his hauberk. After detangling himself from it, he put his tunic back on and then went outside the tent. There was no breeze, none at all, and the sweat trickled down his back, ribs, and legs.

All he needed was a bit of air, and he'd go back and arm himself again. The castle defenders mostly stayed out of sight, afraid of the longbows being used by the Gaultic archers in Benedict's camp.

A squire brought him a drink of water in a leather flask, and the king gratefully gulped it down and then handed it back.

"My lord!"

Benedict turned and saw one of his knights approaching through the haze of smoke. Sir Gordon. "What is it?"

"I've just had word, they think the wall may be breached tonight!"

"That is good news!" Benedict said. "What happened?"

"Some cracks have appeared in the northwest corner. Another direct hit from the trebuchet, and we think it'll go down. If it crumbles, we could get inside and end this bloody siege!"

"What does Captain Horace think?" Benedict asked. Horace never exaggerated or succumbed to wishful thinking.

"Ask him yourself! This way."

Benedict walked with him, crossing the rocky ground that had been trampled so many times it only yielded dust instead of weeds. Smoke drifted into view again, blocking their sight of the tents and pavilions for a moment. Walking farther, they came to the trebuchets that had been launching stones at the castle.

Captain Horace was also sweating profusely. Finding boulders big enough to hurl against Tatton Grange had been a challenge. Wagons and horses were constantly trying to drag them to the contraptions.

Benedict slapped the timbers of the waiting trebuchet. "Think we'll breach the walls tonight, Captain?"

"I dunno, my lord," said Horace gruffly. "It depends on how quickly those lackwit men can drag over stones large enough to hurl." The captain frowned. "Where's your hauberk?"

Benedict shook his head. "I was too hot. I left it in the tent."

"Go put it on, my lord. We're too close to the walls." He punched Sir Gordon on the arm. "Why'd you bring the king out here without armor!"

"I didn't notice!" Sir Gordon complained.

Benedict turned as he heard a wagon wheel creak. "Ah, some more boulders are coming."

"Crossbow!" someone shrieked.

The bolt struck Benedict in the shoulder. The force of it knocked him off his feet, and he went down into the dust, pain gouging his arm. There was a shuffle of men all around him, and he began to choke on the dust it wafted into the air. The knights grabbed him and dragged him away from the trebuchet, shouting for help. Bows twanged as arrows hailed down at the one who had fired on the king.

"Get a barber! Get the king's barber! Hurry!"

Benedict was dragged back to his tent, and someone splashed water on his face. "My lord! How is it? Does it pain you greatly?"

The pain was bad but not terrible. And yet, as Gordon and another man lowered him onto his pallet, a strange tingle shot down his arm. His heart began to beat erratically.

"Where's the barber?" someone shouted.

Benedict grabbed Gordon with his good hand and pulled him closer. "Bring . . . the chest . . . to me."

"What chest? What do you mean, my lord?" Gordon asked, his voice thick with worry.

"The one on the table," Benedict said through clenched teeth. His whole left arm was numb. He felt agony unfurling within him. He'd been wounded before, but not like this. This was something else.

It was poison.

Gordon brought over the chest that contained the Wizr board.

"Open it," the king gasped.

Gordon did, revealing the board. Benedict had looked at it earlier that day. The poisoner piece had been in Pree. But now it was at Tatton Grange. Alix . . . the Occitanian king's poisoner was there.

"He's here, my lord! The barber is here!"

By the time Benedict sat up, the pain was excruciating. His tongue tingled in his mouth. He reached into the chest and moved the piece representing Ransom, dragging it to Tatton Grange.

"Close the lid," he gasped to Sir Gordon.

"My lord, lay back," said the barber worriedly. "I need to pull the crossbow bolt out."

Benedict ignored him. Looking into Gordon's eyes, he said while suppressing a groan, "Take it to Lord Ransom. Guard it with your life, Gordon. Do not fail me."

Sir Gordon blinked and nodded. "I shall do as you command, my lord. I'm sorry. I didn't notice you weren't wearing your hauberk. It's my fault."

Benedict shook his head. There was a coppery taste in his mouth. "It's my fault," he said.

"I'll get it out, my lord," the barber insisted. "It will hurt, but we must get it out so the wound doesn't fester."

Benedict wanted to laugh.

"I'm already a dead man," he muttered angrily.

AUTHOR'S NOTE

When I first pitched this series to my publisher, I said it needed to be four books long because Ransom would serve four different kings. As I've stated previously, many elements of Ransom's character are based on a historical person who did many of the deeds described in this series. He reminded me so much of Owen Kiskaddon; and his feats of duty, loyalty, and bravery convinced me he must have been Fountain-blessed. His experience of getting wounded in the leg while standing alone against impossible odds wasn't creative license in *Knight's Ransom*. It really happened.

For this book, there wasn't as much history to go on, so my imagination was able to run wild, especially in terms of Ransom's connection to Constance of Brythonica, another historical figure, whom I mentioned very briefly in the previous Kingfountain series. For me, one of the most poignant scenes of this book is when Constance prayed for Ransom, despite her own heart aching. That scene was inspired by an early story written by Frances Hodgson Burnett, which has a similar scene that is so moving it made me cry. There is something compelling about one who, while suffering their own personal heartbreak, reaches out to comfort someone else. Constance embodied that trait, and I enjoyed writing her for that reason and also because she often reminded me of Sinia Montfort.

I really enjoyed developing Ransom and Claire's relationship in this book. Their love story has been so fun to write. This is the first time

I've woven family life into my stories without big time jumps, and it has brought back memories of when my kids were very little and all the mischief they'd get into. My wife and I donated some old dressers this week, and as we unloaded them at the donation center, my wife stopped to snap a picture because our son had scratched one of the drawers with stars and a smiley face the day I'd assembled them all those years ago. He's now a senior in high school and about to graduate and (if he gets his wish) serve a mission for our church in Japan. Remembering that precocious moment brought a smile to our faces as we gave the dressers away.

While I was writing this series, some traumatic things happened in the lives of our family and friends. Nearly my entire family got COVID-19, and other events happened that broke our hearts. But as my new friend Morgan Gendel has said, and it's something I've known in my author journey but not in the same words: a writer squeezes characters until you see how they really are as people.

That is why Ransom Barton isn't just a character to me anymore. He's real.

ACKNOWLEDGMENTS

So many people are involved in the process of writing and editing my books. I'm grateful to Adrienne, Angela, Wanda, Dan, and others who make my books as professional as possible. I also have a loyal cadre of first readers (Shannon, Robin, Sandi, Travis, and Sunil) who give me early feedback on the books to make them better. I especially want to thank Sunil for saving me from making a blunder in Hindi in this book. When he read Noemie's dismissal of her servants, he warned me that Google Translate had failed me, and I'd inadvertently dropped a very bad word into my book. We had a good laugh, and he taught me how to say the same thing another way that couldn't be misinterpreted.

When I hear from my fans, it always means a lot, but sometimes a special thank-you note comes out of the blue. Or in this case, out of the smoke. This one came from Laura, who sent me an email that really touched me. Many of you know about the terrible wildfires that ravaged California last summer. Several of my friends were impacted by this tragedy. Well, Laura sent me a note saying that she was surrounded by forest fires. In some twist of fate, she'd read the spin-off Covenant of Muirwood series and my Kingfountain books before learning about the original Legends of Muirwood series. She bought the audiobooks but didn't start listening to them until last summer when the fires came. She found some comfort in these lines: *"Have you ever seen a forest burn, child?" "I have not." "There is nothing left but char and ash. Everything left behind is soulless and void. There is nothing living—or at least that is how it seems. But from the ashes and from the char, new seeds sprout and grow. The forest renews itself. It takes time, but it happens. There is both good and evil in this world. If we did not intervene here, the grapes would all turn wild. They would all become sour, you see. The Blight is merely a culling. A chance for a rebirth."*

I'd written these lines years before, but in that moment, they were especially meaningful to Laura during the pandemic, fires, and a hurricane that bore her name.

All I can say is that sometimes words come to us in exactly the moment we need them most. And she was gracious enough to send me a picture she took, a few weeks later, of the beloved monastery at St. Mary's knoll, which was part of the inspiration behind Muirwood Abbey. She hikes one of my favorite parks regularly and sees the view all the time.

Thanks, Laura. Hopefully, 2021 has been a better year for you and for us all!

ABOUT THE AUTHOR

Photo © 2016 Mica Sloan

Jeff Wheeler is the *Wall Street Journal* bestselling author of *The Immortal Words*, *The Buried World*, and *The Killing Fog* in the Grave Kingdom series; *Knight's Ransom* and *Warrior's Ransom* in the First Argentines series; the Harbinger and Kingfountain series; and the Muirwood, Mirrowen, and Landmoor novels. He left his career at Intel in 2014 to write full-time. Jeff is a husband, father of five, and devout member of his church. He lives in the Rocky Mountains and is the founder of *Deep Magic: The E-Zine of Clean Fantasy and Science Fiction*. Find out more about *Deep Magic* at https://deepmagic.co, and visit Jeff's many worlds at https://jeff-wheeler.com.